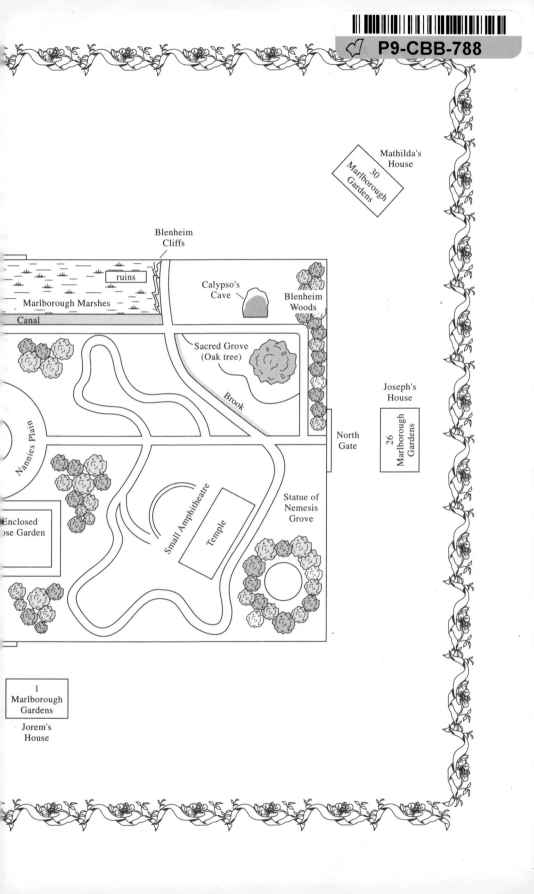

Mathilda's
House

30
Marlborough
Gardens

Blenheim
Cliffs

ruins

Calypso's
Cave

Blenheim
Woods

Marlborough Marshes

Canal

Sacred Grove
(Oak tree)

Brook

Joseph's
House

26
Marlborough
Gardens

Nannies Plain

North
Gate

Enclosed
ose Garden

Small Amphitheatre

Temple

Statue of
Nemesis
Grove

1
Marlborough
Gardens

Jorem's
House

CITY OF CHILDHOOD

CITY OF CHILDHOOD

Valerie Townsend Bayer

ST. MARTIN'S
NEW YORK

Design by Sharleen Smith

Library of Congress Cataloging-in-Publication Data

Bayer, Valerie Townsend.
     City of childhood / Valerie Townsend Bayer.
         p. cm.
     ISBN 0-312-06926-X
     I. Title.
   PS3552.A85878C5   1992
   813'.54—dc20   91-33240
                                  CIP

First Edition: March 1992
10 9 8 7 6 5 4 3 2 1

To my beloved grandchildren
Robert, Jonathan, Jacob, and Naomi
and to my academic mentor
Michael T. Hanifin, Ph.D. (1939–1987)

Descendants of Josephus Isaac Forster (Faustus)

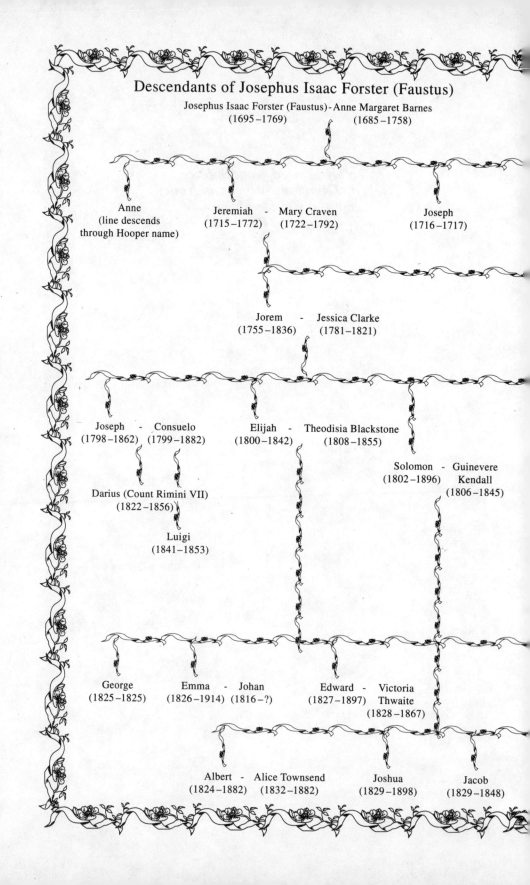

Josephus Isaac Forster (Faustus) - Anne Margaret Barnes
(1695–1769)   (1685–1758)

Anne
(line descends
through Hooper name)

Jeremiah - Mary Craven
(1715–1772) (1722–1792)

Joseph
(1716–1717)

Jorem - Jessica Clarke
(1755–1836) (1781–1821)

Joseph - Consuelo
(1798–1862) (1799–1882)

Elijah - Theodisia Blackstone
(1800–1842) (1808–1855)

Solomon - Guinevere
(1802–1896)   Kendall
       (1806–1845)

Darius (Count Rimini VII)
(1822–1856)

Luigi
(1841–1853)

George
(1825–1825)

Emma - Johan
(1826–1914) (1816–?)

Edward - Victoria
(1827–1897)   Thwaite
       (1828–1867)

Albert - Alice Townsend
(1824–1882) (1832–1882)

Joshua
(1829–1898)

Jacob
(1829–1848)

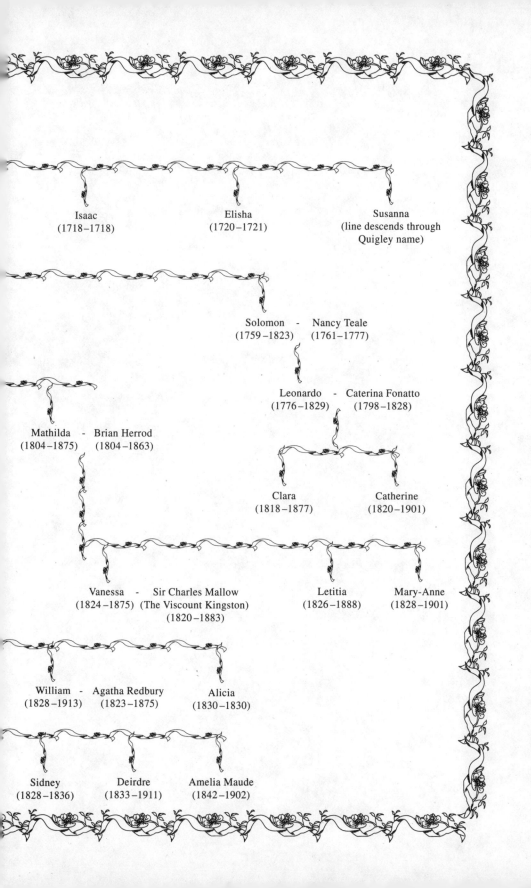

Isaac
(1718–1718)

Elisha
(1720–1721)

Susanna
(line descends through
Quigley name)

Solomon   -   Nancy Teale
(1759–1823)   (1761–1777)

Leonardo   -   Caterina Fonatto
(1776–1829)   (1798–1828)

Mathilda   -   Brian Herrod
(1804–1875)   (1804–1863)

Clara
(1818–1877)

Catherine
(1820–1901)

Vanessa   -   Sir Charles Mallow
(1824–1875)   (The Viscount Kingston)
(1820–1883)

Letitia
(1826–1888)

Mary-Anne
(1828–1901)

William   -   Agatha Redbury
(1828–1913)   (1823–1875)

Alicia
(1830–1830)

Sidney
(1828–1836)

Deirdre
(1833–1911)

Amelia Maude
(1842–1902)

PART
I

PRELIMINARY
COMMUNICATIONS

The real constitution of things is accustomed to hide itself.

—Heraclitus, Fr. 123,
trans. Clara Lustig

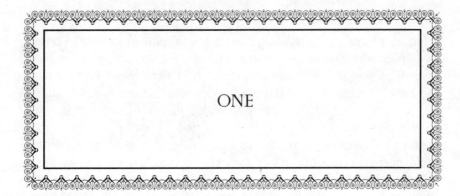

ONE

WE NO longer see anyone anymore. No one at all. Except for people like the postman, the greengrocer, or a repairman come to fix a cracked window . . . people of that sort. What I mean is that we are no longer interested in society, in belonging to what exists out there: the world at large. We have no time for it. We are far too busy with *them*.

We go to the Gardens every day, no matter what the weather is like, and wander, hand in hand, down its gravel paths from the Great South Gate to Blenheim Heights, where Darius led his cousins into battle. It is a ritual that Lowe and I enjoy, and we remind one another that it was "here" that Emma was taken prisoner, "here" that Albert's fleet was burned . . . but one could go on forever, there are so many points of interest in Marlborough Gardens.

Afterward we return home and enjoy a simple tea in the Parlor of Glass Domes, where we read out loud to one another excerpts from the children's archives (another ritual).

This afternoon there was a downpour. Everything was drenched. The sky—a sheet of gray. But Lowe and I walked hand in hand to Blenheim Wood, feeling the pleasant weight of the cutting shears in our pockets.

Vegetation is fierce in Marlborough Gardens. Abnormally active. Vines and weeds seem to grow overnight. We work like common laborers to maintain even a semblance of order. Today we spent the entire afternoon deep in the woods hacking and slashing away at the leaves and stems that were encroaching *Leda and the Swan* and threatening to devour *Europa and the Bull.* Agreeably fatigued, we returned home just in time for tea.

We have no servants. We are not fond of strangers in Marlborough Gardens. I made the tea, Daucus, which comes from wild carrots, one of Mrs. Farnley's recipes.[1] And sandwiches: cucumber and watercress. We drank and ate as always in a companionable and affectionate silence. A brief respite from our tasks. But there is still so much to do! And everything seems to require far more time than we allocate for it. One doesn't wish to complain, but, for example, the classification of female artifacts—what we hypothesized would take us six months at the most to complete, took us an entire year![2] It was only last week that we finally completed cataloguing all of them.

Yesterday I placed them in the Parlor of Glass Domes, on the two library tables that stand on the far end of the room, much to Lowe's annoyance. She complains that it gives the room the air of a catafalque.

Emma named the room, by the way, a sly reference to her mother Theodisia's shell creations that were housed here (and still are) under, of course, glass domes.

Nothing has changed. The room is exactly the same as when mother and daughter were alive: the same Brussels carpet, the same wool-worked footstools on which we rest our feet, the same two chairs made of carved rosewood on which we sit on either side of the fireplace. Sameness, steadfastness, continuity—these are the qualities we cherish in Marlborough Gardens.

I stare at Lowe's stern, grave face. She's no pink and white beauty—dark complected, her skin is sallow, she has the face of a Sybil. Her eyes are enormous, deep set, dark, and hooded.

It is Lowe's turn today to read out loud from the archives.

Her voice is hooded too, and dark like the sound of a cello. Once more I hear the familiar story. . . .

---

1. Georgiana Farnley (1798–1896), Elijah and Theodisia's housekeeper, par excellence, at 43 Marlborough Gardens. "Daucus carota, L. (Queen Anne's lace) a diuretic and a stimulant"—so wrote Mrs. Farnley in copperplate besides its name.—*R. Lowe*

2. A partial list of the artifacts can be found in Reference Note C, page 61. —*R. Lowe*

City of Childhood[3]

I

RETURNS

L AST night I dreamed I was a child again, that I had returned to Marlborough Gardens where, once upon a time, my cousins and I played when we were children.

Thrust out of the bosom of God, I began my flight through the still, dark universe toward the planet Earth, until at last beneath me shone the white alabaster city of my childhood.

Carried on currents of air, I glided back and forth over the city. Remembering . . . a rush of myriad thoughts winding through my brain like the wind that was streaming through my hair. In its center lay Marlborough Gardens winking and shimmering, an immense emerald in a blaze of green light, as beautiful and enchanting as it always had been.

Tears came to my eyes, and I wept. I saw everything as it once was: the woods sloping to the marshes, the marshes stretching to the lake, and on the hill opposite the woods, the temple, its white marble stone now amber colored in the moonlight. Close by, hidden in the partial shadows, stood the single grave. . . .

All was silent: the moon, the stars, the trees. A swan, coming out of one of the hidden coves of the lake, glided past me on the silver surface. In a thicket a bird began to sing. And then another. In the east the sky filled up with plumes of pink. Morning was breaking. Soon all would pale before the dazzle of the sun; the dream would end and I would awaken as always next to my beloved . . . for like all dreamers I knew that I was dreaming, that in reality I was an old woman living in a villa a thousand miles away and half a century later.

---

3. *City of Childhood* is an account of Emma Forster's tenth year in Marlborough Gardens, from April 1836 to August 1837. It is sometimes written in first person, and sometimes in third.—*R. Lowe*

＊   ＊   ＊

City of childhood. It was indeed that. A separate universe. For though we lived with our parents, we had our own suite of rooms: the day nursery, the night nursery, the school room; our own retinue of servants: nannies, undernannies, upstairs maids, and as we grew older our own governesses or tutors; and like a separate polity we had our own concepts of law and order, crime and punishment, our own ideas about what constituted joy and what constituted pleasure.

We were twelve cousins in all: the offspring of my father Elijah, his two brothers, Solomon and Joseph, and their younger sister, Mathilda.

Collectively we were a handsome lot: fair skinned with high coloring. Our hair, various shades of blond, ranged from my flaxen, straight tresses to my cousin Albert's thick, bronze-colored locks. But it was the color of our eyes that stamped us consanguinean. The family called it "the Forster blue," but Vanessa, Aunt Mathilda's oldest daughter, described it as "the color of the heavens on a cold clear night."

There were two exceptions: Vanessa herself and our Italian cousin, Darius. In Vanessa's lovely face framed by hair the color of antique gold, her eyes shone forth a lavender blue. As for Darius, they were not blue at all but brown, as lustrous as the pelt of a beaver.

We were all born, all twelve of us, in the same room in the same bed in our Grandfather Jorem's house at One Marlborough Gardens. "It will give them a heightened sense of kinship," he was supposed to have said. And indeed I do believe that he was right, for there existed among us a kind of telepathic communication as if we were animated by a single mind, like a flock of wheeling starlings, or as if we had been hatched from the same egg, like the Dioscuri, for instance.

The city ran like clockwork, hedged in by the strictest routines that never varied.

The day began punctually at six A.M. From that point onward every second was accountable as if time were a commodity that must display a daily profit.

Between the hours of six and seven there were elimination, ablution, and morning prayers. Between seven and half past there was breakfast (Spartan): cold porridge and one slice of unbuttered bread. From eight to nine, a walk around the Garden at a brisk pace regardless of the weather; at five minutes past nine precisely, not a second sooner, not a second later (each of our nannies carried a pewter watch in the right outside pockets of their coats), we entered Marlborough Gardens to meet with one another, my cousins and their nannies, on a flat expanse of ground known to us as Nannies Plain.

What we called free time was between fifteen past nine and half past eleven. We were allowed to wander off on our own then, either to Blenheim Wood, or to Marlborough Marshes where we played Trafalgar[4], or to Swan Lake where my cousin Albert kept his fleet of ships, or to the sunken garden where we might play tag among the stone nymphs. Only Vanessa and her two sisters, Letitia and Mary-Anne, were content to remain on Nannies Plain with their nurse, an elderly woman named Nanny Burden.

We loved Marlborough Gardens. It was our paradise, our Eden, an abiding passion that remained with us all our lives. My brother Edward once wrote to me from Edinburgh, where he was staying for the year (he was in his forties then), "Do you still recall those blessed idle days when you and I, Emma, would lie for hours, side by side, in Blenheim Wood, the floor a carpet of bluebells and violets, and stare up through twig and bough, transfixed, to the brightness beyond? Somewhere in my mind, Emma, I know I have recorded every scent, every configuration, of that sacred place."

At eleven forty-five we returned to our separate homes for the second meal of the day—a Spartan lunch: a cold piece of meat and one slice of unbuttered bread. After lunch we returned to the Gardens where we played on Nannies Plain until an hour before teatime.

We hardly ever saw our parents except during the one immutable and steadfast tie: afternoon tea. At half past four, washed, brushed, and combed, we paid our daily visit to Momma's drawing room, where we were served tea, but-

---

4. Trafalgar: a game Albert, Solomon's oldest son, devised, and which the cousins played almost every day until their Italian cousin, Darius, came home from school and taught them other games to play.—R. Lowe

tered bread, and a bit of conversation. At bedtime there might be a visit from either or both parents, long or short depending on our parents' busy social schedule. But no more than that . . .

On Monday, Wednesday, and Friday afternoons, I and my female cousins visited with Mrs. Bottome, the minister's wife, in her parlor where she taught us embroidery and needlework. At the same time my brothers and their male cousins were instructed by Reverend Bottome of St. Giles' Church, in the rudiments of Latin and grammar, to prepare them for Warrenton, the public school they were to attend, the one their fathers had attended before them.

In the beginning, when Marlborough Gardens was first created, only five houses surrounded it (Grandfather Jorem's, Elijah's, Solomon's, Joseph's, and Mathilda's), but as the years passed Grandfather Jorem leased the remaining land to various affluent but well-connected strangers and by 1836, the year that I am writing about, there were more than fifty families other than ours whose children (if they had any) had the privilege of playing in the Gardens. But we, being natural xenophobes, largely ignored them. We were the Lords of Marlborough Gardens, a race apart, and we meant to keep it that way.

We were bright, imaginative, badly brought up children. And strange, as children generally are. That is, we saw visions and heard disembodied voices, regularly. . . .

My "worldly" knowledge did not include the fact that I, Emma Forster, was a member of a large, powerful, and illustrious family, that my parents enjoyed a brilliant social life, or that I lived in a city called London, which for that brief moment in time was the hub of the universe. No. My world was only as large as the dimensions of the day and night nurseries. And Marlborough Gardens. The only authority in my universe was a woman called Nanny Grindal. And just as I thought that the kettle that Nanny Grindal boiled her water in for afternoon tea was the "ideal" kettle from which all other kettles had evolved, so I assumed that Grindal was the "ideal" Nanny-Daemon from whom all Nanny-Daemons were formed.

My first memory is one of light: the oyster-white light of the nursery. Opalescent, shimmering, luminous . . . hermaphroditic. It was against this moist and secretive light that Grindal's black uniform first declared itself, my first presentiment of evil.

I was a quiet child, capable of extraordinary dignity, and yet by nature enormously passionate. By the time that I was ten years old, I already had accepted certain truths as if they were natural laws, like gravity for instance. My mother did not care for me. My father loved me. My nurse, Nanny Grindal, hated me.

I was ugly.[5] I was unlovable. The two facts were defined and established in multitudinous ways by Nanny Grindal, the lethal gospel worming its way deeper into my mind year after year. But worse than that, far worse, was the fact that I was plagued with the idea that my persecutor was right: I *was* ugly and unlovable—and stubborn and disagreeable, besides.

It was my father's love for me that kept me from despair. Every evening, unless he was traveling on business, he would visit my two brothers, Edward and William, and me in the nursery before bedtime. Being somewhat of a dandy, he would first pose in the doorway for a few seconds, seconds that seemed endless to me, to be admired by Grindal and her assistant Tansy, but then immediately afterward he would call me to him, saying: "My dearest Emma, come and give your Poppa one of your best and finest of kisses," and I would run to him as fast as I could and stand before him in complete adoration. Waiting . . . when in a dizzying curve of upward motion I would find myself safe and nestled in his arms, my face brushing against his silken whiskers, greedily inhaling his delicious bouquet of whiskey, tobacco, and a cologne that smelled of crushed carnations. And the terror, the awful terror, that seemed to be an integral part of me, would miraculously drain away. . . .

※   ※   ※

Lowe stops here. She places the leather bookmark, one of Vanessa's efforts, carefully along the inside of the page.

It is dusk. The room is in near darkness. Only details stand out: the gilt threads of the drapery, the hanging crystal prisms,

---

5. Emma had a nevus, the size of a guinea, situated on her left temple that Nanny Grindal called Satan's mark.—*R. Lowe*

the gilt on the entwined serpents. . . . What little light there is has a greenish hue to it coloring Lowe's slender fingers and transforming Lowe's black cap of curls into bronze-colored ringlets.

Lowe's hair. I make the calculations: I shall have to cut it— she wears it exactly one eighth of an inch above the tips of her lobes—yes, in one week . . . on April twenty-third . . . on the Day of Arche.

After a light supper—some vegetable broth and a bit of poached turbot—we walk to the Lodge where we return the manuscript to its shelf in the Secret Room behind the screen where the archives are kept.

My name is Harriet Van Buren. I am an American, an Episcopalian, born in Cleveland, Ohio, in 1898. Rachel Lowe, my companion, is an English Jew, born in Paddington, London, in 1900.

Some people might say that we are obsessed, or even mad, that we have foolishly given up our lives to ghosts. Perhaps, but it suits Lowe and myself. Isn't that what really counts?

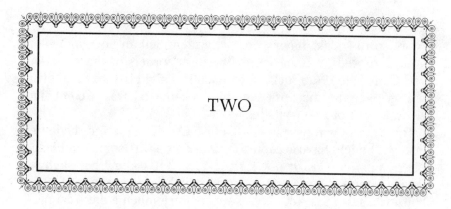

TWO

An invisible connection is stronger than a visible one.
—Heraclitus, Fr. 54,
trans. Clara Lustig[6]

MARLBOROUGH GARDENS, 1935

W HO I am and what I did before I became a caretaker of Marlborough Gardens is really quite unimportant except, perhaps, to illustrate the hidden springs of chance. . . .

Briefly then: twelve years ago I was working as a curator in the Cleveland Museum—my particular province was English landscape; my special focus, John Constable—when a colleague of mine, Clive Grundey, informed me that (miracle of miracles) there was an opening on the staff of the prestigious Teleman Art Institute in London, England. He told me he would have applied himself, "But 't'weren't my bailiwick," is how he put it. "It's landscape, it's British, it's yours."

I remember that I was eager to be engaged, an appointment to the Teleman staff being considered in our field somewhat akin to receiving a knighthood or a D.B.E. And so, ostensibly, I went to London to apply for a position. I say "ostensibly" because I know better now (there are no such things as coincidences). The fact that there was a real possibility that I might be the recipient of such an honor made the prospect even more attractive. I was only twenty-five, but the year before I had pulled off an artistic

---

6. Clara Forster Lustig (1818–1877), Greek and Latin scholar, journalist, and book reviewer. Emma Forster's second cousin, once removed, and her governess from 1838 to 1842.—*R. Lowe*

coup, so to speak, having correctly identified an anonymous oil sketch, tucked away in one of the dark corners of the museum, as a Constable. Pure luck, of course. The night before I had been poring over the master's sketchbooks: the oil was a combined enlargement of two of its leaves.

But I didn't win the post. A Denise Crowell received the laurel instead. I might have accepted their decision with some semblance of equanimity were it not for the fact that I knew her slightly, having attended her coming-out party in Southampton in 1918 on her uncle's estate. Actually, we were very much alike, two peas in a pod: wealthy fathers' only daughters, spoiled and stuffed full of artistic pretensions. So then, why her and not me? That rankled. I began to brood over it.

Impulsively, I decided to remain in London. I could do as I pleased. I was, after all, financially independent, having a more than adequate income from two trusts.

Both my parents were dead: my father whom I had adored had died when I was fifteen and my mother, one of the Tennessee Olcotts, had died giving birth to me. My only close relative was my father's sister, Aunt Jenny, a tiresome invalid. I cabled her and the museum that I would be staying on for "an indefinite length of time."

Still brooding over the rejection, and bored and lonely (I avoided the few friends I knew in London), it became my custom to prowl through the streets until I was exhausted, at which point I would board a bus, any bus, and ride to the end of the line.

One day I boarded a bus and it took me to Marlborough Gardens. It was as simple as that. Or was it?

As usual, I was deep in a jumble of confused thoughts when I heard the driver's voice, really more of a shout, say: "Miss! Miss! 'Tis the end of the line!"

"Where am I?" I asked.

"Marlborough Gardens is where you be! Will you be getting off here, or will you be staying on? The return trip will cost you thirty pence . . . to be paid in advance."

I stepped off the bus.

"I shall walk home," I said to him through the open door.

"Oh. And where may that be, Miss?" I named a street in Belgravia and he laughed. "Well, now, if you be home by evensong, I should be surprised." A second later he banged shut the door and roared off.

I was alone.

*   *   *

Marlborough Gardens. I shall not attempt to describe it. I shall let Emma, Albert, and Jorem do that; I simply cannot do it justice, never having seen it in its pristine state. Though I knew immediately, standing in front of the partially opened gate—an enormous wrought-iron affair with a large and curious shield attached to its center—that I was on the threshold of something utterly unique. Incomparable. Like the discovery of the Dark Continent, or the fabled Kingdom of the Sleeping Beauty. From where I stood I could see a monstrous overgrowth of vine and nettle.

I did not dare go in then. Instead I walked around the fenced enclosure that, unlike the ordinary London square, was a full half mile in each direction. The size of a small park, I thought. Peering from time to time through the rusted palings I caught glimpses of statues so encumbered by wild vegetation that I could not even determine their sex, much less their identity.

What had happened here? I wondered. Why had the gardens—a thing of considerable beauty—for that was immediately apparent, despite the gross neglect—been allowed to disintegrate into this junglelike ruin? It was unlike the English, whose sensibilities were so finely attuned to tradition and history, to allow the savage elements to have their way.

Having circled the garden once, I decided to walk around it again. This time around, just inside the North Gate on a rise of ground I spied a temple; and with a shock I recognized it as a faithful copy, though smaller, of the Parthenon itself.

Twilight was beginning to fall. The Gardens blazed in the last brilliance of the sun: green leaf, black stem, twig and bough, and sculpted figures now shone all copper and bronze. Watching the last rays of the sun enclose the temple in an aura of ripeness, endowing the dead stone with mysterious life (sensuous, erogenous), I thought of Watteau and Cythera, of lovers and their mistresses, of words of love murmured to the sound of lutes and guitars. A world where no anxieties existed. Empty of strife and struggle and . . . rivals.

There was a sudden scent of roses and a flight of starlings sped across the pink-streaked sky. A rising wind began to carve the opalescent clouds into galleons, chariots, and celestial cities while beneath, the earthly garden shimmered in its field of burnished gold. I stood there spellbound, allowing the enchantment to do its work inside me.

Later that evening, alone in my rooms, I told myself that the reason the Gardens had had such an effect on me was because of my curious emotional state. Disappointment had rendered me vulnerable. Rejection had unbalanced me. I don't believe that now. You see, I know the truth.

A row of Georgian houses faced the Gardens. They too were in a state of ruin, but their basic splendor, like the Gardens, had endured. They seemed empty, abandoned. Tenantless. Were the Gardens and the houses a sort of capricious folly then? Or had some awful catastrophe occurred? Like Pompeii, for instance, destroying utterly, without warning, a way of life that had once been luxurious and beautiful?

There was something uncanny about Marlborough Gardens. Something mysterious. Suddenly I had the feeling that if I did actually choose to walk home I might never find my way to Belgravia, or if I did, I might never find my way back to Marlborough Gardens.

The shadows deepened. I began to feel cold. My thin, cloth coat was not warm enough for a chilly spring evening. Reluctantly, I made my way back to the bus stop and to the Garden's entrance, which I had already named in my mind: The Great South Gate.

Standing at the bus stop I looked across the road and saw (for the first time) in the front garden of one of the houses a wooden sign attached to a post stuck in a cinder heap. Something was printed on it that I couldn't make out. I crossed over to take a closer look:

FREEHOLD
CHALMERS LTD.
ESTATE AGENTS
1078 OXFORD STREET

And lower down, in the left-hand corner, there was a barely legible phone number scribbled.

The structure was clearly moldering. An upper window gaped. The oculus was gouged. Most of the sashes were gone, and those that remained were broken and needed paint. Cornices were missing, and one side of the facade was blackened, as if there had been a fire. The front door was missing too. In its place wooden planks had been hammered into the door frame. But the ad-dress—43 Marlborough Gardens—carved into the stone lintel above the door and adorned with acanthus leaves was intact.

On either side of the makeshift door were tall, wide windows. In each were reflected, in a dazzling display of silver and ebony shapes, the wild trees and shrubbery of Marlborough Gardens. For a moment it seemed to me as if someone inside were watching me, but I realized it was only an odd trick of light. No one lived there.

Moldering, "worn to the bones," still, I thought to myself, it is the most beautiful house I have ever seen.

A few moss roses had survived the cruel neglect. I reached over the dirty, rusted railing and picked one bloom. Holding it lightly, tenderly, in the cup of my hand, I stared at the house, and I knew, I was absolutely certain, that I would live there someday. And until that time no other place would satisfy me.

That afternoon I made a promise to myself that I would not inquire as to its price, not until I was ready to buy it and live there, though what I meant by "ready" I didn't know. I would leave it to chance whether or not it would still be available then.

THREE

If one does not expect the unexpected, one will not find it out.

—Heraclitus, Fr. 18,
trans. Clara Lustig

MARLBOROUGH GARDENS, 1935

Lowe and I enter the Gardens by way of the Great South Gate. It is early morning and there is a heavy mist. We pass the sunken gardens, the muted nymphs. Beyond, wreathed in coils of fog, is the rose garden and the single grave. How pale the roses are. Ghost roses. We come to the lake, once swan filled, and stop to feed the "duckies."

The lake is covered with a pale green scum. Liverwort and duckweed choke the shaggy beds of floating nymphea. Bulrushes and codlin's and cream grow out from the curved banks, and from the deepest depths, like a revelation, rises the algae-encrusted statue of the old horse tamer himself, Poseidon.

Reckless women that we are, we throw all of our crumbs into the water at once. The duckies know us and the water churns as they paddle towards us. We are quite alone, Lowe and I, in this still, small pastoral world.

We are on our way to Blenheim Wood to picnic in the Sacred Grove where the oak tree stands.

Sitting in the checkered shade underneath the boughs of the tree, we unpack our lunch: fillets of haddock packed in dill, dry biscuits, and a bottle of wine.

Primroses open their blossoms on the edge of the glade while moneywort creeps with its blossoms over the damper soil in the denser shadows. The oak tree wades in a blue mirage. The earth is free of time. And throughout the glade rings the voice of the nightingale. Our bottle finished, we lie down side by side on the blue carpet and fall asleep.

At dusk we awaken. Are we late? Are we too late? Oh, we must hurry, hurry to the temple! Quickly we follow the winding paths alongside Blenheim Brook, crashing through black nests of twigs and dense undergrowth. Our veins filled with wine, we sing the ancient hymn: "Oh the earth is a thicket of roots!/Oh what is the root of all roots?"

Out of the wood we stand scratched, bleeding, wine-flushed. We brandish our makeshift staffs all covered in vine and ivy. There, across the gravel path, stands the Temple of the Virgin, the Parthenon, burning in the last rays of the sun. Wide, shallow steps cut into the hillside lead up to the dark entrance. In front in a semicircle stand the backless benches made of stone. On summer nights, a hundred years ago, a band played music on those steps. . . .

The temple is cold inside. Someone has stolen Medusa's eyes. We are glad for it, for it is frightening enough to have to stand in front of the great goddess herself as she gazes down at us out of her alabaster eyes. We stay and perform the ancient rituals until the moon completes her journey across the central aperture.

✻   ✻   ✻

I phoned Mr. Chalmers after my aunt had died. Even across an expanse of three thousand miles he set my American teeth on edge. I knew the type only too well—an English toady. I cut through his sycophantic burbling and explained rapidly who I was, what I wanted, and that I would be in London within the month when I could see him in person.

I severed my American connections and sold the family mansion in Shaker Heights far below the prevailing market price, a fact that enraged my father's lawyer, a patriarchal type. But I am not fond of patriarchs and so I informed him that firstly, he was not my lawyer, secondly, I had not asked him for advice, thirdly, I had no intentions of retaining him, fourthly, I intended to reside in England, and fifthly, that if in the future I felt the need of legal help I would hire my own counsel.

The trip over on the *Queen Mary* was uneventful for the most part. From Liverpool I took a train to London, and from the station a cab to Oxford Street. It was a gray, chilly morning. London appeared dirty and dismal. I could not help but wonder if I had not made a ghastly mistake.

Mr. Chalmers's office did not dispel the notion. (It was singularly unimpressive.) Nor did Mr. Chalmers, whose two hundred pounds were squeezed into a suit far too small for him. His opening words did not reassure: "Imagine! Madam coming straight here from the station! Ah, you Americans, much like impulsive children, aren't you?" (Did he expect me to agree?) "But you must be anxious to view the house, *toute de suite,* as they say. *N'est-ce pas?*"

The man was a fool and *both* his accents were abhorrent.

"I should like to know the price first, Mr. Chalmers."

He quoted what I thought was truly an exorbitant price. I reached for my purse and gloves, which I had reluctantly placed on his worn and stained carpet, but as I did he rose and came toward me. His face was flushed.

"But, my dear lady, you are not aware then that the price includes *two* establishments. . . ." His breath was bad; he had had fish for lunch, I could smell it; his teeth were a shambles. "You see, Madam, there is a house behind the main structure. A lodge. But the term is not really suitable. It is nothing less than a millionaire's caprice. And both edifices stocked with the most priceless antiques! And both houses in superb condition though I will grant you there may be need of a few minor repairs." His plaintive voice had become a shade insolent as he sensed my renewed interest. "But if the property does not suit Madam, we have others we can show that might suit her better. Marlborough Gardens is, after all, as you Americans say, 'off the beaten track,' *n'est-ce pas?* . . . May I inquire how you chanced upon it?"

"Mr. Chalmers, I am pressed for time. If I am to see it at all, we'd best leave now." His explanation had satisfied me.

We drove to Marlborough Gardens in his car, Mr. Chalmers maintaining an air of *armour propre* throughout the journey.

"We shall have to enter via the rear door, Madam, the front being boarded up," he said as he parked the car.

He held open the door for me, and I stepped out of the car. The street was empty. I noticed that the Great South Gate was closed. It was noon. The sun was at its zenith, but today its glory was hidden by a thick shield of clouds. It would rain soon.

As we walked toward the rear of the house, I noted with satisfaction that the house was deeper than I had expected. Directly behind it there were what looked like the remains of a kitchen garden and to the right of it a group of forlorn-looking trees. As for the lodge, that stood some distance away. The property was much larger than I had realized. A brick walk, badly in need of repair, joined the two houses. I remember thinking as I glanced at the lodge: uninteresting and unattractive.

Standing at the top of a short granite staircase, Mr. Chalmers withdrew an iron key from his coat pocket and fitted it into the rusted lock of the large oak door. It slid in easily enough, I noticed. I followed him through a grim Victorian kitchen, a grimmer pantry, and a dark narrow corridor that led into a spacious well-proportioned central hall.

As we went through the house, he insisted on describing everything (all in superlative terms): the wainscotting, the swag, the Jacobean ceilings. . . . I could only hope that by remaining silent I might dampen his commercial enthusiasm. My irritation was mounting steadily as I listened.

As we moved from the second floor to the third, there was a sound of thunder. Moments later it began to rain.

We were in the nursery in the rear of the house. Lightning flickered through the room. I could see that it all needed painting and plastering as well. And a new floor. Some of the boards were missing. Mr. Chalmers had placed himself at one of the casement windows, his back to me. It occurred to me that he might have been an actor once. One could hear the director say: "Stand there, old chap, it will be effective." Just then he turned around and beckoned me with a plump forefinger to join him. I did. It was raining hard now, and the group of stunted trees that I had glanced at momentarily some moments earlier looked even bleaker than before from this angle.

"I venture, Madam, that those apple trees"—was that what those poor things were?—"ancient though they be, shall still bear succulent fruit." It was May and they were still almost leafless. "I vow your cook—for you shall have a staff, *n'est-ce pas?*—shall be delighted with them. And she, good woman—"

I cut him off without a qualm. "Shall we leave, Mr. Chalmers? I believe I told you I was pressed for time."

"Leave!" sputtered Mr. Chalmers. "Leave! But Madam, you have not even seen the lodge. Truly you have not been fair—"

"I have seen enough to suit me, Mr. Chalmers," and now I

confess I hesitated a moment or two out of pure malice, while watching Mr. Chalmers's face crumble. His old friend, Failure, was standing by his side ready to embrace him once again, before I concluded my sentence. "You see I intend to buy forty-three Marlborough Gardens. *Toute de suite . . . n'est-ce pas* as they say."

I could not help but smile at Mr. Chalmers's obvious relief.

          ❋   ❋   ❋

Money truly works wonders.

What might have taken six months or more to accomplish, for there was despite Mr. Chalmers's disclaimers a great deal to do, was done in a matter of six weeks.

I paid for the house in cash, which brought tears to Mr. Chalmers's eyes, and in the following week hired glaziers, carpenters, painters, and stone masons to refurbish and restore the main house. I decided to leave the lodge alone. It didn't interest me. Oddly enough, neither did the Gardens.

I moved in on September 28, 1927. My personal belongings were next to nothing. For some reason I had felt compelled to give away almost all of my possessions, as if I were entering a religious order. All that was left were some books, a few clothes, an oil painting of my father, and a cherry-wood wardrobe that he had made for me when I was a child. On its sides and top were painted Queen Mab's kingdoms of fairies and elves. I hung the oil in the master bedroom and placed the bureau underneath. I was delighted and in good spirits as one usually is when one does exactly as one pleases.

As to what I would do in London now that I was physically established, I hadn't a clue. But I wish to make it clear that from the very beginning I knew that I must take care of the house. From the start I not only had a sense of duty, a feeling of moral obligation as it were, but I also understood somehow that it was my assigned task to "caretake" the house, to be its "guardian." As if it needed one. Required one. As if it were sacred, as sacred, let us say, as the ancient grove of Diana on the shores of Lake Nemi.

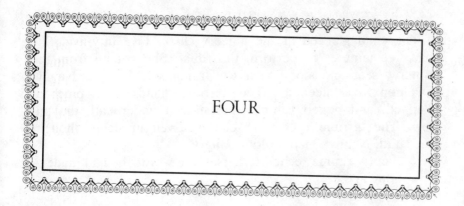

FOUR

MARLBOROUGH GARDENS, 1935

WE have been confined to the house these past few days, Lowe having caught a chill when we were in the temple. But there's enough work for us to do inside. Sewing for instance: yesterday I finished mending Emma's riding habit, which had a long rip in the skirt. This evening I plan to work on Vanessa's ball gown, a lovely thing, an embroidered India muslin with wide moiré stripes. I do hope I shall finish it in time so that Lowe may wear it this coming Sunday when we go to the Tower. Time passes so quickly as I listen to Lowe read out loud—it will be morning before I know it. . . .

City of Childhood

V

THE DAY THE CHILDREN MET DARIUS [7]

APRIL 23d, 5:55 A.M.

EMMA, a thin, small child, her straight flaxen hair done up in rag curls, sat in front of the open window that overlooked the apple trees. They had come into bloom the day before but their beauty did not touch her.

---

7. Since the fall of 1929, Harriet and I have worked together with   *cont.*

The child glanced at the nursery clock. Five fifty-five. She had five minutes to perform the ritual. She got up from the window seat and stood next to Grindal's bed where Nanny-Daemon was sleeping. The terrible hands that pinched, slapped, and poked Emma were hidden underneath the pillow. The terrible eyes were closed. Even in sleep, thought the child, Nanny-Daemon looks angry.

Silently Emma recited to herself the words she had made up long ago:

> *I am watching you, Grindal,*
> *And you do not know it!*
> *Gouge out her eyes! Rip out her tongue!*
> *Smash her teeth, one by one!*
> *I am watching you, Grindal,*
> *And you do not know it!*

The young woman stirred. Her long black hair glided across the white coverlet like a wave. The child glanced at the clock. Almost six. In seconds it would strike the hour.

In what was almost a single movement, the child put herself into the bed that stood alongside her nurse's, and swiftly drew the covers up to her chin. Just as the last chime sounded, Grindal turned herself over, sat up, and yawned. Then suddenly she flung herself out of bed.

The second part of Emma's ritual began. From beneath lowered lids she watched as the "daemon" removed her nightgown and ambled over to the looking glass (I am watching you, Grindal, and you do not know it!), which hung over a low, broad bureau on the far side of the room. Disgusting, thought the child as she watched the nurse gazing at her reflection, those moon-shaped blobs . . . those nipples . . .

---

a remarkable singleness of purpose: checking and rechecking the material, writing and revising it, choosing the relevant, and discarding the rest. Above all establishing connections that heretofore were hidden like some lovely woman's painted fan which upon opening discloses a unique and total universe. Still there have been some minor problems. Despite the abundance of material, there remained mysterious hiatuses . . . unexplained lacunae. For instance: *City of Childhood* is an incomplete manuscript. There are chapters missing. We have dealt with this the best we could.—*R. Lowe* like wax candles stuck in dirty dough. Her gaze shifted downward to the lower part of Grindal's flat belly . . . that was even more disgusting, that triangle of dark curly hair. And positive proof that Nanny Grindal was a monster as the child had suspected all along. Emma had told her brothers, Edward and William, about it—they slept with Tansy, Grindal's assistant, in the alcove of the night nursery—but they didn't believe her. But who could believe such a thing! Once she had seen Grindal slip her long, carrot-colored fingers into the hair and at the same time stroke her breasts. But not this morning.

She watched as Grindal washed herself and brushed her hair, which she braided and then twisted around her small oval head. (Gouge out her eyes, rip out her tongue!) She watched as Grindal put on her drawers and her chemise (smash her teeth one by one!), don her petticoats and her black uniform, and, bending over, lace her shoes (I am watching you, Grindal, and you do not know it!), watched as Grindal withdrew a freshly starched apron from the top bureau drawer, and watched as she twisted the apron strings into a stiff bow. (And you do not know it!)

The young woman, taking a last look at herself in the glass, stuck out her tongue and smiled at herself, then walked over to Emma's bed and stood there quietly.

This was the worst moment of the day. Emma's body tensed. She whispered to herself: "You are a dead tin soldier lying in a box. You are dead, quite dead. You can feel nothing. Nothing can hurt you. Nothing! Not even Grindal."

"UPUPUPUP!" came the raucous command, "OUT-OUTOUT! UPANDABOUT! OUTOFYOURBED!" and then the covers were snatched from her in one fell swoop. *That* was really the worst moment. Then the order: "Get your potty and go about your business!"

The child scampered out of bed. All dignity lost, she withdrew her potty from underneath the bed and lowered herself onto the cold porcelain ring. As she tinkled (Grindal's word), she began to pray, "Dear God, please fill my potty with farmer's gold today."

"Farmer's gold" was the euphemism Grindal had made up to describe the children's bowel movements. If there was none in the potty, Grindal would say: "What! No farmer's gold today! What would the world come to if every child behaved like you, Emma? Answer me that!"

What indeed! Emma used to ponder the question anxiously. In her mind's eye she envisioned a mob of angry farmers, their rakes and hoes held high, marching to Marlborough Gardens, chanting: "Farmer's gold! Farmer's gold! We will not leave until we have it!"

She was still on her potty when her brothers, together with Tansy, came into the day nursery for their breakfast.

Edward planted himself in front of Grindal. He had the frank and open air of a child to whom a continuous series of messages, overt to subtle, had been relayed: "You are special, you are the elder son, you are the heir!" But to his credit he had an innate sense of justice. He was Emma's champion against Grindal.

On the whole the children were loyal to one another, sensing instinctively that there were two separate species (albeit one genus) in the nursery: adults and children. And so they often banded together against the troop of servants who, for the most part, ruled their lives.

"I've had the most splendid dream, Nanny. I dreamed that the Calcutta Ghost came to Marlborough Gardens.[8] To Blenheim Wood, in fact, where he went straight to the old oak in the Sacred Grove and placing his hand on its lowest branch took an oath never to terrify the Calcutta children again. 'I have learned my lesson,' he said. 'I am quite ashamed of myself. And I do hope that I shall be forgiven.' What do you think of that, Nanny Grindal?"

"Not much, Master Edward. Liars and cheats do not change overnight. Let me see your hands."

She was curt with him at times; that was her nature; but she never beat him or locked him in the closet as she did Emma. He was the heir, after all, and possibly, Emma sometimes conceded, she actually liked him.

"Good morning, Nanny Grindal," said Daisy, one of the upstairs maids, as she carried in a large tray and set it on

---

8. The Calcutta Ghost was a character in one of Grindal's fairy tales. Grindal was a tyrant, but she had a genius for telling stories. Her imagination unspoiled by reason could, in a twinkling of an eye, plunge the children into worlds of terror, violence and beauty that held them spellbound.—*R. Lowe*

the white, painted table that stood in front of the cold grate. "Cook says it'll rain 'fore dark. Couldn't straighten out her legs this mornin'."

"If I want a weather report, I'll ask for it," said Grindal as she motioned the two small boys to sit down. After the perfunctory grace, "Forwhatweareabouttoreceivemaythe-Lordmakeustrulygratefulamen," Tansy tied their bibs around their necks.

"And Master Edward. What did he do this morning?" asked Grindal, as she sat down next to the nine-year-old boy.

"His usual, Nanny Grindal," said Tansy. "But William . . . now his did seem a bit green to me this morning. I reckon he might be coming down with spring sickness."

During this dialogue the children ate their porridge, silently putting one spoonful after another into their small mouths. The daily conversation about their respective eliminations seemed neither strange nor untoward. Nor did they really listen; it was the daily interchange between the two women.

"Best be safe than sorry. Daisy, hand me Dr. Boot's elixir. There, you stupid girl, on top of the bureau . . . and the spoon next to it."

The maid handed the tonic and the spoon to Grindal, who walked over to William. She opened the bottle and poured the foul-smelling stuff into the large spoon. "Open your mouth, Master William." He did. "Wide! . . . Wider!" and the spoon tipped its contents into the small gaping mouth. William let out a groan. "Swallow!" He did and it slid down his throat like a cold worm.

"Isn't Emma having breakfast today?" asked Edward.

"Not until she's done her farmer's gold," came the cool reply.

"But that's not fair, Nanny. Sometimes it's awfully hard to do. Isn't that right, William? William! Do speak up! And take your fingers out of your porridge. Nanny, he's got his fingers in his porridge. . . ."

William took his fingers out but said nothing. He was deep in thought, wondering about Cook's legs. How crooked were they? And did they bend to the left or to the right? Might they even be twisted into corkscrews? He would dearly love to see them. Perhaps Daisy would be kind enough to take him later in the day to see Mrs. Lovesley's legs. Sometimes she was . . .

"William!"

"You can't," said William because he had heard the question after all, even though he hadn't answered right away, and he added, for he knew what was expected of him, "Edward's right. Sometimes it's awfully hard to do."

But just as William responded, Emma came to the table, her prayers having finally been answered.

"What!" shouted Grindal. "How dare you! How dare she! Look at her! Who told you that you could have your breakfast? Who told you that? Answer me! Did I, Tansy? Did I, Daisy?" They shook their heads. "Well, I shall teach you a pretty lesson, Miss Emma"—and getting up from the table she swung at the child with her right arm as she continued shouting—"how dare you! Oh how dare you!" but Emma ducked just as the arm completed its arc and in so doing fell against the edge of the table and cut her forehead. It began to bleed. Immediately. Profusely.

Grindal, her face crimson with rage, came out from behind the table, and dragging Emma by her arms as if she were an oversized doll, took her to her bed where Grindal turned the child over on her lap and began to beat her with her slipper.

The child felt nothing at first but then her buttocks began to feel on fire and she started to scream. They looked on in terror, all of them—Daisy, Tansy, Edward, and William— as Grindal's arm swung up and down. Like a bloody metronome, thought Tansy.

"Stop it! Stop beating Emma!" cried Edward running over to them. "If you don't stop, I shall tell Poppa and he shall have you beaten! You . . . you . . . you . . ."—the child struggled to select an insult that would devastate his nurse— "you . . . you . . . you common slut!"

What had come to mind was the epithet his father used when speaking of his Aunt Consuelo, his brother Joseph's wife, a woman his father "detested." "I detest her! I detest her!" his father would shout after she had left the house.

And then Edward added for good measure, "Do not overstep your place!"

Grindal stopped. With her arm still raised and her shoe still held in her hand, she said in a low hoarse whisper, "Master Edward, calm yourself. You can see for yourself that your sister's not really hurt," and she dumped Emma on the bed next to her.

It was true. The cut had stopped bleeding, and except for a slightly stunned expression on her face, he could see that his sister seemed to be her old self again.

Leaving her there, Grindal walked over to the potty and looked down into it. Her apron was streaked with blood. She looks like a butcher, thought Daisy. "What's all the fuss about anyway? She's done her farmer's gold. You stupid child . . . why didn't you say so in the first place? Here, Daisy, take it away."

Daisy lifted up the chamber pot holding it away from her nose. Behind her face, a smooth blank mask, Daisy was thinking how she couldn't wait to tell Cook and Mrs. Farnley how Miss High and Mighty had been put in her place. And by Master Edward himself! Oh, she could kick up her heels and dance!

They were a full fifteen minutes behind schedule. The children were dressed quickly, as if nothing had happened, but when Tansy put Emma's spencer on, she whispered in her ear: "You're a wicked little girl. You've upset your nanny. God shall punish you in due time."

But Emma couldn't have cared less. She was not to be punished. A miracle was taking place. She was not to stay home, not to be locked up or confined to a corner in the nursery and made to stare at a wall for hours. Instead she was to be allowed to accompany her brothers as always to Marlborough Gardens. Why? She didn't know and she didn't care.

Grindal's questions rang out: "Do you have your swords? Your ships? Your flags?" "Yes, yes, yes," came the answers. "Then form a line." And so the children and the nurses—Grindal leading, Tansy taking up the rear—formed a single file and marched out of the nursery, across the landing, down the stairs, out of the house, and across the street toward the Great South Gate of Marlborough Gardens.

APRIL 23d, 8:55 A.M.

Albert, Sidney, and the twins Jacob and Joshua (Solomon's children) enter Marlborough Gardens by way of the Great North Gate. Behind them follows Nanny Jakes, a pale young girl holding the hand of their sister Deirdre, a plump pretty child of three. Albert, Solomon's heir, is leading the group. At the age of twelve he is passionately in love with Guinivere, his mother.

Underneath Albert's right arm is a box that contains his most precious possession: a fine and detailed replica of Nelson's flagship, the *Victory,* a hallowed object, to be guarded if necessary with his life. He allows no one to touch it. Yesterday he had permitted Joshua, but only for a moment, to run his forefinger down the mizzenmast. This morning Sidney dared to touch the *Victory* without Albert's consent. Albert hates Sidney. He has hated Sidney as far back as he can remember. In revenge he broke off the head of one of Sidney's wooden soldiers. His mother has promised to take care of the *Victory* for him when he goes to Warrenton. He hates thinking about Warrenton. She has told him that she will place the ship in the cabinet that stands in her sitting room. Between the porcelain shepherdess and the bisque cat. He knows his mother loves him best of all. He knows it for a fact though she has never told him so and he trusts her . . . though she failed him once. . . .

It happened the day before his fourth birthday. He remembers every detail.

Momma spent the entire day with him. Alone. A rare pleasure. She had kissed him often, stroked his hair, his skin . . . he recalled vividly her soft pink lips on his . . . At teatime she had broken her lemon tart in two and shared it with him. Then holding his hands in hers, she told him that God was sending them a gift, "a sister or a brother whom you shall love, dearest one, and who in turn shall love my dearest one, Albert." But even as he listened, he knew it wasn't true, and the bit of tart that he still held in his mouth turned to stone. Why was she smiling? he wondered. But he said nothing. Young as he was, he had shrewdly gauged the look on his sweetheart's face: she wanted him to want what she wanted. Instead of answering, he had lowered his face.

In due time Sidney had arrived, "God's gift," a small, red, screaming thing, and Albert instantly hated the gift as he knew he would.

His brother Sidney catches up to him on the gravel path. Albert stares at him with unmitigated hatred, and then turning his handsome head away, gazes into the vacant sunshine. . . .

Suddenly in front of Albert, standing on the gravel walk (why he can almost touch him!), is a scarlet-coated dragoon, his face hidden by his helmet that has fallen forward over his face. Who can he be? wonders Albert, though there is no doubt in Albert's mind as to who is lying at the dragoon's feet. It is Sidney. Badly wounded. He watches as the blood flows from Sidney's wound (a chest wound) and drips onto the gravel. It reminds him of something. Of what? Of the bronze droplets on the curious shields that are tied to the Garden's gates. Suddenly he hears the whinnying of horses. Of course! He, the dragoon, and Sidney are on a battlefield! Albert watches, entranced, as the dragoon draws his long sword out of his scabbard and plunges it deep—deep!—into Sidney's heart! A beatific smile breaks across his handsome face.

Sidney, who has been watching his brother intently, lets out a sigh. Thank God! Albert has forgiven him. He loves Albert. Sometimes he thinks he loves Albert more than he loves Momma, if that were possible, though he knows for a fact that Momma loves Albert more than she loves him, Sidney.

"And you are not to climb the tower, your Momma said. It needs fixing," said Nanny Jakes. We are there, then, thinks Albert. At Nannies Plain. He doesn't remember walking here, but we are here, he concedes, for there are the stone benches on which all the nannies sit, and there are the grass lawns with the strange statues that frighten him, and in the distance the winter garden.

The vision shrinks as he answers, "Yes, yes, Nanny, I understand," and disappears from view as he puts down his box carefully, and sits next to it on the bench directly facing a large equestrian statue. The Duke of Marlborough. His father has told him that.

Sidney sits down next to Albert. As he does, Albert immediately picks up his box and moves two whole benches away. Albert is waiting for his cousins Edward and William. He loves Edward. I shall love Edward until the day I die, he tells himself. He waits patiently. They are late this morning.

Out of the corner of his eye he sees Vanessa and her two sisters, Letitia and Mary-Anne. They are walking towards Nannies Plain followed by their nurse, Nanny Burden. He hates all three of them. They do nothing but sit on the benches, though sometimes they stroll up and down the paths, their arms around each other's waists. He knows that Vanessa is beautiful because his mother has told him that she is. "An unearthly beauty," that is what his father once said when speaking of her. What did it mean? he wondered. No matter, he still doesn't like her. She is unkind. She is not like his beloved Guinivere. He doesn't like Emma either. He's quite certain she's the cause of Edward being late. But who could like Emma? Sometimes he feels sorry for her, though. He remembers Vanessa's reply when Emma asked her if she could join her and her sisters on one of their walks. "Yes, when pigs fly."

Sidney begins to count the pebbles between his boots. I shall never touch the *Victory* again. Never! Why had he done it? But he really doesn't understand. Albert *did* smile. But if Albert has forgiven him why did he move away? He doesn't feel comfortable when Albert is angry with him. It worries him. He must do something about it. Looking down between his boots, he decides to himself that if there are more than fifty pebbles between his boots Albert will forgive him before they play Trafalgar.

One . . . two . . . three . . . He is quite optimistic. It seems to him as if there might be more than a hundred pebbles. . . .

APRIL 23d, 10:00 A.M.

The cousins are sitting in a circle in the ruins of Marlborough Marshes behind the remains of a curved wall.

Yesterday Sidney found another coin. He brought it home and put it in one of the two cardboard boxes Jakes allows him to keep under the dresser with his other "finds": a piece of thick orange glass with lovely scalloped edges, three buttons made of tin, a lady's comb with two broken teeth, nine coins with foreign letters on them that not even Poppa understands, and a long gray feather that he thinks might have once belonged to a dodo.

His most prized possession he keeps in a box of its own. It is a torn scrap of paper, a fragment of an advertisement that blew into his hands (miraculously) a year ago on his way home from the Gardens, and which Nanny Jakes, after much difficulty, deciphered and read out loud to him. He has learned the words by heart:

> *D. Godfrey begs respectfully to thank his friends for past favors and to inform them that his hotel will now be found complete with every comfort and accommodation. Table d'hôte daily on arrival of the swift cutter from Glasgow . . .*

What are the past favors? Sidney wonders. And what are the comforts and accommodations? Sometimes he envisions himself arriving on the "swift cutter" and receiving these mysterious "comforts and accommodations."[9] When things look hopeless (when it seems as if Albert will *never* forgive him), he recites the mysterious words "every comfort and accommodation" to himself. Somehow it soothes him. He does so now. . . .

Trafalgar begins: Albert their leader assigns them their roles.

"You shall play Collingwood," he says to Edward (Collingwood was Lord Nelson's best friend), "and three British tars and two gunners." There are only eight children so each child must play double and triple roles.

"And you shall play Villeneuve (Nelson's enemy)," he tells Sidney as he removes the *Victory* from its box and places it on a long flat stone where it shall remain until the end of the game. Sidney plays only one role: the enemy.

"Joshua shall be my aide-de-camp, and one midship-

---

9. Such are the devices children use to sustain themselves in a world with few comforts and no accommodations.—*H. Van Buren*

man, and one quartermaster. William shall play Hardy . . .
William!''

William nods. Why won't they leave him alone? He always
plays Hardy. He knows what he has to do. An interesting
insect has just come up out of the ground in front of him.
It has six legs, two wings, and antennae. But he can barely
see them since all of it is wrapped up in some sort of thread,
and it is struggling. He wonders should he leave it alone or
should he bury it?

What the children liked best about the game Trafalgar was
the Awful Moment! *And* Nelson's death scene.

"Then came the Awful Moment!" their fathers had told
them, "when a French sharpshooter in the mizzentop of
Villeneuve's ship picked out our gallant Lord Nelson and
fired! And the ball penetrated into the regions of the spine
and our poor Lord Nelson was carried to the cockpit where
he died!"

Nelson's death. Albert did it so well. Poor, brave, noble
Nelson! Felled by the wicked blow. They would carry him—
Albert/Nelson—all of them, including Villeneuve/Sidney, to
a declivity in the ground known to them as the cockpit, next
to the long flat stone on which the *Victory* rested.

Oh how they loved it when Albert/Lord Nelson, his face
a perfect mask of courage, recited the famous words: "Kiss
me, Hardy"—and William/Hardy did—"I am a dead
man. . . . Thank God I have done my duty!" and then sank
back ever so slowly onto the ground. They never tired of it.

The roles are assigned. Albert has not mentioned Emma.
Sometimes he allows Emma to play, but only as a prisoner.
But today he's angry with her. It was her fault, just as he
had thought, that they were late.

"What about Emma?" asks Edward. He's promised
Emma he would stand by her if Albert excluded her from
the game today but his heart is thudding. What if Albert
refuses to let her play? What should he do then?

"There are no girls allowed in His Majesty's Navy," replies
Albert coldly.

"But you allow her to play sometimes, nevertheless."
Must he persist? he wonders. He must. He has promised.
Taking a deep breath he says: "If you don't let her play,
why then I shan't, and if I don't, neither shall William."

The die is cast! Oh how he hates Emma! It does not occur to Edward or for that matter to Emma or William that they could play Trafalgar by themselves. How can they? Edward cannot envision himself as Lord Nelson. That is Albert's role. He, Edward, is Collingwood.

Surprisingly, Albert concedes. "All right. She can play today. You may play a prisoner, Emma. Now shall we begin—"

"I don't want to play a prisoner. I want to be an English officer . . . like Edward and William."

Albert is rendered speechless. He feels quite dizzy. He can say nothing. He cannot move his tongue, his mouth is dry. The children are silent.

It is Sidney who breaks the silence. "You can't be an English officer. You can only play a foreigner who is either a prisoner, or a foreigner who is not a prisoner. But you cannot be an English officer. That is a rule of the game."

How dare Sidney help him! How dare he! Anger starts Albert's juices flowing; he turns to Emma, "You may—but just for this once! remember that—play an English officer."

The children have been so engrossed in the discussion that they haven't noticed the figure of an older boy standing at the far end of the wall who has been watching and listening to them all of this time. He steps forward now.

"Oh, in heaven's name! Why don't you let Emma play Emma. Emma Hamilton. Your mistress, Lord Nelson." He nods in Albert's direction. "Or have your Poppas withheld that bit of information in their account of England's most distinguished hero?"

Like the limbs of a single animal the children move closer together. Who is he? they wonder. This . . . this . . . strange boy. Or is he a man? They can't decide. He's not dressed like a boy. That is, he's not wearing a sailor costume and a straw hat and streamers. No. The boy/man is wearing a brown velvet suit, a brown velvet cloak, and a soft gray hat with a long feather stuck in its brim, and is clutching in one of his yellow-gloved hands a silver-tipped cane. Not that their fathers would wear anything like that. But neither would a boy.

After a moment's silence Albert informs the boy/man, "Sir, we are having a private disagreement."

Unconsciously he has imitated his father's most parochial manner. He hasn't quite understood the strange boy's speech but has guessed from the tone of the voice that whatever it meant it was unpleasant.

"Sir! Do you mean you don't know who I am!" He has a boy's voice, the children decide, but the tone is imperious. He repeats the question. No one answers. No, they don't know who he is. But should they?

Suddenly the boy/man lifts his long thin arms over his head, as if to implore heaven (the cane drops to the grass) . . . but for what reason? Then making a fist with his right hand, the boy/man begins to shout in a foreign language. At first it startles the children but seconds later they are delighted. If only he would speak English so that they could understand. Finally, he does.

"Oh, I can't believe it!" moans the boy/man. "Oh, I do not believe it! I refuse to believe it!" The boy/man smites his forehead.

Quite lovely, think the children, though the chap is obviously mad, but ever so interesting, isn't he? Really almost as interesting as Nelson's death scene. Perhaps Albert/Nelson should do that: smite his forehead and shout "I cannot believe it!" Believe what though? And why does the mad boy think that they know him? They continue to stare at him as he continues to shout.

Clearly he isn't a Forster. Not with that black hair! And his skin! What color is it anyway? And those eyes! Enormous! And brown, not blue like theirs. And not only that— they seemed to be burning. But how can eyes burn? And why is the boy/man so angry? Not that they mind, they just want to know: Why? But he is calming down now. He is smiling actually. He is going to say something else. They lean forward to listen. They do not want to miss a single word, a single syllable.

"I am your cousin Darius. I live at twenty-six Marlborough Gardens with your Aunt Consuelo and Uncle Joseph. I am their son. I have come from school . . . I shall stay home from now on."

"Warrenton?"

"Warrenton, of course! I shall not go back. Perhaps I shall

engage a tutor, but in any case I shall not be going back there again.''

Emma blushes. She remembers who Darius is. It was long ago, as long ago perhaps as two Christmases, and she remembers him not because of his strange clothes, though he was dressed oddly then too, she remembers, no, it was because of the cross he was wearing . . . a very large gold cross, the largest she had ever seen. It had hung from a thick gold chain and rested on the middle of his chest. She had been fascinated by it.

Darius had come to their house with Aunt Consuelo and Uncle Joseph on Sunday afternoon. Every Sunday afternoon, all her aunts and uncles and their children came to her house for midday dinner. When everyone had left, Poppa had screamed: "That cross! Those clothes! She dresses him like a Smyrna peddler! He is an anathema!"—whatever that was—"Oh, my poor brother. She will be the death of him. She and her son!"

Emma knows, as do her brothers, that Poppa hates Aunt Consuelo. He calls her "the foreign woman," "the outsider," "the slut!" (whatever that was).

On Sunday afternoons, after coffee, Aunt Consuelo plays the piano, though no one ever asks her to. Her large hands roam up and down the piano keys with an energy that seems to frighten the other aunts and uncles who sit stiffly, forced to listen, their faces absolutely still. When her aunt finishes, she walks to a chair and sits down while they clap, their faces cold and disapproving. They hadn't realized the "infernal piece" had ended. . . . *That* was who Darius was.

Albert offers his hand, "I am your cousin Albert." If the strange-looking boy was really a Forster and he was impolite to him, his father would be angry. "Manners maketh man." His father says that to him often. Aunt Consuelo . . . the boy does resemble Aunt Consuelo. The same-color skin. The same nose: long and slightly hooked. "And this is my brother Sidney." He has decided it would be best to introduce them all. "My twin brothers Joshua and Jacob, my sister Deirdre, my cousins Edward, William, and Emma. We are pleased to make your acquaintance."

The children are relieved: the amenities have been preserved. Now they can play Trafalgar. Or can they? Sidney has just remembered something.

"But if you are our cousin," asks Sidney, "how is it that we have never seen you at Saddler's Grove?"

Saddler's Grove! Of course! Every summer of their lives they went to Saddler's Grove and stayed with Grandpa Jorem. They have never seen him there. Never. Albert feels humiliated. Why hadn't he thought of that?

The boy is angry again. Worse than before. He's very angry. Good, think the children. They listen carefully as the furious words come boiling out: "No one has ever told you then that I, Darius, Marcus, Georgione, Rimini Forster spend my summers on my estates in Italy! I am not like you! I am an aristocrat! A count! A Catholic! In my veins," he holds his long slender arms out to them, "flows the blood of the Riminis . . . once liege men to the Medicis!"

The children are stunned. They have not understood a single word but the sentence rings through their heads: "I am an aristocrat! A count! A Catholic! In my veins flows the blood of the Riminis . . . once liege men to the Medicis." They long to say it out loud. They long to hold their arms out and repeat after him. Still, as Sidney has pointed out, the boy has never been to Saddler's Grove. Saddler's Grove. Nothing can compare to that. That was paradise!

William knows that gentlemen are kind, in particular to those less fortunate than themselves—Momma had told him that quite often—and so he takes it upon himself to show kindness to the boy/man. He moves toward Darius and, placing his hand tenderly on the boy/man's thigh, he says in his sweet high voice: "Do cheer up, Cousin Darius. Perhaps this summer, if you are good, you will be allowed to join us at Saddler's Grove."

Malice, a look of pain, and something else the children can't make out crosses Darius's sharp features. Is it fear? they wonder. He spits out: "*Ignoranti contadini!* I see I am wasting my time here!" And with that he turns sharply on his heels and walks away, his cape in the shape of a giant hoof billowing out behind him.

They watch him leave. Darius Marcus Georgione Rimini Forster. Is he really their cousin? Perhaps, but right now they have more important things to think about. They must play Trafalgar.

Sidney, Joshua, and Deirdre stand at the base of the tower; that is the French line. Albert, Edward, William, Jacob, and Emma stand at the wall; that is the English line. Albert gives the signal (a raised hand) and the game begins. . . .

They play until they hear the church tower clock strike and then wander back to Nannies Plain. They have already forgotten Darius.

APRIL 23d, EARLY EVENING

Emma sat in front of the fire guard, her wet hair hanging over her face (Grindal had washed it after dinner), thinking about something that had happened a week ago. Edward had asked Grindal, "Why does Emma have that funny mark on her temple?"

" 'Tis the devil's mark. 'Tis God's punishment on her because she is Eve's daughter who was a great sinner."

"What was her great sin, Nanny?"

"She ate apples and consorted with serpents," was the mysterious reply.

Ever since that exchange Emma has brooded about it. What did it mean? Did it mean that she was not Poppa's child? The only Eve she knew was the coachman's wife, a kind enough woman. She had once given Emma a bit of pudding. Did it mean that she was Eve's child? And if that were true could she still be Poppa's child? But if she were really Eve's child, a coachman's daughter, did that explain why Grindal hated her so? She was not a gentleman's daughter after all. But Poppa? Did Poppa know? Had anyone told him?

"Oh, do look at her now, Nanny Grindal," said Tansy, "don't she look like the arch fiend himself with them two eyes starin' out at us through her hair? Come along now," she said as she dragged Emma to Grindal to have her curl rags put on.

At seven o'clock Emma realized with a sinking sensation that Poppa was not coming to bid them his usual good night.

Edward had tried to persuade Grindal to let them stay up "just a bit longer, a few minutes more, Nanny. You'll see Poppa will come and if we're in bed asleep when he does, he will be very angry with you. Oh, do tell us a story until then. You haven't told us one for ages."

Will, who had been "naughty" at dinner and thrust into an old high chair and turned to the wall, stopped whistling and said, "Meki! Tell us the story about Meki, the Evil Old Frog from Bristol. I like him. I do like him so very much."

But she wouldn't: "Shan't. Can't. Won't," said Grindal. And so they were put to bed.

APRIL 23d, EVENING

When Elijah comes home that evening, Mrs. Farnley informs him that a letter has come for him by special messenger which she has put on his desk with his other mail (two letters) in his study.

He goes there directly, telling her he does not wish to be disturbed and locks the door behind him. He pours himself a glass of canary from the decanter sitting on the sideboard. Beside it is a plate of fresh fruit, a fruit knife, and a napkin. He drinks the wine and pours himself another glass.

A fortnight ago Joseph told him that Darius was coming home. Because of ill health, he said—tuberculosis was suspected—but Elijah has not believed him. And so he has taken it upon himself to write Dr. Pond, the headmaster of Warrenton, and a friend of his, to inquire as to the exact circumstances of his nephew's what? . . . Departure? Dismissal? Expulsion? He picks up Dr. Pond's letter and puts it down. No, he shall read it last, he decides.

He glances at the other two. The perfumed note is from Moly, his mistress. He recognizes the handwriting. Finley, Moly's maid and a former governess, had written it. Moly is illiterate.

Her real name is Mary but he calls her Moly ever since the first night together when his fingers discovered a small cluster of protuberances inside her upper left thigh. "Moles," she said. But not trusting her, he had lit a candle and inspected them. He called her Moly from then on.

She lives in a pretty little house in St. John's Wood. A bonbon in a candy box. He takes her frequently to Jessie Malkin's brothel, which is situated directly opposite St. Giles' Church on the corner of Wickfield and Collards Lane. It amuses Elijah that during a single evening he might serve with Reverend Bottome on an ad hoc committee formed to close the brothel, and later on have supper at Crockford's, a gambling house, with Lord Fitzcrawford, Jessie's landlord and lover.

A thank-you note. He is certain. He had sent her a gold link bracelet interspersed with garnets. He opens it and reads it. Exactly.

The second letter is from his father, Jorem. He brings it up close to his eyes, examining it carefully. Yes, there are definite traces of tremor. Good. Jorem is aging. He will die soon. Not that Jorem interfered any more in the daily business proceedings of Forster Midland, Ltd., the bank Jorem's father, Jeremiah, had founded some fifty years earlier in the small village of Ashville in the Cotswalds, but it would be better, yes for all concerned, if he were dead, thinks Elijah. A chapter closed, so to speak. Elijah pictures his father in his coffin, the lid open, and himself bending down to kiss the waxen lips. A Judas kiss? Hardly. It had been the other way around. It was he who had been betrayed.

"A matter of honor" is how Jorem had put it. "A commitment to a childhood friend made years ago." A commitment that had been made even before Elijah had been born, Jorem had told him when he insisted that Elijah marry a woman he didn't love. And when Elijah had balked, had asked for time, Jorem had said: "Marry or be disinherited." The threat had sapped his courage and so he married Theodisia, the daughter of his father's childhood friend, a woman he knew he could never learn to love, but whatever love he might have had for Jorem died then. Was it "honorable" to marry someone you did not love?

He cared for no one now, except Emma, his first child, his only daughter. And that had come to him as a total surprise. Why did he love Emma so? He didn't know. But from the moment he had seen her in her cradle with the ugly red mark on her temple—what had the doctors called it? a nevus—he had fallen in love with her. She was so unwanted,

for neither of them had wanted her, he or Theodisia. So
pathetic looking. She had been underweight at birth, so frag-
ile, so needy, so totally dependent that he felt his heart swell
with a love that he knew the moment he felt it would last
as long as he lived.

What did Jorem want? He opened the letter. It was a long-
winded complaint about the passing of the Corporation Act,
". . . and the local administration shall be controlled by the
rabble, if it is passed." Elijah smiled. He hoped his father
suffered every inconvenience.

He is reluctant to open the third letter. He would first
have another glass of wine. He pours it, downs it, and then
has another before slitting open the envelope. He reads it
out loud to himself:

My Dear Sir:

*It is as always pleasing to hear from a former pupil, partic-
ularly one who was admired not only for his intellectual accomplishments but for his physical prowess as well. Hence
it grieves me that our correspondence need be about a matter that has perturbed me greatly. A matter that I fear must
be kept in the strictest confidence. The boy in question,
your nephew, Darius Forster, being still so young, it would
be most deleterious to his future career if the incident I am
about to relate to you was wagged about by careless
tongues.*

*I shall, Sir, spare you the details of the unfortunate oc-
currence except to say that the egregious duty—the substan-
tiation of our suspicions—fell on me as moral arbiter of
Warrenton. I was reluctant, I assure you, but under the circumstances I could not refuse. In the face of possible corruption my duty was only too clear. Subsequently my night
watches confirmed what a student, who shall be nameless,
reported to me. As you must recall, Sir, we have our ways
of controlling and ferreting out such matters.*

*If it can be of any consolation to you, be advised that the
other boy, the son of a Maharajah, involved in this incident
has already been removed.*

*We must be circumspect; judicious; forever heedful of
our Christian heritage and the lessons of our Saviour. As it*

stands now myself, the student, the culprits and their legal
guardians are the only ones who know or need know of
this matter.

I shall look forward to seeing you face en face on
Founding Day. Until then I am, as always, your obedient
servant,

James Jasper Pond, M.A.
Headmaster of Warrenton

Polite. Diplomatic. Even compassionate. But the message is clear: Darius had been expelled for an act of sod-
omy.

His immediate thought is to send the letter directly to
Jorem. On receipt, Jorem will undoubtedly disinherit his
nephew. Elijah is sure of that, and that would mean more
money for himself and his children. But no, he cannot. Not
that he loves Joseph, though he does somewhat; at least he
loved him years ago in his youth when they were children,
but swiftly the images come to mind—Jorem's tyranny, Warrenton, his brother Solomon, his father's favorite . . . Solomon had married the one he loved . . . Joseph
had married Consuelo, the woman he loved. Why not he,
Elijah?

Elijah's eyes narrow. Shall he send it? No, but not out of
love for Joseph. Out of what then? Out of loyalty . . . out
of the remembrance of things past.

Poor Joseph . . . married to the slut, Consuelo, the
woman he "loves." Elijah holds the parchment up to the
flame. He will burn it. But then he changes his mind.
No . . . he shall not burn it; he shall keep it. He picks up
his pen, dates it 23 April 1836, and puts it into the top drawer
of his desk and then, pulling a key out of his waistcoat pocket,
he locks the drawer. Who knows, he thinks to himself, perhaps one day he might find a use for it.

The clock's chimes strike. Soon he shall see his darling
Emma. She will be waiting for him. Artless. Vulnerable.
After one more glass of wine. Yes, his dearest shall marry
some day . . . someone, pray God, that shall love her as he
does, if that were possible. He pours another glass, and
another. Dr. Pond's letter had disturbed him. And his fa-

ther's letter. That too disturbed him. Ashes . . . ashes . . . everything is ashes. Nothing has turned out the way he expected it. Nothing except his financial success. Yes, he expected that. He has achieved that. Five more minutes and he will go upstairs and see Emma. Five minutes . . . but he has drunk too much wine and falls asleep instead.

The glass drops from his hand. The candles all burn down. The fire in the grate goes out. The room turns dark and cold.

❋   ❋   ❋

RESEARCH PAPER NO. 1

MARLBOROUGH GARDENS: Its Creator and Its History

Principal Sources: 1. Jorem Forster's Diary, 1815
2. Jorem Forster's letters to Sir Sidney Ravenscroft, Bart.

Researcher: Rachel Lowe
Editor: Harriet Van Buren

Since the gardens became an integral part of the cousins' makeup, existing as it did just under the inner surface of their collective conscious, its presence buoying them up and sustaining them like some great watery feeding bed, even when in the natural course of events they were forced out of the garden into the welter of social life and its obligations, we deem it crucial to give a history of the Garden and its creator, their grandfather, Jorem Isaac Forster.
To begin with:

"Edward Dowland," wrote Jorem in his diary, "watch manufacturer being unable to meet the demands of his promissory note, I have acquired from him this day, 16 November 1814, one hundred thirty acres of land northeast of the City of London."

It was not until the fall of the following year that Jorem decided to inspect this small windfall. Then he wrote to his friend Sir Sidney Ravenscroft:[10]

---

10. Sir Sidney Ravenscroft, Bart: world traveler, amateur painter, and member of the House of Lords. He was Jorem's only friend.—*R. Lowe*

❄   ❄   ❄

"I immediately ordered my coachman Greenfall to drive me north on Marlebone Road. Remembering Mr. Dowland's directions by some sort of miracle, I told Greenfall to continue north until he came to a bridge with two arches, at the end of which was a fortified house and there, precisely there, to slow his horses down, for just past that, on his left, he would find a narrow road which he should enter, forthwith.

"The day was hot and the air in the coach became stifling, the thickly grown trees on either side of the narrow road acting both as a hedge and canopy, the tops of the branches having interwoven. It was in effect, Sir, like riding through a dark and windless tunnel. I lowered the window and heard, in the distance, the crowing of a cock pheasant and on either side of the carriage the squeaks and rustlings of small creatures as we rode by.

"I am not an easily frightened man, as you know, Sir, but as the vehicle continued to twist and turn, dip and climb, in this unnatural gloom, I wondered whether or not it had been foolhardy of me to come here unarmed. And just as I was about to call out to Greenfall, "Turn about!" momentarily forgetting in my panic that he couldn't, we came out of the wood into the prettiest sight ever!—acres and acres of flat, lush meadowland. Sun drenched. No doubt, Sir, a relic of the days before enclosure. My fear dissipated. I had done well. It was indeed a handsome, albeit small, piece of property.

"Spying a lake in the near distance, I told Greenfall to drive there and stop. When he did, I stepped out of the coach and wandered down to the water's edge, where I dipped my pocket handkerchief into the cool water in order to wipe my face and saw on the surface of the water a swiftly moving shape coming straight toward me. Startled, I looked up to see a black swan flying overhead. No doubt our unfamiliar presence had set it into flight, but it so unnerved me that I dropped my handkerchief into the water, and almost followed it myself.

"After that, I got back into the coach and told Greenfall to drive home, and we did without further incident, except that my mind became occupied by long forgotten and disturbing memories of my youth. In particular, a dream I once had as a young boy.[11]

---

11. Reference Note A, page 48.

Out of nowhere it came back to me as fresh and vivid as the night I dreamt it.

"The point of all this rambling, Sir, is that I have decided to create a garden out of this piece of property, a paradise—a paradise for children. Yes. On your return I should very much like to discuss with you its undertaking."

        ✸   ✸   ✸

Marlborough Gardens took three years to build and cost ten thousand pounds. But as Jorem said, "I have the time, the money, and the inclination." From the moment Jorem decided to build the Gardens he was in a fever to realize it, and discussed the project endlessly with his friend the baronet who in that year was studying oil painting with Henry Fuseli at the Royal Academy.

One day Ravenscroft asked Fuseli if he would recommend a landscape architect to a friend of his, and he outlined briefly Jorem's general plan for his paradise for children.

"Delighted to!" was Fuseli's response. He had someone in mind already. "My most gifted, my brightest pupil! Many a pleasant hour we have spent together studying Homer. And Virgil! And Dante! Kevin Francini. He's a young Italian born in Cork, Ireland, alas . . . a distant relative of the famous Stuccadores. You haven't heard of them? Well no matter . . . the young man is not a landscape architect but he has the caliber of imagination that I believe to be imperative to fulfill your friend's phantasmagorical visions."

Fuseli did not add, either because he didn't know or because he did not wish to, that Kevin Francini was, besides being a brilliant artist, a liar, a cheat—and an opium addict.

It was arranged that Jorem would interview Kevin in his rooms on Hampstead Heath, where the artist lived in a ramshackle house, for it was one of Jorem's contentions that you only truly know a man if you know his surroundings.

The day Jorem came to keep his appointment with Kevin, the young man was on the verge of ending it all. It was only a matter of deciding between a bullet and a rope. As for the appointment, he had forgotten about it.

Kevin was twenty-three years old but had, according to himself, already suffered far too much. A hopeless romantic, he was an unfortunate prey to his own temperament, and suffered wild swings of mood. If at ten in the morning he believed he was a genius (unrecognized), by noon he knew, for certain, in the depths of his heart, that he was a cretin and a failure. At the very moment that Jorem stood outside knocking on his door, Kevin was writing what he believed to be his last words to Fuseli: "To my beloved Teacher, Mentor, and Homeric Companion—" oh, would the knocking in his head never stop?

Jorem, for his part, receiving no answer to his knock, tried the door and, finding it open, stepped inside. "Ah, Sir, are you Kevin Francini?" he asked the young man who was sitting at his desk in front of a narrow window. What a dark, unpleasant room!

Kevin began to tremble. Oh God! dear God! save me . . . save me. . . . Who was that strange, old, fat figure of a man? Could it be an opium vision? Must he before he departed this vale of tears be plagued once more by hallucinations? Had he not suffered enough? The apparition's scarlet jacket began to transform itself into a scarlet hammer that began to pound his skull. And the apparition's gold-topped cane began to burn . . . melt . . . dissolve into a molten flow—and in the center—oh! the awful vision of a pair of demonic blue eyes. . . .

"Are you Kevin Francini?" repeated Jorem. What in the world could Henry Fuseli have been thinking of? The man before him was obviously demented. His coat was torn, his linen unclean, but worst of all—Jorem was sure of it!—the man reeked of vomit! And now, Good God! the man seemed to be having some sort of fit. "Are you ill, Sir? May I be of assistance?" asked Jorem, walking over to him. The young man looked as if he might swoon at any moment so that when he tried to raise himself out of the chair Jorem pushed him back down into it. Best for him to be seated if he were going to faint.

"You are Mr. Fuseli's pupil, are you not? Mr. Henry Fuseli."

Chaos, thought Jorem. Chaos! A jumble of plaster casts were strewn all over the room. Pallet and brushes lay in a corner— had they been thrown there? An easel lay next to it. And paintings, paintings everywhere. Some were sticking out of open chests of drawers, some were lined up against the walls, right side up and upside down, and some were actually hanging on the wall. All unframed. Chaos. Still . . . the room had a strange appeal. And it matched Jorem's inner vision of—of what? An artist's studio? Mad creatures, artists—all of them—diabolical children, was what they were. Yes and thoroughly unreliable . . . for work in a bank, let's say, or at the helm of government, but useful, yes, nevertheless, for certain things . . . yes. Indeed, the man's bizarre behavior coupled with the room's physical shambles in a sense was a seal of authenticity, wasn't it? For who but an artist would live this way?

"Go away!" Kevin shouted, having finally figured out that Jorem must be the rent collector. "Depart! Return to your foul mistress with her pus-infested soul, her heart of lead, go back to that sink of evil and tell the succubus I've no money for her. That I shall be dead soon enough. That she can rent this pigsty to another unfortunate like myself, soon enough. No money . . . no money at all. Do you hear me?" The speech having taken all his efforts, he slumped down even farther into his chair.

Jorem smiled. "My dear Sir, I am not the rent collector, if that is who you think I am. Didn't Mr. Fuseli explain to you that I was to pay you a visit?" Artists! Irresponsible children! "I haven't come, Sir, to take your money. On the contrary, I've come to *give* you money. Now that, Sir, should make you feel better . . . that is, if the two of us can strike a bargain to our mutual satisfaction." Had the young man rigidified? And what was he looking at so intently, just past Jorem's head. "Tell me, Mr. Francini, you are Mr. Francini, aren't you?"—what if he wasn't and he, Jorem, had wandered into the wrong flat—"that oil painting over there . . . pray tell me, is that one of yours?" Jorem pointed to a canvas of a landscape: an enormous blood-colored moon was shining down on a field of strangely shaded and dreamlike flowers.

"Yes," came the distant answer.

"And that one, over there, in the corner. Did you paint that one, too?" Like the other painting, it had an indefinable quality of mystery and calm. A lone woman on the side of a hill was playing a flute while through the branches of a distant poplar a star was rising.

"Yes."

"I am a simple man, Sir," began Jorem with the utmost confidence. "I know nothing about art. I admit it freely. *But* I know what I like when I like what I see. And I, Jorem Isaac Forster, I, Sir, like both these paintings. I believe you are the very man I'm looking for—now hear me out. . . ." And Jorem explained in great length and in great detail the ideas he had previously outlined to Sir Ravenscroft about the Garden he wished to build.

"Paradise County! That is what I intend to call it. Do you like the name, Sir? When I was a boy I used to have a dream, the same dream every night about a garden. I used to call it Paradise County. And a wonderful place it was. And, by God, it looked very much like your two landscapes over there . . . the same feeling at least! Yes. Well, I intend to create it in reality. Paradise County: a place that will stir the hearts and minds of children . . . my grandchildren in particular, though none of them are even born as yet. My intentions are that they shall have in reality what I as a boy only dreamed of! What say you, Mr. Francini? Are you game? . . . Mr. Francini! Are you awake?" The young man seemed comatose. Had he fainted?

"Paradise County . . ." murmured Kevin. Oh, he was so dreadfully cold. If only this odd creature would go away. Perhaps if Kevin humored him he would. Oh, what had he ever done in his life to be tortured like this . . . ?

"Exactly! Paradise County. And as I said before, young man, you need not stint when it comes to money. I am well aware that one cannot create a paradise without spending a great deal of money." Jorem began to laugh. The young man seemed to be coming to, if that was the right phrase for what was happening. Yes, he seemed much more alert in just the last few seconds.

"Your idea intrigues me," said Kevin. His voice was surprisingly firm. "But you must leave me now. *Now*." He began to cough and tremble. "As you see, Sir, at the moment I'm not well . . . the vestigial effects of a bout with cholera this spring . . . What is your name, by the way, Sir? Mine is Kevin Francini. You do have one, don't you?"

"My name? But of course, Sir. My name is Jorem Forster. I am the president of Forster Midland Bank, Limited. A friend of Sir Sidney Ravenscroft."

"How nice. Now please go."

But Jorem would not leave. The room was filthy; the man was possessed, but Jorem was convinced that Henry Fuseli was right— Kevin Francini was the man for the job.

"I shall not leave, Sir, until you tell me that you shall do it . . . shall create Paradise County for me. I *must* have your answer now. Will you? Can you?"

Kevin's eyes grew large and began to glitter and then staring into a world of his own, a world which seemed to be situated midway between the window and the door, he replied, "Will I? Can I? Why of course I can! After all, Sir, I *am* a genius!"

Reference Note A:
JOREM'S DREAM

In the fall of 1932 Lowe and I made a trip to Jorem's birthplace, Ashville, a once-prosperous wool town, at the foot of the Cotswolds.

Very little had changed since Jorem's birth in 1755. The yellow brick house on High Street in which Jorem was born was still standing, as was the chapel at the other end of town, where as a boy he spent all his Sundays, the entire day, listening to his father, Jeremiah, preach; for Jeremiah was not only a banker and founder of Forster Midland Bank, but a church deacon in a small non-conformist sect called the Brethren of the Lamb, the beliefs and teachings of which his father, Josephus Faustus, a goldsmith's apprentice and religious fanatic, had brought over with him from Germany.

We visited the chapel, an ugly, squat building, and the bleak graveyard behind the chapel and found Jorem's grandfather's simple tombstone, and the more elaborate one of Jorem's father, Jeremiah, on which was carved the grim message: "The Storms about the Good Man Rise, Yet Injured Virtue Mounts the Skies, Breaks through the Interposing Gloom, and Mocks the Tempest and the Tomb."

Standing there in the dismal windswept landscape, the air reverberant with Lurid Sin, and images of Hell, we felt the full oppressive weight of Dissent; we thought we understood for the first time Jorem's strange divided response to life: how on the one hand he could create the fantastical Marlborough Gardens, "a paradise for children," and on the other die with the Good Book, his dog-eared copy of *Pilgrim's Progress,* in his hands.

Surely the seeds of Marlborough Gardens were first sown in a dream, a dream that began in the mind of Jorem Forster when he was ten years old, on the night of October 12, 1765, the night of the morning that he began work in his father's bank that stood on Christ Church Road, for that was the day his childhood ended, the day his imprisonment began.

In a letter that he wrote to his friend Sir Sidney Ravenscroft, but which he did not post, he describes his anguish:

"Imagine a young boy snatched, as it were, from his childish pursuits and pleasures, from the ponds, fields, and meadows, from the companionship of his peers, from the sky itself, thrust suddenly into the prison of his father's bank; his boyhood snuffed out and replaced with accounting and bills of lading. Suddenly it was six days of work a week, from seven to seven, and on Sunday, chapel. That young boy, of course, Sir, was myself.

"I was placed at the side of an elderly man, the oldest employee in my father's bank, a Mr. Powers. I was made to sit on a stool too tall for me and my legs, having to dangle, ached. I was made to wear a green eye shade, the edge of which cut into my scalp. I was made to puzzle over long columns of meaningless figures. It seemed to me as if a darkness had swallowed me, that my life heretofore filled with light and cheer had changed for some reason I could not fathom into a dark and gloomy thing, as dark and gloomy as the bank itself. I had the feeling that a death had taken place, but whose death and why did not seem clear. . . . I began to live on the cutting edge of despair—the place where there is no hope.

"Children are strange creatures. It was then that I got the odd notion in my head that I must be a criminal, and my work in the bank a just punishment for my crime—the crime being that I did not love my father. And truly I did not. For though he was a good man, and I was in awe of him, his harshness toward me as well as his wife, my mother, and my two younger brothers had killed whatever love I might have had for him.

"Each night I cried myself to sleep. Perhaps you will not believe me, and you may even laugh at me when I tell you that young as I was I began to think seriously of doing away with myself. I shall never know whether or not these morbid thoughts would have been acted out because something happened that changed my life. You see, Sir, I began to dream.

"I began to dream that I was once more free. Each night I dreamt that I wandered through my beloved fields and meadows of Ashville under the open skies. Everything was the same but everything was different too. The ash grove behind my father's house had become mysterious woods, the fields and meadow were filled with extraordinary flowers, everything was twice as beautiful as anything I'd ever seen in real life; the village pond in which ducks swam was now a dazzling lake on whose surface floated a magnificent black swan. And each morning I awakened with a spark of hope kindled in my breast.

"I told no one about it. Neither my mother, or my brothers, or my friends. It was my secret universe, which in the privacy of my mind I called Paradise County. Each night when I returned to my dream something new had been added. One night the dream chapel was transformed into an ancient temple with a statue of a goddess, though where as a young boy I had ever seen a painting, a drawing or even a sketch of it or her I cannot recall. . . .

"When my father died, need I tell you, Sir, the dream vanished."

FIVE

T HERE are more than a hundred letters from Jorem to Sir Sidney Ravenscroft, who when the Gardens were being created took a grand tour of the Continent.[12] A few examples will suffice to clearly convey the tenor of Jorem's mind.

L. 1, 1817[13]
30 June 1817
Sir Sidney Ravenscroft, Bart.
Auberge des Poissons
Calais, France

My dearest friend: You will be delighted, I am sure, to know that today, this blessed day, the implementation of my dream into fact has been inaugurated! In other words, the Creation of Paradise County has begun. My doubts

---

12. We found the letters sequestered in a game bag and shooting muff of gray linen, Emma's last gift to her father. The letters proved to be both a lucid and graphic profile of Jorem's character, and an invaluable chronicle of the creation of Marlborough Gardens.—*H. Van Buren*

13. Lowe has catalogued the letters in chronological order so that we may place a work's location in the creation of Marlborough Gardens.—*H. Van Buren*

*have vanished—each and every one. I am entirely happy
with my decision.*

> *Yr. obed. servant,*
> *Jorem Isaac Forster, Esq.*

L. 8, 1817
2 August 1817
Sir Sidney Ravenscroft, Bart.
De Huis van de Twee Zvanntjes
Rotterdam, Holland

*My dearest friend: Today I met Mr. Francini in a large
natural cave in the woods that he informed me is hereafter
to be known as Calypso's Cave. He has already begun the
construction of an enormous hearth. She is a Greek goddess. Did you know that?*

*Mr. Francini is a Homer enthusiast and he has advised
me to begin reading him at once! Chapman's translation. I
shall go to the booksellers today. I dare not disobey him.*

> *Yr. obed. servant,*
> *Jorem Isaac Forster, Esq.*

L. 14, 1817
30 October 1817
Sir Sidney Ravenscroft, Bart.
Rue de la Reine
Liege, Belgium

*My dearest friend: Yesterday I met Mr. Francini on a flat-
ish piece of land circular in form, which he calls Nannies
Plain. There on the grass were several odd-looking and
larger-than-life-size statues standing about in the most expectant attitudes.*[14] *What were they? "Nannies," he said.
"Nannies?" I echoed. "Nannies," he repeated. And then
introduced me to them in a manner of speaking rapidly.
Very impatient he was and trembling more than ever.
Nanny Dea and Nanny Demeter are the only names I can
remember, except for the half-horse, half-man figure, which
he called Charon.*

---

14. Today they are shrouded in ivy and resemble truncated trees. We decided
to leave them thus. Some things are better left the way they are. See Reference
Note B, page 60.—*R. Lowe*

I realize of course that I am a figure of fun to him, and that he laughs at me and even mocks me occasionally, but I can't help liking him more and more each day. Decidedly it is one of the pleasures of growing old that one is able to like people who do not like you.

He is so young, so talented . . . so learned. And he is the ideal person for the task—the creation of Paradise County—isn't he? For he is besides being an artist, part child and part lunatic.

Incidentally, the poor fellow has confided in me that he owes Henry Fuseli a sizeable sum of money. I have lent it to him. He did not ask me to, may I hasten to add. But I am convinced that he must not be allowed to work with such a terrible burden on his conscience. Do you not agree?

Yr. obed. servant,
Jorem Isaac Forster, Esq.

L. 22, 1818
4 May 1818
Sir Sidney Ravenscroft, Bart.
Haus Glucklich, Grunewald Forest
Berlin, Germany

My dearest friend: Alas, the work did not go well today. At least not at first. Mr. Francini blamed yr. obed. servant, myself. He called me a blockhead and informed me that I had ruined his life. He said he wished he had never met me and then threatened to kill himself.

It was over what I truly thought was a minor matter, although I should know by now that in Mr. Francini's life there is no such thing as a "minor matter." It concerned the waterworks he is creating for the sunken garden, which is to contain, he says, more than two dozen statues of nymphs: nymphs at play, nymphs in flight, nymphs dancing, nymphs wheeling about . . . and they shall give out, he tells me, when all is completed, over two hundred jets of water![15] *Think of that! It was when I questioned him about*

---

15. Such were the wonders of Marlborough Gardens in the year 1818. Today the canals are choked and the jets grown over with the ubiquitous ivy of the Gardens.—*R. Lowe*

*an aspect of the proposed waterworks and the underground
network of pipes necessary for such an undertaking that
poor Mr. Francini had what I can only call a seizure. I
knew of course that he must be consoled. And immediately!
So I promptly told him that I knew he was a genius, and
that I would do everything in my power to soothe his distress. This seemed, Thank God! to bring him back to his
senses at once.*

*Do you recall, my dear friend, the ruins I mentioned to
you in a letter I wrote you a year ago? The ruins of a
house standing in a large meadow? Well, what do you
think Mr. Francini has gone and done, clever fellow that he
is? Did he remove them? Did he dig them up? No, not he!
He's gone and done the contrary: he's built them up! And
now there's a four and half foot wall where there was none,
behind which some thirty feet away is the foundation of
what, he tells me, is to be a tower, to be known as the
Tower Farfrum—a place where children can play as they
wish. "Far From" their Nannies and their parents.*

O, he is a capital fellow, ain't he?

*Yr. obed. servant,
Jorem Isaac Forster, Esq.*

*L. 43, 1818
6 July 1818
Sir Sidney Ravenscroft, Bart.
Strada Strabico
Casa Chiaro di Luna
Florence, Italy*

*My dearest friend: Today was a special day. I came
down from the City to witness the four shields being attached to the four gates of the garden.*

*They were, if you remember, an entire year in the mak-
ing. And what a hullabaloo there was—we all cheered, the
workmen, Mr. Francini and myself—when the last shield
was finally soldered to the Great South Gate! They are extraordinary, being exact replicas, as you know, of
Achilles's shield.*[16]

---

16. The shields cost Jorem Forster one thousand pounds. They were made
in Manchester in a foundry appropriately named Hephaestus, Ltd. An exact
description of the shields can be found in Homer's *Iliad*, Book XVIII.—*R.
Lowe*

*The work goes at a gallop now except when Mr. Francini
has one of his debilitating fits. Poor man. At times he is so
angry with me, but at other times he assures me, and in the
sweetest way, that I truly inspire him. And may I say, Sir
Sidney, that I believe him.*

> *Yr. obed. servant,*
> *Jorem Isaac Forster, Esq.*

L. 87, 1819
14 September 1819
Sir Sidney Ravenscroft, Bart.
The Castle Louszinsky
Warsaw, Poland

*My dearest friend: Mr. Francini told me last week that he
disapproves of the name Paradise County. He will not have
it, he says. The name is absurd, ridiculous and sentimental.
He will name the Gardens himself, he told me.*

*Alas, shortly after those heated words our Will found two
slabs of stone in the marches:[17] one had the letters* M A R
chiseled on it, the other the letters B *and* O. *Since then he
has got it into his head that this is evidence and proof
(enough for him) that the Dukes of Marlborough once had
an estate on this very spot. On thirty acres! And therefore it
should be named Marlborough Gardens. When I pointed
out to him ever so gently, mind you, that the combined letters could just as well stand for Marlebone, a reasonable
suggestion, I should have thought—the property is adjacent
to Marlebone Road—but need I tell you what happened.
Yes, our Will had the worst spell ever. He fulminated and
frothed. Exploded and detonated. We thought it might very
well be the end of him. And so naturally I desisted. . . .*

But entre nous *my heart was set on the name—Paradise
County. I must confess I was somewhat put out by his attitude but then Fate entered and for whatever reason, alas,
decided to aid, if that is the right word, Mr. Francini in this
matter, rather than myself.*

It happened this way: at the time of our altercation

---

17. In L. 68 (April 2, 1819) Jorem began referring to Kevin Francini as Will,
short for "willful."—*H. Van Buren*

(though I hesitate to call it that) a competition of sculpture that had been arranged by the Prussian Friends of Great Britain ended. Its theme had been The Victor of Blenheim. Yes, the Duke of Marlborough himself! The result: one handsome equestrian statue of the Duke was given to the British government and 242 losing statues of the Duke were suddenly for sale. At reasonable prices, may I add.

Mr. Francini hails it as "an Act of Providence!" and who knows, perhaps it was; he purchased, without asking me, of course, one of the remaining statues—from a sculptor friend of his who had competed unsuccessfully, a Mr. James Titmouse.

So there you are, Sir, Paradise County is to be known henceforth as Marlborough Gardens. But do you know, Sir, the more I say it—Marlborough Gardens—the more I like the sound of it.

What say you?

Yr. obed. servant,
Jorem Isaac Forster, Esq.

✳   ✳   ✳

Marlborough Gardens was never finished. Kevin Francini disappeared during the spring of 1820. At first Jorem did nothing. But as the weeks went by and there was still no word or message of any kind from Kevin Francini, Jorem decided to make another visit to Hampstead Heath.

After knocking for some time (the door was open as usual), he entered. Kevin was not there. But all his belongings were. Jorem debated for some time: should he or should he not go through the man's belongings before he began a search?

He found many strange and wondrous things among which were a silver tray, a lamp, and a pipe whose purpose his friend the "world traveler" eventually explained to him. Kevin's addiction to opium did not offend Jorem, but something else he found did, at first.

In the bottom drawer of the broken bureau he found a collection of bills tied loosely together. Poring over them he realized that these must be the original bills for material and workmen's pay. Upon adding them up, they came to considerably less money (two hundred and forty-six pounds less, to be precise) than the totals Kevin had presented to Jorem.

He went home and after thinking about it wrote the following and last letter to his friend:

L. 103 1820
1 May 1820
Sir Sidney Ravenscroft, Bart.
The Inn of the Russian Bear
St. Petersburg, Russia

My dear friend: I have sad news to relate. Our young friend has vanished. Where to? And why? No one knows.

And now I must divulge an even sadder fact: Mr. Francini apparently felt compelled to make a larger profit for himself than that to which he was entitled. To put it bluntly—he saw fit to cheat me. At first I was distressed but I'm no longer. You must believe me, Sir, when I tell you that in no way do I feel cheated. . . .

When you return from St. Petersburg we shall walk arm in arm together through the Gardens and you shall swear to me that though you have traveled the world over and seen the most beautiful things the world can offer, still nothing can compare to Marlborough Gardens—that it truly is the eighth wonder of the world!

Imagine, Sir, if you will, a garden that rivals paradise and is divided like paradise into four parts. A rectangular design, transected by water routes and paths, containing a sunken garden, a forest, a lake, a temple, a winter garden and a cave beside statuary, rare shrubs and plants of every kind.

No, I have not been cheated. My only fear is that the young man has either been murdered or foolishly in one of his tempestuous moods has done away with himself. The young are so very vulnerable, are they not?

Yr. obed. servant,
Jorem Isaac Forster, Esq.

AN AFTERWORD BY RACHEL LOWE

Less than a year after Kevin's disappearance, Jorem acquired an estate called Saddler's Grove in a small market town in Essex. Jorem's wife, Jessica, died there. She was laid to rest in the graveyard of the country church, St. Swithins, just outside Saddler's Grove. A tombstone inscribed with the words, SO I AWOKE AND BEHOLD IT WAS A DREAM, marks the spot.

Jorem had not loved her. But she had been what he had wanted: a nonentity; a quiet, submissive, obedient woman. He said of her: "She did not displease me."

Her children remembered her, but only dimly. She was the woman who wept easily, the woman who had lived apart from them in the London house in two bleak cold rooms (none of them could ever recall seeing a fire in her grate), the woman to whose bedside they had been brought from time to time, and in whose presence they had been cautioned to be still, silent, and respectful. A tiny slip of a woman with a persistent cough, like the peep of an abandoned fledgling. She had been nothing to them, a wraith, unlike their father, Jorem, whose domineering figure had penetrated every facet of their being and of whom until his death they stood in awe and even terror.

In the spring of 1826 Jorem moved to Saddler's Grove and from that day until his death he never set foot in Marlborough Gardens again. However, though Jorem removed himself from his "creation," he lost neither contact with nor control of his "subjects." As each grandchild was conceived, a letter was sent to the expectant father. Each of these letters contained the same message.

When Consuelo, Joseph's Italian wife, became pregnant with Darius, his first grandchild, Jorem dispatched the following note to his son:

My dear Joseph,

I pray you regard the following not in the light of a request but rather as an order, or if you will, a decree.

Firstly my heartiest felicitations.

I have dismissed by post your physician, Mr. Finley, and have informed your new physician, Mr. Coombes of 32 Barrett Street, Leicester Square, of your wife's condition. In receipt of this letter you will please have your wife re-

*moved to 58 Marlborough Gardens, into the master suite,
where she is to remain until the birth of my first grandchild.*

*She may, if she so wishes, take her personal maid with
her. If you wish, you may visit her once or twice a week.
But no more than that.*

*I shall not be crossed in this matter, in any way. If you
have any qualms, Sir, about obliging me, I advise you to
consider the following: 1. From whence cometh your bene-
fices; 2. The Fifth Commandment; 3. Wills can and are re-
vised as often as the said legator may desire.*

> *Your affectionate father,*
> *Jorem Isaac Forster*

Throughout the years Jorem maintained the house at One Marlborough Gardens with its own staff of servants who kept it clean
and well stocked with food as if his arrival was imminent, and
Mrs. Capacity, Jorem's housekeeper, traveled to London once a
month to oversee and ascertain that her high standards of do-
mesticity were upheld.

After the birth of three more grandchildren—Vanessa, Albert,
and Emma—two more edicts followed relating to his grandchildren:

"*1*. When Mrs. Capacity comes up for her tour of in-
spection, she will collect for my perusal a monthly report on
my grandchildren's progress, said report to be written by
each set of progenitors.

"*2*. My grandchildren are to spend every summer at Saddler's Grove until they are of school age." (The exception
was Darius who, as Jorem put it, "because of his wretched
foreign attachments will have to spend his summers with his
loathsome relatives.")

And such is human nature that what seemed eccentric in the
beginning became as time went on a "hallowed family tradition."

*   *   *

For the most part, his sons and daughter seemed satisfied. There
were no coup d'états, no palace revolutions, no organized revolts.
Only Elijah longed for Jorem's death.

Reference Note B:
THE STATUES ON NANNIES PLAIN

There are eight statues on Nannies Plain, all of them marble. All of them were executed by one or another of Kevin Francini's friends whom he knew from the Royal Academy of Art. They are done in a neoclassical style overlaid with baroque and mannerist traces.

Some of the statues were so overgrown with lichen and ivy that it was difficult to determine the sex. They form an oval on one of the inner perimeters of Nannies Plain, an area of approximately one hundred feet in circumference.

1. Artemis of Brauron. Brauron is an ancient shrine of the moon goddess Artemis in Attica. This statue is on a pediment. Her elongated arms encircle a young boy and a young girl. She has a high, narrow waist and very long legs. She is wearing a peplos and a short cape over her shoulders.

2. Bona Dea (the good goddess). An Italian deity. Six feet tall. She carries a scepter in her left hand and a wreath of vine leaves in her hair. A large stone wine jar filled with stone snakes stands on her right.

3. Charon. One of the Centauri. Represented as rising up in the front of a horse's body and four legs. He was the master and instructor of Greek's most celebrated heroes, Actaeon, Jason, Castor, Polydeuces, Achilles, and Asclepius.

4. Demeter. Daughter of Kronus and Rhea. Goddess of agriculture. Foundress of law, order, and marriage. A seated statue, her throne is carved with her emblems, poppies and ears of corn. At her side is a basket of fruit; on her lap is a little pig. In her right hand she holds a torch.

5. Gaia (Greek word for "earth"). Greek Goddess worshipped as *kovrotrophos,* "nourisher of children." The statue is larger than life size. She wears a chiton and sandals. The drapery is carved in broad shallow folds. (It is the only statue we have cleaned and repaired.)

6. Hecate. Goddess of the night, the lower world, ghosts, and magic. The three-figured statues stand back to back. Each figure has its special attribute: a torch, a key, or a sword.

7. Rhea. Mother of the Olympian Gods. Called Mother of the Gods. On Nannies Plain she is enthroned between lions.

8. Silenus. A satyr. The rather ugly, squat statue is of a thick-muscled old man wearing a loincloth. Pot-bellied, snub nosed, and with pointed ears, he holds the infant Dionysus.

Reference Note C:
THE FORSTER FEMALE ARTIFACTS

As the complexity of the job and the variety of artifacts became clear to us, we consulted contemporary books of the period to better understand and appreciate the breadth and width of the accomplishments of the Forster women. We have listed a few of our sources: *The Art of the Shell* by Holly Hamilton (London: Longmans, Brown and Green, 1843); *Elegant Needlework for Ladies* (London: Wark and Lock, 1835); *The Englishwoman's Handiwork* by Mrs. Evelyn Jones (London, 1842).

Our primary problem was one of identification, since so many of the pieces were unsigned, but as we persevered we became increasingly skillful at matching the artifact with the individual artist, and our decisions were corroborated in a variety of ways by "internal" evidence. The exact position, type, and condition of the artifact that we discovered in the main house and the lodge were recorded by R. Lowe and can be found in her monograph entitled *Catalogue of Female Forster Artifacts*.

A considerable number of artifacts remain. Theodisia's (Emma's mother's) handiwork alone could suffice as prime stock in several gift shops today.

She had an enthusiasm for carving wool, which was a "raised wool" technique used for cushions and fine screens. There are four sculptured pieces extant: *Parrot and Fruit; Flowers and Fruit; Stag and Tree;* and *Rabbit and Cabbage*.

And an enthusiasm for making tea trays: there are thirty of them, all signed with her characteristically flamboyant *T*. Besides that, there are six needlework carpets, dozens of petit- and grospoint cushions, two large tapestries, twenty beaded bags, eight painted handscreens, fourteen egg warmers, innumerable pincushions, as well as a single wreath made of human hair.

But it is her thirteen shell creations that are her "Meister-

stücke." They are truly extraordinary. Each floral arrangement—
a single rice shell forms each petal—is set in a delicate porcelain
vase. We found them carefully preserved under their narrow glass
domes in Theodisia's sitting room, renamed by Emma the Parlor
of Glass Domes.

Emma's productivity is also astonishing considering the fact
that it spanned only the four years when she was between the
ages of six and ten (1831–1835). During that time she managed
to make a half a dozen embroidered braces, four embroidered
cigar cases, five tobacco pouches, ten pairs of embroidered slippers, and one gamebag and shooting muff of gray linen. All were
gifts for her beloved father, Elijah.

Emma's cousins Vanessa, Letitia, and Mary-Anne are represented by three wall pockets, eight work stools, two plant holders,
and four umbrella stands; their mother, Emma's Aunt Mathilda,
by varying kinds of baskets made of leather (dampened sheep-
skin), and textured twigs and cones, and Bohemian beads, and
Guinivere, another of Emma's aunts, made three gilded palm-
leaf fans, one wax flower grouping composed of moss roses, and
one wine caster.

There are also more than a hundred samplers stitched in silk
and wool with ethical and uplifting mottos, which are the collective output of the female Forsters.

There were two exceptions to this female industry: Consuelo,
Darius's mother, the Contessa Rimini, and Clara Lustig, Emma's
second cousin and governess.

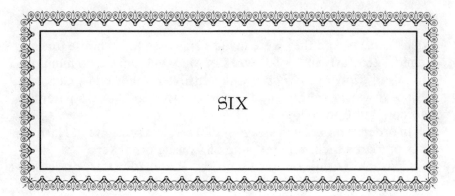

SIX

H<small>ARRIET</small> made the tea this afternoon, pennywort, "an aid in clearing the kidneys," wrote Mrs. Farnley, and served Twocake (Zweikuchen), a Forster savory that was a flat, covered pastry filled with bits of beef, pork, and onion, a delicacy of Upper Hesse, in western Germany.

In their most complacent moments, the Forsters tended to forget their humble origins, in particular, Josephus Faustus, the journeyman who emigrated from Germany in 1710 and changed his name to Joseph Forster almost upon arrival. But even a casual glance through Mrs. Farnley's recipes reveals the Forsters' taste for what the French call "cuisine bourgeois," that is, boiled beef and pork specialties.

This morning we went to our dig in Marlborough Marshes, a stretch of land just inside the West Gate. We made some interesting discoveries: in Stratum II we found a variety of fragments which though damaged and with parts missing, we identified as weapons used by the cousins during their civil war (May 1837), a war which they referred to among themselves as the Marlborough Wars. As you see, our work proceeds in diverse ways. . . .

As we have mentioned, *City of Childhood* is an unfinished manuscript. There are chapters missing.

Presumably the children met their cousin Darius several times (at Elijah's Sunday afternoon dinners, or in Marlborough Gardens, etc.) before they were invited en masse to his house for the famous tea party in the last week of May, but there is no mention of this in *City of Childhood*. Chapter Five is followed by Chapter Nine, in which we are suddenly introduced to Darius's parents, Joseph and Consuelo.

In order to make the passage smoother, less precipitate, Harriet has prepared a curriculum vitae of Consuelo Forster.

Consuelo (Anna Louisa Francesca Rimini) Forster, or as she was known in her circle, the Contessa Rimini, was a well-known composer, music teacher, and voice coach as well as a composer whose works were frequently played in her native Italy and in England.

CURRICULUM VITAE

PERSONAL: Consuelo Rimini Forster, the daughter of Count Rimini VI, was born in 1799 and died in 1882. She was married to Joseph Isaac Forster, an English banker, in 1820. She had one child, Darius, Count Rimini the VII.

EDUCATION: She began the study of piano at the age of five, under the former Director of Music for the court of the Grand Duke Leopold of Florence, Italy. At fifteen she began her studies at the University of Bologna, under Mattei. She also studied under Zingarelli at Lareto where she wrote a treatise called "The Canon and the Fugue."

COMPOSITIONS:

Eight for piano
Ten sonatas for piano and flute
Eleven trios for harp, violin, and cello
A mass in B flat for a four-part female chorus and organ
A Stabat Mater
Many sonatinas, rondos, and minuets

SONGS:

"Canto d'Amore" e "Tre Canti di Shakespeare"

OPERAS:

The Princesse de Cleves, performed for the first time at La Scala in 1842. It was reviewed by one of the leading critics of the time, Senor Tavaldi, who said of it, "The work as a whole has the unity of style and of emotion worthy of the finest Greek tragedy."

Jane Eyre, libretto by her son Count Darius Rimini, performed at the Paris Opera in 1861. "Rich and complex, it captures the nervous brilliance and dreaming poetry of the original work," wrote Monsieur Gravet of the *Figaro.*

WRITINGS: Her two books, *Essays in Musical Analysis* and *The Art of the Harpsichord,* are still extant.

As for her place in musical history: Monsieur Gravet in an article entitled "Modern Composers" said: "The Contessa Rimini has a secure place. She will not be the 'Forgotten Master,' for her music appeals not only to the musical elite, but also to the common people. Bold and original, it is the music of the future."

Gravet's article was written in 1872. Her music is still being played and performed today.

City of Childhood
IX
THE FOREIGNER

CONSUELO, her fingers flying, was developing the opening movement of the *Appassionata.* The headlong energy of the music throbbed through the house, into Darius's room where he lay on his bed, supine, his eyes open, staring at the patterns of light—reflections of the fire that burned in the hearth—that played on the carved ornate ceiling, into the study where Joseph sat staring at nothing, holding his breath as the player began the recapitulation, making the hairs on the back of his neck stiffen, as he waited, for the tonic chord that would lead to the long, sustained, menacing dissonance.

Would she leave, really leave? Joseph wondered. She had threatened to leave and never return. If she left, he would follow. Or he would keep her here by force. Oh, he was so confused; no, he thought, *not* by force, oh no, he would keep her here by capitulating as always. By surrendering his pride.

But it was his fault, wasn't it? His shame. His burden. He loved her but he did not love Darius. That was the truth . . . but no, that wasn't true. It wasn't! He loved them both. Yes, both but . . . But what? He loved his wife (she mustn't leave, he wouldn't let her!). He loved Darius, not as much, no, but he loved him. Then what was it? But of course he knew, he had known it for some time, known it even before he had acknowledged it to himself. He loved them but not together.

What did that mean? Did it mean anything? Yes, it did. He loved each of them separately. Apart. He loved Consuelo; he loved Darius, but not both together. Not mother *and* son. Is that what he meant? Yes . . . yes, that was closer to the truth. . . . Elijah? . . . Did he feel that way about Edward? . . . No, he didn't think so. And Solomon? . . . Solomon seemed to love Albert more than he loved his wife. If he could only speak to them about it. Impossible of course . . .

Inviolate in her universe of music the player mustered up her remaining strength to meet the demands of the coda, and the music swelled into a deafening, tumultuous, unquenchable torrent of the final measures . . . *sforzando! sforzando! sforzando! fortissimo!* . . . Silence!

Joseph rose and walked across the room. No. He would wait for her here. He walked back to his chair and sat down. Soon he heard the staccato sound of her high heels moving quickly toward the study. Everything she did was *vite! vite! vite!* Would she come in to see him? To speak to him? No. She passed the door. He heard her go up the stairs. She was going to see Darius! Not her husband but Darius. He was seized with jealousy again.

When Darius was born, Joseph knew immediately that he had not wanted a male child, a reproduction of himself. As Darius grew up, Joseph felt uncomfortable with him, a discomfort that increased as he saw the strange camaraderie that developed between his wife and son. They behaved as equals. What mother and child behaved the way they did?

But worse than that, they made him feel as if he didn't belong here, in his own house. Joseph tried to like his "son" (it was his duty, wasn't it?) though he never called him son even in the privacy of his thoughts. He couldn't *bring* himself to do it. And now this disgrace . . .

He heard Consuelo come down the staircase again. And then he realized that of course she hadn't gone to see Darius; she had gone to bathe and change her clothes! After a performance like that she was always drenched in sweat. . . . But she passed the door again. Where was she going?

Unfortunately he loved her with a passion that time had not dimmed. He had wanted her from the very first moment he had seen her twenty years ago at the English Embassy in Florence. He was there as a guest with Elijah. Jorem had sent them on a grand tour as part of their education as gentlemen.

She had come with her father, the Count Rimini, a reptilian, ancient creature, shifty eyed, world weary, his bone-thin body dressed in satin and laces. And after the reception she had played the harpsichord—her own. It had been carried in for her—Couperin, Rameau, Bach, and a composition of her own, a sonata in F minor.

He had fallen in love. He could still recall the exact moment the arrow of love had pierced his heart. It was during the Bach sonata for harpsichord, violin, and flute when the page turner who was also manipulating the hand stops was not quick enough for her. She had pushed him away calling him a fool while continuing to delineate the line clearly as she played the rest of the composition by heart. It had caused no pain then, no; on the contrary it had been a pleasurable sensation. He had told Elijah as they strolled in the Piazza Santa Croce later that night that he had fallen in love. Yes, in love.

But when after meeting her for the third time he had timorously declared his love to her, she had laughed in his face. She would never marry. "I am married to my music. Find someone else."

He left Florence but came back four more times to ask her to marry him. The fourth time, her father the count promised him that he would, as he put it, "deliver the wench into wedlock," that is, if the young gentleman would be so kind as to pay the count's current gambling debts, "a mere three thousand pounds, my dear fellow!" Joseph returned to England and spoke to Jorem, who had already looked up the Riminis in the Almanac de Gotha and liking what he saw gave Joseph the money. It pleased Jorem to have his oldest son marry into aristocracy, albeit Italian and penniless. And so they were married.

On the first night of their honeymoon, as soon as they were alone Consuelo told him that her father had said that if she refused to marry the Englishman he would break her fingers. Every one of them. She said she had threatened suicide. Joseph hadn't dared to ask her why she hadn't done it. Nor did she tell him. But she had made him promise that night that he would never place any obstacle in her life as an artist. He had promised as she knew he would. For she had married him finally because she knew her will was stronger than his. He had promised not knowing really what the promise meant—he only knew he wanted her—but he soon found out.

The first thing she did was abbreviate their honeymoon. It had been a romantic idea of his to travel with her to Russia. But how could she! she screamed. For God's sake how could she? She was in the middle of a dozen compositions. The journey would take at least three months! She couldn't afford to leave the piano that long! Didn't he understand that? She was a composer, a pianist: to begin with she had to arrange for a piano for the English house, and she had to find out about the acoustics. What if they weren't any good? However, she told him, if he wanted to continue the honeymoon alone, she was broad-minded, she would understand, she would make the sacrifice, yes! *But* as far as she was concerned, she was leaving for England tomorrow. *Pronto! Pronto!* Did he understand? *Capiche?*

When the issue was settled, to her satisfaction of course (the music room completed, the piano—the most expensive Broadwood in London, not that the money had mattered to him—placed in the room she had selected on the ground floor facing south), he discovered (at first to his amusement) that London town was seething with Italian musicians. The tribe of Clementis, the tribe of Novellos, the tribe of Geminanis. And then there were the English men and women who studied with the Italians, all of whom seemed to consider his house theirs. So that from morning to night there was a continuous flowing fabric of sound in the house. And the sopranos! Dozens of them! Italian, Russian, Spanish, French . . . overdressed, overpainted, and screaming their heads off! And when he demurred and complained, as he did at times, she reminded him of his promise.

In time he became used to it—the Bohemian atmosphere. It was Forster Midland Ltd., the bank with its decorum and stability, that began to seem alien. Occasionally he thought of explaining this to his brothers—this strange transposition of ideas—but as he felt their increasing contempt for him, mingled with pity, he refrained. But everything, their contempt, the singers, the constant sound of music, everything would have been all right had it not been for Darius.

They had quarreled last night. Consuelo had refused to discuss the headmaster's letter. She had threatened to leave for Florence with Darius immediately. Tomorrow! May first. Her usual departure date was a month later: June first. He had begged her not to go. Begged! But she had refused.

"No!" she had screamed at him in Italian, "I will not stay in this country, in this house, in this room! not a moment longer than I have to!"

As always, her fists had come down on the table—outrageous creature!—her hair had come loose, the hairpins falling around her, a metal shower . . . "I cannot survive in this country! It is a tomb, a Protestant tomb! It has no composers! No artists! No writers! Only bankers, bankers, bankers, people who make money!"

Once in the early years of their marriage, Joseph had been foolish enough to point out to her that Shakespeare, a man she professed to admire (hadn't she set some of his poems to music?) was an Englishman. But she had set him straight immediately.

"Shake-a-Spear! But that is not an English name! Shake-a-Spear! Has anyone heard of any other English gentleman called Shake-a-Spear. English gentlemen are named Mr. Johnson, Mr. Blake, Mr. Marlow, even Mr. Dryden. But Mr. Shake-a-Spear? No! My dear Joseph, surely it must be obvious even to you that the gentleman was *not* and *never*

ever was an Englishman! No, never! A Rumanian perhaps. Or a Yugoslavian . . . yes, in those countries gentlemen have strange names."

The door opened. She came in. She was frowning.

"Darius tells me you do not speak to him. You pass him on the stairs as if he were dead. Why? He is your son. Have you disowned him? Because a headmaster writes you a letter that you must come to school and then he tells you, this little headmaster, that your *son* he touches some boy's penis." She used the Italian colloquial term. Joseph shuddered. "What idiocy! Only an Englishman can take such things seriously. My dear man, do you not think I did not touch a penis by the time I was six years old. My brother's penis (God rest his soul), my cousin's penis, the footman's penis." Would she ever stop saying that word? "And *see* them! They were always peeing on the estate: in the bushes, on the lawn, in the lake . . . everywhere! And my cousin Antonio, he did not touch a boy's penis? And they his. He was *normal*. Darius is *normal*. He feels the *power* of his sex. Not like the English. He will know how to make love. Yes, Darius is your son. You will talk to him, you will write Headmaster Pind, Pound, Piddle, whatever his name is, you will tell him he is a *stupido! uno carnivero vampiro!* You will do this or Darius and I will go and never return! Never!"

As usual he noticed that she was intoxicated by her own speech. He admired and envied her for this. Throughout the avalanche, the invective flood, she had walked up and down the room, wildly moving her arms, placing her strong hands on and off her bosom. Now she sat staring in stony silence.

"The boy—"

"He is not 'the boy.' He is your son!"

"My son—there, does that satisfy you?—is mistaken." He said it calmly enough but the words "never return"—he felt like rushing to her, tying her up; he would not let her go unless she promised to return!

"Darius is *never* mistaken. Darius is a psychic. Yes"—her voice was low now—"he would make a perfect medium." Joseph shuddered again. "Yes, Darius, he has the intuitive genius of a mind reader . . . like my uncle Georgio. Yes, he knows what we are all thinking." Her voice rose: "If he says that you do not speak to him, I believe him. He also says that you hate him . . . no, not hate, he did not say that. No, he says you do not *care* for him, *that* is what he tells me. Well then I believe him! Darius notices everything . . . he is like my uncle Luigi in Fiesole—"

"I do not care to be excluded."

"Oh. I do not care to be excluded," she mimicked him, "and what does that mean? What does that mean? You think we exclude you? You think when a mother and her son they speak to one another, study together, *succor* one another, yes, that we exclude you? We may not love one another? Yes? Only *you* are to be loved. Is that not so? Tell me when have we said to you, 'Joseph, you cannot join us'? Ach, you are impossible! I only want to compose and now all this nonsense . . . too much of my energy it takes. . . . I don't care what happens to either of you!"

"Exactly."

"I am selfish, yes? But I must be. If I am not for me, who · will be? Tell me! You! You will tell me, 'Consuelo, my dear, take all the time you need. Think only of yourself.' You will *not!* No, you are jealous! Of my work! Of my son!" She sat down. "Why don't you take up painting again, Joseph? Your drawings they have some flair. Yes, you have a small talent. You should cultivate it."

He said nothing. Let her vent herself. He knew from experience that contrition would follow. What energy she had! he thought wearily. He looked at the clock on the mantelpiece. In another half hour dinner would be served. Though in this household one could not be sure. She couldn't, she *didn't* manage the servants. And the new majordomo, what was his name? Ricci, far too young for the position, she had imported from her aunt's estate in Rimini. Well, Ricci had quickly ferreted out the lay of the land, hadn't he? Instead of disciplining the other servants, he had joined them in their sloth and disobedience.

"I have been cruel, Joseph . . . selfish . . . forgive me, Joseph. I am distraught, distracted, the work it does not go well." She waited for him to speak, but he said nothing. He knew he should in his own best interest. But he couldn't; at the moment he disliked her too much.

"Ah now *you* are cruel. You have no heart, no blood," she said starting up again, "you are made of stone. Stone.

But your silence it is *not* imposing, believe me. Keep your silence." Then suddenly she smiled. "Theodisia, she came to see me this afternoon. . . . Joseph, tell me the truth. Does your brother beat her? She has a beaten look. Isabelle (the Spanish soprano) was leaving. She took her for a street-walker. Oh, I'm sure of it. It was written all over her silly face. *Quella è stupida. Che seccatura. Che stupidaggine!* Would I help her, she dares to ask me! She is arranging a charity ball. Would I play for them? Do you know what I told her? I am too busy for such nonsense. . . . Yes, he beats her; I am sure of it. Ah, she is a fool. *Una perfetta English fool.*"

He let out his breath slowly. The worst was over; she was attacking his family. "An *im*perfect English fool," he said.

She laughed. The quarrel was over. Thank God! No, it was not her fault. It was his. He loved her but he was ashamed of loving her, ashamed of their quarrels. He knew his brothers and his sister (even his father) laughed at him behind his back, at the way she treated him. And it made him dislike her, dislike himself, even though he loved her. Oh God, yes, he loved her! though he knew his love was not returned.

Shortly after she left the room, he repeated to himself the question he had been given to translate at Warrenton many years ago: "When one person loves another, which of the two becomes the friend of the other: the one who loves, or the one who is loved?"[18] The question had intrigued him even then.

But the evening had ended well for Joseph. She would stay. She had promised to remain until June first, as usual.

---

18. The question comes from an early Socratic dialogue, "Lysis" (or "On Friendship: Obstetric"). The main discussion deals with the nature of friendship. Socrates's mother was rumored to have been a midwife. Socrates described his activity humorously as helping his friends to "deliver themselves of correct ideas." (Theaetetus 149a)—*H. Van Buren*

City of Childhood
XII
THE TEA PARTY

N EAR the end of May the children received invitations asking them to tea on May twenty-fifth at four o'clock at 28 Marlborough Gardens. The invitations were signed "Darius Rimini Forster, Esquire." Underneath in parentheses was written: "Count Rimini VII." It was the first personal invitation the children had ever received. Their parents were initially reluctant to give them permission but finally did so, and notes of acceptance were sent a few days later.

On the twenty-fifty a small phalanx, including three nannies and Vanessa and her two sisters, stood in front of Darius's house outside the gate, several minutes before the appointed time: scoured, polished, and dressed in their Sunday finery.

Although Darius's house looked exactly like their own houses (its facade was duplicated in every detail) it was classified in the children's minds as "different!" All their lives they had heard their parents refer to it as "Bedlam," "The Mad Woman's Dwelling," "The Barbarian's Abode," "The Sorcerer's Lair," so that even before Darius had returned, their curiosity had been aroused and they had longed, if just for once! to be allowed inside. *Now* they had been invited!

The who-should-open-the-gates quarrel broke off precipitously when the front door, at the top of the stairs inside the small garden, opened and inside its frame appeared a creature dressed in challis lace, furbelows, and ribbons, with flaming red hair on which was perched a black velvet hat that trailed pink plumes.

The creature was murmuring, *"T'adore, t'adore, t'adore."* She repeated the words again and again. It sounded like music or the cooing of doves. Clasping her small gloved hands together she placed them on top of her small plump bosom: *"Demain, demain, n'est-ce pas, demain."*

"Mais oui, certainment," they heard their Aunt Consuelo reply from the gloom of the hallway. *"Arrivederci, mia*

cara . . . demain, ma cherie," and their aunt joined the creature in the frame of the light and kissed her on both cheeks, twice. Consuelo's thick black hair, shining with oil, was coiled around her ears. Like twin snakes, thought Albert. She was wearing a green satin dress braided in gold.

Seeing the children grouped outside the gate, she laughed and gave the creature a poke with her elbow.

"Mon dieu!" she said, "What have we here? A children's crusade? . . . *Mais bien entendu.* Of course Darius, he told me, yes, yes, yes, he is serving tea this afternoon for all his cousins in his rooms, I remember all now. . . . *Scusa, scusa."*

"Enfin addio!" said the creature as she floated (you couldn't really call it walking, Emma thought) down the stairs and by the brick walk that bifurcated the garden. Nanny Burden leaned forward and over the gate to unlatch it for her and she passed them in a cloud of perfume.

"Maria! Maria!" screamed Consuelo. Seconds later, a fat but very pretty young woman, Ricci's wife, appeared.

"Conduct the children to where they are supposed to go!" she said in Italian to her, and to the children and their nannies she shouted, "Enterrrr! Enterrr! In, in, come in! Come up the stairs! *Pronto! Pronto!"* They hurriedly obeyed her, moving down the brick walk and up the stairs. Nanny Grindal, the last one in, shut the gate behind her.

As each child stepped across the threshold Consuelo took their outstretched hands in hers and said: "You are to follow Maria," except to Vanessa, whose face she cupped in her hands and holding it there said: *"Bellissima! Angelo,* the face of an angel."

When they were all inside she glared at them for a few seconds and then going down the line like an officer roughly pulled the nannies away from the children.

"Grindal, Jakes, Bur-r-den! You are to follow *me.* I retain all! Darius told me that there were to be *two, two* teas," and she held up two broad fingers. "Yes, a cousins' tea and a nannies' tea. Come now," she motioned to the nannies, *"Marciando!* Follow me! *Pronto! Pronto!* I don't have all the day."

Nonplussed for once, the nannies followed her meek as lambs while the children, feverish with excitement, followed

Maria up the staircase. They were inside the house at last! Though it was more like stepping into a cave, the children thought, it was so dark, and the light in the hallway was so dim. . . .

Darius was waiting for them in his doorway, a smile on those remarkable lips. Pale as always, his dark eyes shone out from under his curiously hooded eyelids. Once more the children realized with a shock of pleasure how very different he was from them! He stepped aside gracefully to let them pass. Inside they stood awkwardly bunched together in the middle of the room. What should they do? Stand? Sit? Move around?

"Follow me," said Darius. And they did.

Darius's suite comprised three large rooms: a bedroom, a sitting room, and a study, separated each from the other by a scarlet portiere that was looped and held back by gold-fringed ropes. The rooms were jammed with furniture: ottomans, chaises, chairs, sofas all covered in cut velvets and brocades, Italian chests, bureaus, armoires, tesselated marble-top tables, lamps, and statuary made of wood, ivory, and various metals. On oversized rich Oriental rugs were strewn smaller rich Oriental rugs. In the study two vitrines housed a collection of light medieval weaponry; in the bedroom a large section of the floor was covered with the most beautiful lead soldiers the children had ever seen, arranged in battle formation.

That someone could live this way! That a *boy* could live this way! The apartment with its ambience of splendor, its multiplicity of forms, its variety, its wealth, overwhelmed them! Here was no Dr. Boot's elixir, no talk of sin or damnation, no cold porridge or greasy mutton. *Here* was a different order of things.

When they returned to the sitting room, Darius said, "Albert, you are to sit next to me. Edward on the ottoman to your left. Emma, you are to sit at my feet. Vanessa, you and your sisters may sit on the chaise in front of the window. The twins on the love seat in front, thank you. William, you're on the floor next to Emma. And Sidney . . . ah, yes, Sidney shall be the sentinel. Take the blue velvet chair, no not that one, that one, yes, over to the door. You are to guard the door—"

"Sentinel?" asked Vanessa. "Guard the door? Whatever for?"

"To guard against intruders of course. Nannies or parents or whoever. No one is allowed in my rooms without my permission."

"But what about your mother? Surely you can't keep your mother out!" said Vanessa.

"Consuelo?" (He called his mother Consuelo!) "She is only admitted when she is invited."

The children looked at one another. The conversation frightened Albert but he was even more frightened of being rude (manners maketh man, said Poppa). "It is hard to believe but it may very well be true," he said finally.

Emma was staring at the "freak of nature," for that was what Poppa had called Darius when the invitation came. He had thrown it on the floor and said: "That freak of nature!" Darius's skin, so smooth and lustrous, reminded her of the cups into which Momma poured her tea. And how very interesting his nostrils were—the shape of almonds. And his eyes—an image of the black-eyed Susans that sprang up each spring in Marlborough Marshes came to mind. And what color were his lips, anyway? Such a deep pink like . . . like what? The cook's cat's tongue. She smiled up at him. He smiled back. How very perfect his teeth were. . . .

William smiled up at him. When would they go into the other room and play with the soldiers? He had never seen so many. He had only five and they were never allowed to stay out. Back into their wooden box they had to go every evening.

"I think I hear someone coming," Sidney said in a loud whisper.

"Bolt the door," Darius said.

Bolt the door! but Sidney did.

A moment later there was a knock on the door and the children heard their aunt ask: "Darius, let me in, please, for a moment. . . ."

"No, Momma. I simply can't."

"But Darius, there is something I've left in your room. I must have it now."

"Ten thousand pardons Momma but you shall have to wait

until my guests have departed. And please, Momma, be so kind as not to bother us again."

There were audible gasps in the room. They looked at one another. At any moment the heavens might fall. *Never* in all their lives had they heard a boy speak to his mother in that way. They waited for Darius to be struck down but nothing happened. Instead they heard their aunt laugh. "Ah Darius. You are cru-u-el, very cru-u-el. Also, I shall have to wait I see."

That was the moment Vanessa wanted to leave. She hadn't wanted to come in the first place. She was not fond of her cousins. She had been horrified when Momma had told her that the outlandish-looking boy she had seen walking about in the Gardens was actually another cousin, a blood relative. "But you must go," Mathilda had said. "If you don't, it might cause a breach. And he is your cousin, after all. You need never go there again."

"Well, now that I'm absolutely sure we shall not be disturbed again I shall sing to you," said Darius. He smiled.

Sing! Edward blushed. Jacob giggled. The children looked down at the floor, up at the ceiling, anywhere but at each other. Sing!

Darius walked towards Vanessa and reaching above her head removed the silver lyre from its brass hooks where it rested on the wall. He began to pluck its strings. Poised there, the lyre half resting on his chest, he seemed somewhat less than human, thought the children, more like an animal. But what kind? They couldn't decide. Half man, half animal. Like one of the statues on Nannies Plain? No, not exactly, but something like them. Now for the first time they noticed an oil panel that hung next to the brass hooks. A small painting, really, only a little more than six inches in length and four inches in width. The paint itself was applied with an almost porcelain smoothness. A winter landscape: a group of women dancing on a snow-covered mountaintop under a pale moon. The women's heads were held back and their robes and long hair swirled in the winter light.

Their cousin stood in the center of the room and began to play: the ancient melody starting up and moving forward on and on by repetition in ever-changing keys. After a while he began to sing. His voice wavered on falsetto and had an unpleasant sound, the children thought. And nasal, very nasal, whining almost. Oh it was very unpleasant, the children thought. They disliked the music. They disliked their cousin. Was he really their cousin? They wanted to go home. On and on and on the music went in its recitativo-like design. Monotonous . . . still, it held time. But would it never end? How long would it go on? How long could it? Their speculations ended forthwith when they heard a thunderbolt of a knock on the door. What now? They were terrified. This is what comes from not allowing mothers into the nursery. They looked fearfully at Darius, all except for Vanessa. She was pleased: they were all going to be punished.

"Unbolt the door, Sidney," Darius said, smiling.

"Must I? I'd really rather not."

"Unbolt the door."

As soon as Sidney slid the bolt back, the door was pushed open by Ricci, the majordomo.

Ricci! Their parents complained about Ricci too. His "ridiculous clothes." How can Joseph allow it! And there he stood in his green velvet and silver epaulettes! Behind him stood his pretty, young wife, Maria, holding a large tray filled with pastries and cups of tea.

Ricci said to Maria in Italian, "Put the tray on the table, stupid." To Darius he said (also in Italian), "The witches are waiting for their brats."

Maria put the tray down on a marble-topped table. When they left, Sidney, on Darius's instructions, rebolted the door.

There were all kinds of pastries: jam, fruit, custard, cream, chocolate, nut, some with green icing on them, some with coconut, some with sprinkles. The children stared longingly. But when they realized they could eat as many as they wished, they crammed the pastries into their mouths greedily and gobbled them up in minutes. It was the first time in their lives they had ever had enough. They licked their fingers and ran their tongues around the outside of their mouths like cats with bowls of cream. Delicious, delicious beyond belief! They gulped down the strange tasting tea. That too was marvelous. Even Vanessa enjoyed herself. What now? they wondered. Would he sing again? They thought they might even want to listen this time. . . .

But it was time for them to leave, Darius told them. Their nannies were waiting downstairs.

They walked home through the Gardens past the already open-leafed trees. What an odd person their cousin was. Did they like him? Had they enjoyed themselves? What was the name of the instrument Darius had played? Why were the women dancing in the snow in bare feet? What was the name of the tea they had drunk? . . . It had burned their tongues slightly. But in all their reflections on the party that day and in their later lives it never occurred to any of them that Darius might have "arranged" the afternoon.

On June first, as always, Darius and Consuelo left for Italy. And the cousins, escorted by their parents, went off to Saddler's Grove.

PART
II

SADDLER'S GROVE

*Things seized together are whole and not whole,
being brought together and brought apart, being in harmony
and out of harmony; out of all things come one and
out of one comes all things.*

——Heraclitus, Fr. 10,
trans. Clara Lustig

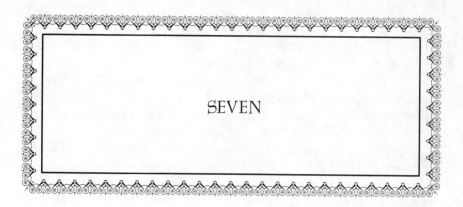

SEVEN

Saddler's Grove is no more.

Nothing material remains except for the thickly wooded countryside in which it once stood. In the winter of 1872 a fire starting in one of the chimneys in the main block spread to the wings and destroyed the house. What was left, a few blackened walls, in time was gradually demolished by the tenants as they used the remaining stone to repair their cottages.

The house and its park were well known. They were mentioned in the *Domesday Book* and more recently in *Travels in Western England* (1835) and *Old Market Towns* (1846).

One of the spoils of war, it was given by William the Conqueror to a Baron De Sadlier for his services to him at the Battle of Hastings. Fortunately for us, in the archives are two accounts of Saddler's Grove, one graphic, one written.

The first is Vanessa's thirty crayon drawings of the Grove done over an extended period, including the delightful pen and bister wash of the Guardian of Saddler's Grove (Jorem's name for it), the rusted knight's suit of armor that stood in the niche of the inner courtyard.

The second is Albert's account from his *Reminiscences of a Happy Childhood*:

"The great thing about Saddler's Grove was its brightness. It was flooded with light. Not a gloomy corner existed, save perhaps in the low buildings that were the stables, but in all the principal rooms, immense windows let in the light of heaven.

"The approach was through lanes bordered with hedges in which the vine and blackberry mingled, past fields of clover, after which there was a sudden turn in the road and before you Saddler's Grove—a stone pile, mellow with age.

"On June first we arrived as always: three carriages and twelve horses, our boots filled to capacity. The women alighting first went to their respective suites to recover from 'the rigors of the journey,' while the men joined Grandpa Jorem in the library for 'a bit of liquid refreshment.' And we (my brothers, sisters, and my cousins), exhausted from excitement and from quarreling with one another, were sent to the 'dormitory,' a large barnlike room fashioned for us by our grandfather in the west wing of the house. First threatened with no dinner if we did not cease quarreling, and then fed quickly, we were fast asleep by the time the stars came out.

"There was a madness in us that summer of 1836. It was as if we knew it was to be the last perfect summer of our lives. All summer long the sun shone in a sky of ideal blue.

"Next year we would leave in midsummer for Warrenton. My cousin Edward and I had been held back, so to speak, so that Sydney, the twins, and William, young as he was, could come with us. So that we would arrive at Warrenton en masse, a block of Forsters, as it were. It was Grandfather Jorem's wish.

"We had heard our fathers speak of Warrenton of course, and we had listened eagerly. Still, it was the unknown. . . . Despite ourselves, the school took on dark and fearful lineaments in our minds. For myself, I remember that each time I thought of Warrenton that summer, each time its shadow drifted toward consciousness, I played more furiously than ever. Here at Saddler's Grove we were safe. Safe in the bosom of our family, in Grandfather Jorem's house: oh, if it could only go on forever, I thought. This perfect summer. This bliss . . . this beautiful and idle time . . .

"That summer of 1836 we went to the abandoned castle and walked on top of the ramparts and roamed through smuggler's caves; we hunted in the tangled undergrowth and fished and lay in the sweet smelling clover, and listened to the bees. That summer we watched the flight of birds, went barefoot, and browned ourselves in the delicious sun and ate Mrs. Capacity's homemade breads and jams and jellies, and all of our lives remembered the acanthus at the height of the summer, its purple spikes glowing against the grey stone wall of the quandrangle."

✳   ✳   ✳

The section concerning Saddler's Grove lay in a separate folder with its own title, "Saddler's Grove: Fragments." A work in progress, a group of episodes that we realized as we examined the material had an underlying structure.

In a few instances we admit to being doubtful as to which fragment logically followed, but on the whole we have complete confidence in our reconstruction of the summer of 1836.

H.V.B.
R.L.

SADDLER'S GROVE: FRAGMENTS

Fragment 1. WILLIAM, HIS DREAM AND AWAKENING

William was dreaming of Warrenton. He knew it was Warrenton because the plaque on the wall read HIC EST WARRENTON. He might not have known it otherwise because the room resembled, in every particular, Reverend Bottome's study. There was the walnut desk, the eight straight chairs on which his brothers and his cousins sat, the glass-enclosed bookcases, the bedraggled turkey carpet with a hole in it, and even the old wall clock. Ticktock . . . ticktock . . .

But instead of Reverend Bottome being seated behind his desk, a stranger was seated there, a man who was surely twice the size of the reverend, whose face was partially hidden behind a full beard and a broad moustache. And there *he* was, William, the dreamer, standing in the middle of the room declining in Latin, the best he could, the noun "to fear": *"Timor, timoris, timori, timorem, timore . . ."* while the man and the desk and the chairs and bookcases and wall clock shouted: "Louder! Louder! Faster! Faster! . . ."

Suddenly there was silence. Complete silence. That was worse, decided William, so he began again: "TIMORTIMORISTIMORITIMOREM—" when the man stood up—oh God, his head almost reached the ceiling! and lowered his left arm, to which a stout rod was attached. Down it came! *BOOM!* It crashed onto the back of the empty chair that stood next to the dreamer. Then William knew with absolute certainty that he, the dreamer, was doomed. That he was to be taken to the smuggler's cave and thrashed, which oddly enough was now located below the reverend's study. The man beckoned. William followed, followed the man down the stairs that led to the cave below, filled with despair, for he now knew who the man was. Oh yes. Reading out loud the sign on the man's back that read HEADMASTER OF WARRENTON! And there, just at the bottom of the stairs, was the door to the cave, the door that William knew even before he saw it would be his exact size.

The headmaster pointed to the door indicating to William that he was to stand there. There! In front of it! Lifting one of his large black boots—for a moment the dreamer thought: why that's one of Poppa's boots!—the headmaster kicked the small door open. Then, placing the tip of his thick rod in the exact center of William's back, he began to prod and push and squeeze William through the door that seemed to be in a state of Heraclitean flux, strangling, shrinking, while in the distance the dreamer heard the furniture chanting: "Faster, faster . . ."

He was almost through the door when he awakened, an unuttered scream dying on his lips.

Fragment 2. GRINDAL, TIGS, AND JOREM

Where was he, wondered William? He was standing in a room that was flooded with moonlight. And was he awake or dreaming? And then of course he realized where he was. He was in the room directly below the dormitory, the room that was used years ago as a ballroom, the room that was kept locked, that no one was allowed to enter. No one. No servant or child at least.

Sixty feet long like the dormitory, it ran the length of the wing. One side of the room was a series of French windows. The few pieces of furniture were covered with dustcovers. Some rugs were rolled up alongside the rear wall.

On the wall closest to William, at right angles to the windows, stood a narrow couch. Its dustcover, William noted, lay in a milk white huddle next to it. On the couch itself were two figures, naked, lying full length, facing one another. Who were they? wondered William. And then he made them out: one of them was Grindal, the other was Tigs (one of the grooms). What were they doing here? No one was allowed in here. Grandfather Jorem had told them that. How dare they disobey him!

Grindal's long black hair was loose. It twisted and curved over her body and over Tig's body like . . . like black ripples on a lake. They were moving back and forth, back and forth, both bodies, like two pendulums of a wall clock: Ticktock, ticktock.

"Faster, faster," William heard Grindal whisper. And then Grindal and Tigs began to moan, as if in pain—oh, were they in pain?—and then from Grindal, William heard a muffled scream, "Ahhh!" and the two bodies fell apart.

The moonlight illuminated their bodies: their ivory-colored torsos, their erect nipples, their slim beautiful hips, and the long attenuation of their thighs and legs. Lying there bathed in the golden light they were indeed quite beautiful.

But William saw none of that. He was staring instead at the patch of thick black hair that grew at the bottom of Grindal's belly, just above her thighs. Emma had been right! She had not made it up. There was hair there! And Tigs, he had hair there, too! Although not as much. But what truly fascinated William, held him entranced, was the sight of Satan's rod (Grindal's name for the penis). It was sticking up out of Tig's nest of hair. Thick and swollen, its tip was wet as if with dew. The lovers lay side by side, their chests moving up and down rhythmically. Tigs's arm, William noted, had slipped off the couch, and the tips of his fingers now grazed the dustcover.

William knew that Satan's rod was never to be touched unless absolutely necessary, like when tinkling. But even then as little as possible. It certainly was never to be seen! Never! Never by any living thing. Never to be even thought of. Suddenly William was cold. Very cold. He thought he might just go back to bed. He would tell Grandpapa tomorrow about Grindal and Tigs being in the room when they weren't allowed in it. No one was. Grandpapa had told them that. And they would be punished. He would tell Grandpapa tomorrow, now he must go back to bed. . . . But he found he couldn't move; he couldn't move at all; instead, the unuttered scream began to well up in him again, and at the same time the thought came to him that, yes, he would like to scream and scream and scream. . . .

And he would have, except that he was yanked, plucked really, out of the room and held fast in someone's arms and the scream died unheard once more. . . .

Held tightly in Jorem's arms, he was carried down the dark hall to the entrance that led to the quadrangle, where Jorem let him down gently, and after patting his head and lifting him once or twice and kissing him, while at the same time motioning him to be silent, he took his hand and leading him through the quadrangle past the Guardian, he took him through the stone archway that led to the fields and pastures of Saddler's Grove.

The night was bright. Standing on the edge of the expanse William could see the wavering silver line at the bottom of the fields that marked the course of the river Alba. Everything, the woods, the fields, the river, the hedges, was clearly defined. The moon was at its zenith. Overhead the stars were dimmed but in the distance over the dark woods they burned brightly.

Hand in hand grandfather and grandchild walked toward a shed that stood in one of the meadows. As they walked, William heard the flutter of wings as bats flew in and out of the hedges. He heard the crickets and the frogs, the scampering of rabbits and hares. Then from the edge of the woods out glided a dark oval shape that passed silently over their heads. "The owl is making his rounds," said Jorem.

Sitting close to one another, they leaned their backs against the shed. William noticed Grandpapa was still in his day clothes.

"Did you know, William, that birds have very large eyes, and that often their eyes weigh more than their brains? Now that's a remarkable fact! And did you know that a falcon can spot a dragonfly more than eight hundred yards away, that is if the light is good and there's a contrasting background like a twig or a cow. Now that's another remarkable fact. . . ."

The boy and the old man talked what was left of the night away, or rather the boy listened as Jorem told him just one more "remarkable fact," talked until the sun came up in a milky sky and the meadow was dew drenched.

Fragment 3. EMMA AND THE PIER GLASS

In my mind's eye I see our group laughing and shouting, and playing our games in the fields of Saddler's Grove, our faces innocent and chaste, as yet unsullied by the slightest strains of inner stress. And yet what remains in my memory is quite unlike these trifling joys.

I can never remember which came first—the finding of the pier glass, or my grandfather's Tale of the Black Swan—but I know they are connected inextricably.

One day, quite by accident, I found myself alone in Saddler's Grove. Momma, my aunts, and their daughters, and all three nannies had gone to visit a neighboring family, the Strooksburys, with whom they socialized in London during the season. My brothers and my male cousins had gone off with Grandpapa to fish in the River Alba.

I was not often alone, except when I was being punished, made to stand facing a wall for hours at a time, or locked in the nursery to "cool my temper," and hence it felt quite strange to be alone. What was I to do with myself? I wondered. At first I began to wander through the house aimlessly, but as I did so I remembered the "treasure" and I became quite excited. Yes, that is what I would do! I would hunt for the treasure that was hidden somewhere in Saddler's Grove!

Every summer for as long as I could remember, Grandfather Jorem had told us about the treasure, a king's ransom he called it, that he had hidden in Saddler's Grove. And on rainy afternoons he would urge us to look for it. "And whoever finds it, boy or girl, it shall belong to. I promise you that." But though we searched every summer we had as yet never found it. Perhaps today, all by myself, I would find the treasure!

There are more than a hundred rooms in Saddler's Grove. Some hours later, standing in a corridor in an upper story that I had never been in before, I realized I was quite lost.

I stepped into one of the rooms just off the corridor. Perhaps, I thought to myself, if I looked out a window I might gain my bearings.

Fragment 4

The window overlooked the quadrangle. There, way below in its niche stood the rusted suit of armor, the Guardian of Saddler's Grove.

Fragment 5

It might be a sewing room, I thought, for there in the corner against the wall was a sewing basket on a table with three chairs drawn up to it. Perhaps the maids came here on Sunday afternoons after church to sew and mend. But then I noticed the film of dust on every surface. No, I was wrong, no one came here.

Fragment 6

As I opened the chest, my heart began to pound; I heard it beat against my ribs; the treasure, perhaps the treasure was in this very chest! But it was empty, there was nothing there. It was when I closed the lid that I caught a reflection of myself in the pier glass that hung directly over the chest.

Fragment 7

I usually avoided looking at my image because of Satan's mark, the dark wine-colored nevus situated on my left temple close to my hairline. It seemed to me that when I looked the only thing I saw was Satan's mark. But this time, instead of turning away, I stared back boldly at my image in the glass and saw that there was no Satan's mark. I felt no fear, not even astonishment, only a keen desire to examine closely this new, silvery reflection.

Fragment 8

I could see that I was not pretty—my forehead was a shade too high, my mouth a bit too wide, my general mien, perhaps, too solemn—but I could also see (the mark not being there) that I was not ugly . . . that I looked like any ordinary little girl.

Fragment 9

I placed my forefinger on my right temple and stroked the skin. The skin was smooth and silky, no longer thick and fibrous. As I stood staring at myself I thought, Momma might love me now, as she loved William . . . as Aunt Mathilda loved Vanessa . . . as Aunt Guinivere loved Albert.

Fragment 10

Suddenly an aching, overwhelming desire rose like a column of fire within me. I longed to be loved. . . .

Fragment 11

From somewhere close by I heard a voice, Grindal's voice, whisper to me, "Come to me, my dearest one, come to me, my dearest Emma, come to me, my love. . . ."

Fragment 12

But even as I stared into the glass, I saw Satan's mark once more.

Fragment 13. A DIALOGUE ON THE BANKS OF THE RIVER ALBA

Albert and Edward were lying on the banks of the river conversing. Albert was telling Edward that he no longer believed in God.

"Not since last spring. You see I have been praying for Sidney's death since then. And he's never, ever, even been slightly ill, not even a little."

"How very disappointing for you," said Edward. How wonderful it was to lie here on the grassy banks with Albert. He loved him so. "But I really don't think you're supposed to pray to God for such things to happen. Poppa says that everything that is good in the world is God's doing and everything evil, Satan's. I don't think that Sidney dying would be considered a good thing. But then I may be wrong."

A damsel fly landed on Albert's hand. He shook it off. "Why does your Poppa allow someone as evil as Grindal to be your nanny?" he asked.

Edward thought carefully before answering, "It's because he's in her power, you see. Much like the Duke in the Tale of the Calcutta Ghost. But she's not evil to me or William. Only Emma." Edward sighed, "I do wish I hated William as much as you hated Sidney. That is really the only thing we don't agree on, isn't it? I have tried but William's too silly. And of course I do know that Momma loves him best . . . but since he's told me he can't abide being kissed by her, I really don't mind if she does. He calls it his 'ordeal,' just like Poppa calls listening to Aunt Consuelo play the piano on Sunday afternoons his ordeal. Perhaps, Albert, Sidney is yours."

"Perhaps. What is your ordeal, Edward?"

"I don't have one as yet. Unfortunately."

"Ever since Grandpapa told him he could bring him his newspaper every day after lunch, he's more cheeky than ever. I hate him. I shall always hate him. Last night I dreamt I strangled him."

A whisper of sound came from high over the marshes to the west followed by quick whistling beats. The boys looked up and saw a swift moving at a great height, its shape outlined against the brilliant blue of the sky.

"Do you think Lord Nelson would be frightened about going to Warrenton?" asked Edward.

"Not in the least."

"Shall you take the *Victory* with you?"

"No. Momma has explained to me that she, herself, shall take care of it. She has shown me the very place she shall keep it—in the locked glass cabinet, in her morning room in Marlborough Gardens. It shall stand between a porcelain shepherdess and a bisque cat. She will have to move everything close together to make room for the *Victory,* but she assured me that she doesn't mind in the least. The important thing, she said, is that the *Victory* be safe."

The church bells tolled the noon hour.

"Shall we go back?" asked Edward.

"We'd better, hadn't we."

As they left, the damsel fly spotting her prey shot out her tongue at great speed and secured her victim effortlessly.

Fragment 14. SIDNEY

Sidney's mother, Guinivere, was one of those rare creatures who found it easier to love than to hate, to be joyful than to be sad, to let go of resentments than to nurture them. She was physically affectionate with her children; they had only to be within the parameters of her arms to be hugged, or kissed, or stroked.

Fragment 15

Shortly after Sidney arrived at Saddler's Grove, something happened to him that made him think that he might be a ghost.

Fragment 16

When Sidney decided that he might be a ghost, he began to pinch himself to prove (to himself) that he either was a ghost or he wasn't.

Fragment 17

Sidney felt more like a ghost at certain times than at other times.

Fragment 18

All summer long we played the games that Jorem had devised for us—Planets, Angels, Smugglers, and Heaven and Hell—in smocks and trousers that Jorem had designed for us.

Fragment 19

When Albert and Edward were chosen to be either the Leader of Heaven or the Leader of Hell, Sidney felt more like a ghost. For when it came to choosing sides, Albert had to call his name out—*had* to! Poppa had told him he *had* to: "Sidney is your brother. You owe your first loyalty to him." But Albert always hesitated. It was in the length of hesitation, those long seconds, that Sidney felt most like a ghost. What seemed endless to Sidney was of course only a moment, but Sidney would think to himself: *Why* is he hesitating? *Why* doesn't he call my name? He *has* to, doesn't he? He daren't disobey Poppa! So then why is he hesitating? But then when Albert did call out "Sidney" (he had to, didn't he?), he didn't look at him.

Fragment 20

Sidney felt that he was different. In some indefinable way he wasn't like his brothers, his sister, or his cousins. They were real; he wasn't. He thought he might be a ghost. He began to pinch himself in places that would not show, like the inner flesh of his thighs and arms. He would take the pale white flesh and squeeze it hard. Hard. In a day or two, when the flesh had turned black and blue, he would stare at it and wonder: Am I a ghost?

Fragment 21

Guinivere was patiently listening to Mathilda complain (as usual) about the "shocking lack of amenities at Saddler's Grove."

They were seated in the library after dinner. Guinivere sat on a hard-backed chair next to the couch on which Mathilda and her three daughters were sitting, all of whom were busily embroidering. The evening was warm. Through the open windows came the cries of Deirdre and the twins playing Angels on the terrace outside.

Fragment 22

". . . and I do hope, Guinivere, that you shall side with me in this matter! It is essential that we stand united." Mathilda glanced down the room at her father, who was placidly reading a book in front of the empty fireplace. Albert, who was standing next to him, was examining with interest an oil painting of a ship that hung above the ugly stone mantel.

"Of course, of course," said Guinivere. Her voice was soothing.

She reached out her hand to Sidney, who stood next to her, drew him closer, and began to stroke his hair. "Of course," she repeated, smiling. Sidney began to move his head back and forth against her fingers . . . delicious . . . while his aunt continued her litany of complaints.

"And yesterday I took it upon myself to confront Mrs. Capacity in person, though 'Miss Insolence Personified!' would be a better name for her. There *are* other animals beside pigs that humans can digest, I told her—pork three days in a row!—and that she was to serve them forthwith or else my daughters and I would prepare for an immediate departure. The wretch's answer? 'When was it then that we would be leaving?' Oh, it's scandalous, scandalous the power he's given that woman!"

Sidney, who was now in a mild state of delirium, was following with his eyes the geometric pattern (cerulean blue) that had been painted above the gold-figured paper that ran the length of the room. As his mother continued to stroke him, his neck, his shoulders . . . his torso was beginning to tingle. On the brink of a swoon he turned his head toward his mother. He wished to declare his love. But as he did he realized that his loved one's attention was engaged elsewhere. He followed her gaze down the length of the room. Albert, of course. He shivered slightly. Guinivere, feeling her son shiver, pressed his body even closer to her and murmured in his direction, "There, there . . . there, there."

Fragment 23

"Vanessa, show your embroidery to your Aunt Guinivere."

The child rose with such grace that it made Guinivere catch her breath. Was there ever hair as golden as hers? Or eyes of such violet blue? She examined the child's work: a spray of lilies on a field of green.

"See how exquisite it is. Each stitch a model of perfection. She is far better at it than I am already."

Sidney moved away. "Good night, Momma," he said.

"Good night, my dearest one," replied his mother, her eyes fastened on Vanessa's work.

Outside the room as he wandered off to bed he began to wonder once more: Am I a ghost?

Fragment 24. SIDNEY AND JOREM

It was Jorem's custom to read his newspaper and smoke his cigar after lunch every day in the library in a chair facing the terrace. Although the lighting of his cigar was reserved for Vanessa, Jorem's favorite grandchild, the task of handing him his newspaper, the lesser distinction, was for the most part evenly divided between Albert and Edward. Except when Sidney took it into his head to compete for the privilege. Sometimes he won, but having fought so bitterly he took no enjoyment in his victory. And besides that his father might rebuke him. "Why can't you behave like the others? Why must you take everything so seriously?" Why indeed.

"Sidney."

Sidney was gasping for breath on the grass. They had just ended the game Planets and all the turning around had made him dizzy.

"Sidney," the voice repeated his name again. He opened his eyes. There stood his grandfather.

"Yes, Sir." He sat up.

"I want a favor from you. I shall only keep you for a moment."

"Yes, Sir."

"It would please me if you would hand me my newspaper today after lunch. Will you do that?"

Up until that moment Sidney had given little thought to Jorem. He knew of course that Jorem was his father's father. And hence his "grandfather." And that Saddler's Grove was his grandfather's estate, as was Marlborough Gardens. And that Jorem was old. Very old. But that meant nothing to him—until now.

"Answer, child. Ah, well, never mind, I see the answer in your eyes. It's yes." Sidney's eyes were filled with tears. "And on reflection, Sidney," continued Jorem, "it would please me were you to continue to be so kind as to hand me my newspaper for the rest of your stay at Saddler's Grove."

Fragment 25

Even Sidney was happy that summer. He had heard his father say on different occasions, "What a joy it is to be alive!" At Christmas last when they returned from caroling, and once on a particularly fine day in autumn when he and his brothers took a walk with their father through the Gardens to Uncle Elijah's house and when Deirdre was christened in St. Giles. Now, for the first time in his life, Sidney thought that he understood what his father might be feeling at the time he said that.

"O what a joy it is to be alive!" Sidney whispered to himself.

Fragment 26. TWILIGHT

It was twilight. The swallows swooped high across the grassy lawn following their leader from tree to tree crying out to one another through a pink and silver sky. The children, dressed in smocks and trousers Jorem had designed for them, played tag with one another, as if in imitation, from tree to tree. Jorem sat watching them in the overstuffed chair that the servants had carried out of the house.

Underneath a hawthorn tree, apart from her cousins, sat Vanessa and her two sisters on a rug stretched out over the fallen white blossoms, their white smocks crisp and startling in the crepuscular light, their golden hair shimmering. They were making flower wreaths from daisies they had collected that afternoon in the meadows.

"Beautiful. How beautiful she is, how truly beautiful," thought Jorem as he observed Vanessa. He watched as she bent her head over her work, the beautiful articulation of her fingers as they manipulated the green stems into knots and smoothed petals, and as they now and then placed the half-formed wreath on her head to test for size. She brushed away a red-gold lock that had sprung forward on to her temple. "Perfection. A second Helen." Mrs. Capacity of course was right when she reminded him of how he had favored Mathilda in the same way when she was Vanessa's age. But he knew for a fact that his love for Vanessa was far more intense, deeper, more profound. An unalloyed joy.

Feeling someone's eyes on her, Vanessa's eyes searched through the luminous air, found his face and flashed him an enchanting smile. Then and there he decided that he would see Mr. Hemsley (the family lawyer) as soon as possible. Yes, his darling was to be left something special, for herself alone: a king's treasure for a golden princess. "Damn Elijah! Damn him!" he muttered. It would incense Elijah, this legacy, for it meant his children would get less. But Jorem thought he understood his son. Elijah was vexed that his father was still alive. Perhaps all sons felt that way. Jorem remembered the strange satisfaction he had felt staring at the corpse of his father in his coffin—he was master now. Yet he doubted that his son Solomon felt the way Elijah did. Or

Joseph. No. Joseph felt only a morbid passion for that foreign woman. . . .

A squabble had started among the tag players. William was having a temper tantrum. As the smallest boy, he was the one who was always "it" but since he couldn't catch anyone, not even three-year-old Deirdre, he didn't want to play anymore. He was cross and tired. The others were trying to persuade him to play one more game, "just one more," but by now he was so incensed he started to jump up and down like a human ball and then he threw himself on the grass shrieking, "I won't! I won't!" while he beat his fists into the ground.

The nannies began moving toward him swiftly but Jorem raised his hand: "*No!* Stay where you are!" He hated the nannies: always fussing at them, restraining them, correcting them, punishing them. He went over to William, who was now sobbing as if his heart would break.

"William."

There was no response.

"William, if you continue to carry on this way I shan't be able to tell you the Tale of the Black Swan." There was instant silence.

"The Tale of the Black Swan?"

"Yes. But you must first promise me not to scream anymore, dear boy. It's ear splitting."

"I promise." No one told stories better than Jorem, not even Grindal.

The children gathered around Jorem. Even Vanessa and her two sisters. They sat in a circle on the grass, their faces lifted toward him, open and vulnerable, a smile on William's tear-stained face.

CREATURE OF LIGHT: THE TALE OF THE BLACK SWAN

Once upon a time there was a black swan named Maartel. His beak was made of coral, his eyes of pink quartz, and the tips of his feathers were painted silver. On Sundays he would dance for the Lord of Creation, spinning and gliding over the clear waters of the Lake of Luria.

One day a spider named Johannah who lived in nearby woods spied Maartel dancing. As she watched, hatred began to well up within her. Generally speaking, she disliked everyone, and was intolerant and uncharitable to all, but Maartel's beauty coupled with his remarkable dancing increased her flow of envy a hundredfold. When it had grown a beard and whiskers, Envy spoke to her.

"Dear Johannah," said Envy, "we both know that you shall not have a moment's peace until you have dragged the swan, Maartel, to the Tree of Death that stands in the middle of the woods and chained him to it."

"Yes, the thought has crossed my mind. But how can I? I am only a small spider and Maartel is a very large, plump, black swan."

"Grant me a moment dear while I ask the Muse to inspire me. . . . Ah! I have it! You must make a net, a large one of pine needles. When it is finished, you must trick him into stepping into it. Then when he is safely trapped, you may haul him off to the Tree of Death."

"Botheration and stale crumpets! What can I say that would tempt that oversized glider to step into the net?"

"Trust me. When the time comes, words will come to your tongue without effort."

And so in a shorter time than it takes to say "Marlborough Gardens," Johannah, assisted by her hundreds of children and dozens of husbands, wove a green net made of pine needles which, on completion, transformed itself into strands of emerald-colored glass that sparkled and shimmered on the forest floor like the essence of the green fire of envy itself.

The following Sunday Johannah put on her robe of jet black trimmed with crow feathers and carrying a parasol made her way to the banks of the Lake of Luria. And there was Maartel: gliding and whirling as usual.

"My dear Maartel," she called out to him. "I do so enjoy your dancing. I want to give you a gift—an emerald glass net—as a token of my appreciation for all the pleasure you have given me by your dancing."

"Thanks, ever so . . ." said Maartel swimming toward her, "but you had best keep it for yourself. I have everything in the world I want. I need nothing more to enrich my life."

Johannah seethed with fury, boiled with anger, bubbled with rage. And to be just to Johannah, I myself feel that Maartel's answer was a wee bit smug. Oh, she couldn't wait until the day when she could chain Maartel to the Tree of Death.

"Yes," said Maartel, "I am the most fortunate of beings. I thank the Lord of Creation every day for my state of bliss. Good day to you, Johannah," he said, standing on the tips of his webbed feet, before he swam away.

That afternoon, Johannah forced all her children and all her husbands to scrub the forest floor, and then imprisoned them and thrashed them with a cat-o'-nine-tails that she spun out of herself while she brooded over the problem. In the last rays of sun, she summoned up the most powerful demon of all—Strife—and he came quickly as he always does when bidden to appear.

"What is it you wish from me this time, sweet Spinnerette? As always, I am your obedient servant."

Being a very bright spider, Johannah presented the problems clearly and succinctly. When she finished, Lord Strife began to laugh. His mouth fell open wide so that one could see all eight rows of his black polished teeth at the same time.

"Forgive me, Spinnerette, forgive me," he gasped. "I really did not mean to laugh but the idea of your trying to tempt Mr. Goody Maartel by giving him something just set me off. You haven't the foggiest notion, have you, of what tempts a Goody, do you?"

Then taking one of Johannah's small furry ears into the palm of his striped hand, he began to whisper into it so that only she could hear the words.

Early the next morning Johannah went to the lake and called out to the black swan who was dancing as usual. "Maartel," she cried, "I need you to do me a favor."

"You need a favor. How wonderful! What is it you want me to do?" said Maartel swimming towards her.

"I need you to help me carry the emerald net I offered you to my cottage in the woods. Neither my many children nor my husbands will help me," said Johannah, wiping away a spider tear with the hem of her gossamer robe. After that there was a veritable storm of spider tears, which are made of black onyx and therefore made a *ping, ping, ping* sound as they fell on the pebbly shore.

Taking her small furry hands into the tips of his black wings, Maartel replied, "Dry your tears, Johannah, I shall help you. And if there is anything else I can do, please ask."

"Terribly kind of you, really, but I can't think of a thing right now, Maartel. But I am sure that after you have carried the net for me to my cottage I shall be able to think of at least nine more things you can help me with."

"Oh, goody, goody. I am so glad to hear that," said Maartel, as he stepped out of the river and onto the land.

Lord Strife was right! thought Johannah as she led Maartel through the woods to her cottage. She went over in her mind exactly what Lord Strife had whispered to her the day before:

"Bloody bores, aren't they, the Goodies? With their everlasting, bothersome habit of always wanting to help! Quite hopeless you know to offer to give Good Maartel that emerald net. Give a Goody something! Never! They won't stand for that. They're the Givers; we poor souls are merely the Givees. They bestow, they donate, they provide. . . . They won't let anyone else play Fairy Godmother, the Friend in Deed, the Good Samaritan! As you can clearly see, they're a thoroughly smug and selfish lot! They're the Helpers and the Givers; we have to be satisfied with being just Helpees and Givees. So this is what you must do to trap that big booby, Johannah. Be a Helpee, and you shall have him!"

They came to Johannah's cottage. In front of it lay the large glittering emerald net.

"It really is quite beautiful," said Maartel, as he picked up an edge of its twisting form, and put it into his coral beak, and then another edge . . . whereupon thousands of legs belonging to Johannah's hundreds of children and husbands tumbled poor Maartel into the center of the net.

When he was in it, Johannah, her children, and her husbands quickly and deftly drew all the edges together into a tight knot. Sitting in the center of his new green cage, Maartel looked startled, but not at all frightened. He inquired mildly: "Why did you do that, dear Johannah?"

But there was no answer. Instead she and her husbands and children began to haul their heavy burden to the serpentine path that leads to the Tree of Death in the center of the woods.

The journey was long. The air grew dark and heavy. As they neared the center of the woods they no longer heard the sounds of birds or animals, or even the wind. Only the sound of the net as it scraped along the forest floor. And now and then, the soft, bewildered moans of the black swan Maartel.

Finally they came to the Steep Ravine, which encircles the earth on which the Tree of Death stands, a tree so tall one cannot see its top. Above it hung a black and starless sky.

Carefully, the spiders dragged their burden slowly down to the bottom of one side of the Steep Ravine and then slowly up the other side. Finally they were there—in front of the Tree of Death. Then they took their emerald ropes that they had carried with them out of their thousands of pockets. Swiftly they lashed the net and its captive to the black, thick bark of the tree. And left. For as evil as they were, the place frightened even them.

A hundred years went by. Long were the days, and long were the nights. What Maartel thought of, how much he despaired, what he endured, only Maartel knows. Against the black tree, the black swan was invisible, except for his pink quartz eyes, which from time to time flickered dully.

Now the Lord of Creation who sees and knows everything knew about Maartel (Johannah, by the way, was devoured by a chimaera on her way home). So in the precise moment Maartel was bondaged to the Tree, his soul flew straight to heaven, and sat there waiting to be weighed on the gold scales of Justice that stand on the Lord's right side.

Placing Maartel's soul on one side of the scale, the Lord of Creation lay, one by one, the weight of Gluttony, Jealousy, Sloth, Greed, Anger, Envy, and last of all Pride. One by one they balanced out—except for Pride.

The Lord reached down, and picking up the weight of Pride turned it this way and that in his luminous fingers until he finally discovered an infinitesimal hieroglyphic, the size of a fly speck, written on one of its myriad facets. Holding it close to his sapphire eyes he read out loud: "He's terribly smug. . . . Oh, well, now a hundred years should remedy that." And that is why, children, Maartel remained tied to the Tree of Death for a hundred years.

But to the day, to the hour, to the minute, the exact second the hundred years were up, the Lord of Creation bent toward Earth and breathing gently on a bud nestled in its bright green leaves created a Creature of Light who flew on her diamond wings up to the Heavens and straight across to the dark patch of sky under which the Tree of Death stood. And as the Lord watched, the creature flew like a bright arrow into the primeval gloom.

"You are free," said the Creature of Light to Maartel as she untied his ropes. "Free to return home."

But Maartel instead of moving remained motionless. Then he began to cry.

"Home?" he moaned, "Oh, I am too frightened to go home. I don't have the strength to go down and up the Steep Ravine that leads to the serpentine path and the Lake of Luria. Please be kind enough to tie me up again. I shall remain here."

"You shall not!" said the Creature of Light. "Freedom and Courage are yours by the right of the Lord of Creation!"

Having said that, she took the form of a sharp sliver of light and flew into the center of Maartel's heart. For a moment, as the sliver punctured Maartel's heart, he felt a wee stab of pain, but only for a moment. Minutes later it occurred to him that it might be a very good thing indeed to start back home.

He knew that at times he might feel lonely, even a bit frightened, and that he might at times be a bit hungry and even thirsty, but he was sure, quite sure, that he could do it. And so Maartel started his journey home to his beloved Lake of Luria.

As for the Creature of Light . . . if you are wondering who or what she really was, why I shall tell you: the Creature of Light that lodged herself and remained forever in Maartel's heart is what we mortals call Hope. Without it, dear children, we would all be tied to the Tree of Death.

*   *   *

The following day the children went home to Marlborough Gardens and . . . Darius.

PART
III

DARIUS AND HIS COUSINS

God is day night, winter summer, war peace, surfeit famine; but he is modified just as fire is when incense is added to it, taking its name from the particular scent of each different spice.

——Heraclitus, Fr. 67,
trans. Clara Lustig

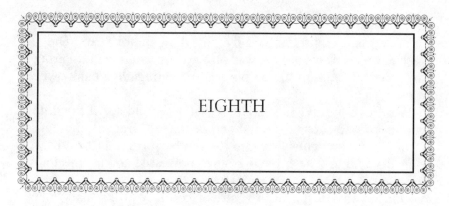

EIGHTH

You would not find out the boundaries of the soul, even by traveling along every path: so deep a measure does it have.
—Heraclitus, Fr. 45,
trans. Clara Lustig

Breaking our custom of dual solitude, Harriet and I[19] spent part of the spring of 1930 on the Continent to see for ourselves Darius's palazzo in Florence and Emma's last domicile, the Villa Aubeitz, in Weimar, Germany. But first we went to Berlin, where we stayed an entire week ensconced in a small hotel near Unter den Linden. We danced till dawn every night in the Cave of Harmony, a cabaret on the Kurfürstendamm owned by a friend of Harriet's, a stout, severe-looking, middle-aged German baroness. Harriet looked perfectly splendid in her tuxedo garnished with her father's diamond cuff links and studs.

On April 8 we left for Weimar.

Upon arrival it was pouring rain. We left our luggage with the proprietor of the White Swan, an inn next to Goethe's house on the Frauenplan. No, we did not wish to inspect our accommodations. No, we did not want refreshments. Just a taxi, *"bitte."* And off we drove through the rain to the villa.

The Villa Aubeitz, situated in one of the city's suburbs, on Ettersburg Hill, is a small estate, only twenty-five acres. The rusted gates were wide open. Our driver, suddenly loquacious,

---

19. See Reference Note D, page 116.

informed us that no one had lived in the villa for years. Did we wish to enter? If we did, he was sure no one would mind. Perhaps the ladies were interested in buying? He thought the bank owned it now.

We drove around the estate. What we could see through the curtain of rain seemed dismal and neglected. But still the house (built in the French style) with its weather-beaten labyrinths, its ruined pavilions, its broken statues possessed for us an almost legendary magic.

On the way to the inn the driver confided to us that "many years ago it was owned by two women, *"die Englanderin und die Italienerin."* Very eccentric they were and when one died, the other one disappeared. A strange business, *"meine Damen, nicht wahr?"*

We intended to stay for at least a week, but our sleep that night was interrupted by gunshots. The next morning the proprietor assured us that it was just a *wilderspruch,* as he called it, and of *no* consequence at all, "no, none at all," between the "pighead Brown Shirts and the pighead Communists and a plague on both their houses!" But Harriet insisted on leaving for Florence that very day. I had never seen her so distracted. I myself wished to stay. After all, Emma had lived here less than thirty years ago. There were all sorts of possibilities, neighbors and servants whom we could interview, and I wanted a look at the land deed and other records. The Germans are so thorough, so efficient. . . . But as I said, I had never seen Harriet so distraught, so I complied with her wishes.

We took the afternoon train to Milan, where we changed to the train for Florence, arriving late that evening in Darius's city.

*   *   *

The Riminis are an old Italian family with roots in several northern Italian cities, but they have lived for the most part in Florence. The palazzo where Darius spent most of his life is a stone's throw from the Ponte Vecchio, on the north bank of the river Arno.

We stayed in a pensione recommended by one of Harriet's Italian friends, a mere hundred yards south of the palazzo, a quiet place with a cool inner court. The day after we arrived, Harriet arranged, through yet another friend, an interview with the present count (Count Darius Rimini the VIII), and a private tour through his celebrated dwelling. But he broke the appointment.

Some days later we received the following note in a cream-colored envelope bearing a familiar crest:

My dear ladies,

My secretary, Senorita Buonaritte, has been advised to receive you and assist and facilitate your purpose in this ancient city in every way.

I cannot, alas, accord you an interview since, like this fabled city, I too am ancient, far too ancient for even such simple amenities as afternoon tea.

Pardon an aged recluse and believe me when I offer my sincere wishes for your every success.
Count Darius Rimini VIII

The count's butler, a young, saucy, ferret-eyed man, showed us into the anteroom: large, cool, dimly lit, crowded with sanctuary and time-darkened paintings.

"Che cosa vuole?" he asked Harriet. *"Come si chiama lei?"* His tone was impudent.

"Mi chiamo Harriet Van Buren . . . sono una amica del Signor Pepato—"

He disappeared through a gilded door. We waited restlessly on two unpadded wooden chairs, Harriet occasionally getting up to look through the long, narrow window that faced the river.

At the far end of the room in the left-hand corner a marble staircase led to the upper floors. Some minutes later we heard the loud *click clack* of heels on the marble steps: Senorita Buonaritte.

"Miss Van Buren? Miss Lowe?" she said, as she came toward us, the scent of her heavy perfume reaching us before she did.

She was not what we had expected: a staid elderly nurse type. Senorita Buonaritte was middle-aged, plump, and a bit tartish. Expensively dressed (in black silk) and bedecked with diamonds in her ear lobes and around her neck, wrists, and fingers. She began her speech rapidly, as if she had rehearsed it. Her English accent was as flawless as her diamonds, but her syntax was impaired.

"Kindest regards from the Count Rimini he sends you. A tour of the palazzo accompanied by the historical commentary I give myself, as best I can. That will suffice you think? Letters of introduction I have taken the liberty to write—the idea of the count—to several of his friends. Their palazzos you wish to visit too perhaps? *Mi capisce?* . . . This room, it has been rebuilt. In fact it has been rebuilt, the whole palazzo. Rebuilt by Count Rimini the Seventh in the last century. Do you hear of him? A monograph on the life of the great Leonardo de Medici he has written. Included a section of it in the Vitelli guide book to Florence since the year 1902. Before you leave, I myself shall a copy give you. Now follow me, *per favore* . . ."

We "regarded" as she suggested the masonry, the mural hangings, the Tintorettos and the Raphaels, the great studded wooden shutters and the innumerable pilasters, in short everything that had contributed to the palace's Renaissance glory. And it was all that we had expected it to be: a work of art.

At the end of two hours we had seen everything except the private apartments.

"Satisfied, you are?" she said.

I looked at Harriet who shook her head. I waited a few seconds and when she did not speak I spoke for both of us. I was quite sure I had read her disappointment correctly.

"Yes and no," I replied. "Thank you for the tour. It was excellent, both informative and gracious, but we are unhappy that there is no portrait of the noted scholar Count Rimini the Seventh. There are so many ancestral portraits, we wonder why there is none of him? Could it be that the portrait is hanging in the count's private apartments? And if it is, is there a possibility of our viewing it?"

She smiled. Her teeth shone in the perennial twilight of the anteroom.

"Ah, but there is one. Here it is not. It is on loan to the Pitti . . . a Veracito[20] . . . a Siennese painter. I will recall," she put her plump forefinger in mock perplexity to her forehead, "Galleria thirty-five, middle center . . . east wall. Of the master

---

20. Antonio Veracito (1827–1901), Neo-Mannerist, follower of Gronzino and Pontormo, known for the elongation of the human figure and the use of the serpentine line. Veracito was one of Darius's protégés.—*H. Van Buren*

I am told it is an excellent example." Thanking her we left and taxied to the Pitti Palace.

We stayed at the Pitti until it closed. In front of the portrait.

The Siennese painter had caught it all: the charm, the arrogance, the sensitivity, and, yes, the effeminacy. It was all there on the canvas before us. There he stood—it was a frontal view— in a brown velvet suit of clothes, a gold fringed sash encircling his epicene waist. His right hand rested lightly on his hip, the cuff's dense lace almost concealing the tapered fingers. In his left hand he held loosely a scarlet lily, the family emblem emblazoned on their heraldic device. Above his head waved a golden banner on which was printed the family motto: *Memoria Tenere.*

Toward the end I became impatient. I have never cared for Darius. At best I understand him as a dilettante, at worst your garden-variety psychopath. A seducer. He tempted his cousins bit by bit with hints of the fabulous, glimpses of the forbidden; . . . still, he must have had boundless charm, which set him apart from ordinary people—one of those people they dub charismatic though lawless would be more apt, someone who can with impunity overide everyday rules, mores, proprieties. But as I said, unlike Harriet, I find the type unattractive.

"My cousin," wrote Emma, "was a markedly refined type, his limbs elongated as in a Mannerist painting; his features a bit too desiccated to be really handsome except for his mouth, which was full and exquisitely carved, the color of a pink camellia. Indeed it reminded me of a camellia afloat in an ivory bowl."

We returned the next day and the next. I began to wonder if one can be jealous of a dead man. Finally I refused to go; Harriet went alone. I grew sullen and impatient. I made threats. . . .

In the beginning of May we returned to Marlborough Gardens. The lilacs were in bloom and the mock orange.

City of Childhood
XIII
DARIUS AND DEE JEE

LONG spears of light pierced the dense bank of gray fog and passed through the eastern window of Darius's study, fell on the maps, diagrams, sketches, books, and celestial charts, fell on the boy who was hunched over his desk, stiff with fatigue and cold. He had been up most of the night, awakened at midnight by his parents' quarrel. Three days ago he and his mother had returned from Florence.

It was always the same the first week they were home. The nights were punctuated by cries and shrieks, bitter accusations, threats, and the terrifying sound of his father sobbing. By the following week there was comparative peace. Had they lost interest in one another? Were they finally exhausted? They boy could never decide which was true. As usual he had detached (with hatred) from the sound of their voices by immersing himself in this work. Translating. A short section of Thucydides. There being sufficient light, the boy blew out the candle and read over his night's translation:

> . . . most of them set to work destroying themselves by piercing their throats with arrows which the enemy had shot at them; others strangled themselves with cords? ropes? from the beds or strips made from their own clothes. This went on for the greater part of the night (for night fell upon their misery) until in one way or another either by suicide or by the missiles struck by their enemy they perished. When day came, the Corcyreans flung the bodies on wagons, laying them lengthwise and crosswise and hauled them out of the city.

He carefully wrote underneath the last words: "Book IV.XLVIII 3, Thucydides, History of the Peloponnesian War. An account of the massacre of the oligarchs on Mt. Istone, a fortress on the western mainland of Greece in 425 B.C., Count Darius VII, 1836."

Done. But should it be cords or ropes? He looked the

word up again in his lexicon, a book that had once belonged to his great uncle, Antonio Platano, who had spent most of his life tracing his family roots back to the Greek philosopher Plato. He had found the book on his uncle's estate in Rimini two summers ago. Small cords, he decided. He ran his pen neatly through the word "ropes."

From below came the sound of the piano. She was already at work then. What time was it? 7:30 A.M. He stretched himself, twisting his thin torso, yawned, and relaxed. He did not fear the day today. Joseph had already started on his trip to Germany on some banking business; the front door had slammed an hour ago.

His father made him nervous. It was not that his father ever interfered with what he was doing. Nor did he encroach on his privacy. Indeed his father rarely spoke to him and he never made inquiries. But the mere thought of his father's presence in the house disturbed him. The boy sensed that beneath the icy formality of his father's manner, his eccentric reserve, there was an agitation of sorts and he suspected that it might be in regards to him. And that disturbed him. He didn't want to be the recipient of any sudden revelation his father might feel impelled to make to him.

Darius was very bright. He knew that. Yet he despaired of ever making himself understood to another human being. Not even to his mother whom he loved above all others. He felt there was something inside himself that was indefinable, something that could not be articulated or transmitted, an integral part connected to his quintessential essence. Yet, paradoxically, what he hoped for most was that it would be possible to do so, to connect, to feel connected (miraculously) to another human being. To end his isolation.

He felt like an exile. He felt he knew how the historian must have felt when after losing the battle of Amphipolis to the Spartan general Brasidas he was banished.

He felt like an exile in England as well as in Italy, at home in neither country, disliked by his English relatives, but also disliked by his Italian relatives. Disliked and ridiculed besides.

Only a fortnight ago his grandfather had mocked him— Darius detested the count—had burst out laughing when Darius had inadvertently anglicized a word.

They were dining en famille: his mother, himself, all his aunts and uncles with his grandfather in an almost bare dining room—his grandfather having sold most of the furniture in the palazzo for money to gamble with. Darius had commented casually on the excellence of the olives when his grandfather burst out laughing and like an evil child began to shout and mimic: "Olif! Olif!" his withered frame suddenly bloated with energy. *"Silenzio!"* Consuelo had screamed at her father, the old count. *"Animali! Vampiro!"* The old count had hid his face like a frightened child in his napkin and then uncovering it with blinking eyes had asked for forgiveness from Consuelo and from the others but *not* from Darius. He would not ask for forgiveness from Darius.

He was eighty-three but they called him *"il cattivo bimbo,"* the naughty baby, for he was still gambling. Consuelo insisted that the servants search him for money before he went out for his daily walk. He would gamble with anyone, for anything. And they did not search only his pockets but his shoes and socks; they even ran their hands under his monstrous wig, fiery red long curls. Once he had hidden a florin in his rectum. Disgusting! Depraved! A sack of depravity! It was because of him that Darius had to live in England! His mother had been *sold* to Joseph so that his grandfather, that sack of depravity, could continue to gamble. It was his grandfather's fault that he was an exile.

Calm, he must remain composed, calm, self-possessed like the other exile who, confronted with the sordid spectacle of human strife, wrote about it and remained aloof. But the anger continued to well up in him, enough anger to destroy the universe. But he must remain calm. . . . he began to stroke his penis to soothe himself. Seconds later he was masturbating. As he ejaculated the face of Dee Jee Marghhadita, the Indian boy, came to him, as it always did. The boy's smooth flesh. Air spun. Slim, elegant like himself, dark-skinned like himself, though a slightly different shade. The boy's cheeks had been carmine as if a thin red glaze had been drawn over a burnt sienna ground. He was prince of a small principality outside of Bengal. Dee Jee's grandfather, a maharajah, had been a close friend of Clive's, the English conqueror who had murdered the maharajah's twin brother and placed him, Shah Jafar, on the throne. Shah Jafar (Dee

Jee's grandfather) had revered Clive; he had called him the God of Justice. It was Shah Jafar who had persuaded Dee Jee's father to give his son an English education. Nothing could be better, could it? And so Dee Jee had been sent to Warrenton.

Poor Dee Jee. He had arrived so eager to please but of course they had not accepted him. He looked like a monkey to them in his Eton-like uniform. Too shocking, really too shocking. It shouldn't be allowed, should it?

And unfortunately he was neither as clever nor as courageous as Darius who had made a special niche for himself at Warrenton the year before Dee Jee had arrived.

Two years earlier, when Darius had entered the second school, he had refused categorically to shine any senior's boots, or fetch for them, or do anything for them. Within the space of a fortnight Darius had been flogged and whipped more than ten times. Once they had hung him outside a window. But he had remained inviolate. And he had told them, quoting Herodotus, "I bow my knee to no man but the Gods." First out of disgust, but later out of respect they had left him alone and eventually he was referred to—it was meant as a compliment—as "the slime-colored chap." But Dee Jee did not fare as well.

On Monday mornings after chapel Dr. Pond read out loud the boys' weekly reports. After reading a bad report from one of the masters, he would say to the boy in question: "Come up to my study afterward." Poor Dee Jee was caned often, but he accepted it with good grace. It was part of his English education, he said. And he might have made a niche for himself as Darius had—he was so good-natured and so fabulously wealthy—had it not been for Reverend Brumsday, whom the boys dubbed "Doomsday." The reverend took an excessive dislike to Dee Jee and began to bait him publicly and to humiliate him at every opportunity. Even so, Dee Jee hung on and continued to fetch and shine boots for the seniors and accept the caning and the extra homework Doomsday meted out to him, even cheerfully. But one day the reverend accused him of cheating on one of his quizzes. When Dee Jee denied it, he told him that he was sorry and that it saddened him but he would have to make an example of Dee Jee because Dee Jee was now beyond the pale, for now he was not only a cheat but a liar besides. The beating would be done by the reverend himself—it was his duty—in the school yard in front of all his peers.

At the appointed hour the whole school assembled in the courtyard. No one was excused. An example was to be set. "Bring out the block!" called Reverend Brumsday to the two prefects, his assistants. To Dee Jee, who looked as if he had a mortal sickness, he said, "Take down your breeches, like a man!" Dee Jee did as he was told. Then the prefects forced Dee Jee to his knees before the block, a solid piece of wood four feet by four feet, draped in black cloth.

The reverend raised his walking cane, a stout walnut rod with a metal tip and a silver handle—there was a hush—and came down with his full strength on the boy's slender naked buttocks. At the end of ten counts the boy's buttocks were a mass of blood. Darius, who didn't like the boy—the boy was a coward and worse, craven—now felt that perhaps he should have what? . . . protected him? Would it have been possible?

Dee Jee began to scream and struggle now. What was he shouting? The boys couldn't understand what he was saying. Was he speaking Hindi? "Hold him down, boys! Hold him down!" shouted the reverend to the prefects. The crowd moaned; it was exciting. *Swish* went the cane; *swish!* Suddenly the boys saw the reverend throw his cane away. "Outrageous! Disgusting!" roareed the reverend. "Take him away!" The boys leaned forward. What had happened? Oh, good God! The boy had defecated. One of the prefect's boots was fouled and so was the reverend's cane! Disgraceful! Oh, he'd never, *never* be forgiven for that!

The prefects dragged Dee Jee away, his trousers still lowered around his legs now befouled with blood and excrement. Beyond tears, thought Darius, as he watched, beyond tears . . .

They lugged him across the courtyard to his boardinghouse; pulled him up the stairs, through the hall, and down the corridor; and dumped him on his cot in his cubicle and left.

Darius started walking into the town, called Little Claybrook, toward the Lion and Lamb, a tavern in which he drank and ate, being unable to stomach the food they served at Warrenton. He wanted rum, lots of it. He walked as far as the bleak houses behind which dug-out and abandoned coal pits lay (Warrenton was situated in northern Leicester, fifteen miles from Coalville) when he realized he had no money with him. He would have to return to his boarding-house and get it.

Cutting across worn-out fields, he came back to Monk's Square, where the school, originally a monastery dedicated to St. Augustine, stood. The gardens that date from the twelfth century were beginning to flower.

He entered Verities, his house. The rank odor of urine and sweat assailed his nostrils. Up the cold damp stairs and down the hall, almost past the Indian boy's cubicle, he went. He looked in. The bed was empty. Where was he? And then Darius saw him. The boy had fallen off the bed and was lying on his back. Presumably they hadn't dumped him on the floor! Or had they? The boy looked dead.

Darius went in, the stench of the feces making him gag momentarily. They hadn't washed him. They hadn't even pulled his trousers up over his pathetic bum. He leaned down next to the boy and felt his heart. It was still beating. Alive then but for what reason? Gently, very gently, Darius turned the boy over on his stomach. A bloody, ghastly mess, blood and feces having hardened and caked. Gagging again and holding his nose, he realized he would have to wash him. There was some water left in the tin bowl next to the cot. First, he would have to remove the trousers. Slowly, care-fully. Removing his own shirt he put one end of it into the water and began to wash the boy. In all he changed the water in the bowl nine times, using the water in the large communal tub at the end of the hall for fresh water, before the boy was clean. Then he went to his own cubicle for a fresh pair of trousers and pulled them up over the boy's delicate shanks, his small dark penis, his small nut-brown testicles.

Throughout the washing, the boy had moaned and then lost consciousness but when Darius lifted up the boy in his arms to lay him on his cot, the boy's eyelids fluttered open.

"Don't be frightened," Darius told him. "It's all over. They won't come back. Just try to sleep now."

"Don't leave me," murmured Dee Jee.

"I won't," said Darius. And he took the boy in his arms and held him throughout the night.

Reference Note D:
RACHEL LOWE

My full name is Rachel Judith Alvarez-Cortez Lowe. I am a Sephardic Jew, a descendent of a famous rabbi, Isaac Alvarez-Cortez, known as Moses of Madrid, the author of a book called *Abiding Traditions,* and called by his detractors *Abounding Lies.*

I was born near Edgeware Road, in an impoverished cul-de-sac, close by the church where John Donne preached his first sermon. My father, a Q.C., his English voice only slightly pervaded by foreign intonations, brought me up neither to marry nor to keep the sabbath, but to educate myself and earn my own money. At twenty-four I was the owner of a bookshop, The Alcharisi, situated near Charing Cross.[21] It was there that I first met Harriet in 1929.

She was searching for a book, she said, a book called *Happy Endings* "written by a Victorian novelist, Emma Forster." Did I have it? It was directly behind her on the shelf. She needed only to have turned around and reached out her hand to have it in her possession. But I lied. I told her that though I had heard mention of it once or twice, I myself had never owned it. In my defense I can only say that Harriet's manner was so arrogant I felt it necessary to refuse her.

She was wearing a Chanel suit made of white wool and trimmed with black braid. In one hand she carried a hat, a white wool tam, in the other a large black bag made of alligator. Both the bag and her handmade alligator shoes were stitched in white leather. Very attractive. Very American. Her thick ash-blond hair fell straight down in a semi-circular sweep a few inches below her broad shoulders. She had the androgynous American good looks that jaded Europeans respond to as exotic. Disdainful. A New

---

21. "Alcharisi" is the name that Daniel Deronda's mother, Princess Halm-Eberstein, assumed in her career as a singer and an actress in George Eliot's book *Daniel Deronda.—R. Lowe*

World snob. Not at all democratic. In less than a month we became collaborators.

Our life together has not been without strife, yet we have remained together. For, as between husband and wife, parent and child, master and servant, there is a common ground: the mythic world of Marlborough Gardens. And at certain times, for want of a better word, we love one another.

City of Childhood
XIV
ALBERT PREPARES FOR SLEEP

A LBERT finished his prayers, got into bed, and waited for Sidney to finish counting his possessions. Sidney always counted his possessions two or three times before he got into bed. Albert could hear him count: my feather, my glass, my message. . . . Nanny Jakes called it an advertisement. Albert recited it to himself, "D. Godfrey begs respectfully to thank his friends for past favors. . . ."

Albert hated Sidney and would until the end of time, but he did understand that those "things" were sacred to Sidney, as sacred as Lord Nelson and the *Victory* were to him, and therefore even though he himself thought of them as rubbish (momentarily he saw the rubbish whirl around the room like juggler's props), he must respect Sidney's wishes in this matter. He understood what "sacred" meant. Ever since speaking to Edward, Albert had stopped praying for Sidney's death.

Through the casement window he could see a few pale stars and a sliver of moon, but they didn't interest him. He was waiting for Sidney to finish putting away his treasures before he prepared himself for sleep. Jakes was a good soul, wasn't she, thought Albert. Not like Grindal. Grindal would have thrown the treasures out—they were rubbish, weren't they?—but then Grindal was evil. Finally he heard what he had been waiting for. Sidney was putting his things back into the boxes he kept under one of the cupboards. He heard

Sidney say his prayers. In a moment he would be in bed.

Albert could never perform his ritual—he didn't know why—until Sidney was in his bed. He felt Sidney staring at him from his bed through the darkness. Their beds were opposite one another, each alongside one of the twin's beds. The twins were asleep already. Jakes slept in the connecting room.

Ignoring Sidney, shutting him out of his consciousness, Albert began his ritual, summoning up from the depths of his imagination the image of Lord Nelson, the man he worshipped and would worship "till the end of time," he whispered to himself.

Almost as he thought it, the image came and stood at the foot of the bed, Admiral Nelson in all his military glory, in full regalia: a blue dress coat, a white kersey waistcoat and breeches, two epaulettes, his medals, and the Star and Garter. Over Nelson's right eye lay the somber black patch. On Corsica—where was Corsica? His father had showed him on the map—French shot had flung debris into Nelson's face, injuring his right eye, leaving it almost sightless. Albert examined the empty right sleeve pinned neatly to the jacket and bearing four bars of gorgeous gold lace. An empty sleeve. It was at the Battle of Tenerife that grapeshot had shattered Nelson's elbow. They had taken him below and cut off, "amputated," his arm; that was the word his father had used. An empty sleeve . . . sometimes Albert thought of the space inside the sleeve, the hollow sleeve, as a secret place, his secret place.

"Good night, Sweet Prince," he murmured, "and may the angels keep you." He had heard that somewhere, he couldn't remember where, but he had liked the sound of it instantly and since then had said it to his "all in all." He liked that phrase too. "All in all." He was Momma's "all in all." "Good night, Sweet Prince, and may the angels keep you." It was important to say it twice.

He placed himself as well as he could in what he thought was the exact center of the bed—so many inches from the head, so many inches from each side, so many inches from the foot—it had to be the exact center. When he was in the exact center, he turned his life and will over to Lord Nelson, his "all in all," and shut his eyes.

He was asleep in moments. Some hours later he was dreaming about the Secor boy.

           *   *   *

According to Edward, the cousins came under Darius's spell without hesitation. But not according to Emma or to William, who was more shrewd in such matters.

William wrote, "I don't think we would have followed Darius if it hadn't been for Albert. It was Albert who delivered us into Darius's keeping, so to speak.

"We needed a leader so when Albert forfeited his role and accepted Darius as his leader we accepted Albert's decisions, and that is the truth no matter what Edward says. And I think Albert did that because of the Secor boy. You see Albert was supposed to fight the Secor boy, but he never did. He was far too frightened of him. Darius not only fought Secor but won . . . and that changed everything, of course."

           *   *   *

When the children returned that fall to Marlborough Gardens, they had almost forgotten their cousin Darius, and when they no longer saw him in the Gardens they did forget him.

But one day in late October—it was after lunch and they had returned to Nannies Plain—they were astonished to see Darius fighting with the Secor boy in front of the Winter Garden.

Their cousin was standing (although he looked stunned) in the center of what seemed like a savage dance that Secor was performing around him. Secor's large fists were curled, and now and then he feinted with them as he pranced around Darius, jabbing the air rhythmically. Darius was jacketless and hatless; his white satin shirt was ripped at the shoulder and one of its lace cuffs was torn off. Albert could see that Darius's left eye was bruised and that the cut above it was beginning to bleed. Secor, though two years younger than Darius, was taller and heavier. He towered above him.

There was a crowd watching: nannies, boys, girls, and gardeners. Some of the nannies were shouting, "Stop it at once!" But every time one of them moved toward the fighters to intervene, Secor's tutor, Mr. Gorget, a big barrel of a man, red faced and dressed in black cleric robes, made a menacing gesture that cowed them. "Stand back!" he screamed if they dared approach. One of the gardeners, Mr. Slocum, kept urging Secor to make Darius "eat dust! Lemme see 'im bleed!"

Albert knew who Secor was.[22] He was the son of Lord Secor, who had died a month ago. It was his young and silly widow, a mere slip of a girl, his mother had told him, who had insisted that her "darling boy" come home from school to keep her company in her grief.

From the very first day Albert had seen Secor in the Gardens—Secor and his tutor Gorget took a daily constitutional around Nannies Plain and the lake—he had known that one day he would have to fight him, that it was only a matter of time. Why or how he knew he couldn't say, but he knew.

Albert never remembered his dreams but he did remember his dreams about Secor. They were always the same: Secor's hands, thick, large, terrible, strong, were always around his throat squeezing his flesh, the large fleshy thumbs pressing on his cartilage, the bone, so that finally he felt he couldn't breathe. He always woke before he actually died . . . but just.

Everyone watched in silence as Secor's right arm kept shooting forward. Over and over again. Closer and closer toward Darius's head, toward Darius's body.

He's going to kill Darius, thought Albert. That is what is going to happen. Oh, he must save him, save him. Darius is going to die. His thoughts raced on wildly: he is going to kill him, kill him, yes, Secor was going to kill him. He must do something. Something! He must scream "stop"! Certainly he could do that! He must run out on the field. Now, right now! He and his brothers . . .

But no sound came from him, no rallying cry, no movement. He tried to shout, to scream, but it was as if Secor's hand were around his throat strangling him. He willed him-

---

22. Secor lived on the north side of Marlborough Gardens. Lord Secor had been one of the first tenants that Jorem had leased to after he had built the first five houses for himself and his family in 1818. It was Lord Secor who had proposed Jorem for membership in the Marlebone Cricket Club (the M.C.C.). Secor's three younger sisters were still at home and played in the Gardens every day.—R. Lowe

self to move, but his limbs seemed paralyzed. Oh why, why, why, did Darius just stand there! Why didn't he do something! Someone Do Something! Something . . .

Secor moved in closer. Handsome. Confident. His head was bent low, his short muscular arms were held at exact right angles to his broad body, his right arm kept lashing out. Again and again. Closer and closer. *SLAM* to the head! *SLAM* to the chest! *SLAM* to the ribs! *SLAM! SLAM! SLAM!*

Albert saw Darius's knees buckle. Backward and forward he swayed. There were more cuts. And so much blood! Why didn't someone do something?

Now Secor moved quickly. Stepping behind Darius, he put his arm around his neck and then took Darius's left arm with his other hand and, shifting himself in front of Darius, moved the frail doll-like body onto his broad hip and then threw him over his shoulder! Albert saw with despair Darius's heels go up, up, up into the air like a lifeless puppet! A moan went through the crowd as Darius's head hit the earth with a thud.

He's killed him, thought Albert. He's killed Darius. Darius was dead! thought Albert in terror. He watched as Mr. Gorget came over to his pupil Secor, a fierce smile on his face; he saw the tutor put his arms around the boy, heard him say, "Well done, Lord Secor, well done!"

The boy walked toward the crowd while the tutor picked up the boy's jacket and his hat. The crowd began to make way slowly, perhaps reluctantly, but steadfastly, for he was the victor after all, wasn't he?

Albert could never remember what happened next. It all happened so quickly. One moment Darius was lying dead on Nannies Plain and the next moment he was alive and running. Running toward Secor, his mouth an open "O," his eyes bulging slightly, his black hair a tangle of sweat, blood, and dirt, he dropped on Secor like some wild beast, pulling and dragging Secor to his knees as if in supplication to the ground! And then he straddled Secor, picked up a nearby stone, and began to beat the boy's head with it!

It was when the tutor leapt on Darius that Albert found he could move. Running onto the field he shouted to his brothers and his cousins to join him; they must save Darius!

Joining him, they all ran onto the field at once, where taking hold of the tutor from all sides they tore him off Darius while Gorget kept screaming: "The boy's a lunatic! Someone help Lord Secor! He'll kill Lord Secor! Someone stop him!" But no one did, and Darius continued to beat Secor though he lay there senseless. Inert. Unmoving. Was Secor dead? Albert wondered wildly. But the boy, his head a sheet of blood, began to moan and Darius stopped of his own accord, as if the noise of the boy's moaning, though a mere ripple of sound, had penetrated the depth of Darius's anger, like a small pebble thrown into a well will break the surface into just a sign of a splash.

Slowly, deliberately, examining the stone as if it were an artifact, he put it down on the ground. He rose and smoothed his hair, buttoned his ripped shirt, and wiped his nose with a spotless white cambric handkerchief that he withdrew from his trousers pocket. Behaving really as if he were alone, thought Albert. For a moment he just stood there. Then looking around he spotted the tutor who was still being held fast by the children and walked over to him.

Seeing Darius approach, the tutor began to whimper, crying softly, "Let me go, let me go." What was Darius going to do now? wondered Albert. Was he going to kill Gorget?

Darius bent his torso forward and when his head was directly opposite the tutor's face, he drew his lips back, stretching them far away from his teeth while he made a fast clicking noise with his tongue. In all the world there seemed to be for Albert only the sound of Darius's clicking tongue and the tutor's whimpering. Then Albert watched as Darius shot his head forward and spat a gob of saliva out onto the tutor's face. Like a crystal it hung there momentarily and then slithered across the gross features of that barrel of a man. Then, straightening himself, still looking at no one, Darius walked over to the statue of Demeter.

At its base lay his brown velvet cloak, neatly folded. On top rested his plumed hat, his yellow gloves, and his cane. Donning his plumed hat, he picked up his gloves, then his cloak and cane and, as Secor had before, walked toward the crowd. Once more they gave way, this time to the grave youth who although his clothes were torn, his nostrils clogged with dirt and blood, his left eye closed, was without a doubt today's victor.

Shortly after that, Albert noticed as he was saying good night to his "all in all," that there was something a bit different about his hero. What? he wondered. It disturbed him. He liked everything to be exactly the same. Every particular. What could it be? What was wrong? There was the patch, the medals, the folded sleeve. He brought the image up closer to him and scanned the features carefully. Something had changed. But what! Ah! *There* it was. Yes, that was it. It was Lord Nelson's eyes, or eye. It had changed, yes, it was darker now, much darker, and rounder too. And the lid . . . it was more hooded, wasn't it? Like what? . . . Like the eyes of Darius! The eyes of Darius were staring back at him out of the face of Lord Nelson.

❊   ❊   ❊

RESEARCH PAPER NO. 2

COUNT RIMINI VII: Darius and His Arrangements

Principal Sources: 1. William's letter from Melbourne, Australia, March 4, 1872
2. Three documents belonging to the files of The London League of Gentlewomen for the Rehabilitation of Fallen Women and Their Progeny
3. Guinivere Forster's household account books, 1825–1835
4. Albert Forster's *diary,* March 8, 1850–1851
5. Emma Forster's *Florentine diary,* June 1854

Researcher: Rachel Lowe
Editor: Rachel Lowe
Commentary: Harriet Van Buren

Introduction

We know that the children began their tutelage under Darius sometime in the early fall of 1836, and that it lasted, in one way or another, until the end of May 1837, about eight months.

However, the manuscript breaks off at this point (Chapter Fourteen) and does not resume again, except for brief episodic accounts and some war notes, until six months later when it describes exactly and at length why and how Grindal was beaten by Maria, Ricci's wife, one afternoon in March.

This eight-month break in time leaves two important questions unanswered: 1. What was the exact nature of the relationship between Darius and the children? 2. By what artifice or trick, or special means if any, did Darius manipulate Nanny Jakes and Nanny Grindal so that he could have access to the children?

For the answers to these questions, we have had to rely on other sources in the archives to reconstruct that crucial passage of time. What follows is a digest of that period gleaned from a laborious and exhaustive comparison of all the available evidence.

Technical Note

Immersed as we have been in mid-Victorian prose, these many years we have noticed on the one hand that we have taken on some of its more treacherous characteristics: a tendency to be verbose, a preference for the convoluted sentence, a positive lust for rolling cadences. But on the other hand we have, generally speaking, tailored the material to a more modern cut.

William's Letter of 4 March 1872 to Albert Forster, from Melbourne, Australia (page 1)

> *". . . Do you recall," you ask, "any of Nanny Grindal's fairy tales? . . . I wish to collect as many as possible for I intend to have them privately printed for the possible amusement and edification of the new generation of Forsters. . . . A copy will be sent to you, in any case. . . ."*

The answer is NO! Forgive the tone for I bear you no grudges (though well I might!)—no grudges at all. I have done far too well for that, as you know—the black sheep positively glitters with gold—but were I to "recall" any part of my childhood (and I don't!) it would be the Marl-borough Wars and Darius and his infernal "arrange-ments."

For by now you must realize (or don't you?) that when Darius crowned himself (you must remember that!) the Grand Duke of Marlborough Gardens, our two watchdogs, Jakes and Grindal, seemed to disappear, as it were, from the face of the earth. I'd give anything to know how he managed that! . . .

Three documents from the files of the London League of Gentlewomen for the Rehabilitation of Fallen Women and Their Progeny

Document A:

Excerpts from the minutes of the LLGW of April 14, Shrove Tuesday, 1825, in which we first hear of Carlotta Jakes.

A REPORT BY THE REVEREND BEAMER JANVERS

On April third of this year, I entered the courtyard off Little Collingswood Street in Bethnal Green, in the parish of St. George.

The court is approached through a long and narrow alley, which has virtually no ventilation. There are sixteen houses in the court, all in various stages of decay, their walls uniformly the color of soot.

I entered No. 31 and, walking through a dark and fetid passage, ascended a few steps and entered the brothel run by a woman known to the police as Mother Morton. She was not there, but her "chicks" as she calls them, eight unfortunates, were. On a small and dirty table stood several bottles of gin.

I handed out our tracts: Tract No. 11, "Earthly Bliss"; Tract No. 23, "The Father Had Made It All"; and Tract No. 42, "The Tree Is Known by Its Fruits"; and imparted, as usual, an invitation to our Wednesday afternoon Morality Tea, given in our Mission

House No. 6 on Wellington Street. I was about to depart when the procuress of this vile establishment entered, followed by what seemed to me a mere child. Said creature was dressed in drab muslin and was carrying a cardboard box, which I suspected contained said creature's entire worldly belongings.

It was then, ladies and gentlemen, that I felt the presence of our dear Saviour Jesus Christ and understood why I was there. I grabbed the dear child and enfolding her in my arms I warned the fiend in human flesh that were she to dare protest, then tomorrow our Trustees, together with the Church Wardens of the Parish, and the local constabulary would march in front of her vile establishment bearing placards that read: BEWARE DISEASED HOUSES.

Subsequently I brought the said creature Carlotta Jakes to Mission House No. 6 where she was duly registered.

Document B:

The preliminary interview of the person registered as Carlotta Jakes at Mission House No. 6 on 3 April 1825, in Bethnal Green.

Interlocutor: Mrs. Mathilda Forster Herrod, Director of the LLGW, School No. 3 in Bethnal Green.

Date: 10 April 1825

Time: 4:00 P.M.

INTER: Your name, child.

JAKES: Carlotta Jakes, ma'am.

INTER: Your age, child.

JAKES: Me sister, Cleo, says I be 'leven, an' she be born the year Jack Truehold beat Bill Waley, an' she say I be born two year after tha'—.

INTER: Silence, child. I shall record your age as eleven.

JAKES: Thankee, ma'am.

INTER: In as few words as possible, child, relate to me
            the history of your early environs, the nomencla-
            ture of your immediate forebears and your sib-
            lings. And answer the following questions: Were
            you ever a probationist? Are you a matriculator?
            Have you ever been an apprentice? Or a handi-
            craft person?

JAKES: [doesn't answer]

INTER: Answer, child. We cannot assist you if you refuse
            to answer. You must answer.

JAKES: Oh ma'am I likes the vittles here ever so much—

INTER: That is commendable, child, but nevertheless you
            must still answer the questions.

JAKES: Oh ma'am I be willin' to answer the questions, I
            be eager to answer the questions if only I knew
            what the questions be.

INTER: Hmmmm. . . . Where were you born, child?

JAKES: I be born in Salford, ma'am. Tha' be on the other
            side of Irwell and tha' be in Manchester, ma'am.

INTER: Born in Manchester. Who are your parents? Are
            they alive or dead?

JAKES: Me poor ole da', 'ee was a sweet potato man on
            the corner of Chantry and River Street, in front
            of the Old Bull Tavern. An' poor man, 'ee was
            knocked down, 'ee was, by a runaway horse, and
            died on his way to St. Bart's.

INTER: Father dead. What was his name, child?

JAKES: Me da's name was Ned, ma'am. An' after, me
            four brothers, they run away, an' three months
            later, Bertie, me mother's darlin', he was fished
            out of the river, dead as an herrin'. 'Ee used to
            say—

INTER: Silence, child. Remember that into a shut mouth
            a fly never enters. Is your mother alive or dead?

JAKES: She be alive, ma'am.

INTER: Her name, child.

JAKES: Clarissa, ma'am.

INTER: Now you may tell me what happened to you after your father's unfortunate demise. I mean death, child, death.

JAKES: 'Twas like this, ma'am. No money comin' in, me mum she starts makin' moleskin trousers, an' wat wid me an' me sister Cleo helpin' 'er we earns mebbe 12 shillins a week, and then me mum she falls in love with Mr. 'arry Topham, the man of many talents.

INTER: The man of many talents?

JAKES: Aye, ma'am. Mr. Topham, stand on 'is 'ead 'ee would from where 'ee would drink off several glasses of gin and lift a man of eighteen stone clear off the floor—

INTER: Silence, child! Remember the fly! Now answer this question and *this* one only: How is it that the Reverend Janvers found you in the company of the woman Morton, at No. 31 Little Collingswood Street, on April third of this month?

JAKES: 'Twas like this, ma'am. Mr. Topham, he loves Mum, he says, but he don't love me or Cleo, an' he says to Mum as how he would take it kindly if we both took off. An' me mum she agrees. So Cleo takes the coach to London where she runs into good fortune in the shape of a Mr. Billy Holt, a seller of corn salves on Oxford Street. So Mr. Topham givin' me the green I takes the coach to London, an' 'twas there at Seven Dials that I meets Mother Morton, an' she be tellin' me, an' widout me askin', where me sister Cleo be livin', an' so I not knowin' London town, I goes wid her, an', tha' ma'am, is how I meets the Reverend Janvers.

INTER: Do you believe in God, child?

JAKES: Oh, that I do, ma'am.

INTER: And in the Saviour, our Lord, Jesus Christ?

JAKES: Oh, that I do ma'am. 'Twas only yesterday tha' I
            looks up from me washin' an' I sees Sweet Jesus
            himself an' 'ee says—

INTER: Silence, child! Remember the fly!

JAKES: Thankee ma'am, I shall.

Document C:

A Letter of Recommendation

30 June 1826

To Whom It May Concern:

*The following is the final report on the completion of
Carlotta Jakes's course of studies at the LLGW School No.
3 in Bethnal Green.*

To Date:

*1. The Above has learned to mend linen, darn stockings,
remove grease spots out of silk and cloth dresses.*

*2. Has learned how to work white satin, clean furs, lay
out clothes and iron them.*

*3. Has learned to clean lamps, candle holders, silver,
brass, and marble.*

*4. Has learned how to make preserves and pickles and
syllabubs of wine and cream.*

*5. Has learned how to stretch curl papers and cut fresh
ones.*

*6. Has learned how to clean grates and light fires with
only seven pieces of wood.*

7. Has learned how to address a lady, titled or otherwise.

*But most important of all, the Above understands that it
is her religious duty to be content with her lot.*

*Furthermore Mrs. Mathilda Forster Herrod, Director of
School No. 3, having taken a special interest in the Above*

*has taught the Above to read. Hereunto the Above has read
with comprehension the following books:*

1. The Art of Preserving Hair, *by Madame de Fleur*

2. Domestic Duties, *by Mrs. Chillingsworth*

3. Advice to Servants, *by Dr. Gregory.*

*To conclude: The Above is an early riser, tractable, doc-
ile, and meek. We are entirely satisfied that the Above has
been rendered suitable for employment, in an apprentice
position in one of the great households connected to the
LLGW.*

> *Sincerely,*
> *Lady Ursula Devanter-Winter*
> *Secretary of the Bethnal Green*
> *Mission House of the LLGW*

Postscript:

The London League of Gentlewomen for the Rehabilitation of
Fallen Women and Their Progeny, or the LLGW as it was fa-
miliarly known, was founded in 1818 by "men of conscience to
prevent the increase of the great evil, prostitution, and to rescue
and reclaim the harlot from the misery and degradation of her
life."[23]

Well endowed, politically conservative, evangelistic in tone,
connected to the Anglican Church but not of it, the League established LLGW Mission Houses, Dormitories and Schools in
some of the worst slums in London, in which the "fallen were
baptized, housed, and educated, so that they need never fall
again."

In 1823 Jorem was elected to the Board of Trustees and from
that year until 1901, the year of Queen Victoria's death, Forster
men and women were associated in one capacity or another with
the League.

We are of the opinion that the above documents were stolen
by Emma when she worked temporarily as secretary to her
brother who was President of the LLGW from 1860 to 1864.

Ultimately the LLGW was self-serving, that is, the League

---

23. Both quotes are from Albert's monograph: "A Short History of the
LLGW: Calm and Resigned, We Fix Our Trust," printed in 1858.—*H. Van
Buren*

became the chief provider of domestic servants for the families
connected with it, Nanny Jakes being a case in point.

———————

Guinivere Forster's Household Accounts

Carlotta Jakes joined Solomon and Guinivere's household
staff in July 1826, having been sent there by the LLGW. She
was twelve years old at the time.

In 1826 Solomon and Guinivere's household staff consisted
of the following: a housekeeper, Mrs. Bridgewater; a cook,
Mrs. Upright; a ladies' maid, Viola Last; a valet, Edward Clift;
two coachmen, Mr. George and Mr. Clarence; a nanny, Nanny
Watkins; her assistant, Emily Leach; three footmen; two gardeners; three housemaids; and one kitchen maid. Jakes became
the eighteenth servant, a kitchen maid's assistant at two pounds
per annum.

Being an obedient and docile girl, she became a great favorite with Mrs. Bridgewater who when she dismissed one of the
housemaids for "rank impertinence" gave Jakes, who was by
then fifteen, the vacated position. Three years later Jakes became the head housemaid.

In 1831 Emily Leach, Nanny Watkins's assistant, who was
pretty and frivolous, neglected to return from one of her bi-
weekly afternoons off. It was Mrs. Bridgewater who suggested
to Guinivere that Emily be replaced by Jakes, who "loves the
children, as they love her." The suggestion was taken and a
year later when Nanny Watkins left the Forster household to
live in married bliss with Mr. Jonas, Lord Secor's butler, the
office of nanny was bequeathed to Jakes. By that time she was
twenty-one and earned all of twenty pounds per annum.

———————

Albert Forster's Diary, 1850–1851 (page 158)

8 March 1850

Today I took my beloved fiancée, Alicia, to visit Nanny
Jakes, who now lives in Paddington in a small house with her
sister Cleo, her brother-in-law Billy, and what seemed to me to
be at least a dozen nephews and nieces.

She told me that she's been "very fortchinatt" for she herself
at last is to be married within a fortnight to the "lustrious proprietor" of a coffee stall on Duke Street.

She is a dear, sweet person and the visit went well until she asked about "Master Darius." She wanted to know everything there was to know about him, she told Alicia, "for had it not been for tha' dear sweet lad, Miss Crowell, I might never have found me sister Cleo."

I did not ask her what she meant by that. I did not wish to know. As for Alicia, it was the very first time she heard his name mentioned. Later when we were alone and she asked about him, she accepted my explanation graciously and without comment. I do think that augurs well for our future life together.

COMMENTARY: ABOUT JAKES

The full truth concerning Darius's manipulations with respect to Jakes may never be fully recovered but there are some legitimate inferences:

1. Darius found Billy Holt, and hence Jake's sister, Cleo.
2. He reunited the sisters and arranged that they see one another on a regular basis.
3. In time Jakes came to feel indebted to Darius, an indebtedness which may have led to a partial dereliction of her obligations with respect to the children.

◆◇◆

Emma Forster's Florentine Diary, an Anecdotal Passage, Slightly Abridged (pages 84–99)

On May 14, 1854, Emma went to visit Darius in Florence, intending to stay a month. She stayed for two years. At the time the diary was written, Emma was twenty-eight years old; Darius was thirty-two.

> Palazzo Rimini, Florence
> 1 June 1854
> 3:00 P.M.

Dinner was over, the guests departed, the family gone to bed, the servants dismissed when Darius took our cups of café Nero and the bottle of Strega out on to the terrace, motioning me to follow.

We made ourselves comfortable on chairs at a table on the part of the terrace that overlooks the ancient yew garden, which was underneath the blaze of a brilliant star-studded pagan sky, an Olympian domain. A mild breeze having sprung up from the west, Darius went to fetch my shawl from inside. When he returned, he asked me if I was tired. "No," I replied.

"Good," he said, "I wish to tell you a story, something I have never told anyone else before . . . apropos, did you recognize Ricci at dinner tonight?"

I told him I had. I could not help adding that I had been taken aback to find him here, at the palazzo *and* at the dinner table.

"He lives here now . . . as part of the family . . . an accommodation. You haven't seen him till now for he's been ill with indigestion. He eats too much."

"Yes. He must be over twelve stone. Quite monstrous, really."

"True, but compliant, Emma, compliant . . . gelded, actually. He's no longer the handsome young man, is he? Well, the story I'm about to tell you concerns Ricci, and . . ." He paused—I remembered how fond Darius was of dramatic pauses—"and Grindal."

"Grindal!" *That* was a surprise. I hadn't thought of her in years. I had almost forgotten her, and told him so.

"Ah how unfaithful we are to our bêtes noires. Would you care for some more Strega? May I pour you some coffee? You must be absolutely comfortable before I begin. It's a fairly long tale and I want no interruptions."

My curiosity was awakened. I assured him on all counts.

He lit a cigar, one of those small, dark Italian cigars, and after taking a puff or two, his face expressionless, he began:

"It happened, let's see, I was fourteen years old. It was the year I was sent home, expelled really, from Warrenton, in disgrace—*extremae dementiae*—at the height of my madness. I had suddenly landed in the bosom of my father's family, an uncomfortable nest, to say the least. I knew they despised me. Particularly your father, Elijah. Ah yes, I knew that. I myself felt I was a pariah, an anathema. . . . I was totally friendless and at the same time far too proud to appear weak or despairing or to ask for help. I have never known misery like that and mercifully with the help of God I shall never know it again.

"Worst of all I feared that what had happened at Warrenton might have destroyed any hope that I might have of academic or scholastic achievement. *Enfin,* there really seemed to me no point in my being alive, and that whole winter and part of that spring I toyed on and off with the idea of suicide."

I began to say something, but he put his finger to my lips: "*Tais-toi,* say nothing. I only want you to listen. Just to listen. Besides, that time has passed and I have survived, and quite well, too . . . as you have, my dear Emma." He took one of my hands and began to stroke it.

"When I arrived at Marlborough Gardens—it was the fall of '36, you remember—Ricci—he was only nineteen, gloriously handsome, and already a part of the household—had been there for six months, I believe.

"He was one of my aunt Celeste's servants. She had sent him to us from her estate in Fiesole with his wife Maria. He was born on the estate, like his father and his grandfather before him. My mother needed a servant. Making domestic arrangements was not one of her talents, so when our latest housekeeper departed, she asked her sister to send someone, and she sent Ricci! He came with his child bride, Maria, and Mother appointed him majordomo. At nineteen! Without his knowing a word of English!

"I was barely home a week when he asked me to teach him English. 'Love English' were his exact words: 'Teach me the words that will make the English ladies love me. I see so much I desire—the golden hair, the pink skin, like nacre, mother of pearl. In my dreams I hold their rosy flesh tight in my arms. I wish to make love to them. All of them. Master, help me. Teach me the Love English.'

"You must understand, Emma, that vis-à-vis Ricci, I was not only his master, but his protector, his confessor, his closest friend. His behaviour toward me—your countrymen would call it 'unwarranted familiarity' and recoil in horror—his behaviour was typical of an Italian servant whose forebears had worked for a family for at least four generations. It was understood I would never injure him. As for him, he was my loyal and faithful servant.

"You see, Emma, he had no idea that I disliked him, detested him really. . . . Instinctively, I hated him. You see I understood he was my enemy, that he might . . . that he could harm me.

"He was stupid. He was self-centered. He was vain. Still, he was one of the lucky ones. He felt at home in the universe, in Italy, in England. I loathed him but I envied him too.

"I put him off the first time. I was too busy, I told him. But he was persistent, and so one day while he was pleading and I

was bored, no, not bored, more despairing than usual, I made
up my mind to injure him. Having come to that decision, the
first thing I did was offer him the reassurance you extend to
people you dislike in the hope that they may continue in their
folly.

"I convinced him that the women he desired with such passion were longing to fall into his arms, that they were eager,
even desperate to hear words of love from him. On hearing
this golden news (we were in my rooms) he undressed himself.
Yes . . . completely. He must show me, he said, 'my most precious possession.' And placed it so to speak under my nose. It
was fully erect. You're not even blushing, Emma, or are you?
The night is your protector . . . shall I continue? . . . Yes? . . .
Thank you.

"Wasn't it remarkable, he asked, its shape, its size, its color?
I told him to get dressed at once. He took no offense. He
never took offense. While he was dressing, he chattered on,
and then remarked in a solemn tone of voice, as if he had
given it much thought that it was his sincere opinion, that an
oil painting of himself, naked of course, would be a far prettier
sight hanging in our palazzo than all those other paintings.
'You know the ones I mean, Master, the pictures of the fat,
lazy *puttane* lolling on her chaise, fondling her private
parts. . . .' Ah, now I have shocked you. . . . Well, I shall continue anyway.

"I told him I would do as he asked: I would teach him Love
English, beginning the following day. Ricci was a fool; he had
played into my hands.

"And now I confess I did something utterly shameful, one of
those malicious pranks, a venial sin, that somehow stains the
soul even more deeply than a mortal one.

"He came to my rooms the following day, eager to learn.
Oh, how he sweated over the foreign phonetics, but he persevered and soon he was letter perfect and was able to recite, in
an impeccable English accent, the phrases I had taught him:
'Your eyes are pools of mud. Your teeth, a row of black and
rotten stumps. Your mouth a putrid swamp' and so on.

"Poor Ricci. They fled from him screaming; though the more
intrepid stayed to slap and one young beauty, he told me (he
told me everything, you see, he trusted me), beat him merci-
lessly with her umbrella.

"Depression followed. After those incidents he could barely
function. Who knows how long he would have remained in that
condition. Please bear with me, Emma; it is an ugly story. It

did not make me happy and certainly God knows I have paid for it, but at the time I could not *bear* his happiness . . . until one day, I saw how I could use Ricci's amorous nature once more to my advantage. It was shortly after I met you and my other cousins.

"I went to his room where he so often lay now in a semi-stupor. 'I have found a woman for you,' I told him.

" 'I don't believe you. I am eleven months in this cursed country and there has been no one for me as yet. Who is she, then?'

" 'Grindal.'

" 'Grindal! That she-dragon! The one that beats your cousin Emma! No, thank you. I know all about her from Maria who knows it from the cook. She is a woman without a soul.'

" 'Perhaps, but it is not her soul that you will be involved with. She has a beautiful body. She is passionate. She is insatiable.'

" 'How do you know that? A mere boy . . .'

" 'I know. Besides I have seen you undress her with your eyes.'

" 'Have you?'

" 'She wants you. She longs for you.'

" 'How do you know that?'

" 'I know.'

"He got out of bed. 'Perhaps you are right . . . but will she have me?' He let out a groan and placed his hand on his flaccid penis. 'This wretched country . . . look what it has done to me.'

"I began teaching him English again, but this time I taught him the proper phrases, all the trite, hackneyed timeworn expressions that vanquish women's hearts, explaining to him at the same time that the other phrases he had learned had been perhaps a bit too ardent for the cool English temperament. He forgave my mistake readily. He trusted me completely. In no time at all he was teaching Maria.

"When I thought he had reached a certain level of proficiency, I arranged to have him meet Grindal in the privacy of my rooms, allowing their lustful temperaments to take their natural course.

"It has been said, Emma, that potassium entertains such a violent passion for oxygen that even under water it burns. So they burned for one another: Ricci for Grindal, Grindal for Ricci. Unclouded by a sense of sin, their passion burned brightest when they quarreled with one another. And they made love wherever and whenever they could: in the Gardens, on the banks of the lake, in the temple, on the forest floor. You see, he told me everything. There are times I have wondered if he ever at the height of their awesome passion murmured the first set of phrases I taught him. I am convinced that he did, just as I am convinced that it brought her to even greater heights of passion.

"On the afternoons that we met in my rooms, I would send Maria on long errands in the city so that the lovers could couple in peace undisturbed in Ricci's rooms. . . ."

Darius's voice trailed off into silence. Somewhere near us, a woman began to sing, her voice, a soprano, ran slowly up and down the tones of a minor scale. I was relieved when she ended her song.

COMMENTARY

After his victory over Secor, Darius apparently began to take a more active interest in the children, though that did not include Vanessa and her sisters.[24]

Darius was convinced from the facts before him that he would succeed in what he wished to do with the children. But the subject matter of life is not predictability; the study of it does not lead to safe generalizations or the possibility of knowing exactly what is the best thing to do.

Chance, coincidence, probability, whatever name you give it, that ever-moving, ever-changing something that some people call God, and that exists between us, among us, in us, but is never fully acknowledged (Lowe calls it "thatness") was present as it is always, and working then as it is now. And so—in the very act of succeeding, for he *did* succeed, Darius lost what he could not afford to lose.

---

24. Vanessa was barely twelve when she first met Darius, so the magnitude of her beauty had not yet achieved its full brightness. Still, from the beginning there seemed to have been a tacit recognition on each of their parts that like stars, they must for their own good remain outside each other's orbits. Like gods and goddesses of old they needed their own appointed regions, the body and its passions for Vanessa, the mind and soul for Darius.—*R. Lowe*

NINE

T HIS spring it rained and stormed for weeks, an unprecedented amount of rainfall, a deluge. Today is the first day that we had the opportunity to traverse the Gardens in order to inspect and assess the damage.

Disaster was everywhere. The Garden was a shambles. Trees felled by lightning lay broken on the wet earth, and one particularly fine oak was actually bifurcated, half of it lying in the lake, the banks of which had overflowed, and half sprawled in the muddy banks. Blenheim Brook was now a raging river rushing furiously over the cliffs into the canal below; its outlines were no longer visible.

When we stood on Blenheim Heights, we were filled with despair. We viewed with dismay the thick florescence of burgeoning weed on the marshes below us that everywhere had strangled ruthlessly and squeezed out our few cultivated plants. In every part we saw corn cockle, field rush, Queen Anne's lace, old maid's pink, and here and there like sentinels in a field of anarchy stood the tall stalks of the yellow-flowered mullein.

Months of work lay ahead! It was while I was trying to coax a feeble spark of duty into a serviceable flame that I heard Lowe remark in her (beastly) authoritative tone: "Look there!"

My eyes followed the direction of her pointed finger.

"There! . . . adjacent to the canal, that white shimmering patch of Queen Anne's lace, within the shadow of the poplar tree. Do you see it, Harriet?"

I loathe it when she plays Socrates.

"I have not been struck blind as of today," I answered.

"Would you say its form was rectangular?"

I said nothing. I would not play "disciple."

"Does it remind you of something?"

"Yes, of how annoying you can be at times."

"I've seen that sort of thing before . . . on a dig in Italy. One spring holiday I joined Lord Pitfield in southern Italy. They were digging up Pompeii. Now observe, Harriet, that that rectangular shape is much taller by far than the surrounding vegetation, is it not?" When I didn't answer, she continued as if I had. "The reason is that the earth's been dug up there at one time or another, so that the roots of the weed, Harriet, have been able to penetrate and move down deeper into the soil, deeper there than anywhere else in the field. Do you see that, Harriet?"

She was right. Though I hated her at that moment I saw exactly what she meant. It was almost a foot higher there than anywhere else. What did it mean? I wondered.

"*That* is a grave!"

"A grave! Lowe, you have a Gothic imagination. It comes from reading Mary Shelley once too often."

"It *is* a grave," she insisted.

"But it can't possibly be. It's far too small, the rectangle, I mean. Why no adult could possibly fit . . ." I stopped.

"Exactly! No adult could. But a child or pet could."

I refused to dig there and then. The matter would have to wait, I told her, until the following day. We spent the afternoon as usual inside working with the material.

Darius Is Crowned and Creates the Order of Rimini

Source: Edward Forster's Diary of Moral Inventory *(pages 73–82). The diary was written in 1851–1852 at the behest of Dr. Garth Blackstone, Wesleyan minister of the Moravian Chapel at Brampton, North Umberland.*

I was nine years old when my cousin Darius proclaimed himself the Grand Duke of Marlborough Gardens. Though it was the last day in November (1836), the day was mild, I remember. The ceremony took place in the center of the Gardens, in front of the equestrian statue. I, my brother William, my sister Emma, and my cousins Albert, Sidney, Joshua, Jacob, and Deirdre formed a semicircle around him.

Darius was dressed as a cavalier in a white satin tunic over which was slung a white and blue braided jacket. A sword hung loose in its scabbard from a brown leather belt that held up blue velvet trousers, and the long white plume of his cocked hat moved back and forth grazing the stone trophy of arms, a collection of jousting lances and armour, that rested at the base of the statue.

He said "I, Darius Marcus Georgione Rimini Forster, grandson of Count Rimini the Seventh, third cousin to the Grand Duke of Tuscany, by the Grace of God, Great Britain, and Italy declare myself on this day, November 30, 1836, the Grand Duke of Marlborough Gardens."

His voice had the rise and fall of an actor's voice, the voice of a siren. And he had an actor's sense of style. When he removed the sword from its scabbard to confer knighthood on each of us, he held the sword straight up with both hands close to his chest and kissed the blade. Then we knelt in turn in front of him.

The accolade, that deceptively light tap on the shoulder with the flat of the sword, felt to me as if I had been touched by a flame! That night, I remember, I examined my right shoulder, carefully, for a mark of some sort. There was none, of course.

"We are now and forever connected. Like the loom and its weaver, the potter and his clay . . . wedded, yes, inextricably wedded to one another into the Great and Sacred Order of Rimini . . . Oh my liege men!"

It was done in a trice, our elevation to knighthood, and we understood without ever once discussing it among ourselves that day or ever, that our life, our future life with Darius, was to be kept secret. Secret from everyone: our nannies and our parents, that it was never to be revealed even under threat of physical torture.

That afternoon (among other things) Darius explained to us his lineage, its ancient and aristocratic roots as compared to ours, descendents of mere yeomen and artisans.

"I am like an artist," he told us, "whose basic substance sets him apart from the others. I have but one responsibility in this life and that is to keep this precious substance intact." It was our task, he said, his liege men, to protect and preserve him.

We were savages compared to Darius. What did we know? A little Latin? A little geography? A little history? All through the benevolent auspices of Reverend Bottome of St. Giles Church, one of the dearest men who ever lived but one utterly without imagination or authority. Essentially we knew nothing. Our servants were ignorant brutes and our parents far, far too busy with their social lives to take time to enlighten us in any way. It was left to Darius to make the unintelligible world—a world that seemed ambiguous, obscure, uncertain, and fearful—intelligible to us.

The meaning of the shields that we had passed every day of our lives—which had intrigued us, but about which we knew nothing—was explained to us by Darius. Darius also explained the temple, who Athena was, who Medusa was. It was Darius who took us to Calypso's cave, where he told us in the most entertaining way the adventures of Ulysses, and who Calypso was, Calypso whose marble lap, we had, heretofore, rested on with such nonchalance.

But all of that, and it was much, might not have won us had it not been for that rare quality he possessed, a quality that is all too rare in teachers; he truly wanted to share his knowledge. It gave him pleasure to enlighten us. And if he demanded absolute loyalty from us in return, it seemed little enough at the time.

It was barely a week after the ceremony that we began collecting tribute from other children beside ourselves who played in the Garden. The idea of tribute also came from Darius: one of the functions of the Great and Sacred Order of Rimini was to collect it, and one of the functions of the sovereign was to receive it.

Perhaps here is a good place to mention that beside ourselves (our clan of cousins), there were more than two hundred other children who played in the Gardens. Though most of them belonged to my grandfather's tenants, there were exceptions. On certain days of the week (Thursday, Saturday, and Sunday) certain children who lived outside Marlborough Gardens were allowed to play in the Gardens too. The greengrocer's children, for instance, Clarence and George Cornwind. And Jessie Malkin's brood, as well as Reverend Bottome's two sons.

How this came about, this mixture of classes, I don't know, but some assumptions can be made. In Jessie Malkin's case I know for a fact that my grandfather served with Jessie's patron/ lover Lord Fitzcrawford on the board of the LLGW. My grandfather could hardly refuse Lord Fitzcrawford's request to allow all five of his bastards the privilege of playing in the Gardens, could he?

In any case our recruits for our two armies came out of this pool of children. But more about that later.

I admired Darius, or rather I was in awe of him but I did not worship him. It was my cousin Albert who worshipped him. We, *I,* hardly existed for him now. His eyes were fastened on Darius. He heard only what Darius had to say.

Thinking back, I believe I might on my own have broken away from Darius because the study of war, which we began almost immediately in Darius's rooms, caused me to have the most frightening dreams and even nightmares. . . .

Since you have encouraged me to bare my soul fully, it is imperative that I confess to you that those seven months of my life (they were only seven) were despite what happened the most vivid, the most exciting in my entire life, even until now.

*   *   *

Among the archives is a green notebook entitled *The Book of Tribute.*[25] A page will suffice to illustrate the tenor of its contents.

---

25. The handwriting is childish but clear. As yet, we have not been able to ascertain the authorship but the admixture, a prosaic account of brutal acts on the one hand, the righteous and puritanical tone on the other, makes us suspect Emma. The uncial script lends further credence to such an analysis.—*R. Lowe*

BOYS	FATHERS	TRIBUTE
Theodore, 13	Rev. Bottome	5 tiger eyes
James, 11	Same	1 wooden carved horse, right ear missing
Clarence, 9	Mr. Cornwind, greengrocer, Chivy Lane	1 gold-coloured ring, yellow stone
George, 10	Same	3 agates & 2 tops
Thomas, 13	Mother: Jessie Malkin	1 pair of cuff links stamped with head of a sphinx
Henry, 12	Mother: Same	1 stick pin, seed pearls & rubies
Charles, 10	Mother: Same	6 shillings
James, 11	Mother: Same	1 garnet bracelet
Fitzroy, 9	Mother: Same	3 gold crosses
Gerald, 9	Judge Adam Torsin, Magistrate	1 leather purse with copper clasp containing one ha'penny
John, 9	Mr. T. C. Peterson, Esquire, Broker	33 foreign stamps
Marcus, 8	Same	1 dagger
Richard, 6	Same	3 tin soldiers

Interspersed among these notations are more sinister ones.

December 10: Today Lucas Albright had his arms bent back by Albert until they almost cracked, he having refused to pay tribute.

March 5: Joseph Lacey, six years old, foolishly refusing to pay tribute was forced today by Albert to eat dirt while being beaten on the head with the stones Albert always carries in his pocket now.

April 10: Izreal Smith-Smithe was made to hang by his thumbs from the oak tree in the Sacred Grove for a full five minutes, and when the naughty boy still refused to pay tribute he was threatened with actual hanging. After that, he surrendered.

There really was not much digging to do; our spades uncovered the small skeleton in no time at all. The earth was soft and pliable, our spades went in effortlessly. The skeleton was not a child, but that of a small dog. No doubt someone's pet.

Beside the skeleton was a leather box, which we pried open. Inside it was a heap of stones and a sling shot. Relieved, curiosity satisfied, we covered it with earth again.

Emma's Weimar Journal, Fall 1883 (pages 1–7)

Yesterday we moved into the Villa Aubeitz. In the course of putting away our belongings I came across Darius's manuscript *The Minotaur's Point of View*. Last night I reread it.

Once I loved him best of all. I have not thought about him or Marlborough Gardens for years.

I was ten years old when I was—I can only describe it as being "seized" with love for Darius. Chaste, of course. On my part I was too naive to encourage seduction, but he had only to touch me a fingertip's worth and that spot, that bit of flesh would ignite and its fire would spread throughout my body. How handsome I thought he was; his slim and supple form even then had the same exquisite grace of a Donatello bronze. . . .

"When one person loves another, which of the two is the friend? The one who loves or the one who is loved?"

I loved my cousin and yet I never thought to understand him.

To be his friend. Nor did I sense his despair. On the contrary, Darius appeared to me as Triumph Personified. When he spoke to me about his despair, for he did sometimes, I remembered that I sympathized but truly it meant nothing to me. I could not see past his dazzling surface.

Only once, and that was the awful day, when he came to say good-bye to me, my father having made arrangements for him to be sent to Somerset Academy, a Catholic school in Wiltshire, did it occur to me that he might be lonely and in desperate need of my help. But I also recall how nervous he made me feel as he babbled on about yet another new and strange idea of his—that we, the Forsters, were connected to a famous German sorcerer, a man called Faustus—and how I wanted him to leave me.

How strange it is that in the first and only time of my life that I loved freely—I expected nothing in return from him—between us there was no tiresome conflict of wills, no petty bickering or bargaining, no fatiguing deceits or disseminations, for it was in my complete surrender to him that I experienced my first and only bliss—I was not the loved one's friend. . . .

Late this afternoon I took a walk (the estate is small, but thank God it has its private places!) to the summerhouse, on the southern border of the property, and sat on its steps. As I watched the sunset, as the glow of light in the western part of the sky began to dim, I saw a vision of myself at ten—slim, proud, poignant, my heart so filled with love for Darius. . . . In comparison, my heart today feels like the stone heart of a peach, all its luscious flesh eaten away.

We met in Darius's rooms at least three times a week. He had arranged everything. We would not be disturbed, he said.

What did we do there? Mostly we listened to him lecture on the art of war. Yes, war. He was a "war enthusiast," he told us, and he called himself a Minister of War.

"War and hunting," he told us "are the only two legitimate pursuits of an aristocrat." From the very beginning of our studies, he had us memorize the maxims: "War is the father and ruler of all things" (Heraclitus) and "War protects us from the corruption which an everlasting peace would bring upon us" (Hegel).

And so under his inspired tutelage we began the study of warfare, which was engrossing and totally absorbing. I look back with some horror when I recall with what alacrity we took to the theme of war, as if we were born assassins.

We studied all its aspects: land attack, sea attack, counter-attack, siege craft, blockade. Within a month's time we could recite in seconds the full panoply of medieval armour, from "armet" to "vambrace"; and discuss intelligently figure-eight shields, matchlocks, wheel locks, and field guns. Nothing has absorbed me as much before or since.

"War is the exemplification of courage," he told us, "the action of heroes, the only true study of human fortitude."

And over and over again he would preach to us about the supreme exultation, the ultimate ecstasy: death in battle.

At night I began to dream of the blare of trumpets, the clicking of bayonets fixed on their rifles, and columns of men being suddenly blown up with powder bags, and over and over again I dreamed of an anonymous headless human trunk flying through the air over a battlefield alive with fire and smoke amid the screams and neighing of wounded horses.

How much did we understand of what he said? Speaking for myself, I think we understood everything. It is truly remarkable how much children can learn once they have set their minds to it.

As time went on, each of us became an expert in some phase of warfare. From the first, my brother William was interested in tactics and in no time at all he learned how to set up any number of battlefields, from Troy to Waterloo. My brother Edward, a more plodding type, concentrated on infantry. Darius and Albert, our aristocrats, studied cavalry together. Jacob and Joshua learned about small arms and trajectories. As for myself, I was absorbed with siege craft. As was Sidney. For once, Sidney and I found ourselves allied: both of us were intrigued, obsessed really, with siege craft, in particular the fortification of keeps and castles.

We would arrive at Darius's house generally around two o'clock. Sometimes Aunt Consuelo instead of Ricci would open the door: "*Avanti, entrez* my *bambinos,* children," she would say in her regular potpourri of Italian, French, and English, seemingly disdainful but amused and in one of her elaborate costumes.

Later in the afternoon as we played our war games—Darius had lead soldiers for almost every military formation—the sound of her music would wind its way up the staircase and down the corridor where inside my cousin's rooms we would imbibe, unknowingly, its muffled beat of high excitement, tragedy, and grief.

A Collection of War Notes, Extrapolated from Emma Forster's War Notebook (1836–1837)

How we love to repeat Darius's words: "the majesty of battle," "the virtue of battle," "the will to fight," "the stern excitement."

"War has a purpose: It decides things."

29 November. Today's lesson: Memorize: A regiment, infantry, or artillery is larger than a battalion and is commanded by a colonel. A battalion consists of two or more companies and is smaller than a corps. A corps consists of two or more divisions. A division is smaller than a corps, and is commanded by a major general.

18 December. Today's lesson: Memorize: Forlorn Hope is a technical term used in reference to a small party of soldiers going ahead of the main storming party to draw the enemy's first fire, and induce them to set off their mines.

Darius told us that he does not care at all for the Duke of Marlborough. He calls him "Churchill." He says that he is the impoverished son of an impoverished politician. He is an "opportunist" and a "parvenu." He much prefers King Frederich of Prussia.

This month (January) Darius read to us from *Caesar's Commentaries;* Blakney's *A Boy in the Peninsular War;* Kinkaid's *Adventure in the Rifle Brigade;* Sir D. Dundas' *Drill Book of 1788* (based on the Prussian system as devised by King Frederich); and excerpts from Sir William Napier's *Memoirs of the Peninsular War.*

Yesterday (26 February) Darius said: "Insolence is more to be extinguished than a conflagration." He was quoting Heraclitus, he said, an aristocrat like himself.

Waterloo's lesson: the importance of ground. "Wellington had a particularly good eye for ground, and he always placed his army into position of the kind he favoured. Were I to fight the Battle of Waterloo in Marlborough Gardens, I would choose to commandeer the western half of Marlborough Marshes. That ground is slightly higher than the eastern half, which slopes to the lake."

"One must develop a lust for combat. Shall the lion lay down with the lamb?"

"Soldiering is a simple view of life. There is an enemy to be fought, a friend to be defended, a leader to be obeyed."

"Armies are for fighting!"

When Darius is not teaching us he occupies his time with family genealogy. He is certain that he is descended from both a Persian king and a Greek historian. It is an exacting quest he says, "that demands pertinacity, energy, and intellectual skill."

Another lesson from Wellington: There are two main requirements for success in battle—information and supplies. The first tells you where to concentrate, the second enables you to remain concentrated.

Darius is very fond of Wellington, makes little of Nelson, and despises Napoleon. "Napoleon rose from the mob. He was not a gentleman." Darius calls himself an "eaupatrid," a Greek word meaning well sired. We are not eaupatrids. Darius says we are "hoi polloi," another Greek word which means many or commoners.

16 April: Darius lectured us today on siege work. He said that the first objective of besiegers of a fortress is to surround it and cut off its communications, to put it under a "blockade." And then by reconnoiter to decide the most suitable method of attack. When these preliminaries are complete the besiegers may open up the first parallel, but great secrecy and speed are required. It is done at night for if the besieged detect the operation they will bring down a heavy fire of guns and mortar on the besiegers, or barrels of boiling oil. . . .

As he speaks, in my mind's eye I envision Grindal. . . . She is the besieged inside a castle; I am the besieger making every effort to reach her. I see myself leading the Forlorn Hope, entering the main body of the castle, and dragging Grindal out of the inner keep where she has fled. Then at sword's point I force her up the tower stairs to the upper reaches of the castle, to the parapet. Then, taking her long, black hair into my hands, I fling her over the side and watch as her body falls slowly and finally smashes on the stones below.

Why do I still hate Grindal when Grindal no longer beats me? Darius has seen to that.

City of Childhood
XVII
AN EPISODE: A HERO'S DEATH

WILLIAM/Kleombrotus, the Spartan King, his face grave and serious, advances northward across the patterned rug with his army toward Thebes (the green leaf-shaped pattern just underneath the table with the claw-shaped feet).

"Leuctra" (south of the table) Darius told them, "lies in the hill of Boeotia, Greece, and forms the southern limit of a plain.[26] The road to Thebes"—a brown flower stalk—"crosses it."

Just east of that road William/Kleombrotus knows that the Boeotian general, Sidney/Epaminondas, and his army are waiting there to engage him in battle.

"Now you do understand, don't you," Sidney says in the tone that William/Kleombrotus hates—the "I am right, you are the wrong" tone—"that each hoplite"—he picks one up, a perfect, two-and-a-half-inch, wooden replica of a Greek

---

26. The Battle of Leuctra, Sparta against Thebes, was fought in July 371 B.C. Sparta, for the first time in one hundred years, tasted the bitterness of defeat. Under Theban blows the hitherto insuperable army collapsed, and with it the myth of Spartan invincibility.

"When the message containing the news of the defeat of Leuctra came, the Spartans were celebrating the 'Gymnopaedia' (boy's gymnastics). The 'ephors' (guardians) . . . gave orders that the festival should continue. Meanwhile each family that had lost a relative in the battle was informed privately. On the next day all those whose relatives had been killed in the battle came into the market place with proud smiles. It was the families of the survivors who stayed at home in shame." (Plutarch, *Life of Lycurgus*)—*H. Van Buren*

infantryman[27]—"is equal to two hundred men. Do you understand, William? That's very important. The last time we played, you didn't remember that, William, and it spoiled everything. You put far too many men in the field."

William/Kleombrotus hadn't. Sidney was a liar and pompous. His father had told them, "Sidney is exactly like your Uncle Solomon. Exactly. Uncle Solomon was pompous when he was a child; he is pompous now; pompous he shall ever be." But William/Kleombrotus counts the soldiers anyway . . . two hundred divided into ten thousand men is fifty. William/Kleombrotus knows that. He knows many things, important things. He knows Momma loves him best of all. He knows Momma dislikes Emma . . . yes, there are fifty, as he knew there would be.

"Fifty," he says.

Sidney frowns. He counts them.

A week ago Darius described the battle to them.

"It is midsummer. Imagine the heat, the burning heat, the sun scorching them. Imagine the sweat collecting, forever collecting under their heavy armour, their heavy metal helmets seemingly oozing down into their heavy breast plates! Sweltering, dripping with sweat and their thirst! The terrible thirst!

"In their right hands the Spartans carry eight-foot spears, with short swords as well for hand-to-hand combat.

"Oh, they had been jubilant enough a few days before when they had captured the port of Creusis and the twelve Theban ships that lay in the harbour, but now for days and days they had been marching through enemy country, unknown land, hostile and filled with snakes and vipers.

"Imagine the dust churned up by ten thousand marching men! Imagine the dust, the terrible dust that crept into everything—their eyes, their mouths, their noses, beneath their nails and into every cranny of their lungs! Finally imagine that day as they marched towards Leuctra, through the hot burning afternoon, through a vegetation that was brown and sick with heat. God! they were so weary, so tired, so very, very tired. And when they did reach Leuctra, imagine how

---

27. Reference Note E, page 152.

they felt when they found their way barred by the Theban army *and* Epaminondas!

"That night they camped on the banks of the upper Asopus." He had shown them on the map the long winding line that threaded its way through the mountains. "The following day the battle that Sparta lost began—"

Sidney/Epaminondas said: "When I lower my hand the game shall begin, but not a moment before. Are you ready?"

William/Kleombrotus nods. He is ready. He knows the battle begins with an engagement of cavalry on the plain below (the turquoise patch) and that his horsemen will lose, for the Spartans "were not known for their cavalry action." He watches as Sidney/Epaminondas lowers his hand. The game begins. He watches as some of his riders are thrown and others clamber up the hill to safety. William/Kleombrotus's horsemen are vanquished. *That* is Phase I.

Now William/Kleombrotus leads his right wing (Phase II) down the slope of the hill (the large violet-shaped leaf). He is a brave soldier. "Very courageous," Darius had said of Kleombrotus, "and of good cheer."

William/Kleombrotus leads his men slowly, bravely down to the plain below (the turquoise patch), past the horses and their riders.

William/Kleombrotus passes a rider pinned underneath his horse. Gasping. Bleeding. He sees the horse's wooden head turn toward him. Sees the white foam as it oozes out of the sides of the animal's red-painted lips. The horse is dying. But he "being courageous and of good cheer" must keep on, and so William/Kleombrotus marches his right wing down to the plains below (the turquoise patch) through the dead and the dying.

Darius had explained to them that "it was the Spartans' habit to outflank the enemy's left wing. They were disciplined soldiers and steady. They marched twelve deep and were always edging as they marched toward the right. They had implicit trust in their fighting comrades on their right. They knew they would be protected—to the death. Then outflanking their enemy's left wing, they would wheel around and roll up the enemy's line. They had done it time and time again until they were the masters of Greece. Until Leuctra and Epaminondas!

"On that day in July, 371 B.C., Epaminondas placed his striking force on the left fifty shields deep. What was twelve deep then compared to fifty! And so they were slaughtered and Kleombrotus, their king and leader fell in battle and died."

William/Kleombrotus is now on the plains, the turquoise patch. William/Kleombrotus knows he is going to die. And soon. At any moment now Sidney/Epaminondas will extend his finger and knock down the soldier who is William/Kleombrotus. Push him over with his finger. And he shall fall either onto his shield or onto his back, dead. He watches his soldier as he waits for the game to end. The soldier's shield had exactly eighteen green spots painted on it. What are they? he wonders. Leopard's spots? Or were they studs? Or nails? One of its coloured greaves is chipped.

"Remember the Immortals!" William/Kleombrotus whispers to himself. And he recites the famous words Darius has taught them: "Stranger, tell the Spartans that we behaved as they would wish us to, and are buried here." He waits tense and anxious. When will Sidney/Epaminondas kill him? To die in battle is to die in glory. . . .

Sidney/Epaminondas reaches out his arm and in one deft movement pushes the soldier, William/Kleombrotus, who falls (this time) on his shield.

"Ahhhhh! . . ." moans William/Kleombrotus, as the sword pierces his side. "Ahhhhh! . . ."

He is dead now, quite dead.

The game is over.

Reference Note E:
THE CHILDREN'S TOYS

Tucked among the pages of the *Book of Tribute* was a letter, still in its original envelope, from the German toymaker Johan Rotnesser in which he thanks Count Rimini for his previous order, and hopes that he is enjoying his recent shipment of a phalanx of hoplites. He then assures the count that he has already "commenced" work on the Victor Emanuel Regiment, the Grenadier Guards, which he promises will be finished before next fall. (The letter is dated 10 October 1836). He ends the letter with the following sentiment:

It is as always an honor to fulfill your orders, and, may I add without seeming presumptuous, a distinct pleasure to do business with you.

> Johan Rotnesser
> Marchebrucke Strasse
> Nuremberg, Germany

It is obvious to us that Mr. Rotnesser thought that he was corresponding with an adult war enthusiast, for it was at that time in history that men began collecting toy soldiers so that they might in their leisure time play out battles for their own enjoyment.

How many soldiers did Darius have altogether? Did he have Lucottes, French-made soldiers, fully rounded and far more realistic than Nuremberg flats? Were they made of lead? Or of the new alloy—tin, antimony and lead? Or were they carved wooden soldiers? Or did he have some of each variety? And who paid for them? Did Darius present the bill to Joseph? Or to Consuelo? Or did he have an income of his own? But these particulars (like so many others) are still unknown to us.

Now and then the archives mention pole horses, cups and balls, tops, ships, and so on, but the comments are generally sparse and nondescript. We know that Deirdre had a "Dutch" doll made of wood that could sit and stand without support whose name was Anna, and that Emma had a "Pedlar" doll that Aunt Mathilda had given to her one Christmas. Were it not for Mathilda's list of her daughters' dolls and Emma's anecdote of "the doll that wept" we would conclude that toys were an unimportant factor for the most part in the children's lives.

Vanessa, Mary-Anne, and Letitia owned, collectively, fifty-two dolls: dolls that had threaded eyes made of white glass; dolls whose bodies and arms were made of soft kid leather; dolls whose heads and busts were made of china and whose hair fell in blond, brown, and red ringlets; dolls who wore blue velvet bonnets; dolls who were dressed as brides, complete with blond lace veils and wedding bouquets of silk roses tied with silk ribbons.

Emma's Memory Journal, 1902

. . . and I would of course have been forever thankful had someone given me one of Vanessa's less sensational dolls, but there was one doll I yearned for with all my heart, that I thought about and dreamt about. It was the doll that was mounted on a gold-fringed rug-covered pedestal . . . the doll that wept!

If she had a name I do not remember it, but I remember every detail of her white satin frock with its velvet and lace trimmings. In her left hand she held the head of a painted puppet; at her feet lay his crushed body still attached to its strings. In her right hand she held her lace-bordered handkerchief, which she moved up towards her eyes and she wept. Wept! . . . a series of mournful cries.

When I first saw the doll—I had been invited over especially to my cousin's house to view it—and first heard it weep, I was convinced that it was real, made of flesh and blood, a real child that had somehow been shrunken, perhaps by an evil fairy, or by the Calcutta ghost. I stared at it dumbfounded!

"She thinks it's alive, don't you?" asked Vanessa. "You do, don't you? Admit it."

I did of course, but though I would not admit it to her I could not deny to myself that to me it seemed alive. When I did not answer, Vanessa turned the figure around and in a somewhat vulgar gesture lifted up the doll's petticoats and pointed to a key in the shape of a lyre that was sticking out of the doll's back. "You are the most absurd creature," she said to me, as she turned the key and the doll wept once more.

From that moment on I never stopped wanting that doll. Many years later, more than forty, I found it in a box filled with other discarded toys in my aunt's attic. I took it home with me and had a servant oil the clockwork mechanism that ran it and clean and repair its costume. Its pedestal being lost, I had another one made and had the doll mounted on it.

When all was cleaned and repaired, I took it to my boudoir where I turned the key and heard it weep once more. But when that was done I put the doll away in the empty armoire of a little-used room and never looked at it again.

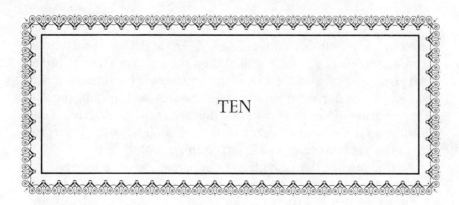

TEN

MARLBOROUGH GARDENS, 1936

DAYS OF hard frost and bitter cold. Wind from the north. There was snow last night. This morning when Lowe and I walked through the Gardens we saw the tracks of small birds and animals.

We walked hand and hand along the lake, its water hidden under a plain of ice, past trees groaning in the wind, toward the marshes where the winter-sweet grows. We cut off a few long branches and brought them back with us together with the bright green flowers of the hellebore.

After a light lunch, we set them in vases in the Screen Room and opened the screen so that we could see the archives as we both worked there in front of the open fire.[28]

Lowe had become quite the expert on Victorian lace. She can speak knowingly of Honiton, Alencon, and Brussels needlepoint lace. This afternoon she began an intricate piece that will be adorned, she said, with roses, lilacs, and poppies. It is to be used as a border for a linen tablecloth, which will cover one of the small marble-topped tables in the Secret Room.

How beautiful the archives are! Over five hundred volumes. A year ago (at great expense) I had the archives bound in Morocco goat skin by Mr. Fernleaf of Oxford Street. It was he who created

---

28. Harriet found the Screen Room, the Secret Room, the archives, and the two letters in the fall of 1928. See Reference Note F, page 168.

our device: a gold-leafed medieval "F" superimposed on a gold-leafed medieval "A." It is stamped on the spine of every volume.

This evening Lowe read out loud from one of Tillotson's[29] sermons: "Consider what a desperate hazard we run delaying our Reformation. Uncertain whether hereafter we shall have Time for it, and if we have whether or not we shall have the Heart for it, or the Assistance of God's grace to go with it. . . ."

At this time of the year, Lowe and I feel the need for spiritual fortification. One gray day follows another. There is no sun, not even a feeble ray. We are locked into the depressing landscape of an English winter.

In December of 1835 there were two deaths in the Forster family. The first was expected, and in certain quarters even caused a considerable amount of pleasure.

The second death was unexpected, and caused the greatest grief.

The first death (Jorem's) was on December 6, 1836. *The London Times* wrote the following:

Jorem Isaac Elijah Forster, London merchant and the founder of the financial house, Forster Midland Ltd., died this sixth of December, 1836. Until the year 1824 he was its chief manager. He was buried at his country seat, Saddler's Grove, near Donnington, a town of great antiquity.

Mr. Forster was a most gifted man. He was not only a brilliant financier, but he was also the creator of the enchanting Marlborough Gardens, situated in the Northeast of London. He was also the author of a series of whimsical books, privately printed, entitled *The True History of England as Seen Through the Eyes of a Field Mouse*. A great patron of cricket in his lifetime, he has turned over a small part of his country estate for the use of cricketers forever.

The service was conducted in St. Swithins in Donnington. The lesson was read by Reverend Bottome of St. Giles, assisted by Reverend Knolly of St. Swithins. The Grave Service was read by Dr. Pond, headmaster of Warrenton.

---

29. John Tillotson (1630–1694). Archbishop of Canterbury. A Latitudinarian. His sermons were Victorian favorites. Albert, like his father before him, read Tillotson's sermons out loud to his family once a week. "He is," wrote Albert on the flyleaf of his book *Tillotson's Finest*, "so endearingly sane, so becomingly sincere."—*R. Lowe*

After the names of surviving family members, an impressive list of mourners followed, among whom were Sir Sidney Ravenscroft, Bart. and his nephew the Earl of Rutledge; Sir Francis Baring; Mr. Nathan Rothschild; Mr. Strooksbury of Strooksbury and Co.; Mr. Russell of Russell and Co.; Sir Lionel Childs of the East India Co.; and Myles Ryder, Esquire, of Canton and Macao.

The Illustrated London News carried the two following public notices:

14 December 1836: A memorial service was held this morning for the late, lamented well-known banker merchant Jorem Isaac Elijah Forster. Sir Sidney Ravenscroft, Bart. amateur painter, publisher of *Country Inns on the North Road,* and lifelong friend of the deceased, gave the eulogy.

2 January 1837: The late financier Jorem Isaac Elijah Forster has bequeathed the generous sum of ten thousand pounds to the charity which he was instrumental in founding, The London League of Gentlewomen for the Rehabilitation of Fallen Women and Their Progeny.

Jorem's will and codicil were read to the immediate family by Mr. Hemsley, Jorem's lawyer, in the library at One Marlborough Gardens on December 12, 1836. Apparently there were some misgivings on Mr. Hemsley's part about both its contents and its form for there is a note appended to the face of the will in Mr. Hemsley's handwriting that reads as follows:

To Whom It May Concern:

Let it be noted first that my late client, Mr. Jorem Forster, died peacefully in his sleep with the book Pilgrim's Progress *open in his hands, his fingers resting on the words, "so he passed over, and all the trumpets sounded for him on the other side." A fitting end for a most honorable gentleman.* Jure divino.

Howbeit I do have some perturbment in respect to both Mr. Forster's will and codicil, though I hasten to add that I personally vouch for the legitimacy of both documents under discussion. Having said that however, I abrogate partial and full responsibility not only for their contents but in particular for my client's eschewment of the time-

*honored custom of primogeniture, and also in regard to the
above-mentioned paper's willful and eccentric style.*

I remain as always,

*Jasper T. Hemsley, Esquire
Solicitor Inner Temple*

Despite Mr. Hemsley's misgivings, Jorem's will is a model of
clarity. It is among other things a meticulous accounting of Jorem's vast holdings, down to the last piglet on Saddler's Grove.

Jorem was an enormously wealthy man. Besides owning Saddler's Grove and Marlborough Gardens, he had stocks in cotton
mills, shares in rubber and sugar plantations, mining investments
in the north of England. In short, he had his financial thumb in
everything lucrative, from hemp to China tea. His stock alone in
the East India Co. entitled him to the maximum four votes.

The sentence (para. 327, p. 12) that stuck in Mr. Hemsley's
legal craw was the one that ended

"and so I leave all my monies, shares, stocks, investments,
and property to my four children (Joseph, Elijah, Solomon,
and Mathilda) to be divided equally among them,"

flouting as it did the law of primogeniture by which the whole of
the property descends to the eldest son alone.

Mr. Hemsley's objection to Jorem's style is justified. The style
is not only willful and eccentric but at certain points borders on
blasphemy. For instance, the first page reads:

My dear children,

*I have enjoyed my life immensely. In particular I have en-
joyed my success. Now that my death is imminent I wish to
share with you a few last thoughts.*

*The Good Book warns us that it is far more difficult for
a rich man to enter heaven than for a camel to pass
through the eye of a needle. Conceivably yes, but what it
fails to mention is the great enjoyment that comes from the
amassing of money, and the even greater enjoyment of
spending the money. I have done both and regret nothing.*

And perhaps it is this sentiment—the honest enjoyment of acquisition and expenditure—that is the best legacy one can leave one's children. But before your collective faces fall, let me hasten to add that I have, indeed, bequeathed all my worldly belongings to my devoted heirs, my dear children.

The will ends though on a more somber note:

Before I begin my final journey to God knows what resting place, I feel compelled to say some last words to my second son, Elijah.

Of all my children, I respected you the most. And feared you the most. Plainly speaking, I saw myself in you and yet, Sir, I did not love you. At least I did not love you as I loved your brother Solomon, nor did I have the sympathy or compassion that I had for your brother Joseph.

And speaking truthfully, it is only now as I stand on the threshold of the next world that that fact begins to lie somewhat on my conscience. For it occurs to me now that I might have to pay, and dearly, too—and only too soon for this most grievous defect of character.

I pray therefore that in the very act of hearing these words, dry as they may seem to you, you might begin to pardon and forgive this old sinner, your father, and pray for the salvation of his eternal soul.

If Elijah did as his father suggested—prayed for his father's soul upon hearing these words—he must have cursed himself for being a fool when Mr. Hemsley proceeded to read out loud to the tense gathering the contents of the lengthy codicil.

JOREM'S CODICIL

My dearest, my most beloved Vanessa,

As an old man who will not pass through here again, I claim for myself one last earthly pleasure: the surrender to complete partiality, the yielding to absolute favoritism. True love is the abandonment of justice. . . .

Therefore I leave to you alone and to no one else—and I give it to you gladly, with all my heart—the King's Ransom.

And now listen, my dearest, as your grandfather tells you his very last story:

Once upon a time . . . I was wandering through my Gardens in the evening when I was importuned by a male servant who insisted I must accompany him to his master's house.

I knew the servant's master, Sir William Saddler, a young man who had come back from India a year earlier with a great deal of money. I had seen him several times at Crockfords, a gambling den where I had watched his reckless play at Hazard night after night.

I went with the servant. It was just as I thought. Saddler needed money desperately. I lent him the money he requested when he offered as collateral his country seat, Saddler's Grove. For some reason I do not know, I did not press him for money when he was late repaying the debt.

Some years passed. Then one night I was called to his home again. As I was led to his bedchamber I could see things had indeed gone badly for him. The rooms in his house were empty, repositories for dust and rodents. My guide this time looked more like a hungry jackal than a servant. He and his co-servants I sensed were only waiting for that crucial moment when their master would be unable to defend himself and they could strip him of all his possessions before fleeing. He was not dead yet, but almost. . . .

Sir William recognized me at once.

"You have not come a moment too soon," he said. "I shall give up the ghost presently. Here . . . take this." And he pressed into my hands a dirty envelope. "Do not argue with me, Sir, there is no time." I nodded, thinking to humor him. "Good! I hope that you can make better use of it than I have!"

And saying that, Vanessa, he turned his face to the wall and in just a few minutes, after a gasp or two, the poor man died. I arranged for his funeral. I buried him. I was the only mourner at his graveside.

As for the envelope, I did not open it. What could he bequeath me? Nothing but debts. But when I moved to Saddler's Grove I opened it; I could hardly decipher the angry scrawl that began with a string of maledictions:

May my faithless wife contract the pox! May my servants one and all die of starvation! May a thousand plagues fall on my creditors! May the earth swallow up my former gambling confreres!

On my death they shall look high and low for the "King's Ransom." High and low the bloodsuckers shall seek, but they shall not find it. I have hidden it too well. They shall pass it, aye, countless times and still not find it.

I ask you, Jorem Forster, where would you hide a King's Ransom. For that is what I am bequeathing you. Why? For the sake of your gratuitous kindness. But it is yours only if you can solve this pretty folderol—this Enigma:

Thou seest me
And yet do not

Pried out of the hilt
Of an Indian Sword

We reside in the silt
Of the arms of our Lord.

Until we meet again then,

Your indebted debtor,
(et dimite nobis debita nostra)
Sir William Saddler, IX

As you can imagine, Vanessa, I began my search forth-with. A King's Ransom! And all mine! What did I care whether it be for spite, or a lark on his part? I was deter-mined to find the fortune.

The first thing I did was strip the chapel of its three effi-gies of Christ and dismantle their arms, but I found noth-ing. Then I began a systematic search, room by room, of Saddler's Grove. A hundred rooms! When after a year I had not found the fortune, I began to think the young man had made a fool of me too, but I was not perturbed. It would happen, I told myself, if it happened at all, and if it was supposed to happen, in its own time. And I forgot *about it. Part of me supposed it to be a jest on his part. He was a sardonic soul.*

But many years later I did find it, and in the oddest way: I was standing in the great hall staring at the pikes, halberds, shields, and the five suits of armour that cluttered the room and walls when for no reason that I could think of, the riddle popped back into my head.

> *Thou seest me*
> *And yet do not*
>
> *Pried out of the hilt*
> *Of an Indian Sword*
>
> *We reside in the silt*
> *Of the arms of our Lord.*

And then I knew, instantly, where the young wag had hidden the King's Ransom.

Can you guess, Vanessa? I shall give you five seconds, no longer.

You are right! Yes, it was standing in front of me, yes, right in front of my nose. Sir William Saddler's suit of armour, Sir William Saddler the First. It was this *Lord, and not our dear Saviour our young friend had meant. Oh, I was sure of it!*

I had the servants remove the suit into my study. Alone I dismantled it. Removing the arms of the armour, I found the chamois pouch wedged in the joint between an arm and the body. I opened it and there *in the silt lay the most beautiful emeralds, diamonds, pearls, and rubies I have ever seen. A King's Ransom indeed!*

For the next few days I kept the pouch in my pocket, taking it out now and then when I was alone to feast on the sight of the jewels. With an odd reluctance, I finally returned it to its snug hiding place, reattached the arm, and told my servants to place the armour in the niche in the east wall of the inner court. From then on, it was known as the "Guardian of Saddler's Grove."

There it remained, eventually to become a rusted eyesore that I steadfastly refused to either restore or polish. No, I

*insisted, it would remain as it was. (Forgive me, Elijah,
once more when I tell you that it afforded me a secret
amusement to witness the scowls that crossed your face
each time you passed the "abomination!" as you called it.)*

*Vanessa, do you recall the game you and your cousins
played in Saddler's Grove on rainy days, the one called
The King's Ransom? At first I decided to give your cousins
and you equal and ample opportunity to find the prize and
divide it among yourselves.*

*But one day last summer I changed my mind and
decided to indulge my prejudices and give this gift, intact,
to the one I loved the most. And so I say to you, Vanessa,
the gift is yours, alone!*

In my defense, I quote Ovid:
*"tanta potenta formae est" (so great is the power of
beauty).*

Farewell, my beautiful Vanessa. . . .

Your first, most gentle, and most loving suitor,

> *Jorem Isaac Forster, Esquire*
> *Saddler's Grove*
> *August 9, 1836*

Mrs. Bridgewater's *Day Book*
  Sidney Garth Forster was eight years old when he died at
6:12 A.M. on 18 December 1836 of complications brought on by
measles. All the Forster children, except Darius who had survived an attack several years earlier, came down with it.
  It began with Deirdre on 30 November and ended with Vanessa on 21 December. But according to Mrs. Bridgewater's
Day Book, Jakes was the first member of the household who
came down with the disease.

  24 November: Today Jakes complained of feeling
  poorly, and to tell the truth, the girl did look bad,
  her eyelids being red, and much coughing and much
  discharge from the nose. I sent her to bed.

  25 November: Jakes very much worse today. When
  I examined her I saw the pustules on the skin behind

her ears, and on her face and chest. 'Tis the pox, or measles, I thought, and so I told my mistress right away so as that she could have the girl moved out of the nursery, though I feared for certain it was too late; all the children having been exposed, they'd all come down with it. . . .

In 1836 the treatment for measles was fairly uniform. The patient lay in a darkened room. Secretions from the mouth, nose, and eyes were removed with a soft cloth which was then either burned or disinfected. The patient's urine and feces were also disinfected by chlorinated lime and buried at least a hundred feet away from the dwelling. The pustules were washed gently with an alcoholic solution and the eyes were flushed daily with a saturation solution of boric acid. Ice bags, wet compresses, and cold sponges were used to reduce the fever.

If the doctor was an Arabist (and Solomon Forster's doctor, Mr. Harlowe, was) the patient was fed a diet with an aim of "extinguishing the heat."[30] Albert, Sidney, Joshua, Jacob, and Deirdre were therefore fed lentils, kid's-foot jelly, and broths made from woodcocks, hens, and pheasants in addition to barley water, the last given four times a day.

Officially Sidney died of "bronchial pneumonia brought on by measles." First he had diarrhea, for which he was given small doses of opium. Then when his high fever continued, a mustard jacket was applied to his chest. One part mustard to six parts wheat flour and some water made a paste that was then spread between two layers of cloth and applied to Sidney's chest until it reddened. But though Sidney's chest reddened, the fever did not break. Instead his bronchials began to fill with "opaque exudate" and abscesses began to form within the intervening lung tissue. Finally the pleural cavities became so filled with pus, the lungs compressed, the walls of the bronchials were destroyed, and Sidney died.

---

30. Basil Harlowe: Born 1794 in Hegelson. Father: Cecil Harlowe, Curate. Became an articled pupil in Manchester to an apothecary, Mr. Henry Flanges. Moved to London in 1823 and joined St. Bartholomew's Hospital where he studied as an assistant to the venereologist, Mr. Thomas Anderson. Dr. Harlowe was a member of the Royal College of Surgeons, a fellow of the Royal Medical Chirurgical Society, and was appointed surgeon to the Islington Dispensary. Particular interest: the reproductive organs and their connection to masturbation. He published a steady stream of papers on this subject in the *Lancet* until his death in 1853.—*R. Lowe*

Albert's Diary, 1873: An Account of Sidney's Death (pages 138–142)

Edited by R. Lowe

I waited outside the sickroom. Sidney had been removed from the nursery four days before to a room next to my parents' bedroom. I was waiting for Momma to come and relieve the night watcher. Poppa had told me that Dr. Harlowe had insisted on a night watcher. "It cannot be your wife," Dr. Harlowe had told him, "for it will only wear her out, and her tears will obstruct your son's recovery."

The night watcher was an old woman. Her eyes were abnormally large; their irises, a faded brown, encircled dark lusterless pupils. Cold, incurious eyes. How could she be better for Sidney than Momma, I wondered, and when I thought of those eyes watching Sidney it made me feel sick.

Two nights before I heard Mrs. Bridgewater tell Jakes that Sidney might die, that his fever wasn't breaking. Ever since then I had been unable to sleep. I was in mortal terror that Sidney might die as I lay sleeping.

I heard my mother open her bedroom door and saw her come down the hall. She was thirty at the time. Although this morning her face showed signs of strain and worry, she generally looked much younger. Hers was a childish face: heart shaped, wide-spaced eyes, plump rosy cheeks, a short upper lip. . . . Deirdre resembles her.

"What are you doing here, Albert dear?"

"I've come to see Sidney."

"You are thoughtful. But you can't, my angel. Your brother's far too ill. Perhaps tomorrow . . . we shall see. . . ."

"I must see him today, Momma."

"Must?" She frowned. "Oh, Albert dearest, do be good. I am so very tired. Besides, Dr. Harlowe has forbidden anyone to see Sidney. He's far too ill. Tomorrow, darling, when he's better. . . . You may see him then. But not today."

"I must see him today, Momma. You don't understand—if he's going to die—"

"Hush, Albert! You mustn't say such things!"

"I need to ask his forgiveness."

"Forgiveness? . . . Oh, Albert dear, you're exaggerating as usual—at a time like this! Forgiveness! . . . Now do be good and go upstairs, dearest one. . . . I promise I shall come to see you later, and we can talk about it then. Now go ahead, go on . . . upstairs."

As she turned away from me to open the door to the sick-room, I caught hold of her dress: "Albert! Let go of me! Let go of my dress!"

"No."

"Albert, you are behaving badly."

"I *must* see Sidney."

My urgency distressed her. I have never known her to be deliberately unkind. She sighed deeply; I could sense her pain. "All right. You may come in, but you must be very quiet . . . and you may only stay a few minutes. No longer than that. A few minutes. Do you understand? No longer than that."

I let go of her dress and picked up the box that I had put alongside the wall hours ago. Holding it underneath my arm, I followed her into the room, which was dark with the drapes drawn and only two candles lit. The room had an unpleasant smell, a mixture of body odor, sweat, carbolic acid, formaldehyde, and gin.

Sidney was asleep in a large bed that stood in the middle of the rear wall, his head propped up on several pillows. His cheeks were flushed, and his damp hair curled into tight ringlets. He looked startlingly healthy to me, although his breath came in short gasps. The night watcher glowered at me.

"I told Albert, Nurse," Momma put her arm around me; she would protect me from angry nurses, from my enemies, from death, "that he may visit his brother—but only of course for a few moments. He understands that. He's promised to behave, Nurse. . . . How is my son this morning?" Her voice broke as she asked the question. She walked toward the bed and the sleeping figure and stumbled on a wet cloth that was lying on the rug. She bent down, picked it up, and walking over to the nurse handed it to her. To me it seemed as if she were sleep-walking. I remember that the nurse took it from her without thanking her.

Sidney began to breathe harder, panting like a small animal in distress. My mother ran to the bed.

"Oh, my poor baby! Oh, is he dying, Nurse!"

"If the fever don't break, Madam, the boy will certainly die."

In an effort to stifle the oncoming sobs, she placed the palms of her hands against her lips and pressed hard. A few seconds later, having succeeded, she bent down quietly and kissed Sidney on the cheek, and he awakened.

"My dearest . . ." and she kissed him once more.

He began to tell her at once how Grandpa Jorem had come to fetch him. "He was standing on the far bank of the river Alba, next to a boat that is always moored there. The blue and yellow one, the one he named Maartel. 'I have come to fetch you,' he said. And he wanted me to come with him, over to the other bank. Grandpa's voice was very low but I could hear every word. He said that if I came with him he would tell me stories, more wonderful than I had ever heard before. Would I come? Oh, I wanted to! And I was about to answer yes. But then you kissed me, Momma, didn't you? And I awakened."

I put the box down on the bottom of the bed and opened it. I lifted out the *Victory*. "I have brought you this, Sidney. It is *yours* now. I am giving it to you." And I placed the wooden ship within reach of his hands.

But though he stared at it for a long time, he did not reach out his hand to take it. He only said: "It *is* the most beautiful thing in the world, isn't it, Albert?"

"Do take it Sidney, please. I have given it to you."

He reached out his hand and then drew it back.

"I cannot."

The two simple words "I cannot" unleashed all the terrifying thoughts that had plagued me for the last two nights, that had kept me from sleeping: It was *my* fault that Sidney was ill, that he was dying, my fault alone; I had willed his death; I had prayed for it; if he died, I would be punished *everlastingly;* it was my fault and mine alone; he must not die; I must save him, but that could only happen if he accepted the gift. Only then, for that is what the Gods had decided. He must accept the gift! He must! Otherwise I would die and be punished *everlastingly.* . . .

"Say that you will accept the *Victory*! Say it!" My voice rose uncontrollably. "Say you will accept it!" Out of the corner of my eye I saw the night watcher move swiftly toward me, her eyes larger than ever. I saw my mother's stricken face. I heard her cry: "Stop it! Stop it, Albert! You promised. . . ."

As I continued to shout, "Say, say that you'll take the gift," the night watcher held me fast in her arms. "Say it!" I sobbed. Her nails dug into my arms as she began to drag me out of the room. But I would not leave. I must not! He shall die and it shall be my fault alone! My fault, alone. I grabbed onto the bedpost. I would not leave, I would *never* leave until he said it.

"I accept. Thank you, Albert."

I heard the words and felt the poison drain out of me. And yes, the notion that I was my brother's murderer has come back from time to time and tortured me, but for that moment, that single blessed moment, there was complete absolution.

"Let him go, Nurse," I heard my mother say.

I watched as Sidney took the ship into his arms and stroked it. "It is the most beautiful thing in the world, isn't it, Albert?" Tears rolled down my cheeks as I nodded in agreement.

Moments later, my brother died, his right hand resting on the *Victory*.

My brother was buried where he wished to be, where Momma had promised him she would when he had asked her, inside the Rose Garden, close to the East Gate.

One night, a month later, when the moon was full I stole out of the house—it must have been past midnight because I heard St. Giles' bells strike one o'clock—and went to his grave. I knelt and prayed. And then when I was absolutely certain that my brother's ghost was present and watching me, I read out loud to the moon, to the stars and sleeping flowers, and to Sidney's ghost the brief message on the new headstone: "Here lies our beloved son and brother Sidney Garth Forster, Yet a little sleep, a little slumber, A little folding of the hands."

That done and over with, I dug a deep, deep hole and buried the *Victory* alongside my brother's grave.

Reference Note F:
THE SCREEN, THE SECRET ROOM, THE ARCHIVES, THE LETTERS

I found the Secret Room, the archives, and the letters in the lodge behind the screen.

I entered the lodge on the morning of 27 December 1927, three months after I had moved to Marlborough Gardens. I had had a series of violent and disturbing dreams, dreams in which I'm sure Emma had a hand, for of all the so-called ghosts, *she* is the most active.

One could walk up and down outside the lodge, search and peer, and not discover or even suspect that it contained a secret room. Architecturally, its exterior seemed absolutely straightforward; it was what it was: a rectangular, granite bungalow. Rather ugly, in fact.

The first floor contained the usual series of rooms on either side of a central hall; the second floor, as one would expect, contained bedroom suites complete with sitting rooms and dressing rooms, all richly painted and decorated, and one rather splendid Victorian bathroom lined with marble; the third floor was a succession of small, dark rooms—the servants' quarters.

Mr. Chalmers had not lied. Nor exaggerated. The rooms were stocked with handsome antiques, and unlike the main house, which was early Victorian and masculine in character, the lodge was French Rococo and exquisitely feminine.

When I first saw the screen, which was on the first floor in one of the back rooms, I took it to be the back wall of the room. A wondrous thing in itself, it stretched from floor to ceiling. A chair made of red lacquer and mounted on a large wooden podium faced the screen. It was the only piece of furniture in the room.

It became a habit of mine—I moved in a small table and a lamp—to read in the room each afternoon until dusk, ever so often lifting my head from the book to glance at the screen. I knew that in and of itself it more than made up for what I once thought had been an exorbitant price for the property.

It was Chinese, intricately carved, gilded, and inset with semiprecious stones. Its wide border contained carved chrysanthemums that were gold-leafed with their lush heads twisting on malachite stems as if a wind were blowing. Inside the border, at regular intervals, small groups of Oriental women made of ivory dressed in their traditional robes wandered through a wooden landscape of pine trees and pavilions, beneath the menace of overhanging crags, along the embankment of winding rivers. Here and there a few delicately arched bridges, made of amber and mother-of-pearl, spanned the river's teakwood sides.

One day I glanced at the screen and saw what I had never seen before: a single female figure standing in the center of one of the bridges, her back to me. Peeping out from her ivory sleeve was her small ivory hand. Like a pet mouse, I thought. Having spied it, I could not seem to take my eyes off of it and then on impulse I walked over to the screen and clasped the small hand in mine. Seconds later the screen began to open and a shimmering darkness unfolded. . . .

Somewhere in one of her journals Emma wrote, "For a woman, secrecy is a way of life, offering as it does the only possibility of her own world alongside the visible one."

It was not a bolt hole, nor a lair. On the contrary, though it was small, it was furnished with choice pieces: one japanned chair; two chairs covered in petit point that glowed with flowers, bees, and various kinds of birds; an upholstered sofa; an escritoire; and three or four charming bibelots. The walls were covered with a rose-colored silk and the domed ceiling was decorated with Putti, garlanded and beribboned, ascending an azure sky. Above a tiled hearth hung an oil painting, a copy of Watteau's *Cythera.* Inscribed in its left-hand corner was the lively signature: *"Apres Watteau que j'adore. Vanessa Forster, 1846."* The whole effect was intensely luxurious, intensely feminine. And there was a fresh scent of lilac as if some lovely woman had just been there and left.

It had its own courtyard, outside its own French window in the center of which, on a marble pedestal, stood a statue of the great goddess herself, her stone tresses curving around her like the waves out of which she rose.

It took me more than half a year to organize the archives—the amount was staggering, as if a literary Atlantis had surfaced—for the Forsters had had a predilection for recording the minutiae as well as the major events of their lives. Some of the material was bound, Emma's novels for instance, in Russian calf, their titles emblazoned in gold-leaf lettering on their spines and covers, but most of it was not. For the most part, the journals, diaries, account books, ledgers, daybooks, bankbooks, notes, lists, letters, brochures, pamphlets, stud books, cash books, and tracts looked as if they had been dumped hurriedly, placed pell-mell on top of one another, on the recessed shelves of two floor-to-ceiling bookcases that stood on either side of the hearth.

There were two letters (written by Emma) on the mantel, beneath Vanessa's copy of Watteau's *Cythera,* in two separate envelopes, one behind the other. I didn't open them until sometime later. Much later in fact.

The first one contained pages that had been torn out of a diary. It was dated 12 May 1882. It contained what I considered a fairly obscure message:

> *I have come home from Albert's funeral (2 April 1882).*
> *A sad occasion, but I must admit there is a real satisfaction*
> *in having outlived him. Still, his death surprised me. His*
> *life was a paradigm of moderation (unlike the rest of us);*

one would have thought longevity his just reward. But as always the Gods are capricious.

Death . . . it is all I think about now. Though it is not the idea of death that disturbs me as much as the idea of dying and arriving in a man-made hell or man-made heaven, whatever the case may be. I am sick to death of this man-made world!

Yesterday I walked through my beloved Gardens once more. Would the aloe plant still be there? My absurd heart beating faster as I raced down the path towards it, remembering that other time when I stood there with my beloved governess Clara (hand in hand) before its full tide of bloom, listening to her incomparable voice lecture on monocotyledons.

". . . a fibrous leafed plant whose flowers are frequently borne in panicles—p-a-n-i-c-l-e—a loosely and diversely branching flower cluster. Its common nomenclature is misleading, Emma. For although it was once thought to flower only once a century, there is in fact no certainty when the flowers will appear, depending on soil, site, and climate, it could take five years or sixty. In the meantime, the plant hoards its stiff fleshy leaves, each terminating in a stout spine, you will notice, enormous food reserves, much like an army preparing for battle. Then, Emma, when it thinks the right moment has come, there is a gigantic explosion! A huge terminal inflorescence—take note Emma—inflorescence, definition: flower head. I would say this specimen of aloe is more than twenty feet tall."

It is no longer there.

Yesterday I went to the temple and stood in front of the great goddess remembering the last time I stood there on the eve of battle, with Darius, my brothers, and all our cohorts, and how we asked her for victory, chanting,

We sing of Pallas Athena, Mighty Defender of cities;
Who protects an army going to war and returning.
Who cares for the deeds of war: cities being sacked,
And cries of battle. Hail oh grey-eyed Goddess,
We shall remember you, oh child of Zeus!

and how she granted it! and glory besides!

Today I made her a votive offering, which she has accepted. She has listened, she has accepted, she has promised, and of her it is truly said: Nothing is promised that is not performed.

The other note was dated seventeen years later:

6 January 1899.

I have a strong premonition tonight that I shall never see this house again, that I shall never walk in the Gardens again, that I shall die on some foreign shore, be thrust into alien ground, and all that I thought and did be forever lost, like Ozymandias, the sands of time transforming all to dust.

Something within refuses to relinquish the life it has known, refuses utterly to vanish into nothingness like a stone thrown into a bottomless lake, its ripples disappearing without a trace. It cries out: I have lived, I have loved, I have suffered, I have experienced ecstasy! It cannot be that all this has happened for no reason. That it was meaning-less . . . something that shall not be remembered.

We only die when we have been forgotten.

Pray, sir, remember us . . . do not desert us now . . .
                                        Emma Forster

When I left the lodge late that afternoon, I remember commenting to myself how quickly the days come to a close in midwinter, for it was already dark as I walked down the flagged path that connects the lodge to the Main House.

City of Childhood

XX

THE ANGEL OF DEATH

"WHERE do you think Sidney went after the Angel of Death came to call for him?" William asked. He was half-leaning on Tansy, his thin body pressed up against her thick legs, but his face was turned towards Grindal. She was the authority.

The children were dressed in mourning clothes, which had been made for them in double haste when Jorem died. The boys wore black arm bands, Emma a black bombazine frock underneath which she wore a black camisole slip. They were in the schoolrooms overlooking the Gardens. They had stayed in this morning, the early morning rain having turned into a deluge.

"Where do you think, Master William?" asked Grindal. She was knitting a scarlet muffler for Edward; the *click click* of the needles jarred on the children's nerves.

Ignoring the question, William asked another question: "What is the Angel of Death? Is it a lady or a gentleman?"

Emma's heart sank. She was sitting in the window seat trying to embroider a pair of slippers for Poppa but feeling everything was useless, this too. Sidney dead! She dreaded Grindal's answer. Looking across the room at Edward, who had lifted his head from a book he was reading, she saw he dreaded it too.

"Now that is an interesting question, Master William. A lady or a gentleman?" She lay her work down and placed her hand on her chin in a mock seriousness. "Oh I shall have to give it all my thought."

Ever since Darius had come into their lives, the children had noticed that Grindal's behavior toward them was better; not that she was kind or affectionate but she seemed distracted, uncaring, and *that* was better. But since Sidney's death she was her old self again. A bit worse, thought Emma.

"The Angel of Death," began Grindal, "is neither a lady nor a gentleman. No, the Angel of Death is a giant caterpillar—lime green with a thin oval head adorned with hundreds of antennae. It stands upright! *And,* Master William, it is an *it*. Yes, the Angel of Death is an *it*!"

Emma turned away her head and stared through the window glass. The downpour continued; it was flooding the Gardens, which appeared all gray and brown through the thick curtain of rain. And then—she saw *it*. And as usual she saw that Grindal was right. It was a giant caterpillar, upright, lime green with hundreds of antennae. It was walking, strolling really, seemingly impervious to the rain, down one of the gravel paths, and it was fanning itself with what? Something . . . Emma strained to see . . . a newspaper? . . . Could that be true? She wondered listlessly as she heard William ask another question. Had it always been there and she had not seen it until this very moment?

"Where do you think he went to, Sidney I mean?"

And was it waiting for one of them? Herself? Or one of her brothers? She turned back to her work and with the greatest care she began to wrap the gold-colored silk thread round and round her long sharp needle, the beginning of a French knot. She pierced the stiff felt successively and drew the thread slowly through the center of the stitched daisy.

"Sidney went to Limbo," answered Grindal.

"Limbo?"

Edward despaired. Why must William ask these questions! He wanted to forget Sidney's death, and quite often he did, though just when he thought he had, he saw (Why? He didn't want to!) Sidney's casket being lowered into the freshly dug grave and the two workmen with sullen faces. Why had the men been so angry? he wondered.

"Yes, Limbo. Looks very much like Nannies Plain, don't it Tansy?" At times like this Grindal liked having an ally. Tansy nodded. Grindal picked up her work again. " 'Cept it don't have those ridiculous statues. No, thank God!" Her voice continued against the *click click* of her needles. "Instead of them ugly things there is a marble dais on one end of the Plain on which the judges sit, all dressed in scarlet robes—their black wings stirring in the breeze."

"That's a lie! It's not true!" said Edward. "Don't believe her. Sidney went to Heaven. Don't you remember Momma told us that and that the angels gave him a harp which he plays and that he looks down on us every day and wishes us well."

Grindal's face filled with wrath. "He is not in Heaven!"

"He certainly isn't," echoed Tansy.

The children cringed. If he wasn't in Heaven . . .

"At this very moment! Right now!"—right now! the children thought in terror as the voice went on relentlessly— "the judges are sentencing Sidney to Pedrogil!" She spelled the word out: "P-e-d-r-o-g-i-l. A recess in Hell built especially for children.

"How often have I told you that Satan hates waste? That he is a practical man, Master William? Yes. Practical. So why then in the world should he use an eight-foot rack for a three-foot child? No. In Pedrogil everything is scaled down to size. There are miniature racks, miniature pits—even the flames are smaller, *but* I can assure you they are *just* as hot, Master William!"

"I don't believe you," said Edward, "Sidney did nothing to deserve such punishment."

"Oh, but he did, my fine laddie. We heard all about it yesterday, Tansy and I. From Nanny Jakes. Oh, he had a long list of sins, beginning with bad eating habits—"

"Nonsense," Edward said, but his voice was weak.

"Well, aren't we all cocky locky this morning. Now *that* was another large sin on Sidney's soul—talking back to Nanny! They've already poured boiling water on his tongue for that—"

"Well then I guess they shall pour it on mine, too, when I die," said Edward with a sudden burst of courage. "Darius told us you were a savage! And I believe he's right!"

But this morning Edward's insult slid off her back.

"Has he now? And did he also tell you that your cousin Sidney was a thief! That he stole coins which they found in a box underneath the cupboard next to his bed! More than ten of them there were! Deirdre said they had been left to her. Imagine that! No one believed her, of course. Let me assure you, Master Edward, that Sidney *at this very moment* is sitting on a small stool *just his size* with a wreath of flames encircling his head that spell out the word t-h-i-e-f!"

The children felt faint. They were shaken. Was picking up coins in the Marlborough Marshes near the ruins, for that was where Sidney's coins had come from, was that stealing? Coins that belonged to no one. Suddenly Edward was worried. He had done the same thing. So had Emma. And William. They all had. . . . The ruins were filled with old coins. Was he a t-h-i-e-f then too? Would he have to sit in Pedrogil like Sidney after he died with a cone of fire encircling his head and spelling out that dreadful word?

"Cat got your tongue, Master Edward?"

"Does taking something from no one," asked William, "is that stealing, Nanny Grindal?"

"There ain't no such thing. Something always belongs to someone. Why do you ask? What have you stolen, Master William?"

"Coins." William's face crumbled and his eyes filled with tears. "I found them in the ruins—"

"Where are they?"

"They're with my soldiers. I only have two coins, Nanny. The soldiers like having money to spend. They've been awfully good since I've given them each a coin."

"Give them to me! Straightaways!"

"Must I?"

"Now!"

"Oh, well, if I must." He walked over to the shelves where his soldiers were kept. "But I'm not the only thief," he said as he placed the two coins in Grindal's large outstretched hands. "Edward and Emma have coins, too. And I do hope they get punished worse than I when they die. I thought it was very mean of them to let me keep only two."

"Well, we do have our work cut out for us this morning, don't we Tansy?" She lay down the unfinished muffler and rolled up her sleeves. "You may spank Edward and William. I shall do Emma."

But she didn't have to go to Emma. Emma went to her without protest. Sidney was dead and the Angel of Death was a giant caterpillar.

As she placed herself on her nurse's lap, she began to wonder if Grindal perhaps, just this once, was right . . . perhaps they were thieves. Perhaps they did deserve to be beaten. . . .

City of Childhood
XXI
GRINDAL GETS A BEATING

GRINDAL herself was beaten publicly in Uncle Joseph's house, in the central hall, three weeks after Sidney's death, on a bitter cold day near the end of March.

I remember every moment of it, every detail! I remember the exact shade of the contessa's dress—moss green and vibrant—in the gloom of the enclosure; the flash of the majordomo Ricci's rings as he lifted his hands to his lips and threw kisses (kisses!); the swift and beautiful movement of Maria's feet as she stalked her enemy, Grindal; the droplets of blood that first pulsed and then fell one by one from Grindal's bosom onto the white slope of her hip . . . and the joy I felt as I witnessed that!

But let me start at the beginning: we met as usual that afternoon at Darius's house. Sidney's death did not interrupt our education. That went on as before except that the empty space next to the door, Sidney's space, terrified us. It was empty and yet it was not: vacant and yet not vacant, it was flooded with our dead cousin's presence. Sidney's death had shattered us. Oddly enough, our grandfather's death (a man we loved far more than we loved Sidney) hardly affected us.

In ways I cannot explain Darius took dominion over that space and with it Sidney's death and our combined terror.

We heard the first screams just as Darius was ending his lecture on sieges. Dressed in our black mourning we were huddled close to one another in front of the open fire in Darius's sitting room. We had heard the lecture several times before—Darius repeated himself quite often. We could in point of fact recite most of his lectures by heart. We knew them as well as we knew Grandfather Jorem's fairy tales.

Just as he finished the sentence "The next morning fire is opened and the guns boom!" we heard Grindal scream: "Ahhieee! Ahhieee! Help! Help!" Darius ran out of the room and seconds later we followed him. We stood beside him on the landing and looked down. We could hardly believe what we saw.

There was Nanny Grindal, bare breasted, standing in torn petticoats, her long arms up over her head in an attempt to ward off Maria's fists that were pounding her!

Maria was shouting: "Whore! Dog! *Never* will you be able to use it again! When I am through with you I will cut it out, cook it, and eat it! *Puttana! Strega! Sanguisuga!*" Her fists rained down blows on Grindal's chest, on Grindal's head, on Grindal's arms.

"Oh help me! Ricci, help me! Oh someone help me!" wailed Grindal as she tried to move away from her attacker. Her black hair was loose and streamed over her shoulders and her breasts. She tried to catch Maria's arms but Maria, filled with a demonic energy, was too quick, too agile. Down down down came the pounding fists. And then I saw her nails tear into the soft flesh of Grindal's breasts. An unholy scream came out of Grindal's mouth. And I watched transfixed as the blood began to flow. God was on my side. My enemy was being punished. . . .

Suddenly we heard laughter! We looked at one another. Laughter! It was the contessa! Where was she? We probed the darker reaches of the hall. There she was! And with her a man and a woman. They were standing outside the door of her studio. The man and women were smiling.

"Help me!" Grindal was screaming again. "Ricci!"

Ricci! Where was he? We searched the hall again, every shadow . . . not there . . . could he be standing directly beneath us? We leaned over the banister. Way over! "Jacob, keep hold of Deirdre!" Albert said.

There he was! Dressed in britches only! Bare to the waist! But protruding from his britches like some swollen and infested finger pointing at something or someone was Ricci's Satan's rod at a sharp right angle to his body. Well, he would certainly be punished for that! And rightly too! But what was Ricci doing now? He was bowing and smiling! How strange! But to whom? We looked around . . . ah . . . to the Contessa. And—she was smiling back!

Grindal let out another shriek. Poor Grindal, how silly she looked. Had she gone mad? She was turning around and around now as if she could not stop. She would collapse soon—it would soon be over—but no, Maria, still in a towering rage, caught hold of Grindal's petticoats and lifted them up with her hands and began to claw at what was beneath. And that revived Grindal.

Breaking loose from Maria, Grindal screamed, "I will kill you! You fat ugly pig! And Ricci will give me a medal for doing it! He told me your breasts hang to your knees. And that your cunt smells like a sewer! You smell like a pig! A pig!"

Maria lunged. Running forward she grabbed hold of Grindal's petticoats and in one masterful stroke ripped them off her enemy. And Grindal stood there naked! Naked. For a moment everything stopped and we all stared at her, including Maria, Grindal's petticoats hanging limply from her outstretched arm.

"*Bravo! Magnifique! Bellissima!*" shouted the contessa's male companion.

"*Bravo, Ricci! Bravo!*" shouted the contessa.

Then Ricci threw kisses, his rings flashing, as he blew the kisses at the contessa and her friends.

But Maria saw him and flew at him. "*Adultero!*" she screamed. As she ran toward him, Ricci, his arms now clasped above his head in a victory embrace, stepped nimbly aside and poor Maria ran into the wall behind him and fell, momentarily stunned. He did nothing to help her up. He merely continued bowing, smiling, and throwing kisses. And Grindal, who had been standing there one hand on her breasts and the other on her sex, flew at him too. "Coward! Deserter!" she screamed. "Traitor!"

Ricci began running. Grindal ran after him. And Maria picked herself up and ran after both of them. Weaving in and out of the marble columns around the hall, they ran— Ricci, Grindal, and Maria, almost knocking down the contessa and her friends. But before they ran a second lap, Maria with great cunning stopped and turned and ran the other way. In a matter of seconds both women cornered him and both began to beat him. But he was stronger than both of them, so he escaped easily and ran out of the hall toward the back of the house, the women following. . . .

We watched as the contessa and her friends tottered and held onto one another, they were laughing so hard. They gasped, they sputtered, they could hardly breathe. "Oh," one of them said, tears streaming down her face, "Oh I cannot breathe! Oh, it is too funny, too funny for words!" She wiped her face with a tiny lace handkerchief that she pulled out from the cleft of her bosom. Then she added: "You'll have to sack him, of course."

"Oh yes, I'll have to sack him. A pity though; he's not a good servant at all, but he is sweet . . . really quite sweet. Darius! Where is he? Ah, there you are." Darius during most of the row had stood on the staircase, his right hand holding his chin, his left arm holding his right elbow, as if in deep thought. "Perhaps you should follow them, Darius. After all, we can't allow that slut to run around naked, can we? Oh, and do take care of Maria . . . such a loyal servant. And Ricci, too. You will do that for me, won't you?"

He came down the stairs. "Yes. I shall attend to everything as usual, Momma. But while I attend to that bit of business you will have to take care of the children." And without looking back at us he left.

"*Dio mio!* The children! Don't tell me *they* are here! Oh my God! They are! What shall I do? They've been here all this time! They were witnesses! What shall I do?" My aunt seemed genuinely distressed and so leaning over the banister I shouted down to her: "You may trust us, Aunt Consuelo! We shall never speak of this to anyone! Honor bright! Our lips are sealed!"

"A thousand thanks, my little Emma. But you have given me an idea. All of you shall be fed sweets, and yes, a little wine . . . to calm the nerves. A few sips, that cannot harm you, can they? Ah! My dear children, what a strange household you must think this is . . . yes? A perpetual opera! Yes? An opera *buffo. Comique.* Is that not so? . . . But your nanny, Nanny Grindal, she is very naughty, isn't she?"

I cried out. "Wicked! She is wicked, Aunt Consuelo!"

"Yes, of course. Wicked. *That* is what I mean." I saw her smile and wink at her friends. "Wicked." She repeated the word.

"Yes. And I am glad Maria beat her."

"Are you now?"

"Yes. And I would like a whole glass of wine, not just a few sips."

"Would you now? But of course, a whole glass of wine it is. It isn't every day we see our nanny beaten, is it, my little one?"

*   *   *

It was cold in the gardener's shed. Even though they were a little tipsy with the wine that Aunt Consuelo had given them, their hands and feet were chilled. They had come from Darius's house to this cold, grim place to honor Sidney's memory and participate in a ceremony that Albert had devised soon after his brother's death. They had been coming for a month on Tuesday afternoons, but as yet they had not told Darius, having sensed he might not permit it: this concentration of feeling on someone other than himself.

A weak silvery light barely filtered through the cracked, smudged windows, soiling everything it touched. The children's scarlet mufflers shone a pinkish gray; their hair seemed a dirty white in this strange light. They looked old and tired.

"Shall we begin?" said Albert.

The children nodded, their heads bowed.

Although the coins had been confiscated, the remainder of Sidney's possessions had not been. Albert had claimed them and they—the feather, the glass, the buttons, the lady's comb—lay in a circle on a wooden table, in the center of which was the advertisement next to a pocket knife. Albert picked it up and read out loud slowly in a solemn voice: "D. Godfry begs respectfully,"—and here the children joined him—"to thank his friends for past favors and to inform them that his hotel will now be found completed with every comfort and accommodation. Table d'hôte daily on arrival of the swift steamer from Glasgow."

Then he asked for a moment of silence and picked up the knife and with its sharp point pricked his thumb, once, twice, carefully squeezing out some drops of blood that he let drop on to the advertisement. Having done that, he passed the paper and the knife to Edward.

As it passed from child to child, Albert wondered how long the paper would last. It was beginning to fall apart from the handling and the shedding of blood. But would another piece of paper, even though the same words would be written on it, would it, could it be considered sacred? As sacred as the words on *this* paper. Yes, he decided. It would be. It would have to be. They could not omit the rite of blood. Sidney *deserved* blood. He wondered if Sidney's ghost was watching. He looked around him and catching a flicker of movement in the shadows he understood it was, just as he also understood that the ghost was pleased with him.

Deirdre, the last one to receive the paper, refused (as always) to prick her thumb. And though they tried to bully her (as always), threatening to exclude her from the cere- mony, she refused. As usual Albert took the paper from her, pricked his thumb again, and said out loud to the ghost: "This is for Deirdre."

Albert now picked up each of Sidney's "treasures" while reciting Sidney's litany: "One treasure, feather; two treas- ure, glass . . ." picking up each item as he mentioned it. When the last one was returned to the table, Albert said "Amen." The ceremony was over.

It was over, thank goodness, thought William. He was cold and hungry and his thumb hurt. Besides, there was something puzzling him and he wanted to ask Edward about it but he had not yet had a chance. There hadn't been any time. They had had to hurry to the shed or Albert would have been angry with them. Dreadful place. William didn't like the gardener's shed. Dark and cold. And so many dead plants and dirty pots. And he didn't like the smell. It re- minded him of death. He watched impatiently as Edward helped Albert put the treasures back into the box. The twins had left already with Deirdre. Deirdre! She had almost fallen off the landing!

Within steps of the South Gate William decided to ask Edward what he had been wondering about in the shed.

"Edward, why did Maria beat Grindal?"

Edward thought for a moment before he answered his brother. Certain things about what had happened puzzled him too. But not wanting to ask Emma or anyone else, he had tried to figure it out for himself.

"I believe Maria found out how wicked Grindal is and when she found out she beat her. And Ricci, I believe he must have beaten Grindal first, but of course we didn't see that. But when he grew tired of beating Grindal, why then Maria began."

That was clear, wasn't it? thought William. Quite clear. *Still* there was something that puzzled William. He asked a second question.

"Thank you, Edward, I do understand that now. But what I don't understand is why they both beat Ricci?"

Why indeed? That had puzzled Edward too. He thought hard. There *must* be an answer. And then it came to him.

"Maria beat Ricci, William, because Ricci had stopped beating Grindal, and Grindal beat Ricci . . . because . . . because Grindal likes to beat people, as you very well know."

Now, that was quite true, thought William. The explanation was really quite simple, wasn't it, once you put your mind to it as Edward had. And wasn't it nice of his brother to explain it to him. If Sidney had asked Albert, Albert would have been horrid. But then William remembered Sidney was dead.

Just before going to sleep that night, William was still thinking about Sidney. And Albert. What if Sidney returned from the dead to ask Albert the same two questions he had asked Edward? What then? In his mind's eyes, he pictured Sidney digging his way out of the grave in the rose garden. First he would brush off the earth, and the twigs, and maybe a leaf or two and yes, some pebbles . . . and then he would walk up to Albert, well not exactly walk, would he? His legs might be very stiff after all this time. Hobble, he would hobble up to Albert and ask the questions, the same two questions. And, yes, thought William, after a while, yes, Albert would be just as kind to Sidney as Edward is to me. For he was quite certain that Albert had learned his lesson.

City of Childhood
XXII
THE CONTESSA'S PEDOPHOBIA

IDNIGHT. Unable to sleep, the contessa lay on her bed, reviewing—for the third time—the conversation she had had with Darius earlier that evening.

It would have been better, she concluded, if it had not happened at all. . . . She had lost control of the situation. . . . A spasm of fear clutched at her heart. *Dio mio!* What would happen to him? . . . to her? She had tried to amuse him. That was all . . . *tout.* Her face drew itself into lines of disgust. Amuse! . . . but she had been afraid, yes . . . she was afraid of him. It was difficult for her to admit, but it was true. She was afraid of him . . . afraid of alienating him. And losing him? Yes . . . no . . . perhaps. . . . What should she have done instead? she asked herself. Sermonize? Insist that he go to school? "Apply himself," wasn't that the phrase? Force him to study! Take a tutor? Impossible! It would have bored him further . . . but those children! Those terrible children! Emma's face swam into view. Leaning over the banister shouting "Wicked!" "A whole glass of wine!" Ah, yes of course, why certainly, my dear Emma! A deranged child. A blackmailer! Greed. Ugly. Horrible, *horrible* child! What *could* he see in her? What could he see in *them?* What sort of life was this for her clever son: an impresario to a company of mad children half his age! . . . Oh, but he was too clever, too clever for his own good . . . yes, far too skilled in mimicry. . . . Of course, *that* was how it had started. . . .

Consuelo had come from Elijah's house, where her husband's family had been assembled to celebrate Elijah's thirty-seventh birthday. Guinivere (*oh, the poor woman!*) had insisted that the party planned months ago take place despite the tragedy. And Guinivere (*oh, the poor woman!*) had come and stayed just long enough to wish her brother-in-law a happy birthday. I could not have done that! Gone!

Stayed! Oh the poor woman! No, I could *not* have done that! But yes, that was how it had started: Darius's door had been open when she returned. . . .

"May I come in?"

"Yes." Darius had put down his book. She glanced at the title: *Lysis*. It meant nothing to her. The cool "yes" had unnerved her. She had begun to jabber:

"You should have escorted me as planned, Darius. You would have enjoyed seeing Elijah resplendent in his new diamonds. He positively reeks of good fortune. My dear, he has not stopped celebrating since his father's death."

That was the first mistake. She should not have said that. It was unsuitable to speak to one's son in that way but she had not heeded the inner warning; instead her mounting unease had driven her to further indiscretions.

"Charming to everyone, except Theodisia, of course. Fool that she is, she stood by his side all evening as if she were his valet. And throughout supper—" Yes, yes, yes it was true she had lost control; she had not been able to stop herself though. It was Darius's eyes; they had been so cold. So deadly cold. Utterly mysterious, she thought, that a being's eyes could be cold one second, and hot another, as if they ran temperatures . . . what had she said next? It came back to her, her nervous rendering: "Throughout supper, Darius, you can imagine Elijah shot his sternest glances down the table at Theodisia, completely cowering the poor woman, so that she started dropping things. First a fork, then a knife, but it was when she dropped her wineglass, Darius, creating a public scandal—for there was the evidence for all to see, a widening deep-red stain encircling her dinner plate—that I thought, we all thought, he would rise and *strike* her!"

Darius had laughed, and she had thought, "Success!" And so she had hurried on in the same vein: "And Aunt Mathilda! You should have seen *her!* She was dressed in black lace and staggering but not from drink—you know she never takes a drop—but from the combined weight of ribbons, tassels, bows, chains, gold, and silver—her feathers alone must have weighed more than a hundred pounds! And her hair! All done in a swirl and a shingle to boot!"

He had laughed again. He was amused and all would have

been fine had she not mentioned Solomon, for *that* had brought out the mimic in him.

He had silenced her then. *He* would describe and "enact" Solomon, he said.

He had risen, her son (her precious son!), had stood in front of her, his feet pointed outward, and he had let out his stomach, puffed his cheeks, and placed both hands on his hips. Clever, clever but it had been the expression on her son's face that had amazed her. He had caught Solomon's soul.

"His clothes as always just a bit too tight for him, isn't that right, Momma? A vain gentleman, our Uncle Solomon, isn't he? And so the burning question on my uncle's mind tonight, as always, was, Shall or shall I not split my beautiful new britches as I sit down for dinner?"

She had laughed to cover her discomfort.

"And Aunt Guinivere." Oh no, he wouldn't dare! He wouldn't!

"Tragedy personified! The pariah at the feast. For what can be more tragic—for a mother at least—than the loss of her son?"

Yes, yes, of course, what *could* be? But said in such a deadly tone. Why? Why had he said it? . . . And with *such* contempt—contempt for whom? Not Guinivere. Herself? But *why?* Why was he angry with her? What had she done? But she had refused, yes, *refused* to be intimidated. Ignoring the barb, she had cut him off. She had plunged headling into an account of the Redburys.

"Cora Lee and Jasper and four offspring, she overweight, he red faced," she had related hurriedly. "Do you remember them? The broad Yorkshire accents. You met them last summer in Rimini at Prince Umberto's villa, well, he, Redbury elder, he is a satyr—oh I am sure of it!—the way he looks at me when his dear wife looks the other way. . . ."

Of course Darius had remembered them. As a matter of fact he would "do" them. Catching every characteristic; exaggerating cruelly. Poor souls, they had the unfortunate habit of wriggling their noses, and so by the time her clever son had finished his charade (if that was the proper word) they had been transformed into half a dozen human rabbits searching for carrots in of all places Elijah's drawing room! She remembered she had laughed, even enjoyed herself . . . somewhat. Then he had begun to yawn. After his second yawn she had bid him good night. "Sweet dreams," she had said. But she couldn't leave him. Why? Why couldn't she leave him? She didn't know why, but she remembered that she stood in the doorway: "Apropos the children . . ."—and *that* was why she couldn't sleep now; it had been a terrible mistake to mention them—"have they recovered from this afternoon's farce?"

"Recovered . . . I wonder if that is the right word. I believe they enjoyed the spectacle though they may not have understood its finer points."

"What do you see in them, *caro?* Don't they bore you?"

"A little. But it passes the time."

"And that ugly little girl, Emma . . . what do you see in her? She is obviously demented. You need only look into her eyes." *That* had been the worst mistake. His reply had been as swift as an arrow.

"You are jealous of her because I love her."

"Love her! But you are joking, Darius!"

"I don't joke about things like that. I love Emma. She loves me. We love one another. *Voila tout, c'est simple.* And unlike you, Momma, she is completely devoted to me."

She had wanted to strike him then and there! She had felt a violence overtake her, a current of rage course through her body, but she had controlled herself, better late than never, she told herself bitterly. She had forced herself to be moderate in her reply, had even honeyed her voice.

"But *caro,* surely you are taking the children a bit too seriously—"

"No, I am not. I am not like you, Momma. People interest me more than music or even art. Music is not my whole life. It never shall be. People fascinate me. But what difference will it make? I shall waste my life, I'm sure, like your father and his father before him."

His reply infuriated her. Frightened her. Why did he say such terrible things to her? Didn't he realize the effect those words had on her? Like her father! Oh, my God! She wanted to drop to her knees then and beg him, yes beg him, not to say such things! . . . those untruths . . . but she had said nothing. Nothing. She had been in control then.

"No, I am not like you. And now, Momma, please leave me. I'm tired. I wish to sleep."

Sleep. She could not sleep. Was he sleeping? she wondered. A film of sweat broke over her body. What would happen to him? She loved him. She did not wish to love him. When he was born she had scarcely paid any attention to him. Strangely enough, Joseph had. But then as he grew up . . . it was during the summers when they were together at the palazzo. From the very first, he had sided with her against her father. He had become her companion . . . her confidante. And he was so bright, so quick, so talented . . . Sometimes she thought she loved him and no one else. Yes, he was the dearest thing to her! She closed her eyes. A moment later she wished he had never been born. That she had never married. Sleep, she told herself, sleep. But how could she? No, there would be no sleep for her tonight.

She got out of bed, lit a candle, and took the stick with her over to the desk (her room was Spartan in its furnishings: a bed, a desk, a chair, a bookcase, a small upright piano). She picked up the book she had been reading the night before: *The Princesse de Cleves*. Reading soon calmed her nerves. She had a special affinity with the author, all of whose novels were concerned with mournful accounts of women who found too late that they had married the wrong man.

Edward's *Diary of Moral Inventory* (pages 103–105)

Darius's power reached his apotheosis after Sidney died.

After his burial we stood in a new world, one in which we had no bearings at all. And we looked to Darius for support. We wanted his approval in everything. We wanted to please him in every way.

About the same time I had a short but decisive conversation with my father. But before I discuss its contents, it is essential that you understand how we felt about Darius . . . how I feel about Darius now.

He did not bewitch us. If I have given you that impression, I have wronged him. When Darius came bearing his apples of knowledge, we were no innocents. Even before his arrival (deus ex machina) we were consummate snobs. We were the Lords of Marlborough Gardens and we felt superior in every way to "the others," the name we gave to those children who were allowed to play in the Gardens but were not Forsters.[31]

We knew the difference between the "poor" and the "rich." Children learn far more from the way their parents behave than from what is told them. We knew the difference between servant and master. Our nannies might scold us and even beat us but we understood that we would be their master one day, as our parents were now.

Darius's values and our fathers' values were not all that different. Our fathers' characters had been molded at Warrenton where concepts such as strength, courage, and blind devotion to Empire (an empire whose mission in history was to "civilize" others) were considered the primary virtues.

Darius's precepts were maxims with which our fathers fundamentally agreed: "Honor must be maintained." "Loyalty to one's friends and harm to one's enemies are the only things that matter." "Justice demands that we respect the natural inequalities of others." How theatrical they look printed on this page, and yet when he said them they carried such conviction.

No, it was not our similarity to one another that attracted us to Darius. No. What magnetized us was that Darius made it clear to us that he *cared* for us, that we were his concern, his special interest.

For instance: the brief discussion that I referred to concerned music. Over the preceding months, listening to Darius play various instruments (the piano, the flute, the violin, the lyre) had awakened in me a desire to play an instrument myself. And I decided to ask Poppa if he might allow me to study with a music teacher, although even before I asked him I knew what his answer would be. And I was right.

"The men in our family do not play musical instruments," he said. When I pointed out to him that Darius did, he replied: "Exactly. He is the exception that proves the rule. Hence, my dear boy, we need no other."

It was the briefest of skirmishes. Poppa, like the true gentleman he was, extinguished all hope quickly and quietly.

---

31. By 1836, forty-eight houses had been built around the four sides of Marlborough Gardens. All were rented to well-to-do families with several children. One of the tenants' privileges was the right to have their children play in the Gardens. According to the census of 1832, there were 248 children in all. Those children who were not away at school played in the Gardens and presumably constituted "the others" that Edward writes about.—*H. Van Buren*

I repeated the conversation to Darius. By that time, we told him everything. He laughed and said (you must believe me when I tell you that he said the following in a totally nonmalicious way), "Your father is incapable of understanding or creating beauty, and he is envious of those who do." (As you see, I have not forgotten his words.) "I shall teach you. Choose an instrument. What shall it be? Choose!"

I chose the violin.

"Bravo!" he replied gaily. "Very soon we shall play duets together."

But we never did; instead . . . we went to war.

City of Childhood

XXIII

GUINIVERE'S GRIEF

G UINIVERE succumbed to grief. She visited her son's grave every morning. It became Albert's custom to accompany her.

The winter had been the mildest of winters, March had just begun, and the celandine that bordered the paths of the garden had burst into bloom and clumps of daffodils came up through the dead leaves.

She allowed the boy to guide her, which he did gently, for she moved, as if she were a sleepwalker, past the hornbeam hedge that enclosed the sunken garden and its nymphs to the entrance of the Rose Garden—a wrought-iron gate inside a wide bricked archway. Above the archway, on a rounded slab of stone, there was a bas relief depicting Cupid handing his gift to Harpocrates (the God of Silence) as a bribe to keep secret the amours of his mother, Aphrodite. "Accordingly, whenever secret matters are discussed, a rose is suspended from the ceiling and what takes place is therefore 'sub rosa,' under the rose," Darius had explained to the children.

Guinevere handed Albert the key that she had clutched in her black-silk glove. The Rose Garden was always kept locked. The children were not allowed to play there.

Turning the key, he opened the gate and held it open for her to pass through. The wind caught at her long veil as she walked down the gravel path. Her caped cloak, too large for her now (she had lost a great deal of weight), made a *swishing* noise as it grazed the pebbles. It was a little less than three months since Sidney's death.

Removing one faded bloom from yesterday's offering, she added the Lenten roses her gardener had cut for her this morning, and then sank to her knees at the foot of the grave where the statue of Cupid had once stood.

She was a brave, courteous, controlled woman, but Sidney's death had undone her. Over and over she saw in her mind's eye his face in those last hours, the sweetness of it, the faith glowing in it, the love. The love for *her*. Although she had told no one, she feared she had not loved him enough. And though she had tried to excuse herself, she had been unable to. His face, the innocence of it, plagued. Her little sweetheart . . . her eyes filled with tears. For one awful moment it seemed to her as she knelt there that the earth had disappeared and she saw him, her son, denuded of flesh, his skull grinning up at her. She began to pray.

Watching as his mother prayed, Albert inhaled the odor of damp earth and fertilizer. In a few months there would be a staggering scent of roses in full bloom and they would be taken by their parents to the Rose Garden where the several varieties would be pointed out to them: the damasks, the bourbons, the Bengals, the Portland, and "in this corner the China roses, which Mr. Miles Ryder brought all the way from China as a gift to your grandfather." They would have golden heads, he knew. Now there were only the bare canes but already some had sprouted shiny new leaves.

On the way to the grave, the boy had felt the awakening, the promise of new life, but staring at his mother, her childish profile almost hidden by the deep width of her black bonnet, he knew that nothing had changed for her. She was secluded in her grief.

He stared at the soles of her upturned shoes. On the right sole there was a man's face, yes, that dark shape, that was a man's beard, and those two spots the size of seeds, they were the man's eyes. The nose was outlined by a crease in the leather. . . . How long would she be? he wondered. He was proud that she had asked him and not the twins, but he was restless. He turned away from her and stared at the bas relief, the verso side: Aphrodite on her couch with Mars. Aphrodite . . . what had Darius told them? Aphros, foam risen . . . then the boy heard his mother say—he had been waiting for it—"and do not fear the dark tonight, my dearest, for I shall be with you in spirit and shall return in the flesh tomorrow morning. . . . Oh my dearest boy!"

It was over. She would rise momentarily. As she rose, the boy caught a glimpse of the black-silk stockings she was wearing underneath the bombazine of her skirt. He held out his hand to assist her. She held on to it briefly and, opening up her black reticule, took out the handkerchief bordered in black lace and held it carefully to the corner of each eye, catching the overflow of tears.

The boy loved her very much but he was angry with her. And angry with Sidney for dying. By dying, Sidney had caused her pain. Sometimes he felt as if he too had died, for he sensed that he hardly existed for her now. But Albert was not a morbid boy, and so he was certain that this would pass just as he knew (though he could not have put it into words) that she still loved him the "best of all," more than Deirdre or the twins or . . . even Sidney.

It was always Albert who decided the way home: the long way through the Gardens or the short way back through the East Gate. Today he decided on the short route. Suddenly he wanted to be alone, away from her.

As they passed through the Gate she began the questions. He dreaded them. They were always the same. Did he remember? they would begin. "So you remember the birthday party? Do you remember the haircut? Do you remember when Sidney was three? Do you remember when Aunt Mathilda?"—a small stock of remembrances. Today it began with the haircut.

"Do you remember Sidney's first haircut? Of course he was always smaller in size than any of you, wasn't he, Albert? And that's why, of course, we didn't cut his curls off until he was way past his fourth birthday. Do you remember? . . ."

He didn't. Truthfully, he never remembered any of the stories. And sometimes he wondered if they had happened at all, if his mother might not have made them up though he knew that couldn't be true. His mother never lied. But what he remembered was so very different. He pretended to remember though; he was afraid she would cry if he told her the truth. This morning the question period was brief. She soon lapsed into a silence, an ordinary kind. Not the other kind. The kind he called to himself, "the Sidney silence," the one in which she thought of Sidney, and no one else. He always knew when she was thinking of Sidney. Once he had taken a flower and pressed its delicate stem, with his forefinger and thumb, from its calyx to its tip, until it was limp and gray. That was what his mother looked like when she was thinking of Sidney, as if the life force had been squeezed out of her. He hated the Sidney silence. He glanced at her sideways. To his surprise, she was smiling.

"Last Sunday," she said, "after the service, Reverend Bottome took me aside and said, 'I must tell you how well your sons are doing with their lessons.' He's quite pleased. He is quite sure that all of you shall be well ahead of everyone else in your form when you enter Warrenton next fall. He feels you've finally buckled down to work. 'Buckled down to work.' Those were his exact words. I told your father and it delighted him."

The boy did not desire credit when it was not due him and so he explained to her that it was Darius's work. "He's been coaching us in grammar and in Latin."

"Cousin Darius? . . . But I wasn't aware that you were seeing him at all."

"Oh yes, Momma. We take classes with him several afternoons a week."

"How odd. I mean, my not knowing. Several afternoons a week?" She stopped walking. She turned to him.

"Yes. Classes begin at two o'clock. Promptly. He's very strict about punctuality. But he's an awfully good teacher."

"Is he? Well, yes, I imagine he is. He's so very bright. It's just that I didn't know. I wasn't aware. You see, no one has told me. Jakes hasn't . . . I guess it's really quite wonderful when you think about it . . . I did wonder what in the world he could be doing in that gloomy household by himself. Well now I know. He's teaching his cousins." She resumed walking.

"Oh he's quite busy, Momma. In the morning he writes his memoirs."

"Memoirs?"

"Yes, the trials and tribulations of his life."

"Oh. Has he read them to you?"

"Oh, no, Momma. They are private. Though he did say he might one day."

She was utterly astonished. Classes two or three times a week! Memoirs! Contact with Darius! Here was a whole part of her son's life she knew nothing about. But it was her fault, of course, she began to chide herself. She had been far too preoccupied with the . . . other one . . . even now her mind resisted the word "dead." A flood of questions and doubts assailed her. Should she question Jakes? And what in the world did Jakes do while the children were in class? Or did she attend them too? Should she tell Solomon? Should she question Albert further? What should she do? Her mind came to the abyss and . . . backed away. It was nothing, of course. Common sense prevailed. But no, not nothing, not exactly that, was it? It was a benefice. For the children as well as for Darius. And even she and Solomon benefited. They had "buckled down to work" Reverend Bottome had said and that had made Solomon so very happy when she had told him. But then she thought of Sidney.

"Sidney . . . Albert, did Sidney attend classes, too?"

"Yes, Momma. And he was very good at his lessons. Quite the scholar, far better than myself. He excelled in grammar. Darius told him if he kept it up he would soon be eligible for a *luo*."

"A *luo*?"

"Yes, Momma. It is a pin that is only given to those students who can successfully conjugate the Greek verb *luo* . . . to lose, disband, destroy, kidnap, ransom. It's very difficult to do. There are ever so many forms. Over three hundred forms, Momma."

She didn't want to ask but she had to: "Did your brother receive his pin?"

"No, Momma. He died just before he would have received it."

"Oh."

The boy looked at his mother as she lapsed into silence

again. Perhaps, thought the boy, if he told her that Darius had given the pin to Emma, for she was almost as proficient in grammar as Sidney was, she would feel better. So he did. But it didn't seem to help for Momma remained silent.

The boy began to feel uneasy. It occurred to him that perhaps he shouldn't have told her anything. By telling her he might have betrayed Darius in some way . . . and the Order of Rimini. He would never have told her anything— he had taken a sacred oath—except for the fact that this had been the first time in such a long time that she had wanted to know anything about his life. Had he done something wrong? Had he betrayed Darius? He scrutinized her closely. She was still silent. What was she thinking of? he wondered, and then he saw the look he dreaded come over her face. She was thinking of Sidney again. Only of Sidney. So that was that. She had forgotten him again. He was quite sure that she had already dismissed from her mind anything he had told her. Poor dear Momma. He took hold of her arm. He must protect her.

As they passed Darius's house he saw the contessa standing at the top of the stairs talking to a man, the same man who had been in the hall that day, the day Grindal was beaten, the man who had shouted *"Bravo!"* She was moving her hands and arms about as usual. She couldn't speak and stand still at the same time, could she? He didn't like her. And he didn't think she liked him. Or any of them for that matter, though she always acted as if she did. She smiled at them, but it was a false smile. Darius insisted (he had taught them how) that they execute a deep bow whenever they encountered his mother the contessa. Homage, he called it, she deserved homage. Deirdre and Emma were taught a deep curtsey.

They were just a few paces past Darius's house—his mother hadn't noticed her sister-in-law even when the contessa had waved at them, she was so deep in her own thought—when something prompted the boy to look back. They were laughing, the contessa and her friend. Laughing at what? Or at whom? the boy wondered. Suddenly the boy was convinced that they were laughing at his mother. Not at him, no, not at him, but at *her*. He was sure of it! Yes, they were mocking her. The contessa's false smile, he could see it from where he was as he continued to walk next to Guinivere, his body stiffening with rage. He hated the contessa . . . hated her! She *dared* to make fun of his mother!

"Is there anything wrong, Albert? I can't keep up with you. You're racing."

"Forgive me, Momma. There is nothing wrong."

He would *never* forgive the contessa. He would never bow to her again!

PART
IV

ARMIES ARE FOR FIGHTING

*War is the father of all and king of all, and some he shows
as Gods, others as men; some he makes slaves, others free.*

—Heraclitus, Fr. 53,
trans. Clara Lustig

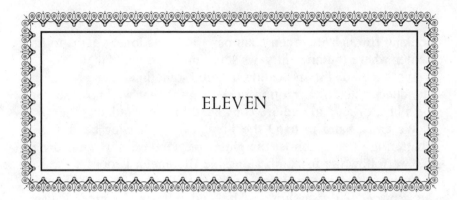

ELEVEN

T ODAY is the Day of Rote.[32]

As is our custom, we have spilled blood, tended the grave, chanted the hymns in the temple, and walked the established routes. All that is left is to perform the cave ritual.

When we first entered the woods (an enchanted place, here all things are possible), it was an entanglement of brambles, shrubs, and bracken; its canopy was so dense that only a few rays of sunlight filtered through to the dank and gloomy place where in the deep spread shadows roamed the ravenous beetle and the ant; it was a home for the predatory badger and the fox, the center of mildew, blight, and rot.

Over the years we have axed, thinned, pruned and felled, and restored the wood to the original dimensions laid down by Kevin Francini a hundred years ago; a wood in which trees, primarily oak and beech, are widely spaced; in whose glades grow the strawberry, the iris, the parsley, the narcissus, the bluebell, and the violet; an alchemist's laboratory where light is converted into gold and silver; a domain in which we have spent whole days

---

32. There are certain sacred days we observe in Marlborough Gardens: Day of Arche, Day of the Hand, Day of Nadir, Day of Advent, Day of Rote—days in which we sanctify what needs to be sanctified in loud speech and quiet songs, days in which we honor the departed dead and connect ourselves with the world of gods and spirits.—*R. Lowe*

walking through its green chambers down its lonely paths to its center where the ancient yews stand in perpetual twilight.

We have sought the children here, sometimes perceiving, in the deeper shadows, motion in the copses that we know cannot be a bird or animal and are convinced that it is indeed "them."

We enter hand in hand the silent woods, leaving behind the chattering of small birds, the glitter of cloudless sky, and single file we follow the footpath alongside Bleinheim Brook.

Spring has come to Blenheim Wood. The banks of the brook are crowded with cowslips, and beyond in the tender green leaves of the beech glow the woodland lilies and the narcissus. Before us runs a hare. Our robes trailing in the wet, fallen leaves make a *shushing* sound. The path is treacherous, slimy and slippery, and Lowe trips over a bulging root but at last we come to the fork in the road. The path that veers to the left leads to the North Gate where Darius's army entered. The path to the right leads to the cave.

We follow it until we come to the statue of Zeus[33] and Antiope in their bower of honeysuckle (their holy thighs entwined, enraptured lovers) where we cross the wide meadow abloom with cuckooflowers to the entrance of the cave, Francini's masterpiece, Calypso's domicile. It was here that the children stored their weapons and discussed strategy.

The light in the cave is extraordinary. The roof and walls are made of polished stone and the floor is a carpet of shimmering pebbles, so the whole gives the effect of an aqueous universe, a liquid void, a chamber at the bottom of the sea; and the sides, acting as an immense mirror, reflect the two great statues of Odysseus and the goddess in multiple shimmering images.

The cave consists of two quadrangular chambers, each over sixteen feet high, united by a narrow passage. The first chamber is the larger. Lowe contends that Francini enlarged an original cave. She has pointed out to me what she considers its natural perimeters. In digging beneath the pebbles, she has found bones, the hindquarters of a ruminant, and some faience beads.

---

33. The forest is strewn with statues of the great phallic God. There are eighteen statues of Zeus as himself and in his amorous disguises in bronze, marble, and limestone. Never was there a more tender-eyed lover, a prettier bull, a more captivating quail. Some are unfinished, chisel marks evident, but all are finely executed, and such things as toenails and fingernails are carved with care.—*H. Van Buren*

As if to define the basic and perennial difference between the sexes, Francini rendered them in two different mediums. Odysseus, the sullen, middle-aged soldier, reclines naked on his hip, his back to the goddess, facing the mouth of the cave in somber bronze, while the goddess seated at her erect loom before her great marble hearth ("bright flames on the hearth did play") is in snow-white marble, her voluptuous form an ideal contrast to the folds of her stone drapery. In her right hand she holds her shuttle. Her stone loom's warp is made of silver threads and the whole thing is so lifelike that one expects the shuttle to slip momentarily from side to side between the threads.

In an account of the Marlborough War, written by Count Maria Alexander Frederich von Hoenfenschtall in Weimar to amuse her neighbor, Emma writes, "Properly speaking, the Marlborough War was not a war, that is, a state of prolonged open-armed conflict. Nor can one describe it as a campaign. It was only one military operation. But let me assure you, my dear count, that though it was a single battle it was by no means a hole in the corner affair. It involved, not including the officer's staff, more than a hundred and fifty boys. . . ."[34]

<hr />

Edward Forster's *Diary of Moral Inventory* (pages 103–105)

The diary was written in 1851–1852 at the behest of Dr. Garth Blackstone, Wesleyan minister of the Moravian Chapel at Brampton, North Umberland.

We stored our firecrackers, slingshots, staves, pebbles, swords, and shields, in short our weaponry, in the second chamber of the cave in oak carts that Ricci made for us. We also kept there our pennons and our red-velvet standard fringed with fine silver bells, approximately a yard broad and a yard and a half deep, that Maria had embroidered and wrought with flowers of green silk and gold. After the standard was finished, we attached it to a staff by cords of red silk and carried it down to Marlborough Marshes to see the wind move it and to listen to the music of its bells.

Our rifle practice took place in the clearing outside the cave.

<hr />

34. Emma's account is included on page 227.

Here Darius taught us to fire our slingshots standing, kneeling, sitting, lying down. At first our targets were natural objects such as tree stumps, then we graduated to a bull's-eye target, and when we had mastered that, we progressed to firing at longer ranges, in particular a life-size wooden silhouette that Darius had made, one that eerily resembled Albert.

How sweetly your words fell on my ears last night, Sir, when you preached no command but "Believe!" And when you said "Regeneration comes of itself. . . . One moment is sufficient!"

Have you read Hobbes? I ask because oddly enough so much of what you preach reminds me of him, though I imagine his *Leviathan* was on the Index when you were a Catholic Priest, and now, of course, that you have become a Moravian you read only Scripture. But, for instance, this morning when you said mankind is totally depraved, that in his natural state he can only behave toward his fellow man with the greatest ferocity, that is Hobbes's view, though Hobbes does not go on to say, as you do, that in Christ we are redeemed.

It puzzles me that Rousseau, who believed that man in his natural state was naturally good but that society corrupted him, nevertheless arrives at the same conclusion that Hobbes did: Absolute authority is best for mankind.

Hobbes says that there are three principal causes of war: competition, diffidence, and glory. The third is for trifles, he says. "A word, a smile, a different opinion, and any other sign of undervalue in their persons, or by reflection in their kindred, their friends, their nation, their profession, or their name."

Briefly, this is what happened: It was because Albert would not bow down to the contessa that we went to war. We were studying Cromwell. The battle of Marston Moor. We had set up Cromwell's army, we were actually singing the second stanza of the Puritan psalm Darius had taught us and that *Old Ironsides*'s soldiers sang before they charged into battle (you see, I remember every detail of that afternoon) when the contessa came into the room.

It was always about a "trifling" matter. That day she complained in her jabber of languages that she had something in her eye. Would Darius remove the "offending object"? I have an obedient nature perhaps, so even as she entered I had risen and made my deep bow. But Albert did not. Nor did he later. When she left, Darius turned on Albert who was still seated and shouted at him, told him he would *have* to apologize.

"You must bow down! You must bow down to her!" he shouted.

But it was as if Albert did not hear him. He remained seated, staring into empty space. "What is the matter with you?" Darius shouted. "Don't you hear me?"

Still Albert said nothing. Speak, speak, I screamed silently. Albert rose and left the room, and seconds later his brothers and Deirdre followed him. I would have followed too, but Emma held me fast.

That afternoon (March 18, 1837) Darius made us swear another oath of fealty to him and at three o'clock we formally declared war on Albert and his brothers.

As we prepared for war, I confess, my enthusiasm for battle grew. I began to yearn in some undefined way for glory . . . for honor. I began to feel tempted to risk myself— but I shall equivocate no longer—in short, I began to lust for war!

❋   ❋   ❋

After lunch (barley cakes and olives), Lowe and I cut the sweet-smelling boughs of cypress that flank both sides of the cave. After lighting the wooden torch and placing them on the small altar in the second chamber and after performing some other acts, we returned home taking the long way through the Gardens.

Perhaps it was the blood that we spilled, or the chanting, or the dances that we performed that heightened our sensibilities, but as we walked home through the Gardens we thought (for one brief moment) that we understood the meaning of the Garden. That beneath its wanton and capricious nature, its jumble of styles, it vagaries and variations, that beneath its more obvious themes of war and peace, old gods and ruined civilizations there was spelled out a more subtle message about the immense difficulty of maintaining one's dreams in a reality one does not understand . . . or can barely tolerate.

❋   ❋   ❋

Edward's *Diary of Moral Inventory* (pages 106–110)

Do you know Kant's aphorism: From the crooked wood of which man is made, nothing quite straight can be built.

You stress a rigorous self-examination; you assure me if I do that it will lead of itself to self-renewal, that I need only be willing.

Why can I not be straightforward with you yet? Why can I

not tell you exactly what it was I did that has made me live in the shadow of guilt ever since I have been a child? I believe you love me and yet—I hesitate . . .

Perhaps as I write of those past events it will come out by itself.

I was explaining to you what I thought were the *belli causae*—by the way, my brother William does not agree with me. I have been writing to him. It is because of you that the breach between us is healing. He says—but I will quote him directly, "We went to war, Edward, because we had prepared for war. Really, it is as simple as that. We had been studying war, we had played at war, and so we wanted to put into action what we had learned on a daily basis for almost six months.

"There was an incident; Darius took advantage of it. As I would have done, as any military man would have done. Darius had the makings of a brilliant general; it is unfortunate that he frittered away his life on nonessentials. War was his real métier. Really, Edward, it was as simple as that."

I agree. I would be a fool not to. But there was another reason, one he may have forgotten or had not realized. I do not believe that William or I or even Emma would have fought were it not for the fact that we sensed that our father had given us his tacit consent. Not that he knew anything. He knew nothing; we had told him nothing, *but* after the drill he began to suspect and on the strength of those suspicions he gave us every encouragement. We had signaled something. He had received the message. And he signaled back to us: if there were to be a contest *we* were to be the victors.

Our army was called the Cordeliers. Darius named us that after a group of Franciscan monks who had successfully repelled the Infidels in St. Louis's reign. Naturally we called Albert's army the Infidels. We wore a white cord around our waist as part of our military costume.

I would like to tell you a little about the organization of our army. It was so devilishly clever, so cunning in a way. A miniature army, a miniature war, a miniature exercise, and so correct in its details, a perfect overture, an *Einführung* for what was to come.

Darius was of course the supreme commander in chief; I was quartermaster general; William was in charge of drill and transportation; Emma was appointed adjutant general, in charge of prisoners of war and discipline, and one of the Malkin boys, Henry, the oldest, was our recruitment officer and paymaster.

A word about the Malkin boys. There were five of them: Henry, Thomas, Charles, James, and Fitzroy. They were the illegitimate children of a whore called Jessie Malkin who ran a brothel in our parish on Wickfield and Collards lanes with her lover and owner of the brothel, Henry Fitzcrawford, the sixth earl of Oxham, second marquess of Beaufort, and the titular baron of Langly. I give the complete title because Darius took such an inordinate interest in the Malkin boys. Though he called them "the aitch-droppers," and offered to teach them English as he taught us Greek, he obviously approved of them. They were, after all, aristocracy.

In one of several strokes of genius, Darius decided not to use the boys from the houses around the park, who had paid tribute to the order as soldiers. Dismissing them as "tradesmen's children," he decided to recruit mercenaries instead, the "armed rabble" as he called it. And so our soldiers were paid: a ha'penny if they showed up for drill and a promise of a tuppence for battle.

Badly clothed, ill fed, the slum children were willing enough to train to be soldiers, to be herded onto the battlefield. "Let Albert have the milksops, the tradesmen's boys," said Darius, "soft, civilized boys, not like Malkin's boys, real savages." We could have had any number of boys but we recruited only sixty.

We had one regiment divided into three companies: the rifle corps, the grenadiers, and the pikemen.

The riflemen wore cockades and old military medals that Ricci had been sent to buy in the city. They were taught by me to care for and load their slingshots with pebbles.

By May first we had accumulated more than twenty pounds of pebbles, which we stored in a cave in Marlborough Gardens. They were kept in wagons, wooden catapults on wheels that Ricci made for us. He also made our pennons and supplied liquor for our army: whiskey for the officers, wine for the troops.

The grenadiers, the strongest and the biggest boys in the regiment, carried their grenades (firecrackers) in a pouch on their right side with a broad belt over their left shoulder in the front of their match case.

As for the pikemen, though we called them men, their average age was ten. They carried both long and short staves.

Such was our army: five staff officers and sixty soldiers.

The first declaration of war was made twenty-four hours after Albert had refused to bow. It was delivered by William to Albert, who was playing with his brothers at the lake. He saluted smartly, William told us, as he had been taught and said, as we had told him to: "We, the Cordeliers, solemnly declare war on Solomon's children and any and all supporters." Then he handed him the note that said the same thing. Albert read it, William reported, and then he laughed, tore it up, and turned his back on him.

"He shall have to beg forgiveness for that too," said Darius.

There were further declarations. But they were all ignored. Albert would not fight. No matter what we did (and there were many provocations), he would not engage.

One day I and the Malkin boys captured Albert's fleet and after breaking his ships into pieces, smashing them to bits in front of him, we burned what was left. But he merely watched us and then when it was over he walked away.

Soon after that, we kidnapped Deirdre. We ambushed her as she was picking flowers in the Marshes. It was Fitzroy who rushed up to her and grabbed her by her arms, which startled her, but only for a moment, for when she saw Emma and myself she began to laugh with pleasure, telling us in her lisping tones how very glad she was to see us, and how she had missed us these many weeks. Could she come with us, please, she asked? Yes, we told her, but she must hurry. "I shall try," she answered. I relate this fiasco to show to you what lengths we would go to make war. We were desperate to fight.

We took her to Blenheim Wood and tied her to the Sacred Oak. We told her she was to stay there like Maartel. That frightened her a bit so we gave her raisins and nuts and sugar candy to eat and William told her the story of Meki, the Evil Frog from Bristol, while we waited for Albert to come and rescue her. And of course when he did come—we had sent him a note saying "Fight or Deirdre shall be tortured!"—she refused to go home with him! Utter and complete humiliation. We who had wanted glory and Honor had been made to feel silly instead!

But we continued with our provocations, our goadings, our aggravations for we knew that sooner or later we would reawaken in Albert's breast his innate enthusiasm for war. . . .

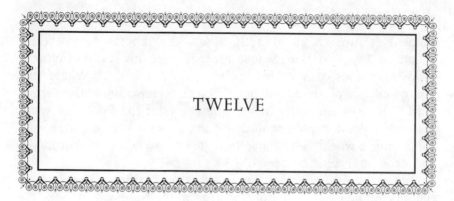

TWELVE

MARLBOROUGH GARDENS, 1936

THE DAY being mild, we decided to take a walk through the streets behind the Gardens. Lowe carries the notebooks in which are listed all the names and locations of the slum boys who fought with Darius on that May morning a hundred years ago.

A quick look at the map of London will show that Marlborough Gardens is situated in the eastern part of St. Giles parish that the broad avenues of Wickford and Beaufort, on which once stood fine, red-bricked, terraced houses, are parallel to the north-south axis of the Gardens. Between these avenues and the Gardens is a small maze of twisted streets and cobbled alleyways on which stood the mean, squat, stone houses of the poor, the source of Malthus's nightmares. It is from these houses the color of coal smoke that Darius's conscripts, Malkin's Recruits, were recruited: Thomas Oakes, Danny Flately, Padric Riley, Michal Flynn . . . there are more than sixty names.

We are indebted to the 1840 census report for the exact location of the homes of the boys who fought in Darius's army, a report compiled by Reverend James Bottome. In and of itself, it is an interesting document, for the reverend like most of the clergy of that time was a fervid Malthusian ("Life everywhere always tends to exceed the warrant for it"—Malthus), which gives the report a flavor of restrained hysteria. With each new birth that is recorded lurks the specter of famine and disease. His remarks and

expletives are strewn liberally across the report—against the
name of Jessie Malkin, whose brothel faced his study window,
and the names of her sons are written "Jezebel!", "Whore of
Babylon!", "White Sepulcher!" "Satan's mistress!" "Fornica-
tor!" He asks anxiously in the margins after the Poor Act was
passed: "What person would not marry with a direct view of
obtaining a weekly allowance or at least a reliance on that kind
of recourse in time of need?"

Not only did he preach on Sundays on Malthus's preventive
checks but he gave bimonthly lectures on the Necessity for Sexual
Continence, and the Necessity for the Postponement of Marriage.
And those in his parish who were willing to undergo the ultimate
sacrifice—the vow of celibacy—were given a bronze medal, quite
handsome with the single Latin word inscribed on it: *Oportet* (it
is necessary).

At sunset we walked to the northern perimeter of the church
grounds and stood in front of the Union Work House (built in
1834). From there, if we look in the direction of the Gardens we
can see the temple on its artificial hill, its white luminosity glowing
across the increasingly depressing space of squalid architecture,
its whiteness ablaze in the last rays of the sun. We return to the
Gardens past the pauper's cemetery, its acres stretching eastward,
row upon row of crosses, unembellished, unadorned.

City of Childhood

XXIV

A DECLARATION OF LOVE

F ROM the very beginning I was my cousin's confidante. "I
am drawn to you," he told me. "We are kindred souls,
Emma, outcasts, aliens." I received the information with my
customary gravity.

One of the very first things my cousin ever said to me was:
"Let me kiss the mark on your temple."

I recoiled. "No," I said, "you must not. It is Satan's mark,
the devil's signature."

"It isn't. It is God's mark of grace, I am sure of it." And

taking my hand gently away from my temple, he placed his lips on the mark and kissed it.

A week earlier, Darius told me that when his father returned from Germany he had been awakened in the early hours of the morning by his parents' fighting. "We had supped *en famille*. It had been a fairly civil exercise. My father had attempted to be friendly with me; on my part, I saw no reason not to reciprocate. Momma was silent for a change. I went to bed that night for the first time with a certain measure of hope; perhaps there would be a change, perhaps we could live together in peace. And then I was awakened. It must have been past midnight. I had been dreaming of you Emma . . . I heard my father shouting. He was completely out of control.

" 'You have gone too far this time!' I heard him say. 'I shall murder you. I shall! I shall! I shall burn down the house with you and the boy in it! And then I shall kill myself!' I heard her laugh and taunt him with: '*Meraviglioso!* A good idea but why not skip the prelude and just kill yourself and Darius and I shall live together happily ever after!' He screamed back at her: 'To have an affair is a disgrace though I might have been able to bear it or ignore it, I don't know which, but to leave your notes addressed to that idiot, to leave them around so that anyone can read them! Not only myself, though that is bad enough! But your son could, your precious Darius!'

"I opened my door. He looked deranged. I could hardly believe it was my father standing outside her door clutching to his breast some papers, presumably the letters that he was raving about. His well-bred face, normally remote, was twisted into the most painful grimace. I closed my door again. I stood behind my door and put my fingers in my ears as they continued. 'Stop!' I screamed, 'Stop!' But they were so involved in their mutual self-destruction, they never heard me."

It was the day after we declared war on Albert and his brothers that Darius proposed to me. He began by talking about Albert.

"You see," he explained to me, "I thought Albert was my creature, that *his* defection was impossible. He would never leave. Never dare leave me, never be capable of betraying me. He was mine to do with what I wished. . . ."

We were in the alcove of his sitting room, which he used as a study. Scagliola columns marked the division between the sitting room and the alcove, and while the sitting room was lush, replete with festoons; carved, modeled, painted garlands of flowers; fruits and leaves; ormolu candelabras; gilt metal chandeliers; and the like, the study in marked contrast was austere. A simply furnished room filled only with marble-topped bookcases on which casts of early philosophers stood.

Darius was such a beautiful boy, so beautifully dressed. I do not think I have ever been attracted sexually to a man since who did not have the same peacock splendor about him. That day he was wearing long woolen gray trousers, and a lemon-yellow, silk waistcoat. One arm in its tight fitting sleeve was flung over the back of his chair; the other close by his side revealed the long olive fingers adorned with a few simple gold rings.

"Come here, Emma." I did. "Kiss me." I did. "You agree that I must revenge myself on him."

"Yes," I replied.

"I love you, Emma. I shall always love you. When we are quite grown up, I shall ask you to marry me. They will not allow it of course. They will say we may not marry because we are first cousins. We shall have to marry in secret. But today I pledge myself to you. Do you, Emma, pledge yourself to me?"

"I do."

"And do you vow to be faithful to me as I vow to be faithful to you always?"

"I do."

"And to love me forever as I shall love you forever?"

"I do."

"And you shall tell no one."

"I shall tell no one."

He sighed and moved close to me. We sat arm in arm until the daylight faded and the room was dark. "You must leave now, Emma," he said, pushing me from him gently. "Remember that I love you."

I left but I could not take my eyes off him and so like some strange insect I walked backward, my arms behind me groping for the doorknob which when I reached it I twisted, and the door opened. The closing of the door had the effect of an amputation.

City of Childhood
XXVII
THE DRILL REVIEW

T HE adults had come, at Darius's request, on a Sunday afternoon to see a drill review, an hour's entertainment, before Sunday dinner at Elijah's house. The drill review was devised and directed by Darius. They would have liked to have refused but could not. Perhaps it would rain. . . .

It looked as if it might on the morning of the drill review, but it didn't; instead the clouds were driven out of the sky by wind, and the sun shone bright and clear on Nannies Plain, on the reviewing stand, and on the regiment of sixty boys standing in three companies in two ranks.

They were dressed in white shirts, black vests, and brown britches. Their tricornered hats were garnished with white cockades and their waists were girdled with white cords. A few weeks earlier they had been bathed and deloused under Maria's vigilant eyes. Today there was a soldierly, respectable look about them.

In front of each of the companies stood their captains: Emma, Edward, and Henry Malkin. Essentially they wore the same costume as their soldiers except over their vests they wore scarlet jackets with copper buttons, each of their tricornered hats held scarlet plumes. In front of them stood William. He was dressed in sky-blue trousers, a white silk shirt, and a blue leather vest. He held a white silk flag on which was stitched in gold the letter C. At the very end of the flagpole, small bells had been attached and they tinkled as William's arm grew tired and trembled. On either side of the regiment stood two groups of very young boys dressed in brown smocks. They carried cymbals.

The gardeners had built the reviewing stand under Darius's careful instructions. It was placed just in front of the winter garden.

On it were three rows of benches and behind that was a row of wooden chairs. The two nannies sat together on the chairs: Jakes and Burden (Grindal had been sent to Saddler's Grove in disgrace). In the row directly in front of them sat Brian Herrod with his daughters Letitia and Mary-Anne, dressed in mourning. But Vanessa, who sat in front of them with her mother Mathilda, was not in mourning. Ever since the reading of the codicil Mathilda had dressed Vanessa in increasingly lavish costumes. The family's criticism fell on deaf ears. Her stock reply was that she was only doing what she was sure Jorem would have wanted her to do.

Today Vanessa wore a skirt of white cashmere with a deep border of azure-green velvet that matched her velvet bodice and her cashmere shawl. Even her silk shoes were azure green. A young Aphrodite. She and her mother, who was dressed in dull purple taffeta, were the only occupants of that row.

In the front row on the right side sat Guinivere, Solomon, and their children, Albert, Jacob, Joshua, and Deirdre. Next to them in the center sat Elijah and Theodisia. On the left of Theodisia sat Consuelo, for once subdued, in brown velvet and a short black, wool mantle. The only touch of color was the orange feather on the brim of her black silk bonnet. Beside her sat Joseph, next to him Darius in his "coronation" clothes. Next to him squeezed into the corner sat Maria and Ricci.

Darius rose and the cymbals clashed. He saluted the soldiers. The cymbals clashed again. Then moving past his mother to the middle of the stand, he went down the short flight of stairs. Quietly, with dignity, he walked out onto the field where he walked down the line slowly, inspecting each boy carefully, stopping in front of one or another of them to say a few words, and then he returned to the stand. The cymbals clashed again. He stood still in the middle of the first step of the staircase, his back to his soldiers, as he explained to the "gracious visitors" that with their indulgence he would now address a few words to his comrades in arms before they began the drill. He hoped it would please the visitors, for he and his men had worked hard to please them. Then he turned to the regiment; the cymbals clashed again. He raised his hand and there was silence.

"Fellow soldiers," he began, his voice grave and author-itative, "it is important to remember, in these times of tur-bulence, that the Code of Drill was first devised to maintain law and order, in the fifteenth century in France, when law-less bands roamed, as they do today. To recall that within the drill are contained the rules for decent government . . . a disciplined government . . . a stable government. Drill is the foundation of good character: stability, steadfastness. Those are the watch words of decency: law, order, . . . justice."

An errant breeze whipped Vanessa's bonnet ribbons into her face. Her mother in a tender gesture caught them and smoothed them down gently over the young girl's budding breasts.

"Instinctively," continued Darius, "all men are patriots. Patriotism is an instinct of a gentleman. Our England, our precious England, is a young empire which one day shall be the greatest empire the world has ever known! But with that status, my dear comrades, goes a solemn sense of obligation. *If* we shall rule others—and we shall—we must be able to rule ourselves. *If* we are to bring to others the glorious tra-ditions of our culture, *if* we are to promulgate the British race, to bring civilization to the barbaric hordes in China, in India, and elsewhere, we must know discipline and obe-dience for ourselves."

Solomon absentmindedly tapped his cane. He was won-dering why his son Albert and the twins were not in the field. It would have done them good. What Darius was saying pleased him. Discipline, obedience, steadfastness—yes, he would speak to Albert about it.

Albert was feeling faint. The desire to tell someone the truth, and the impossibility of doing so had begun to burden him. But he could say nothing, could he? He could do noth-ing, could he? He had taken an oath. Not only had he lost Sidney and Darius (for he still loved Darius), he feared some-how in a way that was beginning to frighten him that he was losing his mother's love. More than anything in the world, he wanted his mother to be proud of him. He wanted her face to glow with the same pride that he saw now in Aunt Theodisia's face.

"But there is another reason for drill," continued Darius's melodious voice. "Soon we shall send forth troops, troops of stalwart warriors to foreign lands where we shall occupy the waste spaces of the earth! There shall be expeditions. What we do here today is but a dress rehearsal for what is to come. Soon we shall be involved in combat, combat in which we shall have the glorious opportunity to die for our country! To plant the seeds of our culture, our religion . . . our traditions!"

Guinivere's eyes filled with tears. "To die for our country . . ." Sidney, Sidney. Oh, she had the oddest feeling—oh, she could not bear it!—that Sidney, her little Sidney, had died for her. Why, why did she think those terrible things? Where did they come from? What was wrong with her? Would she ever forget? Would the pain ever go away?

"We have a destiny. We have a mission. We shall be the civilizing force in a barbaric world. We shall rule others. Comrades, my dear comrades"—Darius's voice broke—"I promise you there shall be battles worthy of you! Many men shall be lost but the gain to humanity will be well worth the price. For—to die in battle is to die in glory!"

Darius removed his hat. On cue the cymbals clashed once more. The drill review began:

"Right by squads!" the captains shouted. Then, "Squad right! Right march! . . . March shoulder arms!"

The boys lifted their poles smartly and advanced down the field, moving into columns of four. At each new order the cymbals clashed.

"One, two, three, four . . ." the officers kept time.

The drill continued through the basic formations: from open column to closed column; from square to echelon, from echelon to square. . . .

"Oh, I do say, look at that!" shouted Elijah. "They have mastered the cordon! *Bravo! Bravo!*"

The squads passed the reviewing stand. The officers saluted.

"Eyes front! Halt!" The boys tramped to a halt.

"Right face! . . . Present arms!"

They stood, the boy soldiers in a perfect square, four deep, facing outward.

"Dismissed!" came the command.

They stood briefly, for a few seconds, and then broke into groups and began to leave Nannies Plain, winding their various ways past the statues.

Elijah had removed his hat and was waving it. "Well done, boys, well done!" he shouted. "Bravo!" He said to Darius who was standing next to him, "My deep-felt congratulations, Darius. Quite, quite remarkable. I am impressed. Impressed." Momentarily he seemed to have forgotten his prejudice against his nephew. "Your speech . . . profound, impressive, yes, quite remarkable." Suddenly he clasped Darius by his shoulders and drew him to his breast. He murmured in his ear, "I am so very proud of you."

Mathilda rushed up to Elijah and interrupted them. "It's disgraceful," she said, her face red and angry, "disgraceful that you have allowed your only daughter to participate—"

Elijah ignored her and turned to Joseph. "My dear Joseph, I do believe your son has come around. I am proud of him today, as you should be also." To Mathilda, who had continued to harass him, he said, "As for my daughter, Emma, I shall do with her as I wish. She shall not grow up to be useless ninnies like yours are already!"

"How dare you! How dare you speak of my children in that way. Brian! say something to him. Now!"

"Oh come now," Brian said peacefully, "let us not spoil the children's fun with one of our boring quarrels. I daresay everyone has a right to rear their children as they see fit. We are all free, I daresay. But . . . well, Elijah, I do think your description of our brood does seem a bit strong."

"You are right," said Elijah magnanimously, "and I apologize." He liked Brian even though he was a poor businessman. He had some sympathy for the man besides that. His sister was a headstrong woman. And yes, Jorem had favored her; just as he favored Emma. . . .

He walked over to the contessa, deciding that he should congratulate her too, the hero's mother, the mother of the speech maker. "Congratulations, Consuelo. I am proud of Darius today. You should be proud of him, too."

She cast him a malevolent look which he chose to ignore. A demented woman. *"Addio,"* she said to Darius as she walked off the reviewing stand, leaving her husband there.

"Albert, come here," said Elijah. "Explain to me how it

is that you have not taken part in this glorious demonstration. I should think that you and your brothers would have been proud to do so. Proud. I confess I am proud of Edward, and William, and Emma, too. Yes, she had her moment of glory, too. And your cousin Darius. *He* most of all. The whole tableaux was quite remarkable. I should have thought that you and your brothers would have been eager to participate. I know if I were a boy again I would have been proud to be a part of this glorious spectacle . . . this glorious achievement! I do hope it wasn't the recent tragedy in your family that prevented you and your brothers from participating. The dead must not take precedence over the living. Besides, had Sidney lived he would have wanted to be part of it. Well, answer me, boy."

Since the drill began, Albert had been dreading this confrontation with his uncle. He knew it would take place. He had been thinking about what to say to him throughout the drill. He admired his uncle; he wanted to be in his good graces. "Proud," Elijah had used the word four times. He gave his uncle his prepared answer: "I am in agreement with you, Sir, but I am more interested in the admiralty."

"The admiralty . . . hmmm . . . Nelson and Trafalgar, I suppose. A worthy interest, of course. Admirable. Well then,"—he smiled down at Albert—"may we expect to be invited then in the near future to a regatta? Perhaps later in the spring?"

"I have not as yet thought about such an event but now that you have mentioned it I shall give it every consideration, Sir."

"And the twins, are they, too, interested exclusively in the maritime?"

"If I may speak for them, Sir. They, too, like myself are enthralled by the sagas of the sea."

Solomon joined them. He had overheard his brother's questions and his son's answers. He loved the way his son had answered Elijah. He had stood up to him, not that he had been cheeky, no, the boy understood that elders were to be respected, but neither had he been craven. His tone, the boy's facial expressions, the boy's words, all had been exactly what Solomon wanted them to be. Yes, thought the father, I am proud of him. He handled himself properly.

When we are dead and gone, he shall be able to handle the business properly. Sidney! Albert would have to do without Sidney now; it would be only the three of them, the twins and himself. Yes, Albert would be able to handle Edward. And William, too. But just before he spoke, the thought crossed his mind again: why hadn't his sons taken part in the drill today? He didn't believe what he had just heard Albert say but he would support him. Perhaps later in private Albert would tell him the truth.

"They've done well today, your boys," Solomon said to Elijah. He did not mention Emma. Her participation had disturbed him but there was no point in mentioning it. Elijah always did as he pleased. "But each of us has a fine set of lads. Mine are interested in the maritime, yours in the military. If we all pursued the same interests, it would be, I dare say, a dull world, wouldn't it?"

But Elijah ignored him. He was hungry. He took out his watch and looked at it. Almost two o'clock. He turned to his wife, said, "Let us go," and holding her by the arm walked past his brother down the stairs.

After his departure, the other Forsters, singly and in groups, left the stand—the day had almost become too warm—and made their way across Nannies Plain toward the South Gate and Elijah's house where they reconvened and dined as usual on one of Mrs. Farnley's sumptuous Sunday afternoon dinners.

City of Childhood
XXIX
TACIT CONSENT

DID Poppa suspect? I often wondered because of a certain incident that took place just after the review. But before I relate the episode I wish to say something about the drill itself, which, more than anything that preceded it— Darius's coronation, the creation of the Order of Rimini, the war lectures, the preparations for war, the declaration of war, the creation of the Cordeliers—described, and extended for me (for us) the reality of our secret life together as children.

On that day, the day of the drill, I clearly saw our "invisible" world operating for once in full view of our parents who, like victims of a conjurer's trick, remained unaware, perceiving only what we had vouchsafed.

I remember the heady feeling, as if I were drunk, the feeling of exultation as I witnessed and was part of Darius's sleight of hand. I am putting into words what, of course, I had no words for then. I remember the singular excitement caused by his placing our secret life in jeopardy, so to speak. For what would happen to us if someone betrayed us? Would Albert, we wondered, in a sort of delicious delirium of fear betray us? Or the twins? Or Deirdre? Or even one of ourselves? The thought made me (us) tremble. The temptation to betray that morning was so strong it was palpable.

But to get back to Poppa: even before the incident, which I shall relate shortly, I believe that Poppa suspected something, at least an alignment of sorts: Darius and his children versus Albert and his brothers.

In the days that followed the drill we waited for Albert to declare war. Surely he would. Would *want* to. Now. But he didn't. The fact that he did three weeks later has remained a puzzle to me to this day. You see I never did find out what exactly brought my cousin Albert to his boiling point.

Somehow I don't believe it was the following episode.

When Albert defected I began to hate him in the same way I hated Grindal. With every atom of my being. I began to dream of laying siege to Albert's house. I dreamt about Albert's stupid fat father, Solomon, and his skinny, ugly mother, Guinivere. Though before this happened they had been my favorite aunt and uncle, particularly Guinivere. I dreamed about starving them out, of laying siege to them and bringing ladders to their house in stealth in the middle of the night and going in through their windows and bayonetting them while their children stood all in a cluster pleading with me not to.

I dreamt of tearing off Guinivere's rings and tearing fat Solomon's watch chain out of his vest, and lunging at my cousins with my teeth, which in the dream were long and sharp—gigantic teeth—that tore at everything. I dreamt of storming the house, shattering the doors with my bare fists. I dreamt of rooms burning and vases broken and how we, myself and Darius, would toast our victory in front of their broken fireplace. Drinking the blood-red wine out of their crystal goblets.

And when Albert rescued Deirdre, stood there proud and calm, and called us children. "You are children," he said, "nothing but children. I am tired of make-believe. I want no more of it." I knew, even then, that what he said was not true. It was *he* who was the child. *He* who had returned to Guinivere and Solomon. *He* who was once more his parent's child. It was *he* who had betrayed Darius, the Order of Rimini, the secret world he had created.

When nothing happened despite our latest provocation (the kidnapping of Deirdre) I took it upon myself to spy on Albert. I was outside the gardener's shed listening to Albert's ceremony when Hollis, one of the gardeners who disliked me, caught hold of me.

"What be ye standing on my boxes for? What they be for, Miss, is not for you to be standin' on. They not be toys. What be ye doin' 'ere anyway? Where be your nanny? An' why, Miss, do they be lettin' you run 'round like a boy? Aye an' I've seen the whole heathen' lot of you runnin' around Blenheim Woods up to no good!"

I tried to wriggle out of his grasp but he held me fast, his fingers digging into the nape of my neck. If only he hadn't shouted, because of course my cousins heard and they came running out of the shed. Albert thanked Hollis for catching me and told him, "We'll take charge now. Jacob and Joshua, take hold of her arms. You may go now, Hollis."

Hollis was a curious soul and he may not have wanted to go but he obeyed Albert. "Yes, Master Albert," he said, and left.

My cousins brought me into the shed where they propped me up on a table on which sat some clay pots and broken shards.

"Well, what have you to say for yourself?" Albert asked. "You've come to spy, haven't you, Emma? What's to become of you? You're a terrible human being, you know. Hollis has told us what you and your brothers and Darius are up to."

I tried not to cry, but the tears came anyway, ran down my cheeks, salty and stinging. He began shaking his finger in my face. "I hate having you as my cousin! I am ashamed of you. Why can't you be like Vanessa? You're absolutely awful looking. And you smell—"

I opened my mouth and clamped my teeth down hard on his wagging finger, clamped down on it so he could not move it. Let him bleed to death. Let them all bleed to death. I would bite them all to death. I heard the crunch of bone. The yell he let out was inhuman but I would not let go. The twins pried my teeth open, but they had to use *all* their strength to do so. He kept on screaming, jumping up and down with pain. Then the blood suddenly spurted out into the air, the drops falling everywhere, a shower of blood. On me, on him, on everything. He held his poor finger cupped in his left hand, roaring like some mad animal. The twins were screaming too. In all the commotion that followed I slipped away. I remember that on the way home I stopped at the lake to wash out the blood that had spilled on my face, my hands, and my dress.

A week later Uncle Solomon came to our house on a Sunday morning after church with the twins. He must speak to Elijah immediately, he told Mrs. Farnley, on a matter of utmost importance and he wanted Emma, William, and Edward to be present. He was shouting so that we heard him where we were in the library with Poppa, who heard our lessons on Sunday mornings after church.

The confrontation between Poppa and his younger brother was brief and to the point. Solomon to his credit did not mince words. He told Poppa how Albert finally had come to him with his finger after it had festered. "That it did not have to be amputated, that septicemia did not occur, is a miracle, Sir. I called Doctor Harlowe who told me in private, after examining it—Albert had told me he had hurt himself accidentally with his pocket knife—that that simply could not be true. Albert, he said, had been bitten, and not by an animal, but by a human being. Did I care to examine it myself? And that was what made it so serious. I did examine it and I saw with my own eyes what Doctor Harlowe claimed, but when I questioned Albert, he denied it. I pressed him but he refused to change his story. It was Deirdre who told me what had happened. 'Emma bit him. She hates all of us and has promised to bite all of us, including me, and I am frightened, Poppa.' "

"Sir, your daughter is mad. I have always thought so. So do others. Emma should be sent away. Locked up in Bedlam. Now, Sir, what are you going to do about it?"

I never admired my father more than at that moment. He had been taken completely unawares, but he never hesitated for a moment.

"Sir, this is a preposterous tale."

"Preposterous?"

"Yes, preposterous. Surely you are not asking me to give credence to a statement of a backward child of four, a statement beyond which there is not a shred of evidence."

"You are truly despicable, Elijah. But I thought you might say something of the sort so I have brought Jacob with me. Albert is still too ill"—he would not admit to Elijah that Albert had refused to come—"to tell you what he told me under oath. Under oath, Elijah! Now do not be afraid, Jacob. Tell your uncle what you told me. Speak up!"

"Sir, Emma without any reason or cause last week on ten April, Thursday afternoon, did bite my brother Albert in the gardener's shed. And when she would not let go—and she would not, Sir—we had to pry her mouth open."

Ignoring what Jacob had said, Elijah seized on something he was quite sure his brother had overlooked.

"And what exactly were you and your brothers doing in the gardener's shed on Thursday afternoon, Jacob?" Jacob quickly lowered his eyes as a pink flush suffused his face. Then my father walked over to his desk where he kept the family Bible and placing his hand on it said, "I bit your son's finger in the shed last Thursday afternoon."

"My God, Sir, what does that mean?" asked an outraged Solomon.

"Oh then you do not believe it, Sir. But yet I have taken an oath, Sir. An oath!"

"Enough. I will hear no more. I have done my duty. You will have only yourself to blame for whatever happens. Come, Jacob." And he left with his children.

After they had left, Poppa locked the library door and turning to us he asked in a low and quiet voice: "Is it true Emma? Did you bite Albert?"

I had not expected that. Fear poured through my body leaving me breathless. I could not answer. I could say nothing. It was Edward who spoke.

"Do you remember the drill, Poppa, to which you and Momma were invited?"

"Yes, of course I do."

"Well, Poppa, they've been angry with us ever since. They blame us for not inviting them to join. They forgot that we did ask them. That it was they who would not join us because they said they hated Darius." I could not believe what I was hearing. My brother Edward was lying for the first time to his father. But so easily, so expertly. "We don't know," he continued, "what happened to Albert's finger, or if someone actually bit him, or how he was injured except, Sir, that it had nothing to do with any of us. Albert has always disliked Emma."

Just for an instant I wanted to tell Poppa everything. I sensed that he didn't really believe Edward. For a moment he looked tired—but I didn't tell him. Then Poppa said: "I am proud of all three of you. If there is to be a contest between you and your cousins, or an 'agon' as the Greeks say, I want my children to know how I feel about winning. I feel the way the Greeks did—that winning is best of all, that in any competition second best is nothing. The Greeks had no prizes for second or third best. There was only *one* prize, only *one* victor."

We thought we understood his message. That whatever it took to win, whether it be underhanded or brutal or violent, that winning—there was only one prize, one victor—that winning was more important than anything else. He and Darius were far more alike than they realized.

Shortly after that, Henry Malkin reported to us that Albert was forming an army. But as I said before, I never did find out what brought Albert to the boiling point.

—⸙⸙⸙—

Edward's *Diary of Moral Inventory* (pages 203–205)

Albert declared war on the Cordeliers on 20 May, 1837. Joshua delivered the message. "Prepare to meet our army on the morning of the twenty-sixty of May on Marlborough Marshes. We will not stop until we are victorious and you are slain."

"He has come out of his tent," declared Darius; he sent back the message, quoting Hector, "You will never kill me—I am not the one who is fated to die."

Up till now I have not spoken to you about how I felt to be fighting against my beloved cousin Albert, the first person I had loved outside my immediate family.

When he left the room on the afternoon that he would not bow to the contessa, I believe that was the most painful moment in my life thus far. I knew that when he left and I did not follow him that I had lost Albert. I did not realize at the time that it might be only temporary. I thought it was forever. On the other hand, when he left and we declared war, there was the promise of war and I became angry with him when he would not play War. For after the Drill Review, and after I felt that my father approved, I wanted war more than ever. Surely Albert would have to go to war now, I thought. I woke up each day expectant. We had insulted him, kidnapped Deirdre, burned his fleet, humiliated him, frightened him. Surely he would declare war; the war game would begin. But still there was no response. Nothing. It was as if to him we had died. We were no longer living. No matter how hard we provoked there was no response. It maddened us; it incensed us. We were driven to despair. Darius glowered, but we did not stop preparing and as the weapons mounted, the strategy developed, and the soldiers (ourselves) became disciplined and eager. We wanted war more than ever.

I don't know when the horrendous idea came into my mind. But I was certain that if it were done (I didn't want to but I must, I must), Albert would finally fight, that it would work, that it would be the key to unlocking Albert's anger.

I shall try now to put into words what I did, as plainly and clearly as possible, though I do not trust words. (During these past few months that I have spent with you, in our daily contacts with one another, a hope had been kindled in my mind and heart that it is possible to be forgiven for any sin that I have committed, for *this* one too.)

One night in May, I, Edward Forster, age ten, stole into the gardener's shed where I took Sidney's advertisement out of its sacred hiding place. I held it in my hands and then deliberately and with malice aforethought lit a match to it and watched it burn. Then I burnt some scraps of paper I had taken with me in case there would not be enough ashes and added it to the small heap of ashes. I then gathered the ashes and put them in the box with the note I had brought with me: "The Cordeliers." I put the box back into its sacred hiding place.

The next day Albert declared war.

As I said, I do not trust words. I shall not give you any reason for doing what I did. And if I have, ignore it for I know only too well how reasons become excuses. And I do not wish to be excused. I wish to be forgiven. There is a difference as you have pointed out to me so eloquently. And I am able to confess since you have led me to the path of faith that believes that there exists in the universe a love so powerful that it will forgive any evil without asking evil to explain itself.

"Forgive me Father for I have sinned . . ."

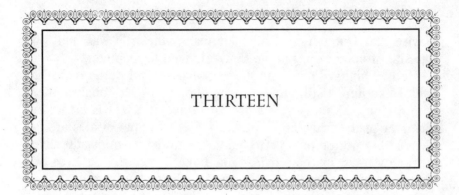

THIRTEEN

MARLBOROUGH GARDENS, 1936

THE following is a compilation of Edward's and Emma's account of the Marlborough War. The first was written for the serious perusal of the Moravian minister, Dr. Garth Blackstone; the second to amuse and titillate Emma's neighbor in Weimar, the Count von Hoenfenschtall.

The Villa Aubeitz, Weimar
16 October, 1884

Our closest neighbor, Count von Hoenfenschtall, rode over today to "chat," but as always it was to complain about his current mistress, an Italian woman. My Beloved[35] pointed out to him that if he insists on an Italian mistress, he must be prepared to put up with temperament. We smile, all three of us. My Beloved is the personification of amiable serenity, and she herself is an Italian woman. It is I who am *"cappricio"*!

The count is a lively gentleman in his seventies and it is on his

---

35. As yet, we have not been able to ascertain the identity of "Beloved." She appears and disappears mysteriously in the *Weimar Journal*. Italian and female, Emma's companion in her old age. But whether it was just that, or an *amitie amoreuse*, or something more intimate we have not been able to learn. This past month, however, we have learned that the villa was left to a woman called Amelia Santori Murray, and that she subsequently sold it to a family called Leutenhoffs. In 1916 the Munich Bank became its owner.—*R. Lowe*

advice that I bought the villa. He claims the villa was built on the site of an ancient temple that belonged to Demeter.

He is a military man, an old campaigner, and perhaps that is why I like him. I still enjoy talking about war. He fought under von Steinmetz, and lost his arm at Gravelotte. He is a former member of the Prussian Cuirassiers. His principal estates are in Prussia but not being able to abide his mother, who is still alive at ninety-three in their *schloss* on Lake Tollensee, he lives on their "summer estate," which is across the valley from us.

In one recent conversation with us, he became so excited that, momentarily I thought he would faint, his rouged cheeks paled. I offered to open up his laces for him, but he told me, "No!" and waved me away.

I thought it best to have him stay for lunch, which he was only too delighted to do. We discussed strategy and tactics, old campaigns, and the battle of Rossbach, in which fought his father, an officer of the famous Fifth Regiment, The Regiment Schwarzen Hausaren. He lost his life at Jena.

For the rest of the afternoon he spoke about von Seidletz, hero of Rossbach. "There are those commanders who have their troops' admiration and respect, and then there is von Seidletz. It was he who had his soldiers' love! They would have followed him to Hell and back."

The count's visit ended with him reciting "The Song of the Sword," Korner's poem, the one that Darius once recited to us. He is "heartsick," he tells me, for Prussia. I know how he feels. Lately my thoughts have all been about England, Marlborough Gardens, and Saddler's Grove. I like him despite the fact that I know he refers to us behind our backs as *"die alte Englanderin und ihre liebe Komaradin."*

Next week he will have another birthday. It occurs to me that my *cadeau* to him perhaps should be an account of the Marlborough War. It would entertain him, I am sure. He has told me often enough that I am one of the few women with whom he enjoys conversing. "You would have made an excellent soldier." Yes, the gift would be appropriate, a witty and amusing one.

The Marlborough War: An Account of a Battle that Took Place on English Soil the Morning of 26 May, 1837

by Emma Adelaide Jessica Forster

Without going into causes and provocations of our enmity—truly it would take too long—let it suffice that my brothers and myself and all of my male cousins engaged in a formal struggle with one another on a field called Marlborough Marshes, a stretch of land approximately one hundred fifty feet long and one hundred feet wide.

I shall attempt to convey the precise course of events, at least up to the point when our armies clashed, for during the action, though we held our line as long as possible, the battle degenerated as it always does into a violent melee in which it is difficult, if not impossible (despite what military historians say), to really know what is going on. But all this you know, of course.

To begin with: properly speaking, the Marlborough War was not a war, that is a state of prolonged open armed conflict. Nor can one describe it as a campaign. It was only one military operation. But let me assure you, my dear count, that though it was a single battle, it was by no means a hole in the corner affair. It involved, not including the officer's staff, more than one hundred and fifty boys . . .

The Battle: PHASE ONE

On the morning of 26 May we slipped out of our houses before dawn, entering the North Gate of Marlborough Gardens at 6:05 precisely, and began our march through the dense fog and cold, through Blenheim Woods, the rank and file dragging our supplies in six or seven wooden carts behind us. Arriving at the Heights, we looked down on Marlborough Marshes.

The slanting morning rays of sun had broken though the bank of clouds and shed light on the large clumps of oxeye daisies, clover, and buttercup. Darius looked through his field glasses. "They are gathering," he said.

You will appreciate that we had, even before the battle began, three tactical advantages: 1. The Marshes sloped (albeit gently) in the direction of the lake, so that the ground on which we were to fight was slightly elevated. 2. A tower that stood on the marshes was on our side of the field. It could be used as a lookout and a low wall close by the tower could be used as our commissariat, our supply station where we could keep our wagons. 3. Our enemy, occupying the western part of the field, faced the rising sun. The sun would be shining in their eyes.

We were quite sure of victory. Perhaps even a bit smug. We had more supplies and more money, and in short we were set up logistically for victory.

We made our way slowly and not without some difficulty down the cliff path to the edge of the field where we set up a temporary camp. Darius, our supreme commander, had taken care to bring a supply of liquor to the field, and just before we formed our line Ricci, our supreme commander's man servant, served up two tots of gin to each officer and two cups of wine to all our soldies. Our supreme commander spoke a few words to us: "Soldiers, this is the battle we have desired. Victory is in your hands."

I remember our grave faces, serious and watchful, as we drank the liquor poured for us by Ricci. After a short speech by Darius, we took our assigned places in the field. It was now a few minutes before seven.

The mists had not yet cleared but we, the Cordeliers, right, left, and center, were in position, our hearts beating—I remember my heart pounding and a wild madness forming deep inside me, and the desire to kill overtaking me—facing an army that though we could not see as yet, we could hear moving into position themselves.

We stood in three main groups in waist-high grass. Darius and his men, three deep, were in the center position, he conspicuous by his black plume and brown velvet tricornered hat, the personification of courage. By the time our line was formed, our blood raced with spirits; we felt fearless.

We had our instructions. "I will begin the attack, but General Henry and General Edward will hold themselves in readiness until I give the signal to advance and break through the center of our enemy's lines. The catapultists on the right flank under the command of General Emma and General William will open up the volleys and the grenadiers on the left flank under the command of General Fitzcrawford will open fire simultaneously.

"When that has been accomplished, both the left and right flanks will be facing the right and left flanks of the enemy. After the attack has begun on these lines, further commands will be given in accordance with the enemy's movements."

We stood there waiting for Darius to give the signal to advance forward. We had decided like Cromwell to charge first. Besides the special weapons of our individual companies, we carried staves and foot-long wooden daggers.

We could hardly contain ourselves, it was the moment we had been waiting for. Suddenly the mists cleared and there before our eyes stood the enemy not ten yards from us. An unholy hatred seized me as I stared at Albert front and center. An unholy desire to smash into pulp his glittering smile as he glared at us. Death to traitors! Death! I said to myself. Let blood flow! Waiting impatiently for Darius's signal, our enthusiasm for battle grew. We would give our lives in order to avenge ourselves! Our lives! Finally he gave the signal and our companies marched with discipline and deliberation across the bare ten yards of open ground that separated us from them, our enemies.

EDWARD'S ACCOUNT

. . . and then I saw them, their flags, their gay pennons, their cockades and caps, and Albert himself. An awful sweat of fear broke out for I knew that no matter how brilliant our strategy was, or how courageous we were, or how much better prepared we were than they, it could not outweigh his purpose, his purpose that was more honourable than ours. I also knew he would never allow himself to flee. That he would fight on and on and on . . . that he would have to be bludgeoned into defeat.

The order came: "Raise staves!" We did. The plan was to go into action as Darius and his company broke the center of the army line. We marched toward each other and for one brief moment there was a tunnel of pikes as both armies clashed against one another, and then I gave my signal and a volley of stones flew through the air, and then another and another. I heard Emma give the order: "Draw the sling!" then "Loose the sling!"

And it was as I thought it would be. Though our strategy and tactics were brilliant, what we had not taken into consideration was the ferocity of the enemy. For despite our lightning advance, they did not flee as they should have, but kept their ground. They went whirling around our flank striking about them with their wooden swords, snarling at us, cursing, showing their teeth.

EMMA'S ACCOUNT

But I speak as if there was order and of course after the initial attack all there was, was confusion. I could see that our line had been halted; some of their soldiers had broken through, some disappearing into our line as into another dimension of space.

Suddenly I was hit from behind at the same time I saw William, smiling, hit a boy with his sword. As I struggled with the nameless boy, I felt my hair being pulled, my flesh being bitten. When I broke loose screaming and snarling, the boy rushed at me again, his pike raised. He threw it and it swerved and then he threw himself at me again. Ferocious by now, I landed blows on his head and his chest; lunged at him; and finally toppled him, the strength of my body being used to its ultimate. My terror, for I did feel that, transfigured, became a desire to kill, to cut, to slash, to spill his blood. I smelled his vomit as it came pouring out of his mouth on me, and I loosened him and moved on.

EDWARD

I saw that William had been attacked by a larger boy. I rushed to his rescue. Their bodies were locked in combat with one another. The boy was stout, heavy, powerfully built. His eyes glittered with rage. His large cruel mouth was twisted into a grimace.

William had dropped to the ground gasping while the boy slashed at him with his sword.

I ran to them. I began to pry their sweating faces apart and then suddenly, overtaken by a homicidal fury, I began punching the boy's head again and again while at the same time watching in a detached way the boy's craven fear, the boy's spasm, the gulpings . . . a voice inside me screaming "Kill! Kill! Kill!"

Two of ours came to help me while four of the enemy came rushing toward us. During what followed, the boy ran away and so did I. I hid in a thicket nearby. Wild eyed, blood splattered. I had forgotten about William entirely. I could make no sense out of what was happening.

EMMA

I was wounded—a sword had torn my skin and flesh at the back of my neck—but I felt no pain; instead I felt an unquenchable vitality. My mouth was dry but I forgot my thirst as I pursued the enemy across the marsh. I ran toward the belt of bushes that separated the marsh from the lake, crashing through the foliage and small boughs. Where was Darius? Where were my brothers? I didn't know, I didn't care! I was fury incarnate, covered with blood and vomit. Wounded, I ran after the enemy. I could smell their fear. At the lake I caught an enemy boy on the banks, threw him in, and held his head below the water. It began to rain.

EDWARD

I had been knocked senseless; how long I lay there I don't know but when I came to a wave of pain ran through me. I reached across my chest, my hand came back red with blood. It had begun to rain. I could see that the western part of the field still had small groups of enemy soldiers holding their ground but that their main strength had already been broken and was fleeing in the direction of the lake. I lay there, my face in the wet grass when James Malkin handed me a message. How had he found me? I wondered.

As much as possible, Darius had supervised the conduct for our fighting. He seemed to be everywhere, his striking uniform seen in all parts of the field. I read the message: "Ricci has fled. Our supplies are unguarded. The enemy has broken through to the wall. Advance there and defend."

It took me a moment to gather my senses. It was when I tried to scramble to my feet that I hurt. Another wave of pain went through me. There was a young boy lying next to me who appeared dead. His cap was gone, his vest ripped. . . .

I went with James. At the wall, Henry and a handful of our grenadiers found the enemy making off with our supplies of fire-crackers and stones.

Then began a free-for-all. There were seven of us and ten of them. During the melee I recognized James Bottome, George Cornwind, John Peterson. They looked crazed and wild, too. I heard an officer scream "Stand fast! Stand fast!" I can't stand it, I thought. This was war then. I must be brave. Gallant to die in battle is to die in glory. I had lost my sword; I picked up a rock and threw it at James. It hit him and his forehead began to bleed, but an enemy boy, one I did not know, knocked me down. As he did, Henry knocked him down, and I managed to crawl out from under the enemy.

Henry had wrested a sword from one of the fallen boys and now with two swords was striking out on both sides. Then John Peterson threw his pike at him, but the pole went crashing by him and hit the wall instead. Then John ran away, and so did George and James. After that we somehow managed to circle the rest of them and drove them up against the wall. We took off our cords and tied their hands together. They were our prisoners now. We would march them to the tower. This was a successful action.

EMMA

I found William. During the fight at the lake, I had lost track of him. I found him behind a clump of bushes near the East Gate. He had undressed himself completely; he had removed his coat, his vest, his hat, his shoes, all of which he had folded up neatly in a bundle beside him. He was smiling and nodding, saying "I shall be a good boy from now on, Grindal. I shall . . . I shall . . . I promised Meki—" while plaiting and replaiting the laces that he had removed from his boots.

I could hear the roars and screams of soldiers, the exploding firecrackers, the clatter of swords. Out of the corner of my eye I saw a small boy crawling toward us, dragging his left leg. But William saw and heard nothing. I dressed him. I told him to give me the laces, but when he wouldn't I let him have them. Then he smiled at me and asked: "May we go home now?" I told him soon and led him by the hand back to the field. William, still smiling, began to cry. I told him I would take care of him, brought him to another clump of bushes, and told him to stay there until I called for him. He said he would. . . .

By now an hour had passed and most of the boys who had lain there stunned and senseless must have either gone off by themselves or those who had been seriously wounded had been picked up by their comrades and taken off the field.

EDWARD

As we marched our prisoners toward the tower, I saw Albert running like some mad beast toward it pursued by Darius. Then Albert ran into the tower. Darius hurled his spear at him, knocking off his cap. I told Henry to watch the prisoners and ran after them. A feeling of rage propelled me, a feeling of being betrayed.

As I ran up the steps of the tower, I could hear the clatter of their boots; when I arrived in the tower room I felt a hopeless fear. I began to tremble. By the time I had arrived, Darius had already attacked Albert. Albert's mouth was bleeding; he looked dazed. "Bow down! Bow down!" screamed Darius. "Bow down!"

A wave of nausea came over me as I saw Albert trying to bow. Where were his brothers? Where were his troops? I had seen them in the field fighting valiantly.

"Do you surrender? Bow down! Bow down!" Albert knelt as well as he could before Darius. Bowed down, his face filled with bewilderment and pain. That look has haunted me from that time on. . . .

EMMA

Hearing the trumpets, I returned to the western part of the marsh just in time to see Albert, his head drooping like a dead phantom, being marched up and down the field carrying the white flag of surrender with his brothers on either side of him. As they went down the length of the field, each signaled their troops (those who still remained) to stop fighting. And they did so, but one of them must have made a threatening movement and one of our troops, keyed up, lashed out and for a moment the fighting began again. But Joshua ran over to stop them, as did Edward.

It had stopped raining. It was over. We had won. I shall never forget that unholy feeling of victory. Our uniforms were covered with mud and blood, our boots were dirty; we were wet and dead tired. But we were exultant and for the most part unharmed, though Fitzcrawford's right arm looked by the way it was hanging as if it might be broken, and though he looked pale like us, he looked happy. We had won. *That* was all that mattered. The sun at its zenith—the battle had lasted almost three hours—drenched the Garden with its brilliant light, shone on the trampled grass and crushed daisies, and on the still forms of the boys who still lay there senseless.

We drank all the wine that Darius poured for us in his rooms. And as we drank, a longing for oblivion came over us and the scenes of battle faded from our minds. Slowly we descended from the heights of fury to a place where there was nothing but blankness.

We slept through the afternoon until early dusk.

City of Childhood
XXX
THE AFTERMATH

NORMALLY we would not have been present, but because my father insisted that we be present at the dinner table on those occasions when he returned from a long trip abroad, we, my brother and I, were there. William was not feeling well.

During the first course of dinner—boiled pork with cauliflower and marrow pudding; a new maid was serving and Mrs. Farnley was supervising—the doors were flung open and our Uncle Joseph stood there. He looked berserk, completely mad, even though, as always, he was dressed properly. There was a finicky neatness about him that he never lost even when he lost complete hold of himself. The madness was concentrated in his eyes; all of it was there, not a drop spilled elsewhere. But his voice was hoarse as he screamed at Elijah, "She has gone! She has left me!"

"Who has gone? Who has left you?" asked my father. "Calm yourself! Speak slowly!"

"Consuelo!" came the roar of anguish. He ran to the dinner table, sat in William's chair, and, his elbows on the table, he placed his head between his hands and began to weep.

"Joseph! Stop it! Control yourself, for God's sake! Theodisia! Mrs. Farnley! Take the children away. Quickly!"

Doing as they were told, the women hurried us out of the room. As we were being led up the stairs, we saw our poppa and Uncle Joseph rushing out of the dining room into the hall and out of the house.

That was the night of the twenty-sixth.

❋   ❋   ❋

Were it not for the servants, we would have known nothing. For neither Elijah, nor Theodisia, nor any of our aunts or uncles ever told us anything about what happened on that night. It was never mentioned and so rigid was the protocol between our parents and ourselves that we could never ask. But it is all we thought about.

And so it was the servants who told us everything, not all at once but in bits and pieces as they learned of it themselves. Daisy, Eve, the coachman's wife, and Mrs. Lovesley, our cook, told us what we wanted to know, though we dreaded knowing.

Joseph had gone mad, they told us, when he had found the contessa's letter saying that she had returned to Florence and would never come back again, that she could no longer exist in England. They said that he had screamed, that he had rushed to her rooms, that he had searched for her over the whole house, that he had screamed her name continuously—"Consuelo!"—that he had rushed to find a gun with which to kill himself and that his servants had had to struggle with him. They told us how his servants had taken the gun away and removed the bullets, and how he had then rushed out of the house to ours.

That was the first bit of news they told us. And then some days later they told us about the letters, two letters, one written to Joseph, the other to Darius. The servants had read them, they swore. They knew what they said.

And then—they finally told us about Darius. Though they hesitated. Should they tell us? We were children, after all. And then they decided they would. And so in hushed tones they began.

In all this madness, they asked us, who had thought of the boy Darius? How it might affect him. We didn't know and so they told us. Elijah! Yes, yes, it was your father who had thought of him and *that* was why both Elijah and Joseph had rushed out of the house that night back to Joseph's house. Rushed up the stairs to Darius's rooms. And when they found the door locked, it was Elijah who had shouted, "Open up!" and had banged on the door. Elijah was the one who had shouted at one of the servants to bring an axe and a knife! "Immediately!" and the servant had. But the boy's father had hurled himself against the door again and again and the door crashed open before the servant had returned.

And there was the boy, your cousin Darius, hanging from one of the beams swaying with an overturned chair beneath him. Was he still alive? It was Elijah who had cut him down. The boy fell to the floor. Was he dead? No, but almost. And the rope, the rope around his neck, which was tied to a heavier, sturdier rope, was his Cordelier's cord. Elijah thought that might have saved him.

We listened, my brothers and I, stunned, dazed. But that was not all, they said; when he recovered and found himself alive, Darius tried to kill himself again, by stabbing himself in the neck, and then they hired someone to protect him against himself, a guard, a big brute of a man, by the name of Malone.

That was the second bit of news.

Finally, they told us the third bit of news: Ricci too had left. He had gone off with the contessa. And then they told us that we knew everything there was to know about the night of May 26.

June first, as always, as if nothing had happened, we went to Saddler's Grove. Never once during that entire summer did any of our mothers and fathers refer or mention to us what had happened on that night.

That summer we hardly spoke to one another and though some of us went to the smuggler's cave and fished, we did it singly. Alone. Mostly we wandered listlessly, thinking our own thoughts. Only William seemed to have some purpose. He searched that whole summer long for Grandfather Jorem, but by the time we were ready to return to London, he realized that Jorem had died and that was what death meant: Grandfather Jorem would never be found at Saddler's Grove again.

When we returned to Marlborough Gardens in August, Daisy told us that Darius had been sent away to a Catholic Academy in Wilshire. A week later my brothers and male cousins went off to Warrenton to begin their summer term as planned.

I was alone now.

Our childhood was over.

A way of life had ended.

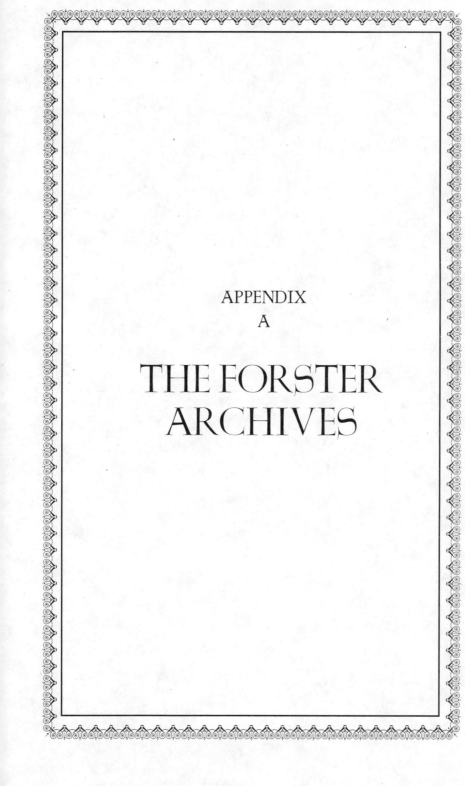

APPENDIX
A

THE FORSTER
ARCHIVES

W E give here as complete a selection as we thought necessary to compile. The selection makes no pretense to be comprehensive, for the material is truly vast. We chose the cited books (we use the word loosely) because they were primary sources.

In dealing with this period (1836–1914), we have found ourselves again and again confronted with the problem of chronology. It might have been expected, for the Forsters were, after all, such indefatigable note takers that certain important dates, for example, the Marlborough War, would be beyond discussion or dispute. Unfortunately that is not true. The most we can determine is a relative order of events, though this may not be apparent within the confines of the manuscript.

We have listed the books, for reasons of chronicity, either in accordance with the subject's birth date or in accordance with the author's birth date. Either way, the book serves as an introduction to character for we are in agreement with Samuel Butler's remark: "Every man's work, whether it be literature or music . . . or anything else is always a portrait of himself."

The following individual listings are preceded by a précis of either the subject or the author or both.

JOSEPH FORSTER (JOSEPHUS FAUSTUS) 1695–1769

Joseph Forster, the founder of the English branch of Forsters, came to England in 1714 emigrating from Rechtdorp, a small town in Upper Hesse, via Rotterdam. He had been expelled from his guild, the Goldsmith's Guild, and his church, The Brethren of the Holy Lamb, when (after having had a vision of the Savior) he exhorted the Brethren to return to primeval innocence by means of nudity and ecstatic love. He left his parents, six brothers, and four sisters behind, but took his awls, his chisels, his files, and his pocket gold scale—the tools of his trade—with him.

Arriving in London, "a yawning pit of Hell," he headed north and arrived in Ashville, a small village at the edge of the Cotswolds. The narrow, crooked streets and half-timbered houses reminded him of Rechtdorp and he decided to stay. He found work with a wool stapler, Wallace Barnes, and when Barnes died, Joseph married the widow, Ann-Margaret, a woman who was ten years older than himself. In the next six years he fathered six sickly children. Two daughters and one son, Jeremiah (1715–1772), Jorem's father, survived. It was Jeremiah who became the founder of the Forster Midland Bank.

In the margin in Jeremiah's bank ledger, dated 1 October 1765, is written, in a clear and legible hand, the following words, "Today my oldest son, Jorem, begins his apprenticeship under Mr. Powers, my oldest and most trusted employee. Praise be to God that all will go well."

Listing: See *The Faustian Root* by Darius Forster, Count Rimini VII.

JOREM JEREMIAH FORSTER (1755–1836)

THE RAVENSCROFT LETTERS (1817–1820)
Letters written to Jorem's friend the Baron Ravenscroft. A selection is reprinted in Research Paper No. 1, page 42. Written in parchment in a bold hand, they consist of one hundred and two letters and fourteen fragments.

THE SOLOMON FORSTER LETTERS (1817–1820)

Written by Jorem to his brother Solomon.

Solomon Forster, Clara Lustig's grandfather, was Jorem's only surviving brother and was an artist, like Kevin Francini. These letters, written at the same time as the Ravenscroft Letters, excoriate artists, calling them parasites, sycophants, and boot-licking, groveling bloodsuckers. The final letter in this series ends with stern admonishments and dire threats: ". . . your lack of discipline! . . . your irresponsibility! . . . your licentiousness! . . . all are abhorrent to me! Do not expect or ever hope that I shall lend you any sum of money large or small!"

The Tale of the Black Swan
The Tale of the Evil Frog from Bristol, Meki
The Christmas Tale / The Journals

by Jorem J. Forster

There are more than fifty journals. For the most part they chronicle the rise of the Forster Midland Bank, but certain pages are scarred with a plethora of cruel and cutting remarks about his children, who have disappointed him, failed him, and betrayed him; and there are final judgments. "Elijah is too cunning, too ambitious for his own good." "Poor Joseph—his base cowardice is repugnant to me." "Mathilda! Why has she monstrasized into a whining, lackluster bitch?" And even Solomon comes under fire. In a journal dated 1832 Jorem notes, "Of late it seems to me that Solomon is beginning to suffer from the grievous sin of complacency."

The fact that Jorem was not at all fond of his own children but was excessively fond of his grandchildren is explained by Lowe in the following way: "There was an 'alchemic' connection between Jorem the father and Jorem the grandfather. Hence the cold and worthless metal of hatred (the alchemist's stone) that was stored in Jorem's heart for his own children in time reached its perfection, and ripened into the gold of love for his grandchildren."

The True History of England as Seen Through the Eyes of a Field Mouse
Three volumes, privately printed, 1824.

The volumes are elegant and inviting, bound in handsome

brown cloth with gilt lettering on the spine. Each contains lavish illustrations by James Titmouse. It adheres to the Protestant ethic: the holy trinity of success, piety, and reform. The protagonist, Harry White, Esquire, is a proper little bourgeois, but the performance is a bit too arch. What is needed is the objective irony of truth that Jorem developed in his later years. It is the first fruit of his retirement.

The Last Will and Testament of *Jorem J. Forster*
   10 August 1836, written on Bristol paper, 43 pages.
   A spirited performance that is invaluable in its attention to the details of Jorem's business affairs. See page 157.

The Codicil
See page 159.

GRINDAL (1815?–1898)

   Grindal was Emma, Edward, and William's nanny. Long after the children were grown, she lived on the third floor of the nursery at 43 Marlborough Gardens. And died there.
   Who was she, really? In Jorem's will there are two mysterious bequests. The first is to a woman named Alice G. Thorpe, the former companion to Jorem's wife, Jessica. The other is to Nanny Grindal. Both legacies are large sums of money. And both have the added proviso that each of the legatees may "remain unto death" at either Saddler's Grove or Marlborough Gardens. Does the G. in Alice G. Thorpe's name stand for Grindal? Was Grindal the product of that trite Victorian sin, the illegitimate child working as a servant in the bosom of her family? Could Grindal have been Jorem's illegitimate child?
   It is all speculation of course—there is no proof, only dark hints, and so far they have led to disappointing dead ends—if it is true *and* William can be believed (see Australian Letters: 10 March 1872), then Elijah may possibly have committed incest.
   The archives make mention of eight other Grindal stories. Although as yet we have not found them, we do have a promising lead.
   According to Emma, Grindal was a born storyteller.

"She was a despot and I hated her but she was my pleasure too. On rainy nights when the wind howled outside, and the moon was covered by dark clouds, she would gather us around the nursery hearth and tell us the most wonderful stories. Her imagination, unspoiled by reason, would plunge us instantaneously into depths of violence and terror that held us spellbound." (*A Memory Journal,* Emma Forster, 1898.)

The Tale of the Two Sisters
The Forster Anthology of Fairy Tales, privately printed, 1876.

The Countess von Cutupp
Grindal's ribald tale. It is the story of the adventures of the countess and her friend Aunt Maria (nineteenth-century cant for female *pudenda*) in an apple-dumpling shop (cant for a woman's bosom).

According to William's Australian letter No. 8, William sent it to Albert with this comment: "I don't expect you'll thank me for this but I have finally 'recalled' one of Nanny Grindal's tales."

Albert did not include it in the anthology.

COUNT DARIUS MARCUS FORSTER RIMINI VII (1822–1856)

We count it as a misfortune that nothing exists in Darius's "authentic" voice, that is, in the form of a diary, journal, or letter. We have searched in all the obvious places. We have even gone so far as to search his former premises—his suite of rooms at 38 Marlborough Gardens.

Receiving permission from the present tenants, a large Indian family that included, besides parents and children, two sets of grandparents and numerous aunts, uncles, and cousins, we spent an afternoon searching the premises. It was an unpleasant experience. *Sic transit gloria* . . . the once glorious rooms were a shambles. Nothing, but nothing, was left of their former grandeur.

Darius, the only son of Joseph and Consuelo Forster, was the charismatic adolescent who became the children's leader during eight crucial months of their lives from October 1836 to May 1837.

The name "Darius" means "holding firm the good" in old Persian. It was the Riminis' custom to christen the first born son Darius, in honor, they said, of their ancestor, a Persian noble who in 401 B.C. joined the Ten Thousand in their legendary march back to the Greek coast of the Euxine Sea.

Whether this bit of family history was true or false is not as important as the fact that it became a family tradition which by virtue of it being told and retold was ultimately transformed into "sacred" fact.

From the very beginning, Darius was intrigued with pedigrees and their various combinations and permutations. But as he grew older, world weary, prone to boredom and despair, the interest became an obsession. All his intelligence, his creativity, and his imagination were ruthlessly channeled into a sustained effort to prove to himself that his original substance was worthy.

The last years of his life were spent proving to himself and to others that certain historic, legendary, and even divine beings were part of his inherited substance. He concentrated on three persons: Thucydides, the legendary Dr. Johan Faustus, and the fabled Minotaur. He became a Florentine joke. His palazzo became known as "The Labyrinth" and the Florentine wags referred to him as "Signore Cornetto" (little horn).

Unfortunately, we do not have the complex genealogical tables he devised but must make do with Emma's occasional references to his final preoccupations, which she notes in a desultory way in her *Florentine Journal.*

Lowe, who does not care for Darius, describes him as a mutation: "The offspring of wheat plants are always wheat plants and nothing else; the offspring of oak trees, oaks. But there are certain types of variations that are produced by deviations in the environment and then an individual will suddenly appear, clearly different from the rest. These are known as mutations. Darius was such a mutation."

A final note: As far as we know, Darius never mentioned his illustrious namesakes, the three historic Persian Kings, Darius I, Darius II, and Darius III, in any of his war lectures to the children. Nor did he ever mention the battle of Marathon in which Darius I was defeated by Miltiades or the Battle of Gaugamela in which Darius III was defeated.

The Faustian Root

Monograph, privately printed, Florence, 1856.

An invaluable manuscript for two reasons. One, it provides the only verifiable information we have about Josephus Faustus; secondly, it introduces a recurrent theme—the Forsters' strange duality of temperament ("Two souls, alas, are dwelling in my breast"—line 1112, *Faust,* Part 1, Goethe), which could without warning remove them from the obedient and disciplined track they were following, and set them on other more dangerous and foreign paths.

The monograph is about the lowly German apprentice, Josephus Faustus, who came to England in 1714 and changed his name to Joseph Forster. It is Darius's attempt to establish a genealogical connection between Dr. Faustus, the celebrated magician who sold his soul to the devil in return for all earthly pleasures, and Darius's ancestors.

Two Curious Tales

Florentine Press, 1849.

This slim volume, bound in vellum, is beautiful by force of typography alone, its type having been modeled on that of Nicholas Jensen, the fifteenth-century printer.

It is dedicated to "Emmathon, the one who understands."[1] The first tale, *The Passion of Panpornia*[2], is a complex story of revenge, not particularly well written, but worth reading for its self-relevatory aspects. What follows is a précis:

Soon after a medieval king named King Perdo[3] marries his second wife, a beautiful woman called Lady Panpornia from a distant country called Minthos,[4] a monstrous serpent appears who ravages the countryside, carrying off young women and young men, first raping them and then murdering them.

---

1. *Emmathon.* Aorist 2, Ind. Act., 1 sg. of the Greek verb, *manthanw:* to understand.

2. *Panpornia* is a composite of two Greek words: *pan,* neuter of *pas,* all (Lat. *omnis*); and *porne,* nominative, prostitute.

3. *Perdo.* Since all of the proper nouns are based on Greek words, we are convinced that Darius is referring to the Greek verb *perdomai,* (to) break wind.

4. *Minthos,* Greek word for human ordure, dung.

Prince Omeunos,[5] Panpornia's son/lover offers to find the reptile and slay him. On his return he informs the king that the serpent has promised to leave the kingdom if the king will give his daughter to Prince Omeunos in marriage. Emmathon refuses. She does not love Omeunos; besides, it has been revealed to her that were she to marry the prince, her father, the king, would be slain.

Enter the hero: Lord Titus.[6] A knight, he has been wounded fighting for the king in a local battle. Exhausted, he has fallen asleep in a nearby wood, only to awaken as a huge and gaudy serpent is coiling itself tightly around his rib cage. With his magical sword, Titus hacks away at the monster, who slithers off taking Titus's sword with him, its hilt twisted in its tail.

Titus follows the path of the serpent to the castle, where a celebration is being prepared for the forthcoming marriage of the king's daughter to Prince Omeunos. The serpent disappears into the vast stone maze beneath the castle. Titus follows the serpent by means of the sparks the sword makes as it is dragged along the stone floor. At the center of the maze Titus finds the serpent lounging, coil upon coil. Titus lifts his magical sword and in one stroke cuts off the serpent's head.

As it rolls toward him, it is transformed into the head of Prince Omeunos. The remainder of the body retains its serpentine form. Titus finds his way out of the maze following the tracks of the sword. Carrying the head of Omeunos, he brings it to the Court and throws it at Lady Panpornia's feet. The lady changes into a fabulous bird and flies away with it in her beak. A day later a wedding takes place. But it is Titus, not Omeunos, who is married to Emmathon. Together they live happily ever after.

The Minotaur's Point of View

An extraordinary achievement. Unlike the first tale, it is basically well tempered and good humored. He tells us everything about Crete, Knossos, the labyrinth, and customs and moral principles in the most convincing manner. And the Minotaur (called

---

5. *Omeunos,* Greek word for bedfellow, consort.
6. *Titus,* Greek name Tituos (Tityos). In Latin, the poet's name for sun.

the Dauphin in the story) is the very model of a Victorian gentleman. It must be read to be appreciated. Sections of it were included by Emma in her novel, *The Metaphysics of Sex.*

A Dissertation on Fatherhood: Ouranos, Kronus, Tantalus et Alii
   An unfinished work. A bitter and excoriating attack on fathers
and fatherhood. As savage and as pessimistic as Swift.

Jane Eyre, a libretto
   In the Biblioteca Nazionale Centrale di Firenze (The Rimini
Collection, 1888).
   A beautiful unification of text and music.
   "Tonight we were entertained at Count Maria von Hoenfen-
schtall's Schloss Brunnen—it has a theater, a masterpiece of Ro-
coco architecture—where we heard Consuelo Rimini's opera *Jane
Eyre.*
   "The title role was sung by Count Maria's mistress, Signorina
Guliana, a fine dramatic soprano. The spectacular ovation after
her aria—Jane has just heard Rochester's voice calling her from
afar and she sings, *'Vengo! Aspettami! Vengo!'* (I am coming!
Wait for me! I am coming!) was no less than she deserved. At
the end countless bouquets and a rain of flowers . . .
   "I did not tell the count that I had once known both the com-
poser *and* the librettist." Emma's *Weimar Journal,* October 1884.

Vanessa Edwinna Forster Herrod (1824–1875)

   Vanessa was the beautiful oldest daughter of Mathilda and
Brian Herrod. An artist, at the age of eighteen she married the
younger son of the Fifth Earl of Grymston, Sir Charles Mallow,
the Viscount Kingston.
   That she was beautiful is attested to by everyone, in letters,
diaries, and poems, for if Albert at the age of ten disliked her,
at the age of fourteen he was stricken with love for her, as were
all her male cousins. Altogether they wrote thirty-six impassioned
love poems to her, declaiming her beauty and calling her by such
names as Aphrodite or Venus of Marlborough Gardens, though
one of William's poems begins "Cruel Athena."

We have Emma to thank for the corpus of work.

The change in Emma's attitude toward Vanessa is one of the stubborn problems that resists solution. It may be connected to Emma's change in attitude toward her mother, to whom she wrote a lengthy encomium in 1859.

DRAWINGS

One sketchbook, 1835, contains forty-three rough sketches in pen and ink. Vivid and candid portraits of all her relatives in various poses, singly and in groups.

One sketchbook, 1838: Several scenes of Saddler's Grove including The Guardian of Saddler's Grove, in black-and-white chalk on tan paper.

Twenty-eight sketchbooks, 1846–1872: Detailed studies and smaller compositions for incorporation into large compositions.

WATERCOLORS (Undated)

The Old Oak in Blenheim Wood, watercolor and gouache on laid paper.

The Duke of Marlborough (the equestrian statue), watercolor on wove paper.

Athena's Abode (the temple), watercolor and gouache on vellum.

Sidney's Tombstone, an oval miniature.

The Winter Garden, watercolor on paper.

Poseidon, on gray silk.

Tower Farfrum, watercolor and chalk on heavy laid paper.

GOUACHE

Twelve copies of twelve Renaissance nudes, including *Memling's Eve,* dated 1844.

Each copy is done on cardboard and wrapped in tan paper on which are written the words, "To my beloved Charles" (Vanessa's husband, Sir Charles Mallow). On one of the wrappers there is an unfinished pastel of a man's face with the letter *C* printed underneath it.

OIL PAINTINGS

Six flower paintings, done with astonishing technical elegance and refinement, are all dated 1848. We have hung them in various rooms in the main house.

Eighteen paintings of a realm that resembles Marlborough Gardens but is even more fantastic, "a beautiful romantic dream that never was, never will be—in a light better than any light that ever shone—in a land no one can define or remember, only desire" (Sir Edward Coley Burne-Jones). We have hung them in various rooms in the lodge.

Before the Fall, 42 by 51½ inches. Unfinished. It is her last painting, on which she worked for five years. We are in Blenheim Wood. In the center of the canvas stands the Old Oak. Strange but beautiful vines twist and curve about its trunk. It is night and the grass, trees, weeds, and flowers (all minutely observed) have been transformed into a moonlight fantasy.

Stretched beneath the tree are two naked figures, Darius and Vanessa, a diadem of daisies in her hair. Surrounding them are their cousins, dressed as elves and fairies.

At first sight the richly textured composition seems abnormally crowded for there are, besides the presence of her cousins and abundant vegetation, innumerable small woodland creatures, flotillas of birds and butterflies. But despite the welter of detail, the canvas has the orderly arrangement of a written page. The eye wanders, as the light directs it, first to the upper left-hand corner, where almost hidden in a ring of foliage is a snake whose human face resembles Charles, her late husband. Then, as the eye continues to travel back and forth across this meticulously painted epistle, we perceive what she intends us to: in the lower-right quadrant of the canvas, an apple tree in *blossom.* And we realize that we are in paradise, "before the fall."

Emma Adelaide Jessica Forster (1826–1914)

Emma was a minor Victorian novelist, the oldest daughter of Theodisia Blackstone, a yeoman's daughter, and Elijah Forster, the president of Forster Midland Bank Ltd.

Emma was a prolific writer. The fact that only one book had been published apparently did not act as a deterrent though it may account for the increasing eccentricity of her work. But despite this outpouring of her emotions, and all her emotions are in a major key, there are irritatingly few facts, except about her childhood. But as she says in one of her journals, à la Keats, "I am not at all interested in facts." All of her *Memory Books* and most of her journals are attempts to reconstruct, sometimes in microscopic detail, the early years of her life. Lowe's response to Emma's humorless concentration on her childhood is, "She certainly took to heart the old man's (Socrates's) maxim—'An unexamined childhood is not worth living.' "

Emma's obsession with her childhood included childbirth. She has written five nativity scenes and though all are wildly improbable, they breathe with vitality.

Happy Endings
London, 1843. A modest sale and a kind remark in the *Athenium*.

UNPUBLISHED WORK
  Misperceptions, 1845
  What Really Happened, 1852
  The Hours Between, 1857
  The Metaphysics of Sex, 1888
  Preliminary Communications (Jane Eyre, Again), 1903

UNFINISHED WORK
  City of Childhood, undated.
  My Mother, The Yeoman's Daughter, 1859
  A Victorian Artist: Vanessa Herrod, 1901
  A Tale of Two Sisters: Pasiphae and Kirke, 1906

ALBERT FORSTER (1824–1882)

Albert was the oldest son, the heir, of Solomon Forster, treasurer of Forster Midland Bank Ltd., and Guinivere Kendall, the oldest daughter of John Kendall, lieutenant-colonel in Her Majesty's army. Educated at Warrenton; entered Exeter College, Oxford, where he read history. Married Alice Townsend (1858), the oldest daughter of Sir John Morrison, baronet and physician. After his father's retirement in 1870, he took over the presidency of Forster Midland Bank Ltd.

The sanest and most balanced of all the Forsters, he was active in the LLGW (London League of Gentlewomen), supported Irish disestablishmentarianism, and was converted to state education, serving on the London School Board from 1851 to 1876.

Lowe has pointed out to me that Albert's diaries "are a reminder that it is a man's faults that make him interesting and attractive—not his virtues."

The Forster Anthology of Fairy Tales
Privately printed, 1872. It is dedicated to Grandfather Jorem, *"Omnia praeclara rara* (all the best things are rare)"—Cicero. A beautiful and moving collection of eight tales by Jorem, Grindal, and Guinivere.

Reminiscences of a Happy Youth
Sections of this were printed in the *Oxford and Cambridge Magazine,* to which he also contributed an essay, "Earthly Paradise," describing the wonders of Marlborough Gardens.

Diaries
There are forty-seven diaries, beginning with his first term at Warrenton. Alas, sanity does not create a vivid style. His is what Lowe terms "the seamstress style: people, places, and events are nearly stitched into one perpetually dull pattern after another." Still, they are invaluable and they provide the indispensable "other point of view."

There are, however, two instances when his style springs to life: in his account of Sidney's death (see page 165) and in his discussion of Darius in his last *Journal* (1881) (see below).

8 February 1881

Common sense leads me to write about a matter that no longer has the power to frighten me. I am well past the fifty mark and a grandfather a dozen times over. It concerns my cousin Darius.

When I was a child not more than four or five, my father showed me, for what reason I cannot recall, an engraving of a strange-looking creature dressed in a richly embroidered coat that came down to his small feet which were enclosed in soft black slippers and white stockings. He held a small fan in his right hand. My father pointed to it and said, "That is a Mandarin, a high Chinese official. He lives on another continent thousands of miles away, on the other side of the earth." It provided me with my first conception of oddity.

When I first met Darius, I immediately thought of the engraving of the Mandarin.

12 March 1881

When I think of Darius now (which I do more and more often), I remember him as he was during the year that I knew him intimately.

He had a clever and bewitching face . . . a classic Mediterranean type with enormous brown eyes . . . wine-colored, fleshy lips, and his black hair shone like some exotic fabric or the wings of some fantastic bird that had flown into the gardens, by pure chance. . . . And yes, his slimness, I remember that too, so very different from my sturdy body . . . I felt gauche . . . maladroit in his presence.

2 May 1881

I was eleven years old when I first met Darius. He was arrogant and prideful, but one felt he had a sense of high purpose. He enchanted me in every way.

We were *all* caught, my cousins and myself, in the brilliant net of his imagination.

But had that been all, I doubt that he would have "captured" us. We hardly saw our parents and though our nannies were kind enough, they were young and ignorant. Darius knew everything!

But had it only been knowledge I doubt that he would have "captured" us. Oh, we might have been grateful but we would not have been moved, shaken. . . . He would not have altered our lives. Even now (as old as I am) I am still embarrassed to declare what I believe it was that bound us to him, but I shall: he made us feel wanted, loved, cared for.

August 1881

I thought I had forgotten the pain caused by my separation from Darius when I was twelve years old. But I haven't. At first, when I made the decision to leave Darius's rooms that fateful afternoon, it felt as if I had stepped out of a long enchanted sleep. But that was followed by the most total and frightening pain I had ever felt so far in my life. And it (the pain) seemed to be in complete possession of my chest so that no matter how I sat, or lay, or stood it would not let go of me. As the days passed and the pain continued, I began to think that I had better tell Momma to send for the doctor, Mr. Harlowe, because I must be dying. . . . But as time passed and the pain abated and I understood that I was not to die, I didn't. . . .

I thought I would never forget Darius, but when I went away to Warrenton, within a month's time I had.

10 September 1881

I had wanted a leader. I had found one. He had ordered me to follow him and I did. Gladly. Blindly. I lost myself in him . . . and now what had been in my heart and mind for so long was over. I was not to see him any more. I was alone. Without Sidney. Without Darius. I was lost . . . lost.

10 December 1881

My life has been a good one. I have been as the Greeks say favored with *tuche,* luck. I have loved and been loved. On the whole I have been happy and contented and, above all, grateful. And yet . . . with Darius I experienced another part of myself, a more reckless self, a more roman- tic . . . Darius was a transgressor. He dared to step outside the limits. I stayed within. . . .

Edward Alexander Forster (1827–1897)

The elder son of Theodisia and Elijah Forster. Educated at Warrenton and Corpus Christi, Oxford. Kept terms at Temple but abandoned law for finance in 1868. Vice president of Forster Midland Bank Ltd. from 1882 to 1897. Member of the Purcell Society and member of a horn quintet (horn and four strings). Organist for the St. Giles Church. Composer of a suite of songs called "Marlborough Gardens." Founded the Orland Gibbons Society in 1880. Published the complete critical edition of Gib- bons's work, including such masterpieces as *The Lord of Salis- bury, The Silver Swan,* and his sacred compositions in F and D minor. The society was disbanded in 1901 but a few local branches survive.

Edward married Victoria Emily Thwaite, the only daughter of a London tobacconist, in 1845. Three years later when she ran off with her young cousin André Boldieu, Edward joined the Moravian church where under the stewardship of Dr. Garth Blackstone, a distant relative of his mother, he began his *Diary of Moral Inventory*. In his later years he became increasingly active in the LLGW.

One last note: At the age of sixteen, he fell in love with Clara Lustig, his brilliant second cousin—scholar, critic, journalist, musician, and Emma's governess. She was twenty-four years old.

Diary of Moral Inventory

Like his cousin Albert, Edward began a diary at Warrenton and continued the habit until his death. Like Albert's the performance is accurate and truthful but a little flat.

WILLIAM MARCUS FORSTER (1828–1913)

William was the younger son of Theodisia and Elijah Forster: Theodisia's favorite. Educated at Warrenton, he left Oxford in his second year after the winter term "to sow my wild oats early," having discovered the exhilaration and excitement of gambling. He was eighteen when he left Oxford and for the next four years he spent his days at Epsom, Ascot, and Newmarket and his nights in Jessie Malkin's brothel with a prostitute named Celeste, one of Jessie Malkin's regulars, whom he eventually married and lived with in one of the mean side streets off Marlborough Gardens.

When she died, he returned to 43 Marlborough Gardens and lived with his sister and mother. For a short time he worked in the bank. In 1863 he married Mr. Jasper Redbury's red-headed daughter. She was a good five years older than he. Much to everyone's surprise, Mr. Redbury approved of the match.

"It is my opinion," he said, "that a man who has gambled and drunk excessively in his youth reaches middle age with a positive thirst for respectability, while those who have begun respectable as they grow older long pitiably to dissipate." And he added to an already handsome dowry a substantial sum of money.

With the encouragement of his father-in-law (William found in Mr. Redbury his ideal father) William turned his back on a controlled and orderly life in London and departed for the wilds of Australia, where he bought thousands of acres of grazing land, several herds of sheep, and in due time (or was it God's time?) became a wealthy sheep farmer, providing wool for the ever-hungry cottonmills of Manchester.

According to Lowe, William was "a garden variety result of English primogeniture, a system which forces the younger sons of wealthy families to go forth into the world and rape, destroy, and plunder so that they may amass the necessary money to re-create the material luxury to which they were accustomed growing up. It is called 'building an empire.' "

Stud Books

In between the lines of pedigrees and in the margins of the pages there are dozens of notations. All of them pertain to betting and women. We have only three stud books, but according to these William bet more than twenty-five thousand pounds, won more than a hundred thousand, and lost more than a hundred and fifty thousand. Lowe cleverly deduced that the ever-present initials *TB* did not stand for the disease tuberculosis but for his mother, Theodisia Blackstone, who apparently staked him time and again.

Unlike Edward who seemed to have no strong physical desire for women, William, as the French say, had a constant need of a bed.

He recorded his seductions in racing terms. For instance, copulation is "jockeyship," "brisk gallop," or "a good mount." He speaks of his prowess as "racing her hard," and "running her three times," while he praises her performance as a "good pacer," or "great at the start, great at the finish." He refers to women generally as "a cart horse," "a false starter" or "a local entry," "a fine filly," or "off her form," "ready for the knackers." But Celeste (his first wife) is referred to as the "immortal mare." He speaks of her as being "owned, bred, and trained by me."

The Australian Letters

There are a dozen. They stretch from the beginning of the year 1872 till the end of that year.

Re Grindal: Australian Letter, 10 March 1872

I do not wonder that when Christmas came around this year and you gave old Grindal an unusually handsome gift you enraged Emma. She always had a jealous nature.

It is my opinion that Emma hated Grindal not because of the so-called beatings she was supposed to have meted out to her but because Poppa, who had an eye for women, had an eye for Grindal, and I suspect that he may have bedded her once or twice.

If you remember, our Grindal was a full-breasted, sensual woman, the kind Poppa found impossible to resist— you do know about Moly, don't you? She was tall and had blue eyes so dark they were almost black, "a fine figger of a woman," as they say.

Were you privy to a certain bit of family gossip? It was well hidden . . . even I am not sure of the details—Edward burned so much when father died—I sometimes wonder did I dream it? . . . that tiny slip of paper tucked between the pages of a dreary bank ledger. Just a name really . . . Alice Grindal Thorpe, the name of our grandmother's companion. Was Grindal the child of Alice Thorpe? And if she was, who was her father? Grandpa Jorem's legacies to both of them left no doubt in my mind, at least.

At any rate, as I said, I thought her a handsome woman. Actually, she resembled Poppa, at least I always thought so.

One day (I was at home during one of the hols) she tried to seduce me, I suspect she realized I was no longer a virgin (thanks to the whores of Swan Street). Have I brought blushes to your conservative, white-whiskered cheeks? No, we did not make love but there was a decided sexual thickening of the air. However, I stayed clear. I had the distinct impression (there was a bit too much of the boa constrictor about her) that a fourteen-year-old boy should be gobbled up in one bite.

JACOB FORSTER (1829–1848)

Jacob was the older of the identical twins born to Guinivere and Solomon. He was educated at Warrenton and the Royal Military Academy, Sandhurst. Received his commission in 1846. Sailed for India in 1846. Was severely wounded but distinguished himself in the first Sikh war, 1848. Promoted to Captain. Killed on 14 September by a sniper while guarding the Lahore Gate during the siege of Lucknow, which lasted a little short of 150 days. Victoria Cross awarded posthumously.

The Guinivere Letters
A series of letters written by Jacob to his mother.

JOSHUA GAIUS FORSTER (1829–1898)

The younger of the identical twins born to Solomon and Guinivere Forster. Educated at Warrenton, student at Royal Military Academy, Sandhurst. Military historian, held a chair of history at London University. In his *Battles of India,* which included the siege of Lucknow, he writes about his brother Jacob:

At dawn on 14 September four enemy parties undertook to force an entrance at various gates into the city. Three gained a footing, butchering in cold blood the gallant defenders, but at the Lahore Gate the fourth party after a long and treacherous battle was bloodily repulsed. During this gallant struggle Captain Jacob Forster was mortally wounded by a sniper as the enemy, broken and disordered, fled. On 20 September Lucknow was once more in English hands.

Married Elizabeth Anne Nash, the daughter of a lieutenant general who had been Jacob's commander during the second Sikh war.
In his time he was famous principally because of his controversial series of articles published in the *London Times Review* (1874) entitled "The Moral Necessity for Combat." Certain battles are examined in relation to the "history of moral progress," the gist of his argument being that had it not been for certain hard-fought and hard-won military victories, "our Christian way

of life as we know it, enjoy it, and live it would ne'er have come to pass." He received a knighthood in 1888.

Decisive Battle of India, London, 1867.

"The Moral Necessity for Combat,"London Times Review, 1869.

CLARA FORSTER LUSTIG (1815–1877)

Clara was the clever, younger granddaughter of Solomon Forster, Jorem's younger brother, who managed despite Jorem to become a minor success as an early-Victorian animal painter. By confining himself to the painting of dogs and horses, Solomon Forster contrived to have a small but unfailing patronage.

We have included Clara for though she does not figure in the *City of Childhood* her presence in Elijah Forster's household changed the course of all the Forsters' lives. We are now in the process of editing an account of the intricacies of the fervid and impassioned relationship between Emma and Clara, which Emma wrote about in her "roman a clef," *The Metaphysics of Sex.*

The Rosewood Box Letters
Two hundred thirty-three letters written on cheap letter paper to her brother-in-law, Johan Lustig, between the years 1838 and 1842. We have made extensive use of them in *The Metaphysics of Sex,* Emma's fourth novel, which we have begun to edit.

Two articles published in the *Blackwood* magazine: Volume XVII, No. 6 and Volume XXXI, No. 3, 1839.

1. "The Natural but Unfortunate Consequences of Being a Monster's Mother." A witty and trenchant analysis and assessment of Mary Shelley's literary career.
2. "The Moral Imperative of Ireland's Tragic Plight." A devastating attack on England's policies during the famine of 1847.

More than a dozen book reviews published both in *Cornhill Magazine* and the *Westminster Review,* including a book review of Mrs. Gaskell's novel, *Mary Barton.*

The novel's opening sentence is "I know nothing of Political Economy or theories of trade . . ." Clara's merciless critique proceeds from that opening statement and crucifies the reverend's wife precisely on that point.

All of her later articles and reviews are signed "Troxilias," the Greek word for "block and tackle." Diogenes Laertes reports in his *Life of Socrates* that Alcibiades, speaking of Socrates's wife Xantippe, says, "Some people may find Xantippe's bitching and nagging unendurable but as for myself I'm accustomed to it; it's like hearing a block and tackle joined together" (trans. by Clara Lustig).

APPENDIX
B

EMMA'S NATIVITY SCENE NO. 4: MY COMING INTO THE WORLD

Outside the room, the men, father and son, were quarreling as usual; inside the room, the midwife, Thorpe, a clean sensible woman in her early forties, was so absorbed in her own thoughts that she hardly heard them. She was muttering to herself: "First 'twas false pains," which she had been sent for two days ago. "Nothin' but wind pent up in the bowels causin' the guts to twinge and grip." And then yesterday they had sent for her again telling her the water had broken. She had come quickly and the woman, young and fair, complained woefully of great pain in her loins.

First ordering the servants to open all the drawers and the closets to make the birth easier, the midwife then ordered the woman to keep standing as long as possible, holding onto a table, if need be, and finally had ordered the husband, Elijah, out of the room, despite his protests. What did men know about pain and childbirth. Nothing! They were of no use standing there, incapable of doing anything, their faces filled with fear. When he had left she had told the woman she could cry out now, as loud as she pleased.

Thorpe put her fingers up the wet and bloody dilated vagina to the mouth of the womb itself, coming in contact with the membrane.

"Fools! The waters broke indeed! Fools! Must have been a bit of piss she passed. But thank God it had not broken yet! 'Twas not to be a dry birth." But she had known all along, hadn't she? Easy pregnancy, difficult birth. 'Twas always the same. Funny how it always felt like an egg without its shell. Through it she felt the top of the baby's head. Mentally she crossed herself, as she always did, in the presence of God's handiwork. Inside the womb the powerful muscles contracted and heaved again. Theodisia screamed. Good, thought the midwife, the labor was beginning in earnest. But at the same time she heard the angry male voices outside the bedroom shouting at one another. God help us! Had they no sense! She suspected it was about her. Had she not told the old man Jorem to get someone else? But he had insisted and she had complied, as always. She had never yet refused him anything. Tender and cruel, he was, tender and cruel. And you'd never know which, would you? The woman screamed again, the scream cutting through the midwife's thoughts.

"Grindal!" she growled menacingly, "give her the laudanum now! Now!" Damn that idiot girl, why hadn't she done it before? Hadn't she brought it in particular, and the oil of sweet almonds, for hoarseness.

And now, unexpectedly, the waters broke. Gushing, they came smelling of urine and ammonia, discolored with scarlet blood. She asked for clean linen and placed it under the young woman's buttocks. How old was she? she wondered as she worked. Not more'n seventeen, she'd heard. A wealthy yeoman's daughter from two towns away. A light sweat made the midwife's pleasant, blunt-featured face glisten as she began to concentrate on the delivery. Still, it bothered her to midwife this woman. It should have been someone else. 'Twas not her place to do it.

Telling the woman to "Push down!" with the ends of her broad-tipped fingers, she pushed back the neck of the womb gently to ease the delivery. The woman screamed. "Push! Push down . . . that's a good girl . . . that's a darlin' . . ." she encouraged, as she saw the child's head advancing through the opening of the womb. Ah, it was in the passage now. In a moment or two it would crown.

When it did, the woman screamed again. A noisy wench, weren't she? But the child was out of the privities at last. The worst pain, the midwife knew, was over now except for the after mess. She relaxed and seated herself on the stool in front of the woman's wide-open legs to receive the child, though still holding onto the neck of the womb to help the newborn bairn slowly inch

The mammer, a short stocky man, selected by the village priest for his piety, health, and personal cleanliness, followed her somewhat sheepishly past the two men into the room. A few minutes later he was bending over the new mother and expertly sucking out the milk of both breasts while the newborn babe lay alone in her cradle screaming to be fed.

APPENDIX
C

EMMA FORSTER: NOVELIST

AN APPRECIATION BY RACHEL LOWE

A FULL discussion of Emma's novels does not lie within the confines of this article but a few remarks need to be made. There were problems.

She was a Victorian woman. The subject of female Victorian novels—the many-splendored reward of subservience—was not however (except for *Happy Endings*) her subject matter. Her subjects were the fulfillment of the heart and how envy makes the world rotten, the ecstasies of physical intercourse and the pain of sexual jealousy, and the issue of being a female artist in a man-made world.

Of the six novels she wrote, only the first one, *Happy Endings,* was published. Its subtitle was *The Danger of Misperceptions.*

The novel begins with a brief homily on the dangers of misperceptions and how they can be avoided. The first sentence reads: "If we but bow our heads and turn our cheeks gladly, again and again and willingly too, shall we not be transported to the pinnacle of pure radiance and the faultless purity of noble perception: the ideal goodness of God's world?"

She was seventeen years old when she wrote her first novel. It was completed in less than six weeks. She was in love and believed her love was returned. It was the last work of its kind. Thereafter she wrote if not from a pinnacle of disillusionment then certainly within sight of its summit.

The name of the second novel was *Misperceptions*. Its subtitle was *The Danger of Illusions*. She goes on to expose the deep-rooted antagonism between the sexes, and examines sexual relations in all their subtle ramifications. All the horror and humiliation of abandonment are spelled out. We are no longer living in "the ideal goodness of God's world" but in the evil of man's world. It was written after the man (Johan Lustig) she loved had disappeared. The contents are exactly the same as the first novel's contents: the vicissitudes of young love. But in this new and diabolical mirror the illusions "created, adhered to, and disseminated by my foolish contemporaries" are destroyed.

She submitted the novel to the same house that published her first novel. It is amusing to read her editor's reply to her manuscript, couched in the language of the day:

> *My dear Miss Forster:*
>
> *Thank you for sending us your second novel,* Misperceptions. *We have read it with pleasure.*
>
> *However, we regret to inform you that due to the state of our economy our lists are temporarily closed, and we foresee that if "hard times" continue there will be even less output next season.*
>
> *Under the circumstances, might it not be, we wonder, a time in which you might wish to reassess the wisdom of a literary life at all, and all the perils that such a life might entail for a young lady such as yourself? The stress of too much intellectual activity on a young mind cannot be overemphasized.*
>
> *Thank you for submitting the novel for our perusal. As we have stated, we were most grateful for the opportunity to read it.*
>
>> *Most sincerely and with best wishes,*
> > *Richard Travers, Esquire*

One can almost see the peculiar smile that William describes as her "wolf" smile cross Emma's face as she reads his reply.

From then on, she accepted the fact, saying, "I was emotionally and intellectually before my time." It is a miracle that she did not dry up artistically—after all an integral part of the creative process is an audience. The first four are dedicated to Darius, the last two to the Beloved. Perhaps an audience of two sufficed.

There is much I could discuss but I have chosen to discuss only her last essay, "Lilith and her Kin," and her last novel, *Preliminary Communications.*

In "Lilith," Emma confronts the problem of female creativity in a world women had no part in creating.

Using the myth of Lilith—the woman who before Eve was Adam's mate and who, unwilling to forego her equality, disputed with Adam the manner of their intercourse—Emma returns to the scenes of her youth, in particular Marlborough Gardens, her grandfather's creation, and explores once more their psychological and emotional significance to her. It ends with a sober investigation on the "unpremeditated" damage caused by Jorem's codicil on her development as a woman, in particular the codicil's last words—"so great is the power of beauty."

"I was not beautiful," she writes. "I was born plain and small and disfigured. According to my grandfather's standards, I was therefore considered powerless. And yet I knew I must wend my way, struggle through somehow to self-completion, without the power/weapon of beauty, that weapon that tempers, subdues, and even occasionally vanquishes the male, for despite my looks I was ambitious, aspiring, enterprising, even . . . predatory. (It has always seemed strange to me that in the Christian world love and war are antithetical while in the pagan world they—Aphrodite and Mars—are lovers.) Having no beauty, what power worth did I have then?

"Though it galled me to have to bend my knee to any masculine value, this one to me seemed particularly unjust."

Then she examines Jorem's gift of the King's Ransom in relation to Vanessa, pointing out that had it not been for the gift, which made Vanessa independently wealthy, she might not have attracted the charming wastrel and aristocrat Sir Charles Mallow, the Viscount Kingston who not only spent her King's Ransom fulfilling his own desires but betrayed her sexually with a younger woman soon after Vanessa's "power of beauty" had faded.

"Of what value was the gift then?" she asks brutally.

It was the *Studien über Hysterie*[7] that inspired her to write her last novel, called *Preliminary Communications (Jane Eyre, Again)*. It is a comic and satiric reworking of that novel, which she had read and studied in her youth.

Emma's neighbor Count Maria von Hoenfenschtall, who was among other things an amateur psychologist and an admirer of Charcot, gave her the book *Studien über Hysterie* to read two years after its publication. The book purported to be an investigation of forms and symptoms of hysteria "with a view to discovering their precipitating cause" and a description of a new procedure (psychotherapy) that would cure the disease.

Part I of the *Studien,* called "Preliminary Communications," is a discussion of hysteria's physical mechanisms: The origin of hypnoid states, Breuer and Freud claim, ". . . would seem to grow out of daydreams which are common . . . and to which needlework and similar occupations render women especially prone." In their hypnoid states they are as insane as we all are in our dreams. "Whereas however our dream psychoses have no effect upon our waking state, the products of hypnoid states intrude into waking life in the form of hysterical symptoms."

Part II of Freud and Breuer's *Studien* is a compilation of five case histories, all of women patients, of course; Part III is a theoretical discussion by Breuer; Part IV, by Freud, is on the psychotherapy of hysteria.

In Emma's version of *Jane Eyre,* the young governess takes off with the "madwoman" Bertha Mason and leaves behind Brontë's hero Edward Rochester.

Taking its structure from the *Studien,* the first chapter is entitled "Case 6, Mr. Edward Rochester." The narrator is a German doctor, Doctor Nebelig (literally Dr. Foggy) who is on vacation in the north of England in the year 1895.

It begins except for minor changes exactly like Freud's Case 5 (Fraulein Elizabeth von R.), weaving back and forth in time as it relates the traumatic events of the patient's life (Edward Rochester).

"In the autumn of 1895," the doctor writes, "I was visiting a colleague of mine in the north of England when I was

---

7. *Studien über Hysterie,* Joseph Breuer and Sigmund Freud, German edition, 1895, Leipzig and Vienna: Deuticke.

asked by a doctor I knew to examine a man who had been suffering for more than two years from blindness. When making his request he added that he thought the case was one of hysteria, though there was no trace of the usual indications of that neurosis. However, after many examinations he had not as yet discovered a physical cause for the blindness.

"He told me that he knew the man slightly and that during the last few years he had met with many misfortunes and not much happiness.

"Firstly, his wife, a middle-aged madwoman by the name of Bertha Mason, had run off with his young ward's governess, a young girl by the name of Jane Eyre. Sometime after that, his beautiful manor house Thornwood burned to the ground. And after that, his housekeeper, a distant relative of his, a Mrs. Fairfax, succumbed to a heart affliction of long standing after a confinement. In all these troubles and in all the nursing involved, the largest share had fallen to our patient."

It is clever. It is malicious. It is savage.

The actual therapy begins with Rochester visiting the doctor five times a week in his hotel suite, which is elaborately described. Rochester's initial resistance is followed by transference, which in Rochester's case is manifested by a sexual dependence on the "good doctor."

In the chapter entitled "Unconscious Ideas and Ideas Inadmissible to Consciousness," Rochester relates to the doctor how he was forced to watch—he could not move, he complains bitterly, being afflicted, as he says, with a sudden and enigmatic paralysis—*forced to watch* the two women, Bertha and Jane, make love with one another in the attic of his beautiful manor house, Thornwood.

The scene is worthy of Zola, the degree and description of the women's sexual passion echoing the violence of the original *Jane Eyre,* and it also clarifies the underlying sexuality of the prototype.

In the closing pages of the novel, the doctor skillfully traces the seeds of Rochester's hysterical blindness and other hysterical symptoms (auditory disturbances, deafness, dizziness, fatigue, headaches, disturbances of smell, walking disturbances, idées fixes, neck cramps, anorexia, depression) to that very incident. The good doctor, quoting Freud, explains to Rochester, "In the

first place I am obliged to recognize that insofar as one can speak
of determining causes which lead to the acquisition of neuroses,
their etiology is to be looked for in sexual factors" . . . and begins
to probe, delicately, his patient's androgynous proclivities as manifested by the patient's penchant for dressing up in women's cloth-
ing, for example, Rochester as the gypsy fortuneteller.

The book ends as the *Studien* ends with Freud's immortal dialogue spoken in the novel by Rochester and Doctor Nebelig.

> "You tell me yourself," said Mr. Rochester, "that my
> illness is probably connected with my circumstances and the
> events of my life. You cannot alter these in any way. How
> do you propose to help me then?"
> I answered him as best I could.
> "No doubt," I said, "fate would find it easier than I do
> to relieve you of your illness. But you will be able to convince
> yourself that much will be gained if we succeed in trans-
> forming your hysterical misery into common unhappiness."

Emma Forster's work was completely unknown in her time. She
does not mention that fact though it must have been difficult for
her to bear. Her characters stand outside her century. She was,
like Darius, an exile in a male-dominated world. Yet she was
more alive in her time than her contemporaries, more aware of
its problems. Her style was uneven, confused, uncertain, even
unpleasant at times, but her vision of the world she lived in had
greater depth than did the work of her contemporaries.

She was, unlike them, an original.

APPENDIX
D

THE FORSTER ANTHOLOGY OF FAIRY TALES

Editor: Albert Forster

With illustrations by Vanessa Forster Herrod

Privately published in 1872

Republished in 1938 by Mantike Press with an introduction by Rachel Lowe

TABLE OF CONTENTS

INTRODUCTION

THAT our lives evolve out of the roots of our childhood is probably one of the most remarkable insights of the twentieth century.
Fairy tales are a part of the story of childhood.

The Forster children were told fairy tales by their grandfather
Jorem, Nanny Grindal, and Aunt Guinivere. These tales were of
course extensions of their secret fantasies and aspirations, the
private language of their unconscious.

Conceived in the primitive and archaic code of dreams, a fairy
tale is a mirror of a child's unconscious logic: a bisexual world,
rife with dreams of incest and other polymorphous sexual satisfactions; a world in which giants, dwarfs, and ghosts exist; in
which animals, birds, and trees converse; in which magic is an
everyday occurrence, and anger, terror, and heartbreaking despair cohabit comfortably alongside the wildest joys and libidinous
satisfactions. As Djuna Barnes said, "Children know something
they cannot tell; they like Red Riding Hood and the wolf in bed!"[8]

For the children, Marlborough Gardens was peopled with characters from the fairy tales. The oak tree where the Calcutta Ghost
lay "forever and ever" was a sacred and awesome place. They
sought Meki and Lord Rolly in the lake and in the brook. Emma

---

8. Djuna Barnes, *Nightwood* (New York: New Directions, 1937).

and Deirdre, even Vanessa, were certain they had seen Elizabeth Vole.

As the children matured, the conscious connections to the tales were repressed, but by that time, they had become part of the sinew of the children's minds, an unconscious ligament connecting them to their vital powers. "Creature of Light" (the tale of the black swan), became the mainstay of their instinctive minds, sustaining them with courage and hope throughout the more desperate passages of their individual lives.

R. Lowe
Marlborough Gardens, London
New Year's Eve, 1938

The Tale of the Two Golden Cockerels:
Guinivere's Tale

Once upon a time, many years ago, on the western coast of France, in the province of Brittany, there lived a young widow, Madame de Fleur, and her two young sons, Armand and André, in a cottage on the edge of a moor. It was a thatched cottage with mullioned windows and eaves that sloped down at certain points almost to the ground. Green vines and creepers clung close to its whitewashed walls.

The widow and her two boys took care of cows, pigs, chickens, and geese, besides cutting wood and drawing water from a well. And though the widow mourned her late husband, and the boys their poppa, they were happy and contented with their life for they loved one another.

Every Sunday after church Madame de Fleur and her sons would go to the moor that lay behind their house to visit Captain de Fleur, who was buried there under a stone called The Pillar of Blood. When weather permitted, they would picnic on raspberry tarts, a food that the widow adored. Her boys, whom she called her golden boys, would be dressed in the most splendid of military uniforms that were the exact replicas of their father's uniform. He had died a hero's death in some distant battle fighting for his king. They chatted mostly about how they loved one another. And so the time would pass.

One Sunday as they were munching their tarts, a very handsome dragon, eight feet tall, whose name was the Baron de Chasseur, spied the widow and fell immediately in love with her. He lived in a stone castle several leagues away. He had come to the moor today for a bit of hunting, desiring a brace of pheasant or grouse, or even a clutch of thrush, having killed much of the wildlife in his vicinity.

He began to court her. Each day a new gift would arrive at the widow's cottage. I shall tell you just some of the most interesting ones: a live cat and a live dog who danced minuets with one another, a toy housemaid in cap and apron who dusted and washed dishes, an articulated horse with a peacock on its back who spread his tail and looked to left and right for applause, and a small silver stove with silver pans and a kettle that prepared its own dinners. But the young widow, remaining faithful to the memory of her departed husband, returned each and every gift accompanied with a polite note of refusal.

On reading the notes, the baron's scales, which were the color of green apples, would turn bright red with anger and a billow of smoke would come forth from his large emerald-colored nostrils. One day, having received the widow's sixteenth refusal, he called for his court magician, a very old toad called Wattles.

The baron demanded a spell that would change the widow's mind. The magician thought for a moment and then right before the baron's eyes created a porcelain box on the four sides of which were printed in gold letters these three words: DO NOT OPEN.

It was brought to the cottage by the baron's messenger, a young water moccasin, that night when both children were asleep.

The widow unwrapped the package and set the new gift on the table to inspect it. She had her pen and paper already laid out on her small desk to write her note of refusal when she read the words DO NOT OPEN. She promptly opened the box. Inside the box was the most delicious raspberry tart she had ever seen or smelled. She promptly ate it and just as promptly forgot not only her husband but her two children, André and Armand.

Later that evening the baron came to call and when he asked for her hand in marriage, she consented and went away with him that very night.

The following morning the children, finding their mother gone, went out into the world to look for her, first to the church, then to the market, then to the moor. When they could not find her in any of these places, they decided to widen their search; they packed a light lunch and then crossed the moor and entered the woods.

Now, a young witch called Do Tomorrow What You Cannot Do Today lived there, and on the day that the children entered the woods, she was practicing three spells that her mentor, an old witch called Do Yesterday What You Cannot Do Today had given her.

She had already done the first spell, transforming a frog into a prince; and the second spell, transforming a prince into a frog, when she spied André and Armand. Clapping her hands in glee, she recited the third spell, and within the length of a sneeze, they were transformed into two golden cockerels, exactly alike, except that one had a gold fleck in one of his eyes, and the other a silver.

Then she took them to sell at the market, where later that day the baron bought them as a gift for his new wife, the beautiful widow, now known as Lády de Chasseur.

The lady was delighted with her cockerels. She would take them on walks with her and tell them stories. How beautiful they were. How obedient. They did remind her of something or someone. Oh, if only she could remember! But she could not, for she was still under the court magician's spell.

As time went on, the baron, seeing how enamored his young wife was of the cockerels, became jealous. One day he told her that the court physician, a magpie called Winter, told him that the only cure for his gout would be for him to eat a golden cockerel's heart. Since she had two of them, would she give him one?

That night alone in her room she wept. How could she choose between them? She loved them both. But before she could make up her mind the cockerels spoke to her. They addressed her as Lady de Chasseur. "Lady de Chasseur," they said, "do not trouble yourself with this problem. We shall make the choice between ourselves." After thanking them, she fell into a deep sleep.

As soon as she slept, Armand held up two straws and asked André to pull one of them out of his claw with the understanding that the cockerel who drew the shortest straw would make the sacrifice. André pulled the short straw out of the claw, and on seeing it exclaimed, "Thank you, God, for granting me the shorter straw!" But Armand, in the meantime, had managed to break off his length of straw. He held his up and said, "No André, mine is shorter yet." And so Armand told his mother, the Lady de Chasseur that it was he, the cockerel with the silver fleck in his eyes, who was to be sacrificed.

In the kitchen the cook took Armand out of his cage and cut off his neck. Then she slit open his carcass and withdrew his heart, which she put into a roasting pan and cooked, basting it from time to time with a bit of ginger water. That evening she put the dish on a silver platter and sent it upstairs to the great hall where the baron, his knights, and his lady were waiting for dinner.

"Ah," said the Baron, "just the thing for my gout," and he cut off a small piece of the heart with his knife and fork. Tears came to the lady's eyes as she watched the baron put a small piece of the cockerel's heart into his mouth. But just as the baron clamped down on the small piece of flesh with his enormous copper teeth, Armand sprang forth from between his teeth, fully clothed and fully armed. Raising his sword high, Armand drove it through the dragon's heart and killed him. The spell had been broken the moment the copper teeth had touched the cockerel's flesh. Of course, had the baron's teeth been made of iron, or ivory, or wood, or stone, or glass, or pewter, or anything else, Armand would have been eaten. The baron's knights, who hated him, wept with joy, as did the lady.

As for André, who was still a cockerel . . . they took him back to the young witch in the woods, who for a half a crown and a promise that on All Hallows Eve she could come to their cottage and practice changing chickens into pigs, pigs into geese, and geese into cows, reversed the spell, and the widow and her two golden boys lived happily ever after.

The Tale of the Two Sisters: Grindal's Tale

Once upon a time there was woman called Rosamunda who wanted a child. So she did the usual things: she took mincemeat, snippets of foxglove, and the molar tooth of an eel, and stirred them together and added a pinch of pearl powder beause she wanted a female child and put them in a large iron pot. To all of this she added exactly six and an eighth ounces of seasoned rainwater and left it to simmer on her stove while she went marketing for her food for the day.

On the way home from market she passed a two-headed frog and a bird with three beaks and saw a dark cloud hovering on the horizon in the shape of a six-footed beast. It made her quite thoughtful and she hurried on home. The moment she entered her cottage, she knew something terrible had happened. She hurried into the kitchen, ran to the stove, and looked inside the iron pot. The baby was burned. Stupid Rosamunda had made a terrible mistake: instead of putting six and a quarter ounces of water into the pot, she had put in only six and an eighth ounces of water. Carefully she lifted the child who was still alive but scorched out of the pot and lay her on the cool tile floor and wrapped her in her grandmother's silver cloak. The baby fell asleep almost immediately.

The following day Rosamunda unwrapped the baby and those parts of her body that had not been burned had been transformed into silver by the cloak, which is why Rosamunda named her Agura, which means "silver." Agura grew up playing with rabbits, chipmunks, moles, and a colony of finches that lived near and about the cottage; she made a special friend of a fieldmouse called Carlotta. Agura was quite happy for she did not realize how ugly she was with all those red burns on her face and body.

One day Rosamunda decided to have another female child, but this time she took the precaution of not leaving the cottage until the process was over. In less than three hours she lifted a newborn baby girl out of the iron pot. This time she wrapped up the child in her grandmother's cloak of gold and laid her on the tiles. The following morning when she lifted the child out of the cloak, she decided to call the child Aurum, which means "gold," because the baby's hair, skin, eyes, and even nails were all the color of gold.

Rosamunda and her two daughters Agura and Aurum were happy with one another because they were kind to and thoughtful of one another. The village parson, a dignified old dog, would refer to them in sermons as "that dear threesome who know their place and are contented with the very little that they have, an inspiration to us all." On church holidays when the villagers would vie with one another to supply the church with gifts of food, Rosamunda and her two daughters would outdo them all. They always made the most terrible pies called Terrible Pies because they were made from berries plucked from Terrible bushes. And true to their name, they had a terrible taste, and really only the villagers of Mopera (that was the village's name) enjoyed eating them.

One day a witch who had just arrived from the moon knocked on Rosamunda's door. She wished to have a cup of tea, she said, to tide her over the last lap of her journey to the middle of the earth. Agura opened the door since Rosamunda had gone out.

"Do come in," said Agura, "and sit down. Would you like a cup of tea?" As you see, Rosamunda had brought her up to have perfect manners.

The witch, whose name was Lebentot, looked at Agura with some curiosity. "Are we acquainted? Have I seen you before? Were you ever in the land of Kalopia?" When she saw Agura shake her head, she said, "Or Shaligreen? . . . or Tovera? Well, no matter, it will come to me when it does, for I know I have seen you before."

After drinking her cup of tea, the witch shook out her long black cloak. Flakes of fire sparkled and then fell as embers to the tile floor. "Give me some bread, child, and I shall be on my way . . . unless"—she moved towards Agura and stared deep into her eyes—"unless . . . you need something from me. I ask, for I see in your silver eyes that you long for something you do not have. If you tell me what it is, I promise I shall provide it."

Before she knew it, Agura told Lebentot what she herself until that moment had not realized was in her heart. "I want to have," said Agura, "the smooth golden skin my little sister Aurum, who is asleep in her cot in the other room, has. Would you like to see her?"

"Oh, there is no need for me to go into the other room. I see her clearly enough. She is beautiful. Perfect. The very opposite of you. Ah! Now I remember . . . it was many years ago, but I remember everything now! You almost came to us years ago, but your mother, Rosamunda, snatched you from right underneath our noses. Oh, we were very angry; had she come home only a few moments later you would have been ours! My companion Astar, who guards the territory we rule, was furious! Fate has brought us together again."

Now the witch withdrew from one of the folds of her cloak a square of cooked dough with many different kinds of seed pressed into its surface and put it on the table. Then she withdrew a looking glass from her cloak, which though it was not larger than a chipmunk's paw reflected entire objects so that when Agura glanced into the mirror she could see herself from top to toe in miniature.

"Every evening when everyone is asleep you are to take a bite of this delicious cake. When the cake is finished you shall see by looking into this glass that your wish has been fulfilled. Then you are to come to the hazel wood, the one that is a mile down the road, on the left, and call my name, 'Lebentot!' and I shall come and teach you how to fly, how to transform birds into bees, bees into nettles, and nettles into wine."

That evening when everyone was asleep, Agura took out the cake, which she had hidden underneath her bed, and took a bite of it. A form of happiness that she had never felt before stole over her. Every morning she would gaze into the small glass, and it seemed to her as each day passed, that her skin was becoming more and more golden. As golden as her sister Aurum's skin. At the same time she saw that her sister, Aurum, was beginning to pale, that she was listless, and a few days later when Agura had taken the last bite of cake, Aurum died.

Rosamunda, grief stricken, went to the village to discuss with the coffin maker, a kindly otter, the kind of coffin she wanted for her daughter Aurum. Together they decided on a small coffin made of birch wood almost the same color of Aurum's hair, skin, and eyes.

The moment Rosamunda left the cottage, Lebentot stood in the doorway and said to Agura, "Well, I have provided for your desires, now you must provide for mine."

"What do you want me to do?" asked Agura. She was a little frightened because the look on Lebentot's face was very nasty.

"Oh, nothing that will be too difficult for you to do. Your village, Mopera, happens to be in the way of some project we have planned for our autumnal ball. We would like you to burn it down. It's standing in our way."

"But I can't do anything like that! Besides, why can't you? After all, if you can change my skin from silver to gold I should think it would be easy enough for you to burn down Mopera." Poor Agura in her state of shock was not thinking clearly.

"There are certain things we can do and certain things we cannot," replied Lebentot.

"I shall never do it. Never!"

"O yes, you shall."

"Never! Never! Never!" repeated Agura.

"Oh, you shall do it. If not right away, in time," said Lebentot, vanishing as she heard a key in the lock and Rosamunda entered. The only thing that was left of her presence was a single ember that glowed at Agura's feet.

That night Agura promised God that she would never do what Lebentot wanted and went quietly to sleep.

The next day as Agura was working in the garden transplanting a Terrible bush, a hand came out of the freshly dug ground and Carlotta, the fieldmouse who always helped Agura garden, ran over to examine it. Beore Agura could do anything, the hand reached up and grabbed Carlotta, and holding the mouse tightly in its palm disappeared back in the earth again. First Agura heard a terrible squalling and then, far worse than that—silence.

The next morning when Rosamunda had gone to visit the coffin maker again, Lebentot came through the door.

"Out! Out!" cried Agura, and she pushed the witch through the door and quickly shut it. But when she turned around, there was Lebentot warming her hands by the fire. "Now, we'll have no more of that, shall we!" said Lebentot and then from the folds of her cloak she removed a large piece of cardboard on which was loosely sketched the plan of the village. "Now, if you start a fire here," she pointed to the cobbler's small house, "that will go up in seconds and with it the butcher's house next to it, why that will go up in flames too—"

"God is listening and he will punish you. I have told him all about you."

"Have you now? For your information, God is a distant relative of mine."

Just then they heard the key in the lock and as Rosamunda entered Lebentot vanished.

That night Agura prayed: "God Seeall and Knowall, help me. And do punish Lebentot."

Sitting beneath the earth, between some ancient oak-tree roots, Lebentot and Astar her friend discussed the matter.

"Stubborn, very stubborn the girl is," said Astar, blowing smoke rings that floated to the ceiling of their cosy cave. "Don't care much for people like that, not really. It's a great fault being stubborn, I always say. 'Cause we could have the ball elsewhere; I know a fine fat young boy that would burn down his town for a lemon tart, he would, but you've got your heart set on Mopera, don't you?"

"Indeed I do. She really does belong to us. A mere accident that she isn't ours actually. We'll have to tighten the screws."

"Hmmmm . . . I did think Caper Carlotta would do it," said Astar looking at the tail of the dead fieldmouse caught in the oak roots. "The girl has no feeling, no feeling at all."

"We could try Raze Rosamunda," said Lebentot. "I've been told that little girls are usually very fond of their mothers."

The next day when Agura was picking some Terrible berries of the Terrible bush, she found a note attached to one of its branches which read: "If you do not do what we want you to do something terrible will happen to your mother." Quickly Agura took her pen and bottle of ink out of her pinafore pocket and wrote in the margin of the notepaper: "What is one life compared to thousands?"

"Hmmm . . ." said Astar, reading the note in the cosy confines of their cave, "a very difficult girl. The girl has no feeling is what I say—"

"Oh but she does! I have just remembered the *one* person for whom she *does* have feeling!" said Lebentot and she left Astar sitting there alone.

The next morning Agura rose as always, humming cheerfully. As always, she took out her small mirror to admire her new golden skin and found instead the old skin, silver, scarlet, and puckered. "Oh, what has happened? What has happened?" moaned Agura, holding onto the back of a chair for she was quite dizzy, and then she began to cry.

It was in her third hour of crying that Lebentot appeared holding in her webbed fingers a familiar square loaf with many different seeds on it. She placed it on the mantel of the fireplace. Agura looked at the loaf, as if it was the only thing in the world worth looking at.

"It is yours," said Lebentot, "*if* you do what I have asked you to do."

A terrible pain shot through Agura's body and though she said "No," her voice was weak as if she was dying.

"Well then," said Lebentot in a brisk tone, "there is a little girl down the street who said she wanted it. I shall give it to her," and she started to put it back in the folds of her cloak when Agura said in a very strange voice, "Leave it here, Lebentot . . . I shall do what you want."

"Do you promise?"

"I promise."

And that is how and why the village of Mopera was burned to the ground, killing all the inhabitants including the parson, the coffin maker, Rosamunda, and Agura. All the inhabitants, except Agura, went to Heaven where they met Aurum and Carlotta, who showed them around and were by and large quite helpful to the new arrivals.

Agura went to Hell and suffered the Tortures of the Damned for Eternity. From time to time, Rosamunda and Aurum would send her by special messenger Terrible pies, for you see they have Terrible bushes in Heaven too.

C.

The Tale of the Calcutta Ghost: Grindal's Tale

Once upon a time there was a ghost called the Calcutta Ghost because he was born in Calcutta, a city on the other side of the world.

Before he was a ghost, when he was a young man he came to London, in 1823, to make his fortune, but since he was lazy he did not. He spent his days lolling about Marlborough Gardens, though he wrote his mother and father long letters about how hard he was working.

One day while walking through Marlborough Gardens (17 June 1827 at 10:00 A.M.) a large bird fell out of a tree onto the young man's head and he dropped down dead. The gardeners buried him underneath the Sacred Oak in Blenheim Wood. After he was buried, he rose from the dead and joined the other phantoms who lived in Marlborough Gardens—the ghouls, goblins, elves, pixies, trolls, ogres, and minor devils.

For a time he was very good, that is, he obeyed all the Ghostly rules, called the Neveralways rules, of which there are many. I shall only tell you a few:

1. Always wear a clean robe and a clean nightcap.
2. Never drink or imbibe in wine.
3. Never appear before sunset.
4. Never float, rise, or levitate on Sunday.
5. Never masquerade as a changeling or a bugbear.
6. Always be polite to wood nymphs, mermaids, cherubs.
7. Always carry your psalmbook.
8. Never frighten or eat children.

But one day quite by accident the Calcutta Ghost frightened a child, a plump five-year-old child who had been left in Marlborough Gardens after sunset by his nanny who had forgotten all about him. And it so delighted him—the silly child screamed and carried on so, it was really quite a treat to watch—that it put him into the way of thinking how he might just "try" another one. But, how many nannies could be relied upon to be so conveniently forgetful? wondered the Calcutta Ghost. Not many. But there were children who left their nannies, weren't there?

Therefore, he decided to buy an alarm clock from a fellow

ghost who lived nearby on Wicklow Street, paying two shillings and ten pence for it. On a Monday evening he set it for twelve noon the following day (6 October 1834).

The next day when the alarm woke him, he jumped out of bed—did I tell you that he lived in the tower room of Tower Farfrum? Well, he did—and rushed down all 156 steps of its staircase, and rushed down the gravel paths looking here, there, and everywhere for some silly child who had been foolish enough to leave his or her nanny so that the Calcutta Ghost could frighten him or her. Much to his delight, he found one almost immediately, walking through the marshes toward the lake. He crept up, slithering through the grasses, and passed the child, whereupon he hid behind a tree and waited. Just as the child passed the tree, he darted out and shouted in a loud voice: "Hoo Hah! Hoo Hah!" and then darted back again to watch from behind the tree the effect of this visitation.

Oh it was wonderful! to see how the child's hair stood on end, how he changed color, how he shivered and trembled, how his teeth chattered, how he started weeping and crying "boo hoo, boo hoo." And so he did it again, darted out from behind the tree and shouted, "Hoo Hah! Hoo Hah!" and this time he added to the effect by raising his long bony arms and wriggling his long bony fingers. When the child fainted, he left him lying there on the path and went to look for another one.

He had more fun that afternoon terrifying children than he had had for the last seven years. Oh, he could not wait until the following noon! But of course someone told (someone always does) Squire Humphrey of Whitechapel, their beloved leader and mentor, and the Calcutta Ghost was summoned to the squire's quarters, a jam factory on Jerusalem Lane.

Now you may or may not know that ghosts are very fond of jam, in particular those flavors that begin with W, such as Waggish and Whimper, Wild and Wicked (everyone's favorite). They won't put up with Wretched or Wrinkle or Wrong or Writer for they all begin with R's, don't they? They're not the wreal thing, are they?

But to get back to our story, there sat the Calcutta Ghost shivering with fear in the squire's anteroom which was jammed full of jars of jam beginning with the letter W. In less than a half an hour the squire came in holding in one hand a long-handled spoon and in the other an open jar of Wise.

"By the way," said Squire Humphrey, prying open Calcutta's mouth and pouring some Wise into it, "would you like some of this? It might do you a bit of good, old thing." Then the squire crammed his own mouth full of Wise and said, "You'll have to Stop! you know, you'll just have to Stop! old dear. It's unfair, ain't it, to take advantage. Not much the Livelies can do about us. Us bein' dead 'nd all that. Why quick as a blink we're through the crack in the door, or window, or slidin' through the key-hole . . . so havin' so much power, old mate, we can't let it go to our heads, can we? Noblesse oblige an' all that. So it's only fair that we be on our best behavior, ain't it? So go home, old dear, and stop all this nonsense; otherwise we'll have to de-phan-tomize you. I myself don't fancy lying underneath an old oak tree for the Rest of Eternity. Do you?"

In plain English what the squire meant was that if the Calcutta Ghost persisted in frightening children, he would have to spend the rest of his death lying forever and ever underneath the Sacred Oak tree in Blenheim Wood.

The Calcutta Ghost was not really bad except that he did like having his own way. But don't we all? Well, anyway, he was not eager or willing to give up the idea of scaring children (even after his spoonful of Wise). It was just too much fun. Furthermore, he had even contemplated eating one or two of them, they looked so plump and juicy, but on the other hand he didn't want to have to die either. It was a dilemma, as they say.

One night, it was past midnight (3 November 1834 at 2:00 A.M. to be exact) and the Ghost was roaming about in the Gardens thinking about all of this when he spied the duke of Marlborough Gardens, a very wealthy but greedy old man, who lived in the manor house just outside the North Gate, hurrying down one of the gravel paths that led to the lake. The duke was carrying a large sack filled with gold coins. At the edge of the lake the duke waded into the water, and the Calcutta Ghost, who was sitting on one of the branches of one of the willow trees that grow by the edge of the lake, watched him as he waded over to the rock that sits in the middle of the lake and saw the duke open it by pressing one of its facets and deposit the sack of gold coins inside it. Then, straightening up and looking all around him, the duke scurried away.

The following night the same thing happened. And the following night after the following night the same thing happened. On the fourth night the Calcutta Ghost confronted the duke just before he stepped into the lake. "Hoo Hah! I've been watching you."

"Oh," said the duke falling to his knees, "if you don't tell anyone what you've seen, I shall reward you handsomely. I shall buy you as much jam as you want," said the duke, the duke being knowledgeable about ghosts and jam.

"I shall tell," said the Calcutta Ghost, "unless you promise to do what I tell you to do. If you don't promise, I will tell your two uncles (the viscount of Blenheim Wood and the earl of Nannies Plain) and they shall make sure you share your gold."

As I said, the duke was greedy. He certainly didn't want to share his gold so he said: "I shall do anything you tell me to do! Anything."

And *that,* dear children, was how the Calcutta Ghost forced the duke to frighten the children of Marlborough Gardens between the hours of 10:00 A.M. and 2:00 P.M. on alternate Mondays, Wednesdays, and Fridays.

When the duke was caught (31 November 1834 at 2 P.M.), he was arrested and sent to Newgate Prison, where he died.

As for the Calcutta Ghost, not being able to give up his bad habits, he continued to frighten the children of Marlborough Gardens so that the squire had to punish him, and that is why the Calcutta Ghost now spends his death lying forever and ever underneath the Sacred Oak in Blenheim Wood.

D.

The Tale of the Evil Frog Meki from Bristol:
Jorem's Tale

"Then you will come to the wedding, Lord Rolly, and give away the bride," said Meki.

"It's little enough that I can do for my oldest and dearest friend," replied Lord Rolly.

Naturally you are all wondering who these two people are, so I shall start from the beginning and go backwards:

Once upon a time there was an evil frog by the name of Lived Lattimore, though everyone called him Meki, who lived in Bristol in a well-furnished, commodious pond that happened to be on the estate of a Lord Rolly, a bumbling old codger.

One day Meki introduced himself to Lord Rolly, and Lord Rolly, having poor eyesight, took Meki to be a long-lost Etonian friend of his: clasping him to his bosom, he invited him to dine with him that evening.

When Lord Rolly's servants took him aside after supper and told him that he was dining with a "frog," he told them to hold their tongues, which they did though it was quite a messy thing to do. His old Etonian friend Algernon Swinbaine, he told his servants, might look a bit like a frog but in his youth he had been ever so handsome, and he might even sound a bit like a frog but Algernon indubitably was an Englishman for he said "rally" for really, drank tea, and shouted "by Jove" at least twice an hour. He certainly wasn't French as they had so callously implied. Besides, wasn't it impolite to call a Frenchman a "frog"?

As I said, Lived was an evil frog, that is, he knew right from wrong; I mean, there's no point in saying that someone's evil if they don't know the difference, is there? No, Meki knew that though it was proper to consume flies, bees, lizards, mosquitos, anything you could catch, you must not torture them before consumption. Just as he knew that one must give "fair warning" to mice before mauling them, in keeping with the Treaty of Sorts composed and signed a thousand years ago by their ancestors the Real Frogs, which is what frogs call themselves, and Real Mice, which is what mice call themselves.

Meki was also very fond of money. He had a really disgusting habit of kissing each and every one of his coins, which were stamped with the two words *pecuniam amo,* which means "I love money." He kept some of his kissed coins in a large steamer trunk in the hold of his yacht that was moored to a willow tree and the rest in a steamer trunk in the strong room of his magnificent mansion that stood on a cluster of lily pads in the center of the lake.

He was enormously wealthy. Not only did he belong to a great and renowned and ancient frog family, the Batraxos, but he had inherited from his Aunt Maude in Essex vast domains of lakes and from his grandmother in Yorkshire an entire river, besides inheriting from his father the very pond he lived in.

Because of his passion for money, he spent much of his time earning it. He had several mills, for instance, in which his workers ground birds' gizzards into flour, which was then made into bread, and which was called Bauerbrot because it tasted very much like German pumpernickel, though it wasn't.

And several theaters. As you may or may not know, frogs are inordinately fond of the theater and four generations of frogs had already been thrilled by Meki's production of *Salamander the First* and horrified by his production of *The Toad's Revenge.*

He also owned a factory that manufactured handsome, albeit gaudy, green-velvet suits for well-to-do frogs. He himself was a picture of sartorial splendor resplendent in gold and silver vests, embroidered cloaks, and Spanish-leather boots, and on the tip of each of his knobby protuberances, which Fake Frogs call "warts," and Real Frogs call "patches of pulchritude," a diamond was soldered so that when he walked he glittered.

But by now you must be quite peeved and angry. Why mention Lord Rolly, you're thinking crossly, never to mention him again?

Why indeed. Well, dear children, I've been "explicating," "elucidating," and "expositing," as I was taught to do as a child. "Begin in *media res,* the middle of things," they told me, and then go backward (exposit). And I've done it perfectly if I must say so myself. Now since there's just a bit more before we catch up to the beginning, and that's quite hard to do since it's so far ahead of us—it's quite a race—don't waken your friends who have fallen asleep, since there's just a bit more going backward before we catch up, that is, if we do catch up at all. Beginnings are very artful, you see, and you must take a firm hand with them if you are going to get anywhere. When I sneeze, you shall know that the three *E*'s have ended and you can pinch awake your dear friends.

So continuing backward what with pulling the wings off flies, not giving mice fair warning, enjoying himself and never washing his hands, cheating his workmen (which I neglected to tell you), and pocketing the proceeds of charity bazaars, he added to the above crimes a new one, perhaps the greatest crime of all. He decided to get married not for love but for reasons of avarice.

It came about this way. One day Meki's uncle, Uncle Vaulter—who always called him by his Christian name, Lived—a distinguished old bullfrog and magistrate in the next county, came to visit Meki to suggest that it was time for him to be married.

'It's time, young Lived, for you to tie the knot. And I have just the damsel, the young daughter of one of your Aunt Polly's cousins, a lovely young polliwog named Atopia full of ginger and good jumping, pious nevertheless, and eager, *very* eager to start a family of her own."

"Does she have money?" asked Meki.

"She's an heiress, my dear wog, a wealthy heiress."

Now Meki who besides being nasty was very shrewd immediately wondered why if what his uncle said were true, why such a wealthy paragon of virtue had not been claimed as yet, and therefore he asked bluntly, "What's wrong with her?"

Uncle Vaulter turned a deep shade of green. "Well now ahem . . . now that you've mentioned it, my dearest of wogs, there is something a bit wrong . . . you see, old diver, the poor gel does have a slight disability, but really, Lived, it is very slight. Why, my dear Lived, unless I pointed it out to you, you would hardly notice it, I'm sure. Really you wouldn't."

"Out with it, Uncle."

"Well all right . . . well, to put it bluntly, my dearest of wogs, the poor gel has no patches, none at all."

"What! No patches, no patches of pulchritude! None! *That* is a bit odd. Must make her look frightfully funny. Peculiar. Quite different. No patches at all! Not even one."

"Alas . . . only a very small one and that can't be seen since it's hidden behind her right ear . . . oh well, you might as well know the rest. She's not really my wife's relative. She's a foundling. My aunt's cousin, a great sportswoman, found her on one of her cross-country leaps in Hampshire and liking the looks of her took her home with her, though she did advertise at once in the *Croaker's Gazette* that if anyone had lost a child on the afternoon of the twentieth of June between the hours of three o'clock and four o'clock, she had found one. Receiving no reply, she reared her as one of her own."

"Hmm . . . exactly how much money does the foundling have?"

Meki's uncle named a huge sum of money, so huge that Meki that very afternoon worked out the particulars including the date, the place, and the time of the wedding-to-be.

However, as the wedding drew nigh, Meki began to feel a bit uncomfortable. While courting Atopia, he grew to like her somewhat even though she did look strange indeed not having those perfectly wonderful patches of pulchritude.

He began to wonder, why was it that some people like himself had all the luck and others like poor Atopia—which means, by the way, strange and unusual—had so little? Now this was very odd thinking for Meki, who till that point had never thought of anyone's happiness but his own. And how very wretched Atopia must feel without patches of pulchritude, which was the second odd, good thought he had in his lifetime WHICH—Kerchoo! kerchoo!—brings me BACK TO THE BEGINNING! I've caught up as I said I would, now quickly, quickly you must poke awake the sleepers; otherwise we might go *past* the beginning and go backward again!

Are you ready? Good!—which is why Meki asked Lord Rolly who had no patches, being a Fake Frog, to give away Atopia at the wedding, for the third odd, good thought that had occurred to Meki was that Atopia might feel just a wee bit more comfortable at her wedding if someone like herself was present, one who also had no delightful, adorable, wonderful patches of pulchritude.

I shall now repeat the beginning for those who may have forgotten it.

"Then you will come to the wedding, Lord Rolly, and give away the bride," said Meki.

"It's little enough that I can do for my oldest and dearest friend," replied Lord Rolly.

During the wedding Lord Rolly's valet whispered in Lord Rolly's ear on the uncanny resemblance between Lord Rolly's sister

Agatha and the bride Atopia. "My word," said Lord Rolly, "she is an exact replica! Do you think—"

"Indeed I do."

"Do you really?"

"Yes, I really do."

"Could it be?"

"It could."

"Are you sure?"

"Absolutely."

"You have no doubts?"

"None at all."

And this tiresome conversation would have gone on and on had it not been for the beadle, a stern old frog, who threatened to wrap their knuckles with his long stick if they did not stop. However, by this time everyone there was far more interested in what Lord Rolly and the valet had been discussing than in the wedding, so they raced through the ceremony and at the end surrounded Lord Rolly and his valet and begged them to explain the mysterious but annoying conversation. When after a quarter of an hour Lord Rolly still had not come to the point, they threatened to duck him in the lake, which is how the valet ended up explaining the matter.

"Seventeen years ago," the valet began, "my master's sister Lady Agatha lost her very first child in Hampshire where she was spending the summer, on the twentieth of June between the hours of three and four. It was a great tragedy. She never quite got over the loss of Arenea, for that was the baby's name. She advertised in the *Times* and the *Guardian* but alas, there was no reply. We believe Atopia is Arenea. She does so resemble Lady Agatha and there is luckily one way of making sure. The child had a slight imperfection—a small wart, which I understand you call a patch of pulchritude, behind her right ear. If she has one, we're certain it's her."

And of course as we all know, except those who fell asleep through the three *E*'s—exposition, explication, and elucidation— she did have one.

So there was great rejoicing.

After the wedding Lord Rolly, having had such a good time, suggested to Meki and his uncle that they compose a Treaty of Bonafide, which they did. And that is why no Fake Frogs (Englishmen) are allowed any longer to eat Real Frogs—at least in Lord Rolly's district.

Now the moral of this story, and the story does have a moral as all good stories do, is that if you have one odd, good thought, it leads to another, which leads to an odd, good deed, which leads to another, and another. So that before you know it, the world that you live in that sometimes seems such a strange and frightening place, and for want of a better word, evil, can be changed into something far far better.

And, oh yes, there is one more thing: Uncle Vaulter stopped calling Meki by the name of Lived. Now, children, that was another odd, good thing as you will discover, if you take the time to spell the name backward.

Grandfather Jorem's Christmas Tale
or
How the Children of Marlborough Gardens Came to
Believe in Father Christmas

Once upon a time there was a five-year-old mouse named Elizabeth Vole who lived in a small cottage underneath the foot of the first stone nymph in the Sunken Garden in Marlborough Gardens.

She had just finished putting Momma and Poppa to bed after spanking them soundly when she heard a disagreeable sound, as if someone were weeping, and the words, "oh, poor me, oh poor me . . ." over and over again.

Very monotonous. Very irritating.

She poked around the library stacks, the wine cellar, all the nooks and crannies of the saloon but found nothing. The weeping and the words were beginning to drive Elizabeth mad. She was quite sure she would kill the weeper when and if she found him. Or her.

She went out on the veranda where the snow lay deep and crisp and even, as it should on Christmas Eve. That made her feel much better.

Elizabeth, though she was only five, was a self-righteous, pompous martinet who demanded absolute obedience *at all times* from her parents. Otherwise, no roly-poly pudding, no skating on the lake, no treats of any sort. Certainly no bedtime tales of any kind!

As you may have guessed already, things were arranged a bit differently in Marlborough Gardens. That is, in Marlborough Gardens it was the children who took care of their parents. And it really does seem to work out better for all concerned. It is a positive pleasure to meet a well-behaved momma and a well-trained poppa. The children rarely have to scold or spank their parents at all.

Elizabeth finally found the wretched little weeper in a puddle of tears in the cloakroom: an elderly hedgehog, a barrister who worked at one of the Garden's inns, by the name of Henry the Fifth, so named because he was the fifth in a litter of eight.

"Oh poor me . . . oh poor me," wept Henry the Fifth.

"Stop that wretched noise immediately!" screamed Elizabeth.

"Have you no consideration at all? My parents are sleeping! What is the matter with you, anyway? And where is Harold your son? You know very well that you are not allowed to wander around without him. Answer or I shall swat you hard and probably kick you as well, you badly behaved sniveling poppa! And on Christmas Eve no less!"

Now Elizabeth was not always so cantankerous, so testy, but to tell the truth she did not like Henry the Fifth. Harold his son (her best friend) had told her how poorly his poppa behaved. *And* on a daily basis. Henry the Fifth it seems was very fond of eggs, and stole them any chance he could get.

Elizabeth's words struck terror into the hedgehog's heart and he promptly rolled himself up into a tight ball, his spines standing out in every direction.

Oh bother, thought Elizabeth, perhaps she had been a bit too harsh, so she said in more dulcet tone, "Do tell Auntie Elizabeth what is wrong."

Henry peering fearfully out from between the spikes of his coat replied in such a low tone, Elizabeth had to bend way down in order to hear him.

"Harold's made a list of all the bad things I've done this year and there are so many that he's quite sure that Father Christmas will not give me what I most desire this Christmas."

"And what is that, dear Henry the Fifth?"

"A wig. A new wig for court. My old one's positively ratty. My colleagues guffaw and snicker at me when I put it on. But Harold says I do not deserve a new one."

Having said this, the hedgehog began to weep again, which vexed Elizabeth, but she said, "Oh well Henry, if that is your only problem I will attend to it forthwith."

She had to repeat the sentence several times before Henry stopped weeping.

"Moira!" she called. A young piglet came into the hall (Elizabeth's parents' nanny). "I must go out for a while, Moira, to attend to certain matters. If my parents awaken and ask for a glass of water or a biscuit or two, you are to give them this list of Latin verbs to conjugate instead." Elizabeth took a sheet of paper out of her apron pocket. "Now Henry, give me your paw and I shall take you home."

Between you and me and the nearest oak tree, her parents were quite unhappy with her. They really did not like her at all.

For years Elizabeth's poppa had wanted binoculars for Christmas, and momma a pony. But according to Elizabeth there was always a good reason why each could not have it.

After dropping off Henry with Harold his son in his lodge by the lake and after briefly reviewing the plight of a child afflicted with naughty parents, Elizabeth scampered through the snow past the carollers to Ivan Ivanovich's cave in Blenheim Wood.

For as long as Elizabeth could remember, Ivan Ivanovich, an elderly squirrel, had played Father Christmas on Christmas Day.

Legend had it that Ivan had appeared one winter in Marlborough Gardens many years ago without children, that is, with no one to take care of him. And so the children of that time, feeling sorry for him, alone and abandoned as he was, told him he could play Father Christmas on Christmas Day. From that day on he had. And he did look splendid in his red-wool suit with its red-tasseled cap and spectacles, his large sack slung over his back bulging with presents for those parents who had been "good" throughout the year.

Ivan said that he had been born in Russia, in St. Petersburg, but Oscar, a wise old fox, said he was really a tailor from Bohemia. At any rate Ivan had a funny way of pronouncing words.

He pronounced all his *D*'s like *T*'s, and all his *T*'s like *D*'s, as well as all his *W*'s as *V*'s and all his *V*'s as *W*'s. But Elizabeth understood him perfectly or as Ivan would say: "Wery Vell."

Another strange thing about Marlborough Gardens, by the way, was that it was the parents and not the children who believed in Father Christmas. When they were children they knew that Father Christmas was really the elderly squirrel named Ivan but when they grew up and became parents they forgot. How this came about no one knew but it had been this way for as long as anyone could remember.

❄   ❄   ❄

"Oh Elizabed, my faworide taughder!" said Ivan as she scampered into the cave.

Elizabeth proceeded to tell Ivan all about Henry the Fifth's dilemma. "Buy him a wig, Ivan. I shall give you the exact cost of a new barrister's wig. Out of my own pocket," and she pulled out three chestnuts and one acorn.

"Vell, I ton'd know vedder I shoult. Shoultn'd I ask Harolt firsd?"

"No, you should not. *I* am managing the matter. If you do not do as I say, I shall see to it that you are retired as Father Christmas."

As you can see for yourself, Elizabeth was clearly a tyrant.

"Vell dad's a goot reason not to ask Harolt, so I shan'd."

That settled, Elizabeth went home to write her Malefaction Accounts, a list of reasons why Poppa and Momma must not receive their hearts' desires: his binoculars, her pony.

Every year the children gave a ball on Christmas Day in the Winter Garden in Marlborough Gardens. At midnight Ivan would arrive as Father Christmas, peruse the Malefaction Accounts, and draw out or not draw out the appropriate present from his sack.

Good and Bad parents were allowed to attend the ball, but it was the Bad parents of course that had to do all the work: move the plants, tables, jardinieres, pots and trees, out of the way so that the children and the Good parents could dance. It was the Bad parents who had to prepare the feast and the Bad parents who had to clean up. But parents, being what they are, were happy enough just to be allowed to attend the ball.

Elizabeth told her parents: "I really would like to be able to tell Father Christmas that you were good this year. But you were not. I do have to be truthful, don't I? I do want you to know however that it hurts me far more than it hurts you. I am quite sure about that."

At midnight when the bells of St. Giles rang out, Father Christmas walked in, his pack bulging with gifts. The parents shrieked, as parents will, and giggled and laughed as parents will, but when it went on a bit too long Elizabeth took it upon herself to rap the knuckles of those parents nearest to her.

Henry the Fifth cried with joy when Father Christmas pulled out a beautiful barrister's wig and gave it to Henry. Elizabeth received a trampoline, which was quite odd because she had told no one, not even Harold, that the trampoline was her heart's desire. But she accepted it graciously from Father Christmas and said: "Thank you, ever so."

Well, everyone had a good time until three A.M., which is the witching hour in Marlborough Gardens. At that time the truce between the ferrets, weasels, stoats, and foxes and the rabbits, hares, and mice is over. A quarter of an hour before that the youngest ducklings had taken their places at all six doors of the Winter Garden, holding their large timepieces in their small webbed hands.

Three A.M. What a sight to behold. Ah, you should have been there to see how quickly the Winter Garden was cleared—the rabbits, mice, and hares receiving a five-minute head start of course.

As Elizabeth ran home holding her momma and poppa's hands, she thought to herself how wonderful the ball had been. Dear Ivan had been in such good form . . . when suddenly, the un-expected happened, and Elizabeth tripped over a fallen branch.

But instead of falling forward over it, she fell onto her tram-poline, which had fallen out of her hand, and she was bounced high up in the air and landed upside down on a branch of a poplar tree.

"Run!" she said to her parents. From where she was hanging by the tips of her black-patent shoes, she could see the ferrets and foxes running down the road in full chase. "Run home and I promise I shall come home as soon as I can."

Hanging there, the tops of her shoes curled neatly over one of the branches of the tree, Elizabeth began to have upside-down thoughts, which are not at all like right-side-up thoughts. Upside-down thoughts are right-side-up thoughts turned upside-down, you see. A very different ball of wax, as they say.

Now as the upside-down thoughts began to trickle through her mind like honey through a honeycomb, Elizabeth gave them a careful examination: dissecting them, breaking them down, subdividing them, and resolving them into first principles as children are wont to do. And she came to the conclusion that these new and interesting upside-down thoughts were really quite wonderful.

After an hour and five minutes had passed, Elizabeth climbed down, picked up her trampoline, and went home. Arriving there, she wasn't in the least surprised to see her mother riding a pony in the front garden and to see her father hanging out of the nursery window watching for her return with his binoculars. For one of the upside-down thoughts had been how lovely it would be if Momma and Poppa could obtain their hearts' desires.

The following day when she went to visit Ivan, she wasn't the least surprised to discover that Ivan had been too sick to play Father Christmas the night before. For the very first upside-down thought that had come to Elizabeth was: "I believe in Father Christmas . . ."

And so from that day on until now, Elizabeth spends a part of every day jumping on her trampoline and hanging upside down from a branch of a tree in order to fill her head with all sorts of interesting upside-down thoughts such as: "If you have not made a mistake today, you have not really tried; only the dead and the foolish never change their minds; it is better to love than be loved; if you have not been kind today there's always tomorrow."

And Elizabeth spread the Good News or as some people say, the Glad Tidings, that there really was a Father Christmas, which is how all the children who lived in Marlborough Gardens came to believe it too.

THE END